Kate crept quietly up to the third floor, not wanting to be disturbed, and placed the old skeleton key into the lock. She turned the knob and opened the door. She ran her hand along the wall for the light and switched it on, holding her eyes closed for a couple of seconds to give the mice a chance to scamper decently away into their hiding places. After a few seconds she opened her eyes, but what she saw was worse than a mouse. What she saw were—

Pins.

Hundreds of them. Stuck in the walls, the floorboards, the old furniture, the boxes, the desk. Kate felt her heart thump in her chest and felt a brief moment of dizziness shadow her brain before the adrenaline took over and her head cleared. He'd been here. The bastard had actually been in her house. She walked slowly, as if hypnotized, toward the tape recorder situated so perfectly on the pin-studded desk she had no doubt that was where she was supposed to go next. She pressed the play button and heard his voice through the speaker.

Hello, Katherine. I hope you're not too surprised to hear from me. Certainly you didn't think I'd refuse you a second chance, after all we've meant to each other. I'm forced to admit I have a certain weakness for you. You have one last chance, Katherine. One last chance, and I hope you won't disappoint me. I want you to meet me at the old Palace Amusements on the boardwalk. I want you to meet me inside the fun house. We are going to have some fun there, Katherine, you and I . . .

ORDINARY LIVES DESTROYED BY EXTRAORDINARY HORROR.
FACTS MORE DANGEROUS THAN FICTION.
CAPTURE A PINNACLE TRUE CRIME . . . IF YOU DARE.

LITTLE GIRL LOST   (593, $4.99)
By Joan Merriam

When Anna Brackett, an elderly woman living alone, allowed two teenage girls into her home, she never realized that a brutal death awaited her. Within an hour, Mrs. Brackett would be savagely stabbed twenty-eight times. Her executioners were Shirley Katherine Wolf, 14, and Cindy Lee Collier, 15. *Little Girl Lost* examines how two adolescents were driven through neglect and sexual abuse to commit the ultimate crime.

HUSH, LITTLE BABY   (541, $4.99)
By Jim Carrier

Darci Kayleen Pierce seemed to be the kind of woman you stand next to in the grocery store. However, Darci was obsessed with the need to be a mother. She desperately wanted a baby—any baby. On a summer day, Darci kidnapped a nine-month pregnant woman, strangled her, and performed a makeshift Cesarean section with a car key. In this arresting account, readers will learn how Pierce's tortured fantasy of motherhood spiraled into a bloody reality.

IN A FATHER'S RAGE   (547, $4.99)
By Raymond Van Over

Dr. Kenneth Z. Taylor promised his third wife Teresa that he would mend his drug-addictive, violent ways. His vow didn't last. He nearly beat his bride to death on their honeymoon. This nuptial nightmare worsened until Taylor killed Teresa after allegedly catching her sexually abusing their infant son. Claiming to have been driven beyond a father's rage, Taylor was still found guilty of first degree murder. This gripping page-turner reveals how a marriage made in heaven can become a living hell.

I KNOW MY FIRST NAME IS STEVEN   (563, $4.99)
By Mike Echols

A TV movie was based on this terrifying tale of abduction, child molesting, and brainwashing. Yet, a ray of hope shines through this evil swamp for Steven Stayner escaped from his captor and testified against the socially disturbed Kenneth Eugene Parnell. For seven years, Steven was shuttled across California under the assumed name of "Dennis Parnell." Despite the humiliations and degradations, Steven never lost sight of his origins or his courage.

RITES OF BURIAL   (611, $4.99)
By Tom Jackman and Troy Cole

Many pundits believe that the atrocious murders and dismemberments performed by Robert Berdella may have inspired Jeffrey Dahmer. Berdella stalked and savagely tortured young men; sadistically photographing their suffering and ritualistically preserving totems from their deaths. Upon his arrest, police uncovered human skulls, envelopes of teeth, and a partially decomposed human head. This shocking expose is written by two men who worked daily on this case.

Available wherever paperbacks are sold, or order direct from the Publisher. Send cover price plus 50¢ per copy for mailing and handling to Penguin USA, P.O. Box 999, c/o Dept. 17109, Bergenfield, NJ 07621. Residents of New York and Tennessee must include sales tax. DO NOT SEND CASH.

MERCILESS

Michael Cross

PINNACLE BOOKS
KENSINGTON PUBLISHING CORP.

15 NOVEMBER

"If a man could be described as a zoological type, he would be described as a lying animal."
P.D. Ouspensky

"What is truth?"
Pontius Pilate

1

12:03 A.M.

One thousand and one . . .

Through the walls of his cell, for the criminally insane, Snow could hear the keening storm lash futilely against the stone buildings of the prison yard. He had planned his escape three days from now, during the dark of the new moon, but decided to move the date up when a tropical storm off the Carolina coast had been upgraded to a hurricane. He had tracked Christine's progress on the television in the commons room over the last forty-eight hours. Now, as the storm ran itself ashore, it was expending the last of its fury over upstate New York.

One thousand and two . . .

Already the lights in the cellblock had gone off twice, knocked out by high winds. The emergency lights run off the prison's generator were a poor substitute, casting everything in an odd, surreal glow. Only three minutes ago Snow had watched the night guard pace up and down the corridor. Now he stopped two cells away from Snow's and banged on the bars with his heavy-duty flashlight.

''Shut the fuck up in there!'' he shouted.

Snow had taken a deep belly-breath; now he let a little of it out, as greedy as a miser with his gold. He felt his heart beating in his ears, his eyes, even in his swollen tongue. He felt the tracks of two tears drying on his cheeks.

All around him inmates kept weeping and screaming. In the surrounding cells were serial killers and rapists, child molesters and slashers, parricides and cannibals, but here they were whimpering like frightened animals, cowering in their steel cages as he imagined primitive man must have cowered in his cave, all on account of a little thunder and lightning. Human nature never failed to amaze him.

He had stolen the broom handle from a utility closet that afternoon, walking back to his cell a little more stiffly than usual, the apparent result of a fall he had taken earlier that day. He'd made sure that at least two guards had seen him fall as he carried his tray to his table in the cafeteria, and for good measure he'd started a fight with another inmate, claiming he'd been tripped. He'd even been taken to the infirmary, where the nasty gash on his lower leg had been tended. So no one had thought it amiss that he should be walking a little lamely as he returned to the cell from the commons, the broom handle slid down inside the leg of his pants.

One thousand and three . . .

The guard was still standing two cells away, screaming at the man inside, demanding that he shut the fuck up or else, but his threats were having little effect. The guard, a big black man named Earl, had it in for the inmate. The skinny white guy was a former Wall Street stockbroker who'd cruised Harlem for his victims. He had sodomized and strangled six young black boys before he'd been caught. Still, Snow detected a touch of fear in the guard's voice. The storm had everybody spooked. The cellblock, with its weird lighting and lamenting cries, sounded like the bowels of hell itself.

Snow objectively considered his situation. He didn't have much time left. He could already feel the burn in his lungs start, as if he had swallowed lighter fluid and sucked in the flame of a candle. His window of opportunity was rapidly closing. Finally the guard moved on, stopping in front of Snow's cell, moving the flashlight like a frightened eye in a predictable pattern, from the bunk, to the toilet, to the four corners of the cell.

"What the fuck—"

There was no one in the cell.

Snow could sense the man's incredulity from fifteen feet away. The flashlight moved through its pattern again, the eye of light finally falling on the body of the naked man hanging from a broken broom handle wedged high in the corner where the two cell walls came together. Above the twisted sheet that served as a rope, the man's face was swollen blue, his tongue pushed between his teeth, his bulging eyes the consistency of hard-boiled eggs.

"Dr. Snow," the guard whispered, almost as if afraid to wake him. "Dr. Snow, what's going on in there? Answer me!"

Inside his mind, Snow was laughing. What stupid things people said at times like these.

In the gloom, the guard fumbled the radio from his belt. "We've got ourselves an emergency in cell nine. Where's Denny?"

The voice on the radio crackled back. "He's off someplace catching a smoke. What's the problem?"

"We gotta croaker. Who's the shrink on duty tonight?"

"Chang is on the floor."

"Well, you better get him in here. And find Denny, dammit."

One thousand and four . . .

Snow kept his mind alive, working mathematical progressions forward and back, reciting passages of Shakespeare and the *Bhagavad Gita*, remembering the exact details of events that had happened a dozen years before. As if from far away he heard the magnetic lock disengage and the cell door slide back. There were three of them: the two guards, and the slight Chinese doctor named Chang. They seemed just to stare at him for an interminable period of time, as if somehow they were still afraid of him. Death always awed the living. At last the doctor stepped forward, shining a small penlight into Snow's ogling eyes. He grabbed one of Snow's dangling wrists, held it between his warm, sweaty fingers, felt no answering throb in the forked blue veins, and dropped it.

"He's dead," Chang pronounced. "Get him down and send him upstairs to the infirmary. Dr. Abbott will need to make a preliminary examination of the body and fill out a death certificate before we send the remains to the morgue. Anyone see anything?"

Both guards shook their heads.

They were already talking about him in the third person, Snow thought, pleased.

"Well, he wasn't on suicide watch, so I don't suppose anyone's to blame," Dr. Chang said, everyone already attempting to cover his ass. "Heard his appeal was denied, but he was only doing five years max. I didn't figure him for a croaker, though. Jeez, you think you got people figured out, and then they go and pull something like this. Someone get him down . . ."

One thousand and five . . .

The guards proceeded to lower Snow from the makeshift gibbet, the one called Denny grabbing his waist, while Earl climbed onto the bed and with a great deal of effort pushed free the broom handle wedged between the walls. Snow's body nearly fell through Denny's grasp. He could feel the man's revulsion.

They laid him on the bed until two orderlies arrived and transferred him to a gurney and wheeled him out of the cellblock to a freight elevator. Inside the elevator one of the orderlies pulled a sheet over Snow's face.

"How the hell did he do it?" he heard one orderly ask the other.

"Don't know. Found some way, obviously. Man wants to kill himself, he'll find a way."

"Jeezus," the other said. "Can't imagine wanting to die that bad."

One thousand and six . . .

Snow felt the steel box swoosh upward, counted off the

floors as they rang off one after the other. He didn't move until he heard the fourth ring, the elevator still moving, meaning they were between the fourth and fifth floors, counted *one thousand and seven,* and then he broke his trance. He sat bolt upright on the gurney. The orderly standing directly behind him screamed.

Snow grabbed him by the throat. Snow's hands, seldom without a rubber ball or at the very least a wad of paper, which he worked incessantly between his fingers, were as strong as a vise. He crushed the orderly's windpipe in less than two seconds. The second orderly, his face to the elevator door, turned around at the truncated scream, saw the dead man swing his legs from the gurney, and turned white as a hundred-watt bulb. He backed up against the elevator door, his hands out, imploring.

Snow knew intimately the forty-three weaknesses of the human anatomy. He regarded the man before him now as an architect regards the blueprint of a bridge for structural flaws or a grammarian evaluates a sentence for syntactic error. Snow swung his arms around in a large arc, stepped forward, and dropped to one knee. In the Orient they had a rather fanciful poetic name for what he was about to do. They called it "Monkey Steals the Peach." Reaching up with his right hand, Snow slapped the orderly in the groin, grabbing the man's testicles in his iron grip and ripping them free from his body. The orderly slid down the steel door, his dead eyes glazed with shock, his white pants soaked with blood.

Almost as if on cue, the elevator door opened and Snow emerged on the fifth-floor infirmary. He walked down the hall, the thick burgundy carpet swallowing his bare feet, wearing only the strip of sheet like a bizarre necktie. He found himself face-to-face with Dr. Abbott, who was heading for the doctor's lounge. Dr. Abbott had written up a rather uncomplimentary evaluation of Snow's mental status for the parole board. But what was worse, he had said some pretty libelous things about Snow's research.

"What are you doing up here, Dr. Snow?" he said, his

trained voice calm and authoritative, the affected William F. Buckley inflections all in place. His glands, however, were telling a different story. "You're supposed to be—"

"Dead?" Snow finished. "I'm feeling better. Can't you see? I always said you were a lousy diagnostician, Abbott."

The doctor was looking distastefully at Snow.

"You're naked, Doctor," Abbott said.

Snow knew what was really bothering the doctor. In spite of the circumstances, Snow was fully erect.

"Good God, Snow," he said, finally losing his cool. "What is the meaning of this?"

Snow leapt forward and drove his thumbs deep into the warm jelly of the doctor's eyeballs, using his grip to bring the doctor's head down to meet Snow's upraised knee, driving the bone and cartilage of his nose back into his brain. Snow let the doctor's body fall to the plush carpet and padded calmly to the bathroom. There was only one occupant inside, locked in one of the stalls, straining over his stool. Snow listened for a moment, amused. He recognized the voice: it was one of the part-time interns, a decent enough young fellow who'd once answered one of Snow's sexual questionnaires. Snow moved to the small frosted window over the radiator and twisted free the bolts that held the grille to the wall. The bolts had been loosened by a paranoid schizophrenic the day before. He was one of the prison's trusties who had been a plumber by trade before he'd bludgeoned his mother and aunt to death with a wrench. After ten years he'd been given the dubious privilege of cleaning the doctor's lavatory. Over the course of several days Snow had subtlely planted a subconscious suggestion to get the man to loosen the bolts.

Snow pulled the grille away and opened the small frosted window.

There was a gust of fresh air.

"Hey, Garrison," he called out, straddling the sill. "A table-spoon of psyllium husk in your orange juice every morning will straighten you right out."

From inside the stall Snow heard a small, frightened voice. "Dr. Snow?"

Snow jumped from a height that would have killed or at least seriously injured any other man. Instead he landed safely at the foot of the stone wall, crouched by the prison building, and exalted in the sensation of rain needling his naked flesh. He untied the sheet still wrapped around his throat, embedded so deep it almost felt a part of his flesh, and wound it around his hands. He was pumped with adrenaline. He stared out over the grounds of the yard. Less than a hundred yards, a low wall, and then freedom. The barbed wire wouldn't bother him at all.

The storm had built in intensity, howling all around him, the night as black as the unconscious.

It was a good night to go looking for the truth.

And he knew where he had to go first.

2

Kate held the phone to her ear long after the party on the other end had hung up.

She knew that whatever happened from here on out, she would never, ever forget this moment. It was the moment that fate had finally caught up with her. In the silence of the dead line she even thought she could hear it laughing at her. Once, when she was a little girl, she had heard a similar sound. She was on the roller coaster at the amusement park, plummeting down the silver rail at what seemed a thousand miles an hour. She was screaming at the top of her lungs, but strangely enough, there was no sound. Her screams and the screams of the others riding with her had been wiped into one long, empty howl of silence.

She heard the same silence on the other end of the phone now.

Outside, the rain was rushing over the old Victorian house, beating against the windows and breaking over the roof in violent, wind-driven gusts, as if the ocean itself were coming down overhead. Kate had spent the greater part of the day taping the upstairs windows in preparation for the storm. The forecast had originally called for Hurricane Christine to hit the shore area head-on at Atlantic City, about seventy-five miles south, but at the last moment the storm had unexpectedly veered offshore and swept up the coast toward Long Island, leaving in her wake a trail of high winds and torrential rain, but little in the way of serious destruction.

Earlier in the evening, Kate had discovered that one of the windows at the back of the house was leaking water. She had wedged a bath towel between the pane and the sill to staunch the flow. In spite of her weariness, she had been unable to sleep, pacing the wooden floors, climbing up and down the stairs, feeling like Captain Ahab, as the old house creaked and groaned around her like a foundering ship. She had weathered several storms before, including a vicious midwinter nor'easter the year before, but nothing quite like this. Now, as the wind rolled over the house again, bringing with it a fresh load of rain, Kate glanced upward, wondering how the roof was holding up under this latest onslaught of the elements.

She remembered the puzzled look on the real estate agent's face when she'd found out Kate wasn't married, had no children, wasn't even engaged. It was a look that plainly asked the question the old busybody didn't dare to ask: *What on earth does a woman alone want with a house this big, anyway?*

On bad days, when the furnace went out or the plumbing backed up, or the wiring burnt somewhere in the walls and threw the whole house into darkness, Kate asked herself the same question. The house was a money-pit, draining away even her substantial savings. After three years she finally had to admit to herself that it was too big for one person, especially when that one person didn't happen to be a building contractor. Yet ever since her family's yearly exodus from the city to the New Jersey coast for summer vacation, Kate had always dreamed of one day owning one of the grand old Victorian houses by the shore. She'd fallen in love with the turreted rooms, the big front porches, and the fancy gingerbread trim of the big houses. They reminded her of the houses in the

Gothic romances she'd read as a teenager. She had always dreamed of living in one when she grew up. She wasn't prepared to give up the dream just because she didn't have the husband and two children she'd also always dreamed she'd have long before the ripe old age of thirty-nine.

Up until the last twenty years or so, Ocean Grove had been a tightly knit religious community, a camptown built around a church and a huge auditorium where visiting preachers would declare God's word, choirs would sings praises to the glory of Christ, and speakers like Norman Vincent Peale would spread their message of the power of positive thinking. It was the kind of place that still observed the blue laws, where driving was illegal on Sunday, and where you had to sit before a governing council of town fathers in order to gain permission to buy property. But progressive social laws, economic necessity, and the inevitable weakening of tradition as the older generation of property owners slowly died away had gradually relaxed the rules. Now anyone could buy property there. In fact, for a while, before AIDS had made its mark, the town had even become something of a mecca for a rising gay population who thought it somewhat camp to renovate the stately old Victorian homes in what had once been a strict Episcopalian enclave.

Unfortunately the modernization of the town had brought with it some unexpected liabilities. The state had muscled in and turned some of the old hotels in town into boarding homes for mental patients deinstitutionalized from various county facilities. Now this substantial schizophrenic population could be seen shambling aimlessly about the streets, or sitting on the benches by the ocean, or feeding pigeons in the park, mumbling to themselves in what many residents found a most disconcerting manner. It was not unusual to wake up in the morning and find one or two or three such patients sitting on the steps of your porch, drinking coffee. To many residents, this was an intolerable if uncorrectable situation, but knowing from her own research and work that most schizophrenics were not dangerous, Kate remained on friendly terms with many of them. Unfortunately, the majority of her neighbors did not share her enlightened view of the mentally ill. They saw them merely as unsightly eyesores and sought to escape the town as quickly as possible, sending real estate prices plummeting, so that Kate's house was currently worth approximately half of what it had been worth when she'd paid for it.

Still, with characteristic stubbornness, Kate had remained behind with no intention of pulling up stakes and leaving. She had decided to start anew here, to pick up the pieces of her shattered life after a case that had cost her a thriving psychiatric practice and very nearly her own sanity. After three years she had almost convinced herself that she had done it. Now all she had struggled to rebuild had been shattered by a single telephone call.

He had escaped.

Three words torn from her darkest nightmare. The man she had given up everything to help convict, the man she had counseled and then betrayed, the most purely evil man she had ever encountered in more than ten years as a clinical psychiatrist, had escaped—and she knew in her bones that there was a good chance that before long he would come looking for her.

The man on the phone had been unable to give her any details of the escape. He explained that he had a list of persons to contact and it was only his job to call them. Someone, he assured her, would be in contact with her before long. When she tried to press him, he apologized but told her he still had others on his list to notify. Kate could hear the tension in his voice. She was still trying to wheedle any shred of information she could from the man when he hung up, leaving her talking into a dead line.

How? That was the question she wanted answered most of all. It was the only question that really mattered. How could they have allowed this to happen? They had promised. Of course, it was naive to trust in such promises, and truth to tell, Kate hadn't. Not a day had gone by that she had not imagined something like this happening, yet she had somehow convinced herself that she was letting irrational fears get the better of her. It was the same kind of advice that she so often used to give her patients. Now she knew how empty her words must have sounded to them. Fear was real, even if the reason behind it wasn't.

Her own fears, however, had not been irrational. There was good reason to be afraid. Her fears were not based on any paranoid fantasy; instead, they were based on the intimate knowledge she had gained of the power, determination, and self-discipline of a man whose hidden thoughts, dreams, and delusions she had shared for nearly nine of the most terrifying months of her life.

The wind broke over the house again, throwing a fresh wave of rain against the windows, pattering like an explosion of tiny hard peas. Penelope whined, wiggled backward as far as she could, lay her head between her paws, and rolled her big, brown eyes up at Kate. The little golden dog, usually so bright and lively, had taken refuge under the couch, afraid of the sound of the storm. Usually the dog followed closely at her heels throughout the house, but until now, Kate hadn't seen hide nor hair of the dog in over an hour.

She was about to stoop down to pat the dog's head when the phone suddenly came to life in her hand and a disembodied voice cut through the silence, nearly scaring her out of her skin.

It was only the computerized voice of the operator advising her that if she would like to place a call, to please hang up and try again or to dial "O" and ask for assistance. Kate looked up at the clock on the mantel. It was half-past midnight.

Yes, she would like to make a call.

She pressed down the button on the phone, waited for the dial tone, and then called Jeff at home.

12:49 A.M.

Dr. Snow crouched naked inside a stand of stunted trees on a small rise about thirty yards from the tollbooth. He was wet and cold, shivering in the sloshy green grass beneath the trees, his swollen throat throbbing, making it difficult for him to swallow.

For the past three hours he had stumbled his way through the dark and wet, following the highway. He jogged along the shoulder, listening through the rain for the sound of approaching cars, ducking back into the surrounding woods, or diving into a roadside ditch when one came past, and then darting naked toward the space temporarily illuminated by the car's headlights, remembering the terrain with his photographic memory. Twice he had slipped and fallen. The second time, throwing his hands out for support, he had painfully twisted his left wrist. He was streaked with greenish-brown mud, the flesh of his shins torn in a half-dozen places, but he no longer felt any pain. He was free, and that freedom was exhilarating. He knew that now he had to pay its terrible price.

He squinted toward the tollbooth, wiping away the rain that dripped from his forehead into his eyes. When he was planning his escape, this tollbooth had played an important role in his calculations. It was situated on an access road leading southbound to Interstate 87, which would take him straight into the city. The first thing he had to do was get some clothes, hijack a car, and get on the road as quickly as possible. Here he could do all three at once.

Snow watched the shadow of the man inside the tollbooth. He had been watching him for several minutes now. There wasn't much traffic on the road tonight. The storm was keeping away even the few who would normally be traveling the road at this hour. Only one car had passed since he'd been watching. The man inside the tollbooth was eating a sandwich: meat and onions, and some kind of cheese. Snow could smell dead animal fat, vinegar, and dairy every time the wind shifted direction. To an expert nutritionist like Snow, the cloying stench was intolerable.

He stepped out of the sheltering shadow of the trees and dashed quickly over the wet grass. He had crossed half the distance to the tollbooth when he heard a tinny talking sound.

The man inside was listening to the radio; Snow wondered if he had heard the news of his escape.

Snow crouched under the shelter of the toll plaza overhang, feeling doubly exposed in the crackling fluorescent lighting. On the other side, the toll collector was singing to a song on the radio. He was singing loudly and off-key. He had no concern about being overheard. He was alone out here in the tollbooth, protected by the storm and the miles of empty road unraveling in all directions around him.

3

12:50 A.M.

Ralph Annunziato liked being a toll collector. There were a minimum of rules to follow and no one to hassle you, and by working overtime, he had cleared sixty-five grand the previous year. Sure, there was the occasional asshole who gave you a hard time, claiming he had only a hundred-dollar bill for a forty-five-cent toll. And there was the carbon monoxide poisoning that gave him four times the normal risk of contracting lung cancer and heart disease. Twice he'd even been held up. But for the most part, it was a pretty easy job.

Tonight it was even easier than usual. There was hardly any traffic on the road, most people having the good sense to stay put while the storm passed. Since starting his shift two hours earlier, he could have counted on the fingers of one hand the number of cars that had come through and still had a finger left over to pick his nose.

One had been a state police cruiser with news of an escapee from the prison for the criminally insane about fifteen miles north of Ralph's booth. The trooper had given him a description and told him to be on the lookout for the man. No one had reported a stolen car yet, but it was still early. If he saw anything suspicious, he shouldn't hesitate to call it in.

There was always someone escaping from that damned place. Usually they caught him the next morning, huddling under a bush on the grounds, or a motorist reported him wandering along the interstate in a Haldol daze until the troopers came by and picked him up. He wasn't worried. None of them had ever made it this far, and besides, that was what he kept the big knife under the counter for.

Ralph turned up the radio. The song *Hungry like the Wolf* was playing. The rain was thrumming down on the metal roof of the tollbooth, and Ralph felt warm and cozy inside. They said that even an amateur sounded good in a tiled bathroom, but for Ralph's money, he'd take a tollbooth every time. He sounded like Pavarotti inside his booth. Or, in this case, every bit as good as those two faggots in Duran Duran. He picked up the submarine sandwich he had bought at the 7-Eleven down in Warwick and danced with it a moment before taking a big bite, wiping the grease off his lips with the back of his hand.

On the counter in front of him was an open skin magazine. He looked hungrily at the centerfold, of a platinum blonde lying on a fur blanket. She was wearing nothing but white high heels and a come-hither smile. Ralph poured more coffee from his silver thermos and washed down the sandwich. *Yup*, he was thinking, *it sure don't get much better than this* when the naked man appeared in his window.

12:51 A.M.

Less than twenty minutes after she'd called, Jeff Hudson stood on the front porch. He was wearing a yellow rainslicker that was running with water and a pair of large rubber work boots. His curly red hair was tucked under a floppy yellow rain hat. In spite of herself, Kate suppressed a smile. He looked like a six-foot-two-inch banana.

"I came as soon as I could," he said, standing on the throw rug in the foyer and taking off his jacket, careful not to splash water on the hardwood floor. "The bridge from Asbury Park is washed out and I had to take the long way around." He jerked his thumb at the Ford Bronco parked at the curb. "The water was over the bumper in some places. It's really wild out there."

"Thanks for coming," Kate said. "You sit yourself in front of the fire and warm up. I'll get you a dry towel and a cup of hot coffee."

"Sounds great."

Kate gathered up his wet clothes and took them to the downstairs bathroom where she hung them up to drip-dry in the bathtub. Then she went to the kitchen to fix the coffee. When she came back to the living room, Jeff was sitting on an ottoman in front of the fire, petting Penelope. The dog had apparently overcome her fear of the storm in order to greet Jeff. The dog loved Jeff, but that wasn't unusual; Penelope loved just about everyone. What was unusual was that Jeff seemed to love the dog as much as Kate did herself, and he didn't mind the shameless way Kate had spoiled it. Penelope rolled over onto her back and Jeff scratched her pink belly, the little dog's rear leg kicking with pleasure.

"Here you go," Kate said, handing him the towel. She set the coffee cup on the hearth.

"Thanks."

Jeff took the towel and vigorously rubbed his hair dry. In the firelight, Kate could make out the individual strands of gold in his red beard. His hair mussed but dry, he draped the towel around his neck and looked up at her. His serious blue eyes sparkled from behind wire-rimmed glasses. "So talk to me," he said. "What's up?"

Kate always thought that fate must have been working overtime to bring them together. They had met when Penelope was just a puppy. She had brought the dog to the veterinarian with a bad case of kennel cough. She was waiting in the lobby, flipping nervously through a back issue of *Psychology Today*, and found herself in an animated conversation about Jungian archetypes with a red-haired giant of a man sitting beside a chestnut-brown Great Dane. With his strapping build, callused hands, and macho dog, she had him easily pegged for a mechanic or a construction worker. She was completely taken by surprise when the receptionist looked up from behind her desk and said, "You're next, Dr. Hudson." He called her at the college a week later to ask how Penelope was doing. She thanked him for his concern and waited patiently as he worked up the nerve to ask her out.

That was almost three years ago. They had been seeing each other two or three times a week ever since, and though their relationship had grown and deepened during that time, Jeff did not seem inclined to change the arrangement into anything more permanent. He had been married once before, while he was still in medical school, and he never talked about it except to say that they had both been too young, too poor, and too impatient to make it work. As a result he had two children living in California who he helped support but who he got to see for only three weeks of summer vacation each year. His bitterness made him more than a little gun-shy about commitment. Not that Kate was looking for a commitment. Not now anyway. She had more than her own share of skeletons.

Jeff was by nature a solitary man, and that was probably what Kate liked best about him. He was a contradiction in terms, an emergency room doctor who read Laing and Shakespeare. He had the talent and experience to be a surgeon but preferred the hands-on challenge of emergency room medicine. With his flannel shirts and red beard, he looked more like a lumberjack than a doctor, but he spoke about ideas with the passion of a poet. He was very different from the men she had met at the university, men who had cultivated their minds to the exclusion of all else, men who had gone soft and white, men who had forgotten how to use their hands.

She had never told him about what had happened in New York, not the entire story, anyway. It wasn't that she didn't trust him. If she could have told anyone, it would have been Jeff. The fact was that she'd wanted to put the whole damn business behind her, and that seemed impossible if she allowed her past to follow her into her new life. But it *had* followed her. She hated calling Jeff over like this in the middle of the night, hating playing the part of the hysterical female. But she couldn't help it. She didn't want to be alone in the house tonight. It was time to tell him. Now.

"What's up, babe?" Jeff asked again, softer this time. The concern in his eyes deepened when he saw the expression on her face. He touched her arm.

She could hardly believe the words as she said them.

"He's escaped," she said dully, staring through him into the laughing fire.

12:53 A.M.

Ralph recognized him immediately from the trooper's description. "You're hurt, mister," he said, slowly putting down his sandwich. He could feel his heart pounding hard inside his chest. "You been in an accident?"

"Do you know who I am?" the naked man asked. He didn't seem agitated; he didn't even seem particularly insane. It would have been easier if he had. His calm, under the circumstances, was more unnerving.

"No, mister," Ralph said. "Can I call you an ambulance?"

He made a great show of reaching for the phone, while his other hand eased toward the handle of the knife protruding from between two clipboards on a shelf under the counter. The man seemed to be drawing some kind of invisible pattern in the air with his left hand. Ralph found himself following it in spite of himself. He didn't even see the other hand come down, but he heard the bones in his wrist crack like dry kindling, felt the cold pain radiate up his arm and across his chest and explode like white lightning on the left side of his skull. He staggered against the back of the tollbooth holding his wrist in his other hand, staring at the numb, useless fingers, and then back at the naked man, who had jumped inside the tollbooth. "Now," he said, in that same calm, patient voice. "I'll ask you again. Do you know who I am?"

Nauseated by the pain, Ralph found himself strangely mesmerized by the man's soothing voice, his cool gray gaze, the knife in his hand. "Yes," he said quietly. "Yes, I do."

"Good," the naked man said. "You should know that I'll kill you if you don't do exactly as I say. Take off your clothes."

"What?"

"You heard me."

The toll collector was beginning to sweat, smelling of onions and cheese. Snow could see the man's good hand trembling as he fought to loosen his belt, his pants falling to his ankles.

"Don't be afraid," Snow said, his voice almost soothing.

He grabbed the articles of clothing as the toll collector took them off. He put on the man's underwear and pants, his shoes and socks. The clothes stank of the other man's body odor, but the warmth trapped inside felt good on Snow's chilled limbs.

"Are you married?"

"Yes," the toll collector said.

"What's your wife's name?"

"Marie."

"Do you love her?"

"Yes."

"Do you want to see her again?"

The toll collector didn't answer, but his jaw began to tremble.

"I'll ask you once more. Do you want to see your wife again?"

"Yes," the fat man said in a small voice.

"Then what do you look at that shit for?"

"What do you mean?" the toll collector said, sounding like a guilty child.

Snow jerked his thumb over his shoulder at the skin mag on the counter behind him. "*Cavalier*, July 1993."

"*I-I* don't know."

The toll collector was trying to be careful, afraid that Snow was some kind of religious psycho. He was no doubt wondering how the man could have known the name and issue of a magazine that was over three years old just by glancing at the centerfold. "Don't worry," Snow said, as if reading his mind.

He was buttoning the gray shirt to the collar. The shirt was three sizes too large. Snow had to tuck it deep inside the oversized pants. "I'm a doctor, not a religious fanatic. My curiosity is merely scientific. Kneel down."

The toll collector sank slowly to his knees. Snow grabbed the skin magazine and threw it on the floor in front of the fat man. "Pick it up," he said.

The toll collector picked it up. His pale, speckled, hairy shoulders were shaking. He was crying.

"Now I want you to bring yourself to orgasm."

"Please don't do this to me."

The rain was falling on top of the tollbooth, making a sharp, pinging sound, insulating them from the world. Snow felt as if he were in a confessional, only him and this naked, kneeling penitent. "Do it," he said, waving the knife.

The toll collector held the magazine in his crippled left hand. He put his other hand on the shriveled organ between his legs and rubbed awkwardly.

"With feeling," Snow said.

The man rubbed harder, weeping more openly now, his eyes closed, no longer looking at the smiling naked woman in the picture. The rain seemed to pick up, gusting against the toll booth. "Harder," Snow shouted over the sound of the rain. "Harder."

"I can't," the fat man howled. "I can't do it."

"What are you thinking?" Snow shouted.

"Please don't kill me!" the fat man squealed. "I'm begging you."

"You can do better than that. What are you thinking?"

Fear and adrenaline had actually produced half a hard-on. It slid in and out of the man's pudgy hand like a short fat sausage.

"Tell me what you are thinking."

"Please," the fat man wailed.

"Tell me what you are thinking right now!"

"I want to wake up tomorrow morning and hear the birds outside my bedroom window, you bastard!" he screamed.

"Excellent," Snow nodded, feeling the rapture rise from the pit of his stomach. "Excellent!"

He brought his elbow down over the top of the man's head. The toll collector dropped to all fours. Snow brought his elbow down again. The man's skull made a wet crunching sound as the coronal sutures separated and the frontal bones collapsed back into the brain. The toll booth suddenly smelled like a urinal and the floor was slippery wet. Snow swung his elbow down once more and the fat man pitched forward.

Snow stopped, took a deep breath, and slowed his heart rate. The fat man was kneeling facedown, pale butt in the air, as if he were praying to Mecca, the top of his head a red, splintered mess. His nose was in the crease of the magazine centerfold, his left eye bulging from the socket like a skinned purple grape.

Who would have suspected such poetry was locked inside his skull, Snow thought. He looked down appreciatively at the dead toll collector.

It was a tragic but necessary truth.

Sometimes, to taste the sweetest wine you had to break the bottle.

4

12:56 A.M.

"His name is Alexander Snow." Kate paused, searching for the words to go on. She was sitting in the armchair across from the fire. She had not spoken of what had happened to anyone for so long that doing it now was like trying to remember a foreign language. "He was a neurobiologist and experimental psychiatrist, one of the best in the world. His pioneering work on brain-mapping and the problem of memory was considered Nobel material, but some of his methods were suspect by conventional scientific standards. I'd followed his work in the journals for years."

"How did he happen to come to you?"

"Believe me, I was as surprised as anyone. He said he'd read a paper on false memory syndrome that had impressed him and that I came highly recommended. But by whom, he wouldn't say. I had the distinct impression that for some reason he was lying."

"What was his problem?" Jeff was sitting across from her on the hearth. He took a sip of his coffee, one hand lost in Penelope's ruff. The dog lay contentedly between Jeff's feet.

"He wouldn't say. He just sat there in the leather armchair in front of my desk with his hands steepled under his chin, as if he were examining *me*. It's weird, but the first thing I noticed was how extraordinarily long his fingers were. I was fixated on them. I don't know why. He was insane, Jeff. I knew it from the moment he sat down. We're trained not to make snap judgments like that, but the look in his eyes was unmistakable. I can't quite describe it, except to say that it was the look of a man who'd seen too much. Finally, it might have been five minutes, maybe more, he spoke."

"What did he say?"

"He asked me how many times a week I masturbated."

"You're kidding."

Kate shook her head. "I'd encountered that kind of sophomoric hostility all the time. It's not unusual. It's meant to shock or embarrass the analyst, knock him or her off his high horse. But I really hadn't expected such a crude sally from a man of his reputation. I was shocked, but I tried not to show it."

"What did you say to him?"

"I told him I was disappointed in his attitude. That he was certainly under no compulsion to be there and that he was free to go if he chose, but that if he elected to stay, I would appreciate it if he didn't waste our time with childish attempts to disrupt my composure."

"That's my girl," Jeff grinned. "What did he say to that?"

"He just sat there listening patiently and then explained that he had no intention of shocking or insulting me, but that he thought the question perfectly valid under the circumstances. When I asked him how that was possible, he explained that he was merely trying to gauge my level of sexual anxiety. He told me that his was quite high, as he had not permitted himself an orgasmic release in ten years."

Jeff whistled under his breath. "That explains the insane look in his eyes. Christ, talk about being wound too tight."

"He was dead serious. He said he carried a great deal of sexual tension about his person and warned me that I would dream about him that night."

"Did you?"

"Yes, I did," Kate said quietly, wondering whether she should tell him the whole truth, and deciding on telling him half. "I dreamt I was sitting in some kind of dentist's chair and he was reaching down my throat with those long fingers and pulling up what looked like a strip of black videotape, piling it in my lap until I felt nauseated. I couldn't believe I had so much inside me. He started laughing and I woke up in a cold sweat." Kate paused, forcing herself to go on. "It was embarrassing, demeaning. I dreaded facing him in the next session. I'd had dreams about clients before, but nothing like that. I couldn't shake the feeling that he had somehow planted the seed of that dream on purpose."

"Did he ask you about it?"

"Yes. I lied. I told him I hadn't dreamed at all. He laughed, and it was the same laugh I'd heard in the dream. I wondered how it could have been, I mean, he hadn't laughed in the first session. I'll never forget what he said next. 'I bet if we put that tape through the projector we'd finally see what makes you tick.'"

Jeff stopped petting the dog. He looked up, his face somehow changed. "How did he—"

"I don't know, Jeff. Perhaps he's some kind of natural mentalist. Such powers are not wholly explained away by modern psychiatry. Even Jung believed in the paranormal. Maybe it was just a damn lucky guess. I don't know."

"Now, that is creepy."

"Wait. It gets even worse. A week later he invited me to a lecture he was giving on acupuncture—"

"Acupuncture?"

"He had studied for a long time in the East. India, China, Tibet. He employed a lot of what he'd learned in his research. He maintained that he could use acupuncture to release blocked energies in the body where lost memories were trapped, manifesting themselves as various physical and psychiatric disorders. Reich did similar research. Anyway, he demonstrated his technique on a young female patient diagnosed with congenital degenerative nerve disease. She'd been wheelchair bound since she was fifteen. Maybe it was just me, maybe it was what he told me about not having sex in ten years, but I couldn't help but noticing the way he inserted the pins into the atrophied muscles of that poor girl's calves and thighs. He did it . . . almost lovingly. By the end of the demonstration the girl took a few faltering steps before collapsing in his arms in tears.''

Jeff snorted. ''Sounds like faith healing to me.'' He put his mug down on the hearth and Penelope jumped up and started noisily lapping at the coffee. Neither of them paid attention to the dog.

''That's what his detractors claimed. A week later the first woman disappeared. She was a CUNY student, the daughter of a prominent black councilman. Two weeks later a suburban housewife vanished from a mall parking lot in Connecticut. A month after that the abandoned car of a third woman was found stranded along the New Jersey Turnpike. Seven months of therapy, nine missing women.''

''My God, it was him?''

''I don't know exactly how I knew, but I did. And what was worse is that I knew he *wanted* me to know. That was why he'd invited me to that little acupuncture demonstration. He was playing with my mind, gauging my responses. But why? I didn't think he was looking for someone to turn him in. He wasn't the type. What did he want from me? I still don't know.''

''What did you do?''

''A colleague of mine worked with the FBI in preparing psychological profiles of serial killers. I told him my suspicions and he put me in touch with an agent named Tom Lincoln. They told me Snow would never get out. That he would never know it was me who'd tipped them off. The DA, the police, the defense attorney, even Lincoln. They assured me that they would find some way to keep him locked up until they could find the evidence they needed to bury him.''

''Fools. Why didn't they put you in the witness protection program?''

''Because I wasn't a witness for the prosecution. I was an

anonymous informant. I thought I could just walk away, disappear on my own. That's why I quit my practice and moved down here to teach. I thought I had put the past behind me. Until tonight.''

In the fireplace a log shifted, sending a shower of sparks up the flue. Jeff didn't say anything for a long time. ''I had no idea,'' he said finally. ''How could you have kept so much inside you? I wish you'd told me.''

Kate shrugged. ''I wanted to. You don't know how many times I started and just couldn't. I just thought if I didn't talk about it, it all might somehow go away. Strange thing for a psychiatrist to say, huh?''

''Maybe. But not for a human being.''

''I'm scared Jeff. Scared he might come back.''

''You said yourself that he didn't know you had broken confidentiality.''

''That's what they told me. But Snow is no fool. He's had three years to figure out how he was caught.''

''He'd have a hard time finding you,'' Jeff said. ''Besides, I'm sure he's got more pressing problems on his mind right now. Like eluding the police. Anyway, most escaped prisoners are caught within twenty-four hours.''

''I hope you're right, Jeff. You don't know Alexander Snow. He's not like anyone I've ever met before. I know this sounds ridiculous, but I really believe he's not quite human.''

''I'm sure I'm right. You'll see. They'll probably catch him by morning.''

''All the same, would you mind staying the night?''

Jeff grinned. ''I thought you'd never ask.''

1:02 A.M.

Brenda Pilot stared out the windshield at the rainswept highway and back at the man behind the steering wheel. She had once read in *Mademoiselle* that the best way to determine whether or not you and your lover were truly compatible was to spend the weekend together. After three uninterrupted days with Todd, she decided she hated him enough to strangle him if she could stand to have her hands around his throat long enough to deplete his seemingly inexhaustible supply of hot air.

She had chosen an upstate bed-and-breakfast for their romantic getaway. The inn was perfect—stone fireplace, jacuzzi, fourposter bed, gourmet chef—it deserved every one of the four stars in her travel guide. The problem was Todd. He had gotten on her nerves even before they'd arrived. First he got lost no fewer than three times and refused to stop to ask for directions. He wouldn't stop for food or at any of the attractions along the way. He reluctantly stopped at a highway comfort station, but only after she'd convinced him that if he didn't, she might wet the crushed velour of his brand-new BMW.

She wasn't in the mood for sex that first night and he sulked the next day and generally made himself so unappealing that she wasn't in the mood for it the second night, either. He was ungracious enough to mention all the money the weekend was costing him and he hadn't even gotten any. That provoked a terrible fight that finally ended in Brenda relenting to three minutes of unspirited coupling. When he rolled off her he was even more sullen than before.

The clouds started rolling in Sunday morning and the weather reports were warning of the coming storm. The inn advised its guests to stay an extra night and provided a discount to those who did, even offering to make arrangements at a nearby Holiday Inn for those who preferred less expensive accommodations.

Todd would have none of it. He pointed out again how much money the weekend had cost him, as if he were depending on every dollar of his six-figure Wall Street income in order to eat the following week. She had never noticed before how cheap he was when it came to spending money on them. There were a lot of things about him she had never noticed before.

Brenda looked at the side of his face in the halogen lights of the highway. What in the world had she ever found attractive about him in the first place? The flaws that her eyes had glossed over in the first flush of romance now glared out at her as if his features had been drawn by a caricaturist: the receding chin, the hooked nose, the slightly bulbous eyes. On top of that, his hair was thinning in the back and she had found an alarming number of hairs on his pillow each morning. He'd be bald before he was forty.

Todd turned. "What the hell are you looking at?"

"Nothing. I was just daydreaming, I guess."

He snorted. She was thinking of how she was going to dump him and how much she was going to relish doing it. She turned back to the road. The highway looked like a wide gray river ruffled by wind and stitched together by rain. Up ahead she could see the lights of a toll plaza. Todd grumbled. "Can't believe they even have these things open on a night like this." Todd was slowing down, the painted grid making sticking sounds under the tires, the car rolling to a stop in front of the only open booth. He buzzed down the electric window and stuck his arm out, holding a twenty between his fingers. He shook the bill impatiently, waiting for the toll collector to take it. "Come on, already," he shouted. "Wake up in there!"

Brenda screamed as the knife came down, pinning Todd's wrist into the slot where the window disappeared into the door. "He stabbed me," he said. "He fucking stabbed me!" His fingers, still holding the twenty, were twitching. The BMW lurched forward and slammed into the light stanchion.

The toll collector came out of the booth and yanked open Todd's door, pulling him out of the car onto the wet macadam. He clapped his hands over Todd's ears and twisted his head in one swift, violent motion. Todd sat slumped on the ground, his face turned in the wrong direction, the hair at the back of his head brushing the knot of his silk Armani tie. The toll collector looked up at Brenda and calmly walked around the front of the car to the passenger side.

He opened the door and pushed aside her fumbling hands, undoing her safety belt. He grabbed her by the arm and yanked her out of the car onto her knees. "I don't want to die," Brenda whimpered. *"I don't want to die."*

The toll collector reached down and ripped open the front of her blouse, the buttons scattering. She could feel the cold rain on her breasts. "What are you thinking?" the toll collector asked.

Brenda surprised herself with the clarity of her answer. "I don't want to die because of this lousy weekend," she shouted, feeling anger, fear, and even a touch of humor at the absurdity of it all. "He was a lousy lay. *Mademoiselle* was right."

She thought she heard the toll collector chuckle and then she felt a horrible weight at the back of her head that forced her to double over on her hands and knees. She was staring at the ground and saw the buttons of her blouse mixed with blood and had just enough time to recognize that what she was looking at weren't buttons after all but her teeth when the next blow killed her.

5

He had just lost his eighth straight game of solitaire when the call came.

Tom Lincoln had read *A Course in Miracles* and the books on quantum healing by Deepak Chopra. But when all was said and done he was down to playing cards to pass the time. Ironic. He didn't have much time left and yet it seemed to drag on interminably. Part of the problem was that sleep almost totally eluded him now. If he did manage to drift off for a few hours, it was hell to pay upon waking. The pain was ten times worse, especially if he'd been lying down. So he always made sure if he felt sleepy to prop himself up in the easy chair in the corner.

Against the far wall the television was tuned in to one of those home shopping networks. They were selling cookware, and some woman from Ohio was extolling the virtues of that hour's feature item, a set of nonstick bakeware. Every once in a while Lincoln looked up from his desk to watch, but for the most part the television was just a patch of talking wallpaper. The show was live and he liked the fact that there were other people up and about at this hour of the morning. Somehow it made him feel less alone.

Outside the rattling windows the Maine cold had turned the rain that was socking the East Coast to hail. Lincoln listened as it clattered against the pane like the claws of an animal trying to get inside. He lifted the cigarette burning in the ashtray beside him, took a drag, and held the smoke deep inside him for warmth. He was staring down at the red queen who'd done him in, unwilling to concede defeat just yet, when the phone rang. He let it ring one and a half times before picking it up.

The voice on the other end was unfamiliar, but then, it had been almost three years since he'd retired from the Agency. He listened as the other man spoke, giving him the details, his tone calm, clipped, neutral. When the man was finished, Lincoln put the phone back in its cradle, placed his fingers at his temples, and rubbed. His eyes burned as if someone had placed acid on his pupils. The worst part was that he couldn't say the news was totally unexpected.

They were sending a car to get him within the half hour.

No problem.

Just enough time to brush his teeth, splash some water on his face, and tack a note on the front door to the postman to hold his mail. He always kept a small bag packed, a habit left over from his agency days, which came in handy now, in case he had to admit himself to the hospital. He stubbed his cigarette out in the ashtray. Hell, he wouldn't even have to change. He was already dressed. Up until two minutes ago, he'd just had nowhere to go.

1:32 A.M.

In a diner off the interstate, Snow sat in a booth by the window and watched the rain. The diner was empty except for a pair of truckers sipping coffee at the counter, their rigs in the lot outside, and a salesman from Michigan munching on a cheeseburger a few booths away. He had pulled in just after

Snow and parked his brown company sedan right next to the silver BMW.

Snow had found a fresh change of clothes in a suitcase in the trunk and put them on in a service station men's room about six miles back. He was wearing a pair of khaki corduroys and a dark blue pullover. The boy had been a little taller than Snow so the clothes didn't fit quite right, but he was closer in size than the toll collector had been. The sneakers were a particular problem. He'd had to lace them up extra tightly to keep them from slipping off his feet.

Snow picked up his fork and deftly manipulated it with the fingers of his left hand. He put it down and repeated the procedure with the fingers of his right hand. He held out his hands and stared at them in the too-bright light. They were the hands of a healer, the hands of a killer. With them he could repair the tiniest tear in an artery deep inside the cerebral fold or kill a two-hundred-fifty-pound man with little more than a touch at the solar plexus. To Snow, his hands were objects of almost transcendent beauty.

A tired-looking waitress in a stained nylon smock brought his order: a hamburger steak and green beans.

"Are you sure I can't get you some french fried potatoes or rolls to go with that, mister?" she asked.

"No, thank you. You shouldn't mix starches with meat. It isn't trophologically correct."

"Huh?"

"It's an ancient Chinese dietary rule."

"Oh." The waitress shrugged. "Well, is there anything else I can get you?"

She had been pretty once, but too many late nights had taken their toll on her fine skin, etching lines around her mouth and filling the sacks under her blue eyes with darkness. *Yes,* Snow thought, *you can tell me how you go on night after night with nothing but the prospect of another pointless day ahead of you. You can tell me how you do it, what is your secret, what you pray for before you sleep, what you daydream about, what you see when you come. You can let me hear you scream . . .*

Snow held the woman with eyes the color of smoke.

"No," he said politely. "But thank you very much."

With interest Snow watched her buttocks rolling beneath the smock as she walked back to the counter.

Snow ate methodically, one eye on the parking lot. When he was done, he used Todd Scheffield's platinum Amex card to pay for his meal, leaving an extra-large tip for the waitress. She thanked him, her smile making her look ten years younger.

"You have a good night, now."

"You, too," Snow said.

She would remember him if the police came around, and they would, sooner or later, but she would be reluctant to say anything, because he had been nice to her and so few people were. She would feel singled out, as if they shared a special bond. She, too, was an outsider of sorts. She would find it hard to believe that he could really be as bad as the police said. Snow had discovered people generally didn't give a damn what you did to others, so long as you were nice to them.

Fifteen miles down the road Snow saw the interstate sign announcing that New York City was only 175 miles away.

I'm coming, Katherine.

1:33 A.M.

Kate fixed the plastic baby gate in the doorway of the living room.

On the other side, Penelope looked up sadly. Usually she had the run of the house, and that meant following Kate upstairs where she spent the night snuggled in the quilt at the foot of Kate's queen-sized bed. But whenever Jeff came over, Penelope was confined to the first floor.

"Sorry, baby," Kate said.

The little dog trotted resignedly back to the easy chair in front of the dying fire, jumped up on the seat, scratched the worn corduroy a few times, and flopped down.

Jeff followed Kate up the stairs to the second-floor bedroom. She switched on the sconce light near the bureau and the electric candle cast a dim glow throughout a room carefully decorated in a Victorian motif. There was the canopied bed, the antique hutch she'd bought at a garage sale, an overstuffed armchair, and a small wooden vanity. They undressed each other in the semi-darkness, Jeff pulling off her sweatshirt while she undid the button on his blue jeans, working down the zipper. Like an old married couple, they'd done this dance enough times that it had inevitably lost some of its desperate passion, but what it lacked in lust it more than made up for in consideration and gentleness. Each knew what the other liked and went about providing it without awkwardness or uncertainty. Familiarity had its advantages.

She took him in her hand and, walking backward, led him to the bed, sitting down and letting go long enough to lift her legs as he pulled her jeans and panties off.

Kate lay back on the pillows and he covered her nakedness with his large, warm body, his hands on her breasts, fingers teasing a delicious response from her hardened nipples. He kissed her on the mouth, his tongue pushing, slow and insistent, between her parted lips, filling her mouth, soft and pink, a thrilling contrast to the hardness of the burning flesh lying across her right thigh.

She pushed gently at his strong, freckled shoulders and he rolled off her onto his back while she climbed on top, straddling his hips. His large pink cock was standing straight up from its red nest of hair, and she slowly eased herself down the length of his straining erection. She placed her hands flat on his broad pectorals, her nails raking his thatch of chest hair, as he slipped his callused hands beneath her buttocks and slowly lifted her up and then down the hard rod of flesh.

They say that fear and danger are the ultimate aphrodisiacs. Shades of Freud's Eros and Thanatos, the strangest of couples. Kate wondered briefly at the mystery of human sexuality, sometimes beautiful, often perverse, and then was swept up and carried away by the irresistible sensations rising from her body. Jeff was a patient and skillful lover, his hands gentle and knowledgeable; taking as long as it took, reveling in her growing excitement, holding back his own, he brought her to the summit from which she longed to plunge, but in the end just couldn't. He looked up at her, questioning, but she just couldn't fake it tonight, she didn't have it in her. "It's okay," she whispered, "it's okay. I want to feel you inside me."

She reached down behind her and cupped his swollen balls with one hand and with her other squeezed his left nipple. She heard his sharp intake of breath, felt his body stiffen, and then finally felt him relax the control he held over his own sensations, moving swiftly and deeply inside her, reaching up to take her breast in his mouth as he came, hot tongues of white fire inside her, each thrust growing slightly less urgent than the one before until at last she felt his whole body relax under her palms like a wild horse she had magically calmed.

She leaned forward until her head was lying on the hairy pillow of his chest, his penis still inside her, and listened to the slow and patient beating of his heart. Finally, reluctantly, she rolled off him. He put his arm sleepily around her and she could smell the slightly acrid but not unpleasant sweat of his armpit. Kate snuggled closer, feeling momentarily warm and safe, as if nothing could harm her now, trying to savor the feeling, knowing it wouldn't last long. "Go to sleep," Jeff murmured. "I'm here. No one's going to hurt you."

Ten minutes later she could hear Jeff's deep and steady breathing, his big chest rising and falling peacefully beneath her cheek. Meanwhile Kate lay wide awake, listening to the creaking and groaning of the old house and the sound of the mice scrambling around on the unfinished third floor. The first few months after she'd moved in she'd tried to get rid of the mice, setting traps on the dusty floor and windowsills. But the sound of the snapping traps startled her awake throughout the night and the carnage that greeted her in the morning was too much to bear. It was bad enough to see one of the small gray creatures nearly bisected by the copper bar, its insides squeezed out its mouth and anus, but even worse were the ones who'd somehow escaped instant death and were still alive, in many cases struggling to get free. In the end Kate decided it was best to leave the third floor to the mice.

She never went up there anyway, and they stayed pretty much to themselves, rarely venturing down to the lower floors, or at least having the decency to do it when she wasn't around to see them.

A gust of wind rattled the window.

Kate wondered how it had all come to this. After the Snow case, she had completely lost faith in herself as a psychiatrist, in the profession as a whole. Whatever else he had done, he had taken away her belief in herself as a healer, and there was nothing she could do to get it back. She had decided to become a teacher, partly because it was the most logical thing for her to do, and partly because she hoped her experience might somehow help someone else from making the same mistakes she'd made. Deep down she couldn't help but hope that psychiatry might someday make strides in rectifying the hopelessness of the human condition.

She had not told the whole story to Jeff. She had never told the whole story to anyone. Sometimes she wondered if he suspected she was just faking. If he did, he never let on. Did he somehow know she wouldn't be prepared to talk about it? Even tonight, when she'd come closer than ever to telling him the whole truth, she couldn't. She had even gone so far as to tell him the dream about the videotape. The one thing she couldn't bring herself to reveal was that during that dream she'd had the first and only orgasm of her life.

Now she lay awake, her head on the chest of the man she loved, listening to the mice scampering across the third floor, pawing and gnawing through the cardboard boxes holding the audiotapes she hadn't dared listen to in almost three years.

6

The plane had been diverted from its original destination upstate because of the weather and sent toward La Guardia to land instead. The brunt of the storm had already passed Manhattan, but the ride was still full of bumps and drops. Outside the small window, lightning forked the roiling black-and-blue sky as if it would spear the plane like a salad shrimp.

The stewardess walking down the aisle kept a smile on her face, straining to hold it there. The doctor didn't tell him, probably didn't figure he'd be doing much traveling, but Lincoln should have guessed that flying would be sheer torture. Besides the nausea, the pressure building inside his skull was almost unbearable.

He poured out the little bottle of gin into his plastic cup of seltzer and shook a pill loose from the brown bottle he always kept tucked in the pocket of his shirt. He was supposed to take one pill every four hours, and at first he held himself rigidly to the schedule, no matter how bad the pain and sickness, feeling that any lapse would be an admission of defeat, that the disease was getting stronger. In the end he simply surrendered to necessity. The disease *was* getting stronger; he was getting weaker. The only way to bear it at all was to take the pills whenever it started hurting. It was no longer a question of pride. It was a matter of survival.

He put the pill in his mouth, tasting its bitterness, and lifted his left arm to swallow it down with the gin and seltzer. As he lowered his hand again he felt his arm go numb from the shoulder to the fingers, the small cup slipping from his grasp, hitting the tray in front of him, its contents spilling over the side, splashing his shoes and the cuffs of his pants.

"Are you okay, sir?" the stewardess asked, genuine concern replacing the fake smile she had worn only moments before.

"Yeah," Lincoln said, embarrassed. "I'm sorry. It just slipped."

"That's okay. It's been some flight. I'll be back in a minute with something to clean up."

Lincoln stared at his arm like a man who'd been betrayed. That's what dying was like, your body betraying you. He felt the sensation coming back into his fingers and he flexed them a couple of times. The tingle spread to his shoulder, the feeling slowly returning to him. He looked away in disgust, down the aisle of the lurching plane. Around every object was a delicate nimbus of blue light, as if he were one of those psychics who claimed they could read auras, or as if, as the Hindus believed, he could see the life residing in all things, animate and inanimate. He smiled grimly to himself. The idea made him think of Snow. Was it possible the two of them had something in common now?

Lincoln shut his eyes, rubbed them as if he could somehow erase the ominous symptoms with his fingertips. He knew what came next. The huge black hole that obstructed the right visual field, as if someone had blown a chunk out of his world with a cannon. He kept his eyes closed, unwilling to face the truth. The symptoms wouldn't subside until the pill kicked in, and then it would be only a matter of hours before they returned, the time between symptoms growing shorter and shorter as the days went past. Inside his head the pain laughed at him.

Its voice was Alexander Snow's.

1:55 A.M.

Kate lay staring at the ceiling, her mind working in overdrive, knowing that sleep was impossible.

She carefully lifted Jeff's muscled arm from around her shoulder, heavy with sleep, and slipped out from between the sheets. She found her chamois robe draped across the armchair and covered her nakedness. She stooped over Jeff's sleeping form and kissed him lightly on the forehead before creeping carefully across the floor in bare feet to the door, opening and closing it behind her with a barely audible click.

At the end of the carpeted hall was the staircase to the third floor. Kate flicked on the light switch and climbed the short flight of stairs to the landing, unlocking the door with the ancient skeleton key she kept in the lock, and reaching inside to turn on the light, letting the mice scamper away to their hiding places before entering the room.

It was a large, unfinished room extending nearly half the length of the house, the ceiling slanting down sharply to the right. When she was being shown the house, the real estate agent suggested putting in dormers to let in light, but Kate had neither the finances nor the need to turn the attic room into functional living quarters. With only the roof overhead she could hear more clearly the ferocity of the storm, the howling wind, and the fierce, hard hooves of the rain and wonder how many more roof tiles were being torn away. In the middle of the unfinished floor there stood the green plastic garbage container she had set in place earlier to catch the rain already leaking in through a soft spot in the roof. From where she stood she could see that the container was already more than half full. It would be too heavy to carry down herself. She'd have to remember to ask Jeff to do it in the morning.

Here and there she could see other shiny patches on the ceiling and caught the irregular sound of dripping water, but nothing bad enough to cause any major damage, not that there was anything of value to damage in the attic room. There was some furniture from her old apartment in New York too modern to fit in with the Victorian theme of the house, furniture now shrouded in white sheets, the ghost of furnishings past; boxes of old photographs and letters she never looked at anymore; other boxes filled with personal mementoes, things she had no use for but couldn't quite bear to throw away. If she lost the whole lot of it to some accident of fate, she would feel more relief than grief.

There was only one box she was looking for now, one box she had any use for, though she had hoped it, too, might somehow be carried away in some unforeseen accident. Unlike the others, it was unmarked. She didn't need to label it to remember what lay inside.

She carried it from the shrouded form of a white-stone coffee table to the black lacquer desk against the wall on which sat a compact cassette recorder. She had asked for permission to tape their sessions and been denied it, but she had done it in secret anyway, not willing to trust her memory and unable to capture his quicksilver mind no matter how quickly she scratched out her notes, hoping someday to decipher the secret of his mad brilliance. Now that he'd escaped, the box of tapes seemed to be calling to her.

She tore open the box and reached inside the jumbled collection of cassettes, grabbing at random the first that came to hand. She glanced at the date on the label. January 19, 1990, approximately two months into therapy. She placed the tape into the recorder and pushed the play button, sitting back in her old leather office chair, and felt the rude shock of his voice over five years old, speaking as if he were standing just behind her.

"I have held the human brain in these two hands. It weighs less than three pounds and loses its consistency within minutes after being removed from the skull, collapsing into a soggy

gray pudding. And yet this three pounds of gray pudding is responsible for everything from the Cathedral of Notre Dame to the gas chambers at Auschwitz, from the cure for polio to the atom bomb. It can spur us to actions of superhuman selflessness and achievement or lead us to the most depraved acts of violence and sadism. From self-sacrifice to murder, there is nothing under the sun that this amazing organ cannot conceive, and, once conceived, turn into reality.

"Did I call it an organ? The heart is an organ, the lungs are organs, the liver is an organ. They can be transplanted, replaced, and one day even made obsolete by mechanical replicas. The scientific technology is being developed right now. But we will never be able to duplicate the brain. It is not an organ; it is the stuff of miracles, the substance of mysticism, the flesh of God Himself. Those idiots like Dennett and Hofstadter who think the brain is just a machine are nothing more than deluded fools. The brain is not a computer, it does not operate like a computer, nor does it break down like a computer. Their misguided efforts to create a model for artificial intelligence will always remain just that: artificial. Even if science were able to crudely mimic the functioning of a living brain in all its infinite complexity, it would never be able to duplicate the myriad clouds that shadow the functioning of the human brain, giving birth to the phobias, anxieties, psychoses, and neuroses that are the genesis of personality. The point they miss is that it is not the rational but the irrational that makes us human. It is in the inexplicable malfunctioning of his brain that a man manifests his creativity, achieves his greatness. No technician will ever be able to create an artificial brain that suffers. The Buddha was right: our enlightenment begins in the realization that we suffer.

"The neuroscientists, which I counted myself among until only recently, have charted and mapped the human brain with their sophisticated instruments. They tell us the brain is nothing but a pattern of chemical and electrical patterns. Our hopes, our fears, our greatest ideas and our basest fantasies, even love and hate, can be measured and reduced to nothing more *than various observable patterns inside the brain. But I ask, what organizes those patterns? For instance, a psychosis is accompanied by certain very definite and easily recognizable abnormalities in the electrochemical structure of the brain. But are these changes truly the cause of the manifestation of mental illness or merely the observable symptom, just as a tumor is the observable symptom of a cancer but not the cause of the cancer?*

"It has been estimated that the total number of connections in the brain of an average adult human is greater than the number of particles in the known universe. How can anyone seriously propose that our brains are merely machines and that human science can duplicate them? It would require the creation of an entire universe. And yet if our brains are truly the stuff of God, could we not, like God Himself, re-create the universe? You see, I come full circle, speak in riddles, if you will, for it is all an insoluble puzzle to me. At times it seems more like a joke. Are we each really no more than a soup of chemicals interacting with one another? If so, how come no one can reliably predict the outcome of the reaction as we can with any other chemical interaction? Take dreams, for example. In spite of medical science's best efforts, we have not been able to explain away our dreams. If anything, their experiments have proved our need to dream. Why do we need to dream? Can machines dream?

"At the same time, where do 'we' go when we fall asleep at night? How do we wake up the next morning with the same thoughts, memories, opinions, desires? Why don't we wake up as someone else? Or simply with a clean slate? There are hypotheses to explain where information is stored in the brain, but no one has yet explained how this information makes up the coherent and consistent 'I' one experiences day after day.

"I should have warned you from the start; perhaps it's not too late to warn you now. If it is, I can only say I'm heartily sorry for my lack of discretion and professional caution. You have put yourself and your mind in grave peril in accepting me as your patient. I have done no little laboratory work on

*the biochemistry of interpersonal relationships, and my findings
concur with those of others even more expert in the field than
I. The act of learning, which is inherent in any personal interaction, produces a direct physiological change in the neurons in
the brain. You're an intelligent woman. I think you can see
where I'm going with this. The relationship between therapist
and patient changes each person's brain. These sessions,
whether you realize it or not, are quite literally altering your
mind. They are changing the person you are, the person you
thought you were, into someone you know not.*

"*Beware, Katherine.*"

2:01 A.M.

Snow enjoyed the sensuous feel of the torque and hum of
the well-designed engine in the cushioned seat beneath him.
Across the windshield the rain lashed faster than the wipers
could push it away. He held the steering wheel lightly in his
hands, correcting the slight swerve of the car as it was buffeted
by gale-force winds.

This stretch of the interstate was dark, only his headlights
piercing the murky blackness, yet he could see miles beyond
the reach of the beams. In his youth his vision had been poor,
and through medical school it had deteriorated as a result of
too much reading and too little sleep. Yet he had corrected it
himself through sheer force of will and the help of an ancient
Tibetan ideogram upon which he had meditated regularly for
three years. His optometrist recorded the results incredulously
as Snow's eyesight went from 20/400 to a perfect 20/20. His
visual acuity was now far above average. Though conventional
medical science would deny it, Snow had convinced himself
there was nothing one could not accomplish through the correct
application of concentration and willpower.

Snow watched the front fender of the car eating the miles,
the distance between him and his goal, like so many bitter pills
he had to swallow. He thought of demonstrations he'd seen of

Indian yogis deliberately ingesting poison capsules with no ill effects.

He had already killed six people and his peculiar odyssey had only just begun. A favorite verse from the *Bhagavad Gita* flashed through his mind.

> *He who thinks himself a killer*
> *and who thinks it killed,*
> *both fail to understand;*
> *it does not kill, nor is it killed.*

He was not a killer so much as an instrument of death; those he killed did not die but were subject to a random process of transformation.

In the distance, Snow could see the haze of the city's lights sitting on the horizon like the afterglow of a nuclear blast.

New York City.

City of liars.

7

2:22 A.M.

Kate popped out the cassette, put it to one side, and rummaged around inside the box of tapes. She pulled out a second cassette, the label recording a date sometime in the middle of Snow's analysis. Outside the wind rushed over the roof of the house, dropping its load of rain, but the storm was obviously passing, the worst of it over.

Kate let out a sigh.

The house had made it through another crisis more or less intact.

She fingered the cassette a moment and then dropped it into the recorder. She waited a moment more before pressing the red play button.

"All men are liars, Katherine. In fact, psychology could be called the study of lying, for men and women are pathologically unable to tell the truth. In twenty-five years of practice, I've heard nearly everything imaginable—everything but the truth. In every case I've been presented with, the patient has lied to me, holding back some key piece of information, some memory or fantasy that might have effected a cure, if only they had

been courageous enough to face it. I've become so adept at recognizing the chronic lying I hear everyday that I hardly need my machine anymore to detect it. I can see it in a patient's posture, an expression, the most fleeting gesture. With my eyes closed, I can detect it in the very tone of a patient's voice.''

"Why do you think people are lying to you, Dr. Snow?''

"Because it is not so easy to tell the truth. In fact, in most cases, our survival often depends on us concealing the truth, from others, and, even more important, from ourselves.''

"I don't understand. Why would we lie to ourselves?''

"It's simple. Our very identity depends on the lies we tell ourselves.''

"How?''

"The very first, and most pernicious of lies we tell ourselves, is when we say 'I.' What we call 'I' is little more than a fictional character invented out of sheer necessity: it is an illusion to explain the ever-changing perceptions that appear and pass away before our sensorium. Without this fundamental lie we would have no center of being in the world; we would collapse into a riot of meaningless perceptions and thoughts.''

"I don't lie to myself.''

"No? Can you remember what you ate for lunch last Thursday? Where you ate it? The position of your legs as you ate? Can you remember what you were thinking? What the weather was like? Can you do the same thing for the lunch you ate ten years ago last Tuesday? Five years ago? Can you even tell me how many times you touched your face in the last five minutes?''

"Those events are meaningless to me. I have no trouble remembering what is important. Therein lies my basis for a real 'I'.''

"You say you remember the important events, the climactic events in your life. But do you really remember? How much of it are you imagining? Police are familiar with the phenomenon. Six different eyewitnesses to the same crime have six different descriptions of the perpetrator and the order of events in which the crime occurred. In your own experience, how many married couples have you counseled who saw the circum-

stances of their deteriorating relationship in the same way? Do you think they are consciously lying? If not, how can there be such different interpretations of reality? What is the truth? You see, we are all unwitting creators of the fiction that is our lives. We lie: filling in gaps, guessing at detail, speculating, making up events. We tell and retell ourselves a plausible story so that in the end it all somehow fits together.''

''I remember Dr. Snow.''

''It is a lie.''

''I don't agree.''

''I have, under hypnosis, or merely by the mildest form of suggestion, induced memories in patients so vivid that upon awakening they would swear they had actually lived through them, so real that they could even pass one of my E-meter tests.''

''That proves only that you are a good hypnotist. A good liar yourself.'' (Laughter.)

''We are not who we think we are, Katherine. We credit ourselves with an identity we do not possess. We do not possess an integrated consciousness, and without this consciousness we can have no unity, no ego or 'I,' no true self. We are left with only the illusion of consciousness. In fact, we are as insubstantial as ghosts. Descartes said, 'I think, therefore I am.' But we really know nothing about ourselves, and if once in a while we get a glimpse of the yawning abyss inside each of us, we turn away quickly, not daring to admit what we have seen. We go through life like sleepwalkers, and when we awake, we lie to ourselves about what we did not truly experience. We make up facts to cover for this existential void. Almost all we know about ourselves is fiction.''

''Are you a liar, too, Dr. Snow?''

''I am a man. All men are liars. You finish the syllogism yourself, Katherine.''

''Are you lying to me now, Dr. Snow?''

''I've gone beyond normal psychology into the realm of supernormal psychology. I've traveled through Europe, Egypt, India, Ceylon, Turkey, and the Near East, through China, and

even into Tibet. I've witnessed the extraordinary feats of Hindu fakirs who can live buried underground without oxygen for days at a time or inflict upon themselves hideous mortifications of the flesh without apparent permanent harm. I've studied with Buddhist masters who've lived on remote mountain retreats, men who've devoted their whole lives to sitting cross-legged, counting their breaths, until their minds were as empty and yet as powerful as the wind. I've visited Christian monasteries where monks have given themselves over to the total devotion of Christ, enabling them to perform what contemporary science would consider miracles. But there is a price to pay. There is always a price to pay. And I don't mean my two-hundred-dollar-an-hour fee. To follow me, the prospective seeker must be willing to suffer.''

"Suffer?"

"You're no doubt familiar with Zen koans?"

"Yes. They are ancient Japanese riddles presented to students seeking enlightenment.''

"True enough. The profane consider them nonsense, the scientifically minded mystical mumbo-jumbo. The more reflective try to explain them from a philosophical perspective. But do you know the real purpose of a koan? How it works from a psychological perspective?''

"No, I can't say I see the connection.''

"One Zen master described the koan as a way of snatching a stick away from a blind man, to push him to the ground, turn him around, and thereby throw him into complete despair, in which he has no idea which way is right or left, up or down. The koan works that way upon the mind, ruthlessly taking away our 'stick' of intellect and reason. The purpose of the koan is to throw us into blind despair. To leave us with no clue as to up or down, right or left. To throw us into the terror of unreason in which there is only one way out: enlightenment. I'll leave you today with a koan, Katherine. Perhaps you can solve it, perhaps not. It would honor me if you would try, for it's one I've been working on myself for a long time without success. Perhaps you can help enlighten me.''

"I'll do my best."

"Very well. Here it is. How, without reflection, can the eye see the eye?"

2:25 A.M.

In spite of the weather, the dark car sped north along the rain-slick highway into the windy blackness that was upstate New York.

Lincoln stared out the window. The concussive pressure in his head was now little more than a dull throb, an echo of the pain he'd felt earlier, and the visual disturbance was all but gone. The pills had done their job. They would continue working for a few hours more. Up front, the young agent behind the wheel was silent. Earlier, Lincoln had asked him a couple of questions and had gotten only a few clipped words by way of response. The kid was no doubt a rookie, fresh out of training, but he already had the superior act down pat. Lincoln found himself being treated with the same polite deference he himself remembered treating outside "experts" during his old days with the agency.

He looked at the back of the young agent's close-cropped head.

Had it really been so long ago?

Three years.

That was all it took to make him an outsider.

He turned back to the window. The trial had been orchestrated from the beginning. With Snow's agreement, the case had been tried in front of a judge rather than a jury. Lincoln figured Snow would consider it easier twisting one mind instead of twelve. But what he didn't realize was that Lincoln was pulling all the strings he could pull and had one of the toughest judges on the circuit assigned to the case. At the same time, he'd gotten the state to assign its most talented and tenacious district attorney to serve as the prosecutor, a young up-and-comer with none too secret political ambitions who was dedicated to keeping his conviction rate over ninety percent by hook or by crook.

The last thing to consider was Snow's defense, the one thing Lincoln could not control, yet he couldn't have picked a better candidate himself. As Lincoln stared out the rain-lashed window, he still wondered what had caused Snow to make such a grievous error. Was he purposely placing himself at a disadvantage, putting himself as deep in the hole as he could so that his escape would be that much more spectacular, like some kind of psychological Harry Houdini? Or was it just a mistake? No, Lincoln thought, Snow didn't make mistakes. Of all the aspects of the case, this was the one that disturbed him the most.

Snow had chosen a brusque, brash, no-nonsense woman who'd made a name for herself defending the victims of rape and spousal abuse, as well as women who'd taken the law into their own hands against their formerly abusive mates. She considered herself to be on a personal crusade and was generally the kind of one-track, narrow-minded emotional type that Lincoln couldn't abide, but who made an invaluable ally, especially in a case in which the rules were made to be bent. She knew about the information Kate had given him, which led to the raid on Snow's office and the collection of incriminating papers, which constituted the basis of the investigation and the subsequent case against him, but she agreed not to object to the admittance of the evidence or pursue their source, which lay in the tricky legal area of privilege between psychiatrist and patient. Kate had spoken only under the condition of complete confidentiality. She refused to testify in court and made it clear that if she were subpoenaed, she would stand by her professional ethics and force contempt of court charges rather than face Snow. At the time Lincoln could not understand the hold that this man had over people. He would learn that for himself soon enough.

Snow sat patiently through the trial, even as on point after point his own lawyer sold him upriver. He had a chance to speak, to defend the controversial therapeutic practices outlined in his notes, but coming as it did after the harrowing testimony of the only one of his former patients willing to testify, a thirty-year-old woman so broken in spirit and composure that the judge mercifully dismissed her from the stand without cross-examination and with no objection from Snow's counsel, Snow's scientific and theoretical explanations of his radical therapy fell flat. The judge retired to his chambers for less than fifteen minutes before returning with his decision. Lincoln thought he had the case won, but Judge Macklin turned out to be the one wild card in the deck. In spite of his reputation as a hanging judge, he was also eminently honest, and he had smelled a rat from the beginning. He declared Snow to be mentally incapacitated and remanded him to an upstate mental facility for the criminally insane for a period of time to be declared at a later sentencing hearing. Snow's own lawyer was so incensed Lincoln was afraid she might leap from her seat to object, a reaction not lost on the judge, and presumably not on Snow, either.

As they left the courtroom, before his wrists were cuffed behind his back, Snow extended his hand to Lincoln.

Lincoln had hesitated, as one would before picking up a snake, and then reluctantly took Snow's hand, refusing to be intimidated, pretending he considered it a token of honest surrender.

"You won," Snow said. "Congratulations."

Lincoln's mind was a storm of emotions as he looked into Snow's calm, knowing face. Snow knew damn well that Lincoln hadn't won at all, hadn't gotten what he really wanted, which was to have Snow convicted of kidnapping, torture, and rape, even if he could not yet prove murder.

Lincoln had been so preoccupied with anger that he hadn't noticed Snow's peculiar handshake until later, how the doctor had slid three long fingers on the inside of Lincoln's wrist, feeling his pulse. He was only aware of Snow's ice-gray eyes and the matter-of-fact words which came from his thin, colorless lips.

"In six months," Snow said neutrally, "you will be diagnosed with an inoperable brain tumor."

Lincoln felt a shudder even now at the memory. He had dismissed Snow's statement as an attempt to psych him out. But sure enough, four months later, Lincoln began experiencing painful headaches, visual dysfunction, and numbness on his left side. He ignored the symptoms at first, but of course he couldn't forget Snow's words. Had the bastard planted some kind of subconscious suggestion in his mind, similar to the way voodoo priests worked? Two months passed and the symptoms had grown so debilitating that Lincoln was forced to check into the hospital for testing. A CAT scan detected the peach-sized tumor in his right anterior lobe, and more ominously, the tendrils that had spread throughout his cortex and deep inside to his hypothalamus, making the tumor impossible to remove.

Lincoln's first reaction was disbelief, then rage. How had Snow known? Lincoln resisted as best he could the irrational conviction that Snow had somehow planted the tumor inside him, hypnotized him in such a way as to make him grow a tumor. His doctor reassured him that such an idea was ridiculous. No one had that kind of power. Still, Lincoln could not shake the obsessive idea that Snow was in some way responsible. How had he known? It was only while discussing Snow's diagnosis with one of the hospital's young Indian interns that Snow had received a satisfactory answer. It was then that Lincoln remembered and described the strange handshake at the end of the trial, just before Snow had pronounced his fateful words. The intern explained that in India those trained in the Ayurvedic medical tradition are able to determine a person's health simply by feeling their pulse. Though it has been proved such physicians exist and the skill can be learned, it is very difficult to master and Western medical science cannot bring itself to accept its viability. Still, it gave Lincoln the rational explanation he was looking for to explain Alexander Snow, the explanation he needed to remind himself that the doctor was just a man.

Lincoln repeated the phrase as the car raced through the storm to the prison.

He's just a man . . .

"What's that sir?" the young agent asked from the front seat, glancing in the rearview mirror.

"Nothing," Lincoln said, not realizing he'd spoken out loud.

He's just a man, Lincoln whispered this time, the words forming a pattern of condensation on the cold glass and then disappearing.

He didn't believe them himself.

8

Kate was putting the cassettes in at random now, reaching into the box and pulling out whatever came to hand.

She inserted the cassettes one after another, fragments of Snow's monologues blending together into a bizarre patchwork of theories held together by a deceptive thread of reason, like the fevered ramblings of a psychotic.

How easy it would be to believe that Snow *was* simply psychotic, that what he said made no sense. But behind her conviction that the hypnotic voice on the tapes belonged to a man who was completely insane, Kate couldn't help but admit that what he said made terrifying sense. It was in this sense that she sought the path that led through the labyrinth of his twisted mind.

If she could find the secret hidden at the end, perhaps she could figure out why he had escaped from prison and what he was likely to do next.

She picked up a tape dated two weeks before the end of her sessions with him. She remembered the hour well. He was wearing an impeccably tailored Armani suit, his long fingers wrapped around a small green bottle of Perrier, at which he periodically sipped. It was the first time she suspected he might be a murderer.

"*Why do you think we choose to sleep instead of staying awake?*"

"*Because our lives are too easy. If you are in pain, you are aware of everything. Time stands still. Only then are you wide awake.*"

"*But isn't it human nature to avoid pain? Don't we all seek to avoid as much pain as we can?*"

"*That is precisely the problem. The Buddha's First Noble Truth is that all of life is suffering. We can't reach enlightenment until we allow ourselves to suffer. Nothing is more difficult, and yet nothing can create so much inner focus and force as voluntary suffering. Its power is exponential, atomic. The idea is to create an inner force so irresistible it can shatter the immovable object of self. There is no way to do this without suffering.*"

"*And how do we create this state of voluntary suffering?*"

"*The sad fact is that most of us need help. That is where I come in. I help the patient see what there is in himself to hate. When one becomes angry with oneself, one can see many things that were hidden before. The most difficult thing of all is to go against oneself, against one's own views, opinions, and most deeply cherished beliefs. Awakening is not for the timid. Man begins to heal himself from the moment he first realizes that he is not what he has told himself he was. When he sees that he is little more than a helpless worm masquerading as a man, then he is on the way to a cure.*"

"*Self-loathing, a loss of self, what you are describing sounds dangerously close to promoting a nervous breakdown.*"

"*Many people come to me wanting to change. If only they could change they would be happier, healthier, more successful. There is only one thing standing in their way. You cannot change if you want to keep everything. You must be ready to give something up. To even think about changing, one must think about what one would give up. The problem is that no* one wants to give up anything. They all want something for nothing. Well, it doesn't work that way.''

"You're saying that we can't have it all."

"Buddha's Second Noble Truth. The root of all suffering is desire. Our society has lost the idea of sacrifice. Ancient civilization practiced ritual sacrifice. They selected and offered up to the gods in ceremonies of slaughter the most beautiful girl and boy in the village. We regard them as primitive, barbarian. But the fact remains that they understood a key point in the psychology of transformation. You cannot gain anything new unless you're willing to give up something you already have. And often, what you must sacrifice is precisely that which you prize the most.''

"That doesn't seem fair."

"Life is not fair. Nor can any amount of wishful thinking make it so. The chief mistake we make about ourselves is that we consider ourselves one. We are always referring to ourselves as 'I,' and we make the mistaken assumption that we refer to the same person everytime we use the word. Not even Freud, Adler, Jung—the fathers of psychoanalytic theory—could come up with a satisfactory definition of the ego. In reality, we are divided into hundreds, into thousands of different 'I's.' How many times have you acted abominably in some situation or other only to wonder later how you could have behaved that way? How many times have you made a solemn resolution in the evening only to do the exact opposite in the morning? We say we have merely changed our minds, that we lack self-discipline. But in fact, we are witnessing the multiplicity of 'I's' that inhabit us, each with its own claim over our bodies. Whenever you have a thought, it is one part of you speaking. The very next moment, another 'I' is speaking. Each one has its chance at the controls and the inner struggle between them is what makes up your life. Is it any wonder why people lack control over their own lives? Is it any wonder why they are so unhappy?''

"And what is the way to happiness?"

"Buddha's Third Noble Truth: the end of suffering is the

elimination of desire. As you might have already guessed, the first thing we must sacrifice is this ridiculous, flawed, imaginary notion of 'I.' We must correct this lie by any means necessary, including the most radical. 'I' is a cancer that has gone out of control, eating away all that is vital in our lives. We are riddled with 'I.' Try going through a single day without saying the word, a single hour without thinking it, and you will see what I mean. Every breath we take is 'I,' every breath we release is 'I.' We're rotten to the core with 'I,' a mere husk, a walking corpse taken over by this false personality. We are like zombies, like the living dead, repeating a single diseased mantra 'I, I, I.' We are terminally 'I.' As a result, there is no therapy too severe, too harsh, too experimental. We are living in a state of emergency. We are living under a sentence of death. The prognosis is hopeless unless we can somehow uproot this disease at its source.''

''And how often have you been successful at uprooting this 'I'?''

''You ask me my rate of success? You think perhaps I will flinch from the harsh glare of full disclosure? The fact is, as you must well know, that my rate of success is almost negligible. But the cases I have seen are all but hopeless. You ask an oncologist how many cases of terminal cancer he has cured and his answer will be the same. Maybe one in ten thousand, and that one an unrepeatable miracle at that. But no one criticizes the oncologist, even though his methods have been shown to be all but useless, even though a person has about as much chance of being cured of terminal cancer by the best of specialists as he has being cured by drinking holy water from Lourdes or being ministered to by a witch doctor.''

''So you're saying it's a miracle if anyone is saved at all?''

''Yes. The people who I've seen are in as desperate a condition as the patient dying of cancer. Outwardly they may appear to be normal, but over thirty years' experience has taught me that the majority of people who are considered sane are more deranged and consequently more dangerous than those pronounced certifiably insane. The inmates are truly running the

asylum! I speak of the man in the street, of the politician on the floor of the Senate, of the father at the PTA meeting, none of whom ever stops to question his identity, who never realizes that he is basically divided against himself, who never ever suspects that he is ill.''

"But how would one of your 'enlightened' patients deal with ordinary life? Wouldn't he or she become more alienated from his surroundings? Isn't the point of psychiatry to help the individual function within consensus reality?''

"A patient can be dealt with either as a machine or as a human being. Most psychiatrists today favor the mechanical-chemical approach. No doubt they have some superficial success. But at what cost? How can you successfully treat a man like a machine without, in the process, turning him into a machine? Can a man be explained as no more than the sum of his dreams, desires, fears, and hopes or reduced to a series of simple biological chemical changes? Is he just a cog in the social machinery? Or is he not more than that? I prefer to think the latter. You may call me insane, but I cling to the belief that man is alive. But to be alive, we must first be born. We cannot be born until we die, and we cannot die until we come awake. And we cannot awaken until we realize that we are asleep.''

"Dr. Snow, I can't help but feel that your theory is dangerous, not just to the health of the patients, but to society as a whole. I just don't see how your awakened individual would function.''

"Kate, the sad truth is that most men's lives are a series of accidents, one after another, until the day they die. What could be more dangerous than that? Accidents don't happen to people whose lives comprise conscious actions. A man can correctly be said to possess a will only when he has discovered his true self. So long as he suffers the disease of many 'I's' he will move like a weathervane at the whim of every passing breeze. I don't say it to brag, but the fact is that I never suffer accidents. I have no negative emotions: they drain energy. I remember

*every event of my life. Except the most important. That is why
I'm here."*

3:00 A.M.

Dr. Snow exited the interstate at a small town called Warwick.

He drove the BMW down the silent streets until he came to
a darkened strip mall. He turned into the deserted parking lot
and rolled to a stop in front of the ubiquitous hardware store
that is a staple of small, still predominately rural towns filled
with do-it-yourselfers and part-time farmers.

He turned off the ignition and lights and climbed out of the
car. He jogged the ten feet to the storefront, ducking under the
overhang, but still got soaked, water dripping down the back
of his collar, the rain still coming down steadily, occasionally
blown into a horizontal wall by the gusting wind.

The double security deadbolts on the front door, the best the
store had in stock, were no problem to Snow with the clever
manipulation of credit card and car keys. What was a problem
was the burglar alarm. As the door swung open, Snow heard
the sharp-pitched tone of the ADT alarm as both the broken door
connections and motion sensors were alerted to his presence. He
had seen the sticker on the window and figured it was a fifty-
fifty proposition whether the store was truly wired or not.

Snow knew he had forty-five seconds. Forty-five seconds
before the warning signal would turn into a full-scale alarm
that would be broadcast over the telephone line to those moni-
toring the system. They would place two calls. First they would
call the store; failing to get an answer, or someone who knew
the right code, no second-guessing, they would place a second
call, this one to the local police department.

Snow walked calmly to the panel on the wall identified by
a tiny red light flashing in the darkness. The rubber keypads
were numbered from zero to nine. Snow was familiar with the
system. There were four numbers in the code, any one of which

could be used twice. Snow's mind ticked off the number of possible permutations: 10,000.

If Snow had known the man who owned the store, not to mention his birthdate, his children's birthdates, his social security number, etc., he could have guessed the number the man would most likely have chosen with an accuracy that would have convinced an uninitiated observer that something supernatural was at play, instead of the utmost application of psychological logic. As it was, Snow would have to use a different strategy to disarm the system.

He let his long, sensitive fingers play lightly over the numbered pads, feeling just the slightest trace of wear over four of the rubber pads. He was in luck. If whoever had set the code had used a number twice, Snow would have cut the number of possibilities from 10,000 to 256, a significant decrease, but still a daunting number of possible combinations. Yet by wearing down the pads and using each number only once, the man who'd set the system had allowed Snow to cut the number of possible combinations all the way down from 10,000 to 24.

By Snow's internal clock, he still had thirty seconds to punch in the code, which gave him over a second a combination. With his superior manual dexterity, it was no trouble at all. In fact, he hit the correct sequence on only the third try, the panel giving three satisfied little beeps, the red light turning to green, signaling all was clear.

Snow glanced around the dark store, making a mental inventory of the stock lining the shelves. The storm had depleted the supply of candles and kerosene as people anticipated power outages, but there was still enough for what he needed, including four whole shelves of spray paint.

9

Kate listened to the voice on the tapes, her mind wandering. She remembered the circumstances surrounding the trial, which, of course, she did not attend. She remembered the betrayal that had led to the trial. She could think of no better word than betrayal to describe what she had done.

She had betrayed her own patient.

Snow was a murderer, of that she had no doubt. Every instinct honed by ten years of therapeutic practice told her so. She would never have done what she had if she hadn't first been convinced in her own mind. Yet she could not shake her feeling of guilt. There had been a relationship involved, a relationship that went beyond mere professional confidentiality, or the legal wrangling about doctor-patient privilege. It was a relationship quite unlike any other.

No layperson could fully understand the link that developed between a psychiatrist and a patient. It was more than a meeting of minds; it was a meeting of souls. Patients confided in their analysts things they would never tell their closest friends, things they didn't dare speak of even with their spouses. In many cases, they said things they'd spent years unable even to admit to themselves. Snow had been right. By the very act of sharing his story, he'd changed them both forever. Theirs was a very special bond. And she had willingly broken it.

Still, how long could she continue to keep his secret? If only she could have helped him stop, helped relieve his anguish. But how many innocent lives would it have cost? How could she have lived with herself then?

No. There was no doubt in her mind that she had done the right thing. She had taken a violent and insane man off the streets and had him locked away where she hoped he could get the help he needed. No, that was self-deception. She knew perfectly well that he was beyond the help he'd be offered at a prison for the criminally insane. Perhaps he was beyond help at all. She still wondered why he had picked her as his psychiatrist; it was one of the questions he had never satisfactorily answered.

Even though she knew she'd done the right thing, Kate had felt the need to punish herself. In retrospect, she realized that was why she had quit her lucrative Manhattan private practice, broken the lease on her penthouse apartment at a substantial financial penalty, and even severed a fairly promising relationship with a successful Wall Street trader. But she was driven by more than simple guilt to give up the trappings of her superficially successful life. The fact was that her experience with Alexander Snow had caused her to lose faith in psychiatry at the most basic level. She no longer believed in what she was practicing. In light of what she'd learned from working with Snow, she was driven to reevaluate her career. As a result, she was forced to admit that she couldn't say unequivocally if she had ever truly healed anyone, if her methods hadn't always fallen short, if her patients didn't leave just as sick, if not sicker, than when they'd first come.

And so she gave it all up and came to Ocean Grove as if retreating into exile. Strictly out of financial necessity, she accepted a position as a professor of psychology at the local private college, her classes a form of penance. As a teacher, she passed on what she knew to a new generation of bright, naive young psych students who eagerly devoured many of the same theories she had once idealistically embraced as offering salvation to modern man's troubled soul. Sometimes she felt like an old magician giving away the tricks of the trade, revealing the reality behind the illusion, debunking popular therapies, slaughtering many a sacred cow. But in the end, she felt as if she were a better teacher for all that, dispensing to impressionable young minds the antidote to the most dangerous poison of all: that any theory truly explained the mysteries of the human mind.

Meanwhile she had tried put the memory of Alexander Snow behind her for good by immersing herself in her new life. At first it wasn't easy. For months she had troubling dreams of Snow, dreams that took the form of their old sessions, as if his therapy were continuing uninterrupted on another plane of reality. She took pills, tried self-hypnosis, forced herself to stay awake to the point of exhaustion, even took up jogging, but still the dreams came, and worse, they were invariably accompanied by an erotic dimension that left her feeling nauseated and violated.

She did everything she could to exorcise the demons—everything short of what deep down she knew she should do, which was to go to a psychiatrist. But going to a psychiatrist meant reliving the whole nightmarish experience all over again, and that was one thing Kate was unwilling to do. She had thought she had left it all behind her in New York, but she had forgotten the most basic truth of the psyche: you couldn't run away from your problems because you carried them with you. The only way to give them the dodge was to go insane.

Until tonight she had at least taken some comfort in the knowledge that Snow was safely behind bars. Even though hardly a day passed that she didn't consider with cold dread the possibility of his escape, she convinced herself that she was being unreasonable. Lincoln had assured her that the investigation against Snow would continue until they found some solid evidence linking the psychiatrist to murder. Kate let herself believe him: she'd had no choice. The trial hadn't gone according to plan; neither had the sentencing. But both Lincoln and the DA had promised her that Snow would stay put for the maximum fifteen-year sentence. Lincoln himself would personally see to that.

And then came word that Lincoln had gotten sick, an inoperable brain tumor, and been forced to retire from the agency.

Not long afterward the DA ran for public office and got elected, beginning the long climb to the political prize he'd coveted all along. And where did that leave Kate?

All alone with her nightmares. And tonight the worst had come true.

Snow had escaped.

Kate stared at the cassette in the tape player, watching the white sprocket of the tiny reel slowly turning, hardly hearing Snow's voice at all anymore, not the words, anyway, just the tone—smooth, soft, hypnotic. She knew she should turn it off, but somehow she couldn't.

Kate hadn't told Lincoln about the tapes, hadn't told the DA, hadn't told anyone. They were her secret. Why she'd kept them she couldn't say. Was it out of some last remnant of guilt or some lingering, if misguided, notion of professional ethics? Or worse, was it due to some unconscious complicity she felt toward the killer she had betrayed?

She had boxed them up and never meant to listen to them again. But why save them if she hadn't planned, on some lost and forlorn night, to replay them and try to ferret out the answer to the enigma that was Dr. Alexander Snow. She had no doubt that the answer lay buried in the hours of taped conversations she had held with him over that fateful seven-month period, less conversations than monologues, lectures, in which Snow spelled out the twisted mysteries of man's existential soul. What was it that he'd said? He could remember every incident in his life but one. That's why he had come to see her. What was he trying to remember?

And then there was the koan: How, without reflection, can the eye see the eye?

If she could answer those questions, would she finally have found him out? More important, would it exorcise his presence from her psyche? Could it keep her from being afraid?

3:16 A.M.

Snow drove fifteen miles down the road to a row of cheap motel units just off the main highway through town.

The electric vacancy light hanging under the rusty, weatherbeaten sign surged on and off in accompaniment to the rising and falling of the wind, as if unsure whether to invite him in or not. In the lot outside there were a few cars with out-of-state plates, stranded travelers, no doubt, as well as three tractor-trailers whose drivers had decided to sleep out the storm. It was the kind of run-down establishment few people would choose unless forced to by circumstance and lack of options.

At the desk Snow signed in using Todd Scheffield's name and sliding Todd's platinum Amex card across the counter so the night manager could take an imprint. The night manager was in his forties, but old-looking, his eyes red and rheumy, his skin jaundiced, his body narrow-shouldered and thin, with a small pot belly. A flap of wet hair lay across his pasty-white pate like a broad stroke of black paint. Snow spotted one of the causes for the man's accelerated aging between the first two nail-bitten fingers of his left hand, a cigarette butt burned down nearly to the filter. As if on cue, the night manager took a long drag on the cigarette as he ran the credit card through the scanner.

"Some night we're having, isn't it?" he said, trying to make small-talk, his voice cracked by nicotine.

On the counter behind him a late-night movie fought the static on a small black-and-white television. From the dialogue, Snow recognized it as *The Rainbow Jacket*, an English melodrama about horseracing made in 1954, starring Robert Morley, Kay Walsh, and Wilfrid Hyde-White. It must have been a long night.

Snow looked up from the guest log. In Ayurvedic terminology, the man was a pure Vata type, his life burning away as quickly as the cigarette between his fingers. He would live for another five, ten years at the most.

"Terrible," Snow said, returning the credit card to Todd's wallet. "But violence is a prelude to peace, peace to violence. They are two sides to the same coin. All is compensatory. The more violent the storm, the more tranquil the peace. My guess is that we should be seeing some beautiful weather after this storm passes."

"Yeah," the man behind the counter said, getting more than he'd bargained for. "I guess that's one way of looking at it."

"Think," Snow continued, "of how light and free you feel after an outburst of anger. The earth's atmosphere is no different than the psychic atmosphere. Each must restore its balance by any means necessary, even if it requires an occasional explosion of destructive force. It's nature's way of establishing harmony. The Chinese called it the way of the Tao."

The man behind the counter crushed his cigarette in an ashtray littered with twenty-four tan butts. He pulled another from the softpack in his pocket and lit it with a blue Bic disposable lighter. He exhaled smoke, squinting through one eye. "Are you some kind of scientist or something?"

Snow smiled. "I like to think of myself as a teacher."

He had requested and gotten a room at the end of the row of tiny units, nine doors away from the nearest occupant, not that it was likely anyone would hear him moving the furniture around over the sound of the storm. He parked in front of the aqua-green door to room 27 and climbed out of the car, the plastic bag from the hardware store clasped in his right hand as he bent forward against the wind-driven rain.

Unlocking the door, Snow stepped dripping into the room and gave it the once-over, his eyes piercing the gloom. A bed, a nightstand, a pressboard desk, two broken-down armchairs. The air smelled of stale yogurt.

It was perfect for what he had in mind.

Snow shut the door behind him, carefully locked it, and slowly undressed.

Less than twenty minutes later he was sitting naked in an advanced version of the esoteric yoga position known as "Scorpion Poised to Strike." His hips were thrust backward, his legs drawn up behind him, his ankles crossed at the back of his neck, his feet on either side of his head. His arms were held straight down in front of his body, his face showing not the slightest strain in spite of the fact that he supported the entire weight of his body on the knuckles of his fists.

He had unscrewed the cracked full-length mirror from the back of the bathroom door, propping it up in front of him, and it was into this mirror that he stared, calm and unblinking, his body dabbed by reflected flames of the flickering candles, so that in his serene immobility he resembled nothing more than a votive statue. His voice, deep, sonorous, and sounding as if it came from the throats of hundreds of devout monks, shook the window of the room, as he intoned his secret mantra.

Who is sitting?
Who is breathing?
Who is watching?

10

3:35 A.M.

3:35 A.M.

Except for the barbed wire at the top of the red brick walls, the Hudson Correctional Institute for the Criminally Insane looked more like a country club than a prison for dangerously insane felons. It was situated on a prime piece of green real estate in the countryside of upstate New York. The local zoning board, representing a cadre of concerned citizens, had exerted its power to keep the prison looking as little like a prison as possible. No doubt the well-heeled had moved to this quiet oasis in the New York landscape hoping to escape the violence and squalor of the city they had left behind. But the former governor had decided it was only fair that the misery be spread around equally. The prison had been built over their protests, and the evil had followed them out here. As a result, they did the only thing that was left for them to do, which was to make the prison as aesthetically pleasing as possible.

Overly officious, the guard kept the car waiting at the gate while he double-checked Lincoln's credentials, his caution clearly a case of closing the barn door after the horse has escaped. Lincoln snorted in disgust. He was prepared to see a

lot of that behavior in the next hour or so. No doubt the guard
had been instructed to let no member of the press through. If
they couldn't keep the prisoners in, then they could at least
keep the newspapers out. Finally the guard came back from
the small guardhouse, his hand resting significantly on the butt
of his holster. He passed Lincoln's identification back through
the window, stepped away from the car, made a motion to his
partner in the guardhouse, and brusquely waved them through
as the wooden gate blocking the road ahead jerked its way up.

Lincoln was met inside the main building by a short, balding
man with glasses perched on a small, beaked nose, putting
Lincoln in mind of a myopic turtle. He was flanked by two
guards in tan uniforms. The man introduced himself as the
assistant warden. He held out a small, pudgy, clammy hand
which Lincoln took reluctantly, staring over the top of the
man's head, the scalp flaking with dandruff, down the long
hall behind him. He barely heard the man's name, which was
Archibald Whipple.

There were several state troopers talking together, their long
black slickers dripping rain. A couple of men in the cheap, ill-
fitting suits common to undercover detectives stood off to the
side, smoking and comparing notes. A few uniformed cops
completed the scene. Overall, there was a curious lack of action.
They all had that slightly dazed, excited look that people got
after a tragedy. Lincoln could feel the impatience boiling inside
him. No one seemed to be *doing* anything.

"Would you like a cup of coffee?" the little bald man asked.

"I'd like to get started," Lincoln snapped.

"Of course," Whipple said, clearly taken aback. "Where
do you want to start?"

"At the beginning," Lincoln said. "His cell."

"Fine. Just let me get my coat."

They made their way under a covered walkway to the cell-
blocks accompanied by Whipple's two bodyguards, the rain
pinging off the sheet metal overhang offering scant protection
from the wind, which blew the rain against them at an angle.
At the entrance to block C-9, the assistant warden passed a

magnetized card through a sensor and a guard unlocked the heavy door from inside. They took the stairs down to the wing where Snow's cellblock was located, the elevators shut down for precautionary measures, their shoes ringing off the metal, the tight coil of the stairwell making Lincoln slightly nauseated. Two flights from the bottom the assistant warden stopped and ran his card across a second sensor and the lock on the door disengaged. They stepped through the door into a small commons room with a TV mounted on the ceiling, a ping-pong table, and a couple of sofas, both of which looked to be in better shape than Lincoln's own. On the other side of the room they stepped through another locked door and into the cellblock.

The long row of cells were dark, splashed here and there with the harsh glare of wall-mounted spotlights that did less to illuminate the dank interior than fill it with ominous clusters of conspiring shadows. But what was worse was the cacophony of madness that greeted Lincoln's ears: the barks, grunts, and howls of insanity. After the initial shock of being diagnosed with terminal brain cancer, one of Lincoln's first fears had been that the cancer would cause him to go insane. He quizzed his doctor on the possibility and could get no more than a lukewarm opinion that his chances of losing his mental faculties were slim. Still, as Lincoln pressed the doctor, he discovered that the possibility of madness existed. The prospect of insanity frightened Lincoln more than death itself. He'd faced death before in the line of duty, and he'd always faced it eye-to-eye. That was the way he wanted to face it when the end came. He wanted to die with all his faculties intact, with dignity, courage, and understanding. He didn't want to slip out of life a slobbering idiot unaware of who he was. He had promised himself that under no circumstances would that happen. He would end his own life first. Now, standing at the head of that shadowy corridor, the fear came back twofold.

If he didn't know better, Lincoln would have thought he'd stepped into a pen of caged animals, the sounds bearing no relation whatsoever to human speech. The air was rank with the smell of urine, fear, feces, and the sulphur stench of desperation. As he passed the cells, Lincoln caught glimpses of the inmates imprisoned within. From the corners of his eyes he saw them, crouched on the floor, hugging themselves, rocking back and forth on their beds, or simply standing like statues, their knuckles white on the bars of their cells. But in every case it was the eyes he noticed most of all, eyes trapped, eyes damned, seeing visions no one else could see and that could be described in languages no one else could understand. If he didn't know what horrible crimes most of them had committed, Lincoln could almost feel sorry for the poor bastards.

"They know something has happened," Whipple offered. "That's why they're so damned excited. I don't know how they know, but they know. Of course, this storm doesn't help any, either." They stopped at the last cell but one on the block, the assistant warden splashing a flashlight inside. "This is it," he said.

"May I?" Lincoln said, indicating the flashlight.

"Be my guest."

Lincoln stepped inside the cell that for the past five years had been the home of Dr. Alexander Snow. The cell was simple: a thin cot bolted to the floor, a toilet, a chair, a small desk. Still, just being in the cell Lincoln could sense the aura of pure evil the man had left behind: it made the hairs on the back of Lincoln's neck stand on end. On the east wall Lincoln saw a taped piece of paper on which Snow had executed an expert piece of Chinese calligraphy. On the desk he saw a carefully arranged stack of books. Among them were *The Tibetan Book of the Dead, Yang Style Tai Chi Chuan, Chi Kung: Health and the Martial Arts, The Iron Cow of Zen,* a translation of the *Mumonkan,* and several books whose titles Lincoln couldn't make out, as they were written in Chinese. Obviously Snow hadn't gotten such volumes of esoteric literature from the prison library.

"How come he was allowed books in his cell?"

Whipple was visibly irritated. "Really, Mr. Lincoln. This isn't a concentration camp."

"Well, under the circumstances, that's too damn bad, isn't it?"

The assistant warden said nothing. Lincoln's flashlight found the broken broomstick wedged between the corners of the wall.

"I presume this is where they found him hanging."

"Yes," Whipple said.

"And the doctor pronounced him dead?"

"Dr. Chang. A good man. He insists that Snow had no pulse, that he'd been dead for some time. He feels awful about this whole thing."

"I bet he does.

Lincoln followed the assistant warden as he buzzed them through the doors at the other end of the cellblock and passed the guard's station, through another set of locked doors to the freight elevator. The car was stopped at the bottom floor, doors open, two lab techs still inside, collecting evidence. Lincoln saw the chalk outline of the two bodies, the empty gurney on which Snow lay, presumably dead, the dark splash of blood on the floor already looking thick and tacky. "From here he took the elevator to the doctors' lounge," Whipple said.

They took the stairs again, Lincoln puffing and panting, the pain in his head growing larger and smaller with each breath, stopping on the landing to will back the dizziness, taking out his pad and pretending to be taking notes. Instead, he was writing out the numbers from one to twenty and back again, a trick he'd learned to keep his head clear.

The lab techs weren't quite finished with the body in the doctors' lounge.

Lincoln saw the dead man lying face-up on his back, two red pulpy holes where his eyes should have been, his whole forehead sliding down the front of his broken face like a bloody ape.

"Dr. Abbott was going down to the infirmary to sign the death certificate when he ran into Snow," the assistant warden said. "Snow then escaped through a window in the men's room."

In the bathroom Lincoln noted the iron grate propped on the

floor, the window still open as Snow had left it, a puddle of water collecting on the tiles. Lincoln leaned forward and took note of the drop.

"He shouldn't have survived the fall without at least a broken leg," Whipple suggested.

Lincoln pulled his head back through the window and glared at the little man.

"He shouldn't have had the opportunity to try."

The assistant warden seemed glad to finally deliver Lincoln at the warden's office. Inside the spacious room, Lincoln found himself at the hub of frenetic activity that seemed to signify that at least something was being done, even though it was clear that no one knew any more than Lincoln did. The office was occupied by several guards as well as a disheveled old man introduced to Snow as the local police chief and another as the second-in-command of the New York State Police. The warden was on the phone with the governor, a cigar clenched between his teeth. He was a pleasant enough looking man with a broad red face, greased back white hair, and about twenty too many pounds around his waist. He hung up the phone, which immediately began to ring again, and held out his hand to Lincoln.

"I'm glad you're here, Mr. Lincoln. My name's Garvey. Jim Garvey. We've sure got ourselves a situation."

"I'd say that's putting it mildy," Lincoln said, his face hiding nothing.

"Yes," the warden said. "Well, did Whipple here show you around?"

Lincoln nodded.

"Good. Have you got any questions?"

"Just one," Lincoln said quietly. "How the hell could you have let a man like Alexander Snow get away? What the fuck are you running here? A girl scout camp?"

The hubbub in the room died away, everyone in the office seeming to freeze in mid-motion.

The warden regarded Lincoln through narrowed blue eyes,

his face growing redder. He measured his words carefully and then spoke as if taking a particularly nasty-tasting medicine.

"Look, Mr. Lincoln, I've lost three good men to this bastard. I want him as much as anyone. More."

"You had him," Lincoln growled. "And you lost him. I told you what he was capable of. Do you have any idea how many innocent people your incompetence has put in jeopardy?"

The warden was halfway around the desk now, moving quickly for such a big man, his fists doubled up at the end of once-muscled forearms gone to flab like the rest of him. The color of his face had deepened to that of raw meat.

Lincoln stood his ground but was grabbed around the shoulders and turned around by a man he'd not even noticed before, a lanky, square-jawed kid with a blond military brush-cut. He reminded Lincoln of the young agent who'd driven him from the airport, except there was a hardness around the gray eyes of this kid that took away his innocence and made him seem unnaturally older. With just a glance into those eyes, Lincoln knew he was looking at a man who'd already seen something of the darkness of the world.

"Mr. Lincoln, please," the man said. "This isn't the time or the place."

"Who the hell are you?"

"My name is Ryan McCall. And I'm in charge of the Agency's participation in this case."

"I see," Lincoln said, the sudden reminder of his civilian status leaving him feeling momentarily awkward. "You're my boss."

"In a manner of speaking, yes. But I'd rather you think of yourself as my consultant."

"Well, boss," Lincoln said, ignoring the diplomacy. "May I ask, pray tell, your opinion of this meat-headed imbecile here?"

Lincoln could feel the hostility pouring off the warden behind him like a wall of heat.

"I'm not going to stand here and take anymore bullshit from this broken-down Elliot Ness. I don't give a rat's ass who he used to be. Get him under control, junior, or get him the hell out of here!''

''I'll handle it,'' McCall snapped, ice in his voice. He looked back at Lincoln.

''My opinion is unimportant. My job is to recapture Dr. Alexander Snow. But since you asked, my opinion is that antagonism and personal attacks aren't going to get us one step closer to our goal.''

''You're right,'' Lincoln said, impressed by the younger man's composure, but in no way mollified. ''But let's get one thing straight from the start. There's not a man in this room who knows more about Alexander Snow than I do.''

The young agent nodded.

''That, Mr. Lincoln, is why you're here.''

3:51 A.M.

Wake up, Katherine!

Kate started, realizing she must have dozed off, and stared at the tape machine as if it were speaking directly to her. Nonsense, of course. It was just Dr. Snow going on about how the overwhelming majority of people were asleep. Still she couldn't shake the eerie sensation that he was in the room—if not physically, then psychically, that he knew her every move, that she was meant to hear the words he spoke years ago right now, that he had somehow planned it all from the start. Now she really was thinking nonsense.

Still, irrational or not, she couldn't shake the feeling of Snow's malign presence.

''Be on your guard, stay awake, even Christ himself said so, Mark, chapter thirteen, verses thirty-three to thirty-seven. Stay awake, because you do not know when the master of the house is coming—evening, midnight, cockcrow, or dawn: if he comes unexpectedly, he must not find you asleep.

''Reich and Gurdjieff were close to the truth, but one succumbed to his own psychoses and the other allowed himself to be swallowed by the myth of his own reputation. Guru sickness,

*I call it. But had either persevered to the end and had the
courage of his convictions, he would have seen that there is
only one way to wake people out of their terminal sleep, and
that requires the most extreme measures.''*

''What are you saying, Dr. Snow?''

''Pain, Katherine. Pure and simple. The lies are held inside
our bodies and manifest themselves as chronic muscular tension, impotence, frigidity, all manner of physical and psychoso-
matic ills. We must break through the body's armor to the true
memory locked inside the patient's brain.''

''Isn't what you are talking about sadism?''

''Is it sadism when the surgeon cuts open living flesh to
remove the tumor that has insinuated itself into healthy tissue?
To heal is to hurt, Katherine. There is no other way. Disease
has its own life, and if we are to save the patient, we must be
the murderers of the disease.''

''And where do you draw the line, Dr. Snow?''

''Where does the oncologist draw the line? Radical surgery,
chemotherapy, and, in the last resort, experimental drugs. We
must use everything at our disposal in the battle against disease.
Everyone accepts it in the case of physical disease, but they
are reluctant to apply the same standards to mental illness.
Why is that? What lack of courage prevents us from seeing the
correlation? If we could truly wake up humanity we could
eliminate the cause of ninety percent of the diseases flesh is
heir to.''

''And what if the patient cannot 'wake up,' as you say?''

''It is a tragedy. But then we haven't really lost anything,
have we? If you aren't awake, you aren't truly alive.''

''Dr. Snow, as a physician, you can't possibly mean that.''

''Ah, but I do, Katherine. As a physician I have an obligation
not to flinch from the grim truth.''

''And what is that?''

''Sometimes the cure is death.''

11

Lincoln stared down at the body of the girl lying on the pavement, the top of her head showing a visible indentation where the skull had been caved in, her teeth scattered on the asphalt.

A few feet ahead, by the light stanchion, a young man was lying on his back, his head twisted clean around so that you couldn't see his face. His left arm was stretched to his side, hand out, a long, ragged slit like a pair of gaping lips grinning inside his open palm. In the booth behind him Lincoln had already seen the body of the toll collector, his fat, naked body wedged so tightly under the counter they were probably going to have to cut him out.

Off to the side, in a glare of red strobelights, McCall and a pair of state troopers in black slickers were questioning a jittery man standing under a small umbrella, which he struggled to keep from turning inside out with every gust of wind. He was a salesman on his way back from Buffalo. He'd had nothing on his mind but paying his toll, keeping his car on the road, and getting home in one piece when he'd happened to stop at this nightmarish scene. He used one of the pay phones just beyond the tollbooth to call 911. His car, a late-model Toyota, was parked by the phones, the driver's side door still hanging open, from where he'd no doubt stumbled to the phone half in shock from what he'd seen.

The whole picture was clear to Lincoln. The doctor had killed the tollbooth collector, stolen his clothes, and waited for the first car to come along. The salesman didn't know how lucky he was. An hour or two earlier, and it could have been him. Lincoln stared back down at the girl again. Long brown hair, slender, with blue eyes, a girl about the same age as his own daughter. He averted his gaze from her exposed breasts and stared at the side of her face visible through the matted hair. She had been pretty. He could tell, even though the savage blow to the top of her head had distorted her features, pushing them forward and causing them to sag like a deflated balloon.

Snow hadn't even bothered to cover his tracks. He'd made no attempt to hide the bodies, which would have been easy enough, but had left them lying right there in the open, no doubt knowing the first person who came along would spot them, no doubt intending just that. But why? Was this all some kind of grisly game to him?

The rain had washed away the blood and no doubt most of the forensic evidence from the murdered bodies outside, but a team from the coroner's office were moving carefully in and around the tollbooth itself, dusting for prints and looking for blood and hair samples. A pair of detectives were probing the grass beneath a stand of trees with a pair of long black maglites. Just like at the prison, Lincoln had the impression that everyone was moving in slow motion, if they were moving at all. No one seemed to understand that time was of the essence.

McCall turned away from the troopers questioning the salesman and came stalking back toward Lincoln, his head bent against the wind, his trenchcoat flapping around his knees. He straightened up underneath the booth, his blond brush-cut soaked flat against his skull, and wiped his face and head with one swipe of his wet sleeve, making the short hairs stand on end again.

"The guy didn't see anything," he said. "Just drove up to drop his quarters and found the slaughter. No telling how long ago the perpetrator was here."

"Snow. It was Snow."

"No doubt, but until there's a positive ID . . . "

"Here's all the proof you need," Lincoln said, pointing down at the dead girl.

McCall nodded. "Look, I know where you're coming from, but I'm just trying to make sure this goes down by the book."

"I did it by the book," Lincoln snapped. "I know how the book ends. This is the sequel, and I'm going to make sure it ends differently this time, one way or another. I know this is Snow's work, and I want as much material evidence as we can gather. I don't know why he's being so careless, it's not like him, but I'm not looking a gift horse in the mouth. When we nail him, he's going to have the blood of six murders on his hands." Of course, he hadn't been careless enough to leave any identification on the two victims. Lincoln pointed both ways up the highway. "I want this whole area cordoned off, a half mile up the road, a half mile down, and every blade of grass examined and examined again as if it contained the fucking cure for death. Try to get a positive ID on these two kids ASAP. Find out what kind of car they were driving and put an APB out on it immediately. If he's spotted, I want to be informed. No one is to stop him unless the effort is coordinated. That means waiting until he gets settled and bringing in maximum backup. No cowboy shit. Dr. Snow is too dangerous and we might lose him for good."

McCall flushed red beneath his brush-cut. "I know what to do, Mr. Lincoln."

Lincoln didn't miss the emphasis McCall had placed on the word "mister." He ignored the none-too-subtle implications.

"Then do it," Lincoln barked, and turned away.

As McCall dashed back into the rain, Lincoln stared up the

dark ribbon of road that with each passing minute carried Dr. Alexander Snow that much closer to freedom.

4:17 A.M.

Inside the small roadside motel room, the naked man carefully lowered his legs, hitching his shoulders just a bit, lifting himself up a little higher on his white-knuckled fists, and finally coming to rest in the full lotus position.

A small, enigmatic half-smile played on his face lit by the remaining candles as he stared into the full-length mirror and watched his reflection slowly materialize in the glass. For an indeterminate time that could have been a moment or an eternity he had experienced a taste of pure existence. During that time that was no time, in a place that was no place, there had been no right or wrong, no yes or no, no I or Thou. He had totally ceased to exist and at the same time had become existence itself. There was nothing left but the radiance of being, and that being was everything and everywhere at once. Beyond that, no words could describe the experience, though mystics of every faith had tried and failed.

It was but a sip of the limitless, living waters of immortality.

It was a taste of the cure for death.

He sat now in front of the mirror, watching his body solidify around him, watching himself become incarnate. He had the distinct impression of putting on a costume for a part in a drama of which he was but an actor. It seemed to him he had done this many times before, in many different lifetimes, and the strange thing was, he always came back by choice, each time playing a new part. How easy it would have been to escape from the painful dualities of this fallen world into that nameless, disembodied light of pure, perfected existence. What was it that kept him coming back, delaying his own nirvana?

Mercy.

Infinite mercy.

That was it. Mercy for all the poor, suffering creatures who did not have the power to see that they, too, were already enlightened, if only they could be made to see it.

Like the bodhisattvas of old, who had broken free of all earthly attachment, he had taken the Buddha's vow, promising not to leave until he had helped every last soul to escape the endless wheel of desire and pain that was ordinary mortal life.

Did those who persecuted him as an outlaw, a criminal, a madman, not realize who he truly was?

Or were they merely demons bent on destroying his work in order to better keep humanity enslaved?

Did those who sought to stop him truly not realize that what drove him to his work was love—limitless, unconditional love?

Did they not know that no power was greater than love?

Did they not know that to show the ultimate mercy he had to be merciless?

From across the room, he saw the man in the mirror and recognized the face looking back. It was the face his ageless spirit had assumed for this incarnation. He moved the muscles of his face as if trying on a mask and called to himself by name.

"Welcome back, Dr. Alexander Snow."

12

They stopped at a diner about a half-hour from the tollbooth down the interstate. McCall doubted Snow would have been stupid enough to pull into a place so close to the scene of the brutal murders, but Lincoln wasn't leaving anything to chance. He didn't have the time to explain why it was exactly something Snow would do. While the young agent stood by the kitchen, talking to the night manager, Lincoln sat in front at a table next to the cash register, questioning one of the waitresses.

She had the look that all waitresses—and many FBI agents, for that matter—acquired after too many years on the job: the trapped look of frustration, dashed hope, and resignation to fate that betrayed that their lives had not turned out as planned and—man or woman—it prematurely aged them at least ten years. Lincoln studied her carefully. The dark circles and cracked lines bore testimony to eyes that had seen too many late nights, the manicured but chipped nails to vanity given way to the demands of necessity. It was late and the foundation on her cheeks was beginning to cake, settling into the lines bracketing each side of her full but unpainted lips.

On the table in front of her was an empty pack of cigarettes. She was taking an early break.

Lincoln took out a pack of Marlboros from inside his trench-coat. He noticed how her eyes darted furtively to and from the pack, like a mouse sniffing cheese in a trap. He'd never smoked himself, but he'd learned that a pack of cigarettes could be as important to an investigator as handcuffs or a .38.

"Cigarette?"

"Yeah, thanks."

He watched the slight tremor of her hand as she took the cigarette from the proffered pack, the way it moved between her lips as he struck a match and lit it. She inhaled deeply, blew the smoke toward the ceiling, but Lincoln still caught a whiff of it. He hated the smell of burning tobacco; it made his head throb.

"Look, I told you already, I didn't see anything unusual."

"What's your name?" Lincoln asked quietly.

"My name," the waitress said, as if momentarily stumped. "Marty. Martina, really, like the tennis player. But everyone around here just calls me Marty."

"Marty, I've been in this business a long time," Lincoln said, and made himself smile. "You might even say a little *too* long. One thing I learned is that sometimes people see things they don't even remember they've seen. It's not unusual. They're not on the lookout for anything, caught up in the regular grind and all that, things just slip by unnoticed. But I want you to think hard. Real hard. The man we're looking for is very dangerous. He's already killed six people, and he'll kill more if we don't stop him. If you came across him and he didn't kill you, it was merely a matter of chance. Under different circumstances, he'd be as liable to kill you as any of the six people he's killed already."

Lincoln paused, letting the words sink in.

The waitress was staring out the window. Lincoln could see red taillights in her eyes. The license plate, he thought. If only he could read the license plate number between those taillights.

"I say this only because I know that a lot of people have

sympathy for fugitives. In a way, it's only natural. A man on the run from the law seems vulnerable, alone, even afraid. Something inside us wants to believe that he's innocent, that he's somehow been falsely accused. It's human nature to root for the underdog.''

Lincoln sensed McCall coming up behind him; McCall had finished questioning the night manager and was now standing over the booth. Lincoln saw the woman eye the young agent nervously.

Too bad.

Lincoln liked to work this alone. He knew he had to finish quick or the waitress would become completely distracted.

''Though he may seem like the victim now, he's not. The man we're looking for is insane. We don't even know how many people he killed before he was sent to prison. But we need to catch him. For his own safety as well as the safety of his potential victims. He's better off in a facility like Hudson Valley, where he can get the attention he needs.''

Lincoln was actually thinking that the only safe place for Snow was in a pine box, six feet underground.

''Now I'm going to show you a picture of him. It was taken about five years ago, but his appearance won't have changed. If you remember anything, anything at all, no matter how insignificant it might seem to you, it could be of tremendous help.''

Lincoln reached inside his trenchcoat and pulled out an 8×10 black-and-white photograph. The mug shots taken after his arrest were useless. Almost every experienced criminal attempted to alter his appearance when being photographed for the files, narrowing his eyes, jutting his jaw, raising his chin, trying to appear more menacing than he'd appear in ordinary life or completely emptying his face of all expression whatsoever, leaving behind nothing but a lifeless mask. The effects were subtle, but almost always futile, but the idea was to effect enough of a change in appearance as to make a positive ID impossible for a prospective eyewitness. However, in Snow's case, the effect was truly eerie.

When Lincoln first saw the mug shots, he was convinced that there must have been some kind of mistake, that the man in the photo was not Alexander Snow. But a double-check of the records confirmed that it was him, all right. Somehow, Snow had been able to alter his appearance for the camera so severely that he looked like a completely different man. How he did it Lincoln could only guess: a deliberate slackening of the facial muscles, perhaps, or an intimate knowledge of the function of light and shadow in photography. Whatever the explanation, Lincoln didn't like the idea that no reliable photograph of Snow existed in the FBI file. Call it intuition, but he had a suspicion that he'd need one someday.

So he'd hired a professional photographer to capture the real Snow during the trial, stepping out from behind Lincoln in the hallway like an assassin, snapping a roll of film as the doctor was being led into the courtroom. Lincoln still remembered the expression on Snow's face when he'd heard the rapid-fire click of the camera's shutter. The doctor had been caught unawares, but only for an instant, yet it was the instant the photographer needed.

Later, when the roll of film was developed, only one clear picture of Snow emerged; the rest were either blurred beyond recognition or obstructed by a smoky black patch. The photographer could not explain what had happened and Lincoln didn't care. He had his picture of the devil. It was the picture he now laid on the table in front of the waitress.

Lincoln saw something open in her eyes and then slam shut again.

"I don't recognize him," she said.

"Are you certain?" Lincoln asked patiently. "Take a good look."

The waitress took another long drag from the cigarette. "He wasn't in here. If he was, I didn't wait on him. Maybe one of the other girls . . ."

"Okay," Lincoln said and smiled, slipping the picture back into the pocket in the lining of his coat. "I won't take up any more of your time." He turned. "Come on, Agent McCall. We've got a lot of work to do."

"Did you see the way she reacted when you showed her the picture?" McCall said. They were standing outside the diner in a small, windowed vestibule that held three coin-operated videogames and a cigarette machine with a sheet of paper taped to the glass that read, "Out of Order." "I've never seen that kind of pupillary response before. It was straight out of an agency textbook." There was something of genuine awe in the younger agent's voice.

Lincoln watched the rain sliding off the windows. "I want her taken back to the local state police barracks and given a full interrogation. She may have seen the kind of car he was driving, even the plate number. If we can get it out of her, it'll give us a head start. The only alternative is waiting until those two kids have been ID'ed."

McCall nodded.

"As far as what you saw in there, it's nothing unusual. I've seen it a dozen times while interviewing people who've come in contact with Snow."

"What does he do, hypnotize them?" McCall asked.

"Even worse," Lincoln said. "He alters their consciousness."

"You can't believe that."

"Why not?" Lincoln said quietly, lost in the shifting patterns of rain on the glass. "He's altered mine."

4 45 A.M.

Kate could hear the uncertainty in her voice.

And what was worse, she knew Snow could hear it, too. It was as if she were playing a kind of mental chess with a grandmaster and had somehow carried the game far beyond her expectations, close enough to hope she could win, and yet at a loss as to what to do next, playing on mere intuition. On the other side of the board, Snow had been watching her with the intense, clear eyes of a falcon, waiting for that one fatal mistake that would finish her.

She could still see those sharp gray eyes.

She had tried to banish the eerie sense that he was carrying her along, that he was actually playing both sides of the board, that he was merely amusing himself, that he could end the game at any moment. She remembered thinking that even if he had allowed her to come this close out of some perverse compulsion of his own, she might still pull off a surprise move to defeat him, but only if she could keep her heart from beating so fast, only if she could keep her thoughts from racing out of control, only if she could keep her professional composure.

"*What are you saying, Dr. Snow? That any means are permitted? That death is a viable alternative to the human condition?*"

"*Personality is a defense against life: it must be shattered.*"

"*Are you speaking metaphorically?*"

"*Metaphors are a way of avoiding the truth, Katherine. My life and work have been devoted to just the opposite.*"

"*Then why are you being so evasive? I can't help but feel that you're purposely being obscure. Are you afraid of something?*"

"*Have you ever wondered how close we all are to the edge? Certainly you have made the observation that even a slight fever can disrupt our thoughts and perceptions. As R. D. Laing once said, we are all only a few degrees from madness.*"

"*I get the sense that you're trying to tell me something important, Dr. Snow, but you're encountering some inner resistance. It's as if a part of you is concealing another part of you.*"

"*Very astute, Katherine. We all have two brains—a right and a left—each dealing differently with different phenomena. Oftentimes one side of our brain literally doesn't know what the other side is doing. We are, biologically, at least, two different people.*"

"*Which two people are you?*"

"*More than two people, Katherine. Each change of mood can be said to be the emergence of a new personality. I am merely playing at being all the people who inhabit me: sinner, saint, healer, slayer. It's the same with each of us.''*

''I have a problem with that, Dr. Snow. I don't find myself divided against myself.''

''Ah, but you are. For instance, you can feel or believe one thing one moment and another thing the next. If you don't look too closely, you will never notice the logical inconsistency of your thoughts. But if you do look closely, you will realize with a shock that the two perceptions are completely opposed to each other. And that's when the revelation comes upon you: you are populated by numerous I's and no two of these I's have ever even met.''

''Are you trying to say that you're suffering from schizophrenia?''

''In treating psychotics, I realized that the only way to communicate with them was to get in touch with the psychotic in me. Only then could we speak the same language. In the process, I discovered things about myself that changed me forever. When it came time to return to what we ordinarily call sanity, I realized that I had gone 'native.' I remember the language of sanity, I can speak it well enough, but I am no longer sane. For I see in sanity an example of true psychosis, the victory of the 'I,' and in those we ordinarily label psychotic, I see the holiness of divinity.''

''I'm confused again, Dr. Snow. Are you speaking metaphorically? I can't help but feel that you're not being direct with me.''

''Our first act of power comes as children, when we tell our first lie. It's an assertion of our individuality, a way to protect ourselves. But to protect ourselves against what? We fall in love with the power of the lie and soon we are lying all the time, until one day, without even being aware of it, we are lying to ourselves. We no longer know the truth. What am I lying about, Katherine?''

''That's what I'm trying to find out, Dr. Snow. But you have to help me. Only you know the truth, only you can tell me. You're hiding something, Dr. Snow. Something I suspect you

*can't even admit to yourself. Have you ever hurt anyone, Dr.
Snow?''*

"*You disappoint me, Katherine. And up to now you were
doing so well.*"

The tape broke into the sound of Snow's laughter. And that's
when Kate heard it for the first time, like a subliminal message
suddenly stripped of the distracting cover noise. His voice was
sober, deadly sober, neither angry nor amused, but completely,
horrifyingly neutral, as if he were giving the time of day.

"*I know you are recording this, Katherine.*"

4:48 A.M.

Snow drove down the circular approach to the Lincoln Tunnel, feeling like a marble drawn inexorably down the inside of
a funnel.

On his left, in the predawn light, he saw across the gray
waters of the Hudson the famous sawtoothed skyline of New
York City, the top of the Empire State Building lost inside the
haze of heavy clouds. In a few hours the road would be jammed
with commuters on their way to work. Even now there was a
steady, light stream of traffic making its way toward the tunnel

To Snow, New York City was a steel, glass, and concrete
representation of everything wrong with human society, a city
built and sustained by lies. From the politicians in City Hall
to the brokers on the floor of the Stock Exchange to the CEOs
of its megacorporations right on down to the peep shows, street
hustlers, and rip-off electronics stores, it was a city whose every
brick was an illusion mortared together by falsehood. If there
was a god, this was the place he would destroy first. It seemed
only appropriate that in the event of nuclear war, New York
City was considered a prime target. More likely, however, wa
the possibility that the city would just collapse, no longer able
to sustain itself under the weight of its own corruption. There
was evidence of it happening already, as it already had to cities
like Newark and Detroit, leaving nothing in the wake of

illusory existence except a wasteland of bankrupt storefronts, empty lots, and unpopulated buildings.

Rain speckled the windshield and Snow smiled.

He knew what Ezekiel and Jeremiah had felt like when they'd railed against the sins of Jerusalem. Unlike them, he knew it was useless to preach to the multitudes. People could be awakened only one at a time.

And usually, not even then . . .

Slowing down at the tollbooth, he reached into his back pocket and pulled a five-dollar bill from Todd Scheffield's wallet. The tollbooth collector handed him his change. She was a short black woman in a uniform the color of exhaust who bore a striking resemblance to James Brown.

Snow thanked her cordially, but she didn't bother to look up.

He could forgive her lack of civility.

Breathing in the pollutants of the thousands of cars that filed past her booth every day had no doubt atrophied the parts of her brain devoted to higher social functioning.

Snow pulled slowly away from the tollbooth. He saw two black-uniformed Port Authority policemen listlessly watching the sporadic traffic as it passed by in the rain. They didn't give him a second glance.

As he approached the dark hole of the tunnel he felt just the slightest twinge of discomfort. He imagined he saw Dante's slogan at the top of the gate to hell emblazoned on the stone.

Abandon all hope, ye who enter here.

13

Kate stared at the tape recorder in disbelief. She told herself she must have heard wrong, that she must have dozed off, that she must have been dreaming. She hit the rewind button, cued the tape, and played it back.

There was no mistake.

She heard the laughter. And then she heard Snow's voice again: clear, calm, clinical.

I know that you are recording this, Katherine.

How did he know? Had he somehow heard the tape machine hidden in a closed drawer of her desk? Had he somehow spotted the wire or the mini-mike taped to the bottom of her desk? That much was plausible enough. The thing that made the hairs stand at the back of her neck was how he had been able to plant his message at the same time he'd been laughing, and how she had not heard him say anything at all during the session. How had he done it?

Immediately her mind began groping for some logical explanation, each more unlikely than the last. Had he stolen the tape from her and then overlaid his accusation on top of the laughter?

She had no doubt Snow possessed the technical know-how to do such a thing. The problem was, when had he gotten the chance to do it? She was careful to remove the tape immediately after each session, seal it in a dated manila file folder, and bring it home with her, placing it with the entire collection of tapes in a cardboard box she kept hidden at the back of her bedroom closet. Was it possible he'd broken into her house, found the box, tampered with the tape, and then broken into her house a second time to return the tape, all without her noticing? Or was it more likely that he had put her into some kind of trance during the session, causing her to miss the double-speak that enabled him to leave the message on the tape, bringing her back to consciousness after only the few seconds required to make his accusation? Again she had to concede that such a feat of mind control was not entirely out of the realm of probability for a man of Snow's psychiatric talents.

What was equally disturbing was the fact that Snow had bothered to dub the message at all. Why didn't he come right out and tell her he knew she was taping him? Of course she knew the answer. He had purposely planted the message like a time-bomb to blow up in her face at the moment she least expected it, the moment it would have the maximum impact to shake the foundations of her psyche. Still, how had he known that she'd listen to this particular tape at this particular time? Could he really have planned everything right from the start— the therapy, his enigmatic confession, his betrayal, the trial, his escape?

Kate recognized paranoid thinking when she saw it and her line of reasoning at the moment was as paranoid as it came, not reasoning at all, really.

She had fallen into a kind of morbid trance, and now she snapped herself out of it by clicking the recorder off. She stared up at the window and saw a small gray mouse crouched on the warped sill regarding her with blank red-rimmed eyes. At any other time, the sight of the mouse would have caused her to jump up in fright, but now she just held its fearful, beady stare until it saw the consciousness growing in her eyes and dashed squeaking away along the damaged wood, disappearing into a crack in the wall no wider than her little finger.

5:05 A.M.

They had set up temporary headquarters at a Holiday Inn about fifteen minutes east of Rochester. McCall was lying back on the made bed, not having bothered to take off his wet trenchoat.

Lincoln was sitting at a round prefab table by the window punching keys on the laptop computer he'd plugged into his cellular phone, keeping the line to the room phone open. Thirty years ago, when he'd first joined the Academy, they hadn't had all the electronic weapons they had now, and yet it didn't seem any easier to catch the bad guys now than it had then. Were the bad guys getting that much smarter, had lawmen gotten lazy, or had life just gotten so much more complicated that it negated the advantages offered by the information age? They were questions for another time and place. Right now, Lincoln had work to do.

He punched in his access code on the laptop, waited a few seconds for the file to open, and received only a message that the file was still empty. The preliminary results on the autopsies of the prison guards weren't available yet, nor were the reports on the crime-scene data from the investigation at the tollbooth.

Lincoln checked his watch; an Ironman Timex. It had only cost forty bucks, but dammit, on the same battery, the thing had kept perfect time for seven years. He sighed when he saw the number in the digital display. Too much time was passing.

"I'm sorry," McCall said from the bed, "if I came on a little strong before, pulling rank like I did. I hate that shit."

"Don't mention it. You find yourself doing things you hate when you're in charge all the time. It comes with the territory. Besides, I was way out of line. I was acting like an asshole. You don't begin an investigation by making enemies of the people on your team, no matter what kind of stupid pricks they are. I'm the one who should be apologizing. I should know better. The fact is, you're in chrage of this investigation.''

"Well, let's call it even. I may be in charge of this investigation, but without you, I wouldn't know the first place to start. Like you said, you know more about Snow than any man alive.'' McCall grinned, making him look even younger. "Besides, my superiors at the Academy warned me about your, what shall we call it—your diplomatic demeanor.''

"No doubt they told you I was an irascible, insubordinate bastard who could never work well with anyone, with more partners than Liz Taylor and Zsa Zsa Gabor combined.''

McCall laughed outright. "Yeah, something like that.''

"They also told you about my discharge. The cancer.''

The smile was gone. With it the hard, sharp look Lincoln had first noticed returned to the younger agent's eyes. "Yeah.''

"And you still want to work with me. Why?''

"Because of what else they told me.''

"And what was that?''

"That you were the best there ever was.''

Lincoln felt himself blushing, but whether because he was touched or incensed, he couldn't say. He figured it must have been Kirkland who'd paid him the long-distance compliment— Kirkland, who'd been his chief of operations for nearly twenty-five years with the Agency; Kirkland, with whom he'd been at loggerheads on more occasions than there'd been cases; Kirkland, who never so much as cracked a smile, let alone paid him a compliment when Lincoln broke an investigation; Kirkland, who'd never shown the least trace of emotion when he'd informed Lincoln that he would be forced to take a medical discharge. So this was the roundabout way the tight-assed old bastard paid him a compliment. Strangely, Lincoln could hardly help but feel it all the more valuable for that.

Without thinking, he punched a few more keys on his laptop until the emotion passed. That was another disturbing side-effect of his condition: he seemed to get more emotional about things than he'd used to. Sometimes, listening to a sentimental song on the radio or watching a corny movie on late-night television, he embarrassed himself by finding tears running down his face. He didn't feel quite so emotional now, but enough not to want to think too much about what McCall had said. The moment safely past, he felt the old curmudgeon in him retaking control.

"Well, you can't believe everything you hear in this business, kid. The secret is not to go gently into that good night. You put in your time and retire and everyone says what a great guy you were and forgets you in three weeks. You've got to make it dramatic: get taken down by a bullet or a tumor and they're ready to make out you were another Sherlock Holmes. People like a good tragedy."

McCall smiled again, the tension broken. "All the same, I think I'd prefer being forgotten in three weeks. What I still don't quite understand is just what makes this Snow so damn special."

"Did you read the file?"

McCall nodded. "Enough to get the general picture. A psychiatrist involved in some very questionable therapy, but no bodies to hang around his neck. Until tonight, that is. You were lucky to get him put away for as long as you did, but then, from what I heard through the grapevine, luck had very little to do with it. You played the judicial system like a maestro."

"Except for one thing."

"The judge. Well, not even a maestro can be blamed for a broken string. That was merely a matter of chance."

"No matter. It still played wrong."

"I can understand how it must have eaten at you, how it still eats at you, especially now that it's been proved the bastard is nothing but a cold-blooded killer. But why the personal vendetta?"

"Because Snow is evil."

McCall shrugged. "They're all evil in this business."

"You don't understand. Snow *is* evil."

"What the hell are you talking about?"

"Did you see the photograph of him in the file?"

"I saw the FBI mugs and what I presume is a copy of the 8 × 10 you showed that waitress. The two look nothing alike."

"How old would you say Snow was, judging from the 8 × 10?"

"Forty-something. Lose the silver hair, he could be thirty-five."

"He was sixty years old when the photograph was taken."

"Jesus Christ," McCall said, sitting up on the bed. "That was almost five years ago. You mean we're chasing a sixty-five-year-old man?"

"That's right. Let me tell you a story about Snow. About two years into his time, he was sitting in the prison library working on the page proofs of a psychological article he was publishing when he was approached by some three-hundred-plus pounds of psycho with his pants down around his ankles and his jimmy pointing north, looking for someone to play Juliet to his Romeo. Snow calmly took a sheet from the page proofs, cocked his wrist, and when the psycho came close enough, whipped that sheet of paper around so fast the edge sliced right through the meat of his neck. You know how badly even a minor paper cut hurts. Well, this was the grandaddy of all paper cuts. It severed the poor bastard's carotid artery and he bled to death right where he stood before the medics could get to him. Luckily for Snow, there was a trustie shelving books who saw the whole thing and he corroborated Snow's account. The death was ruled an act of self-defense. Maybe that gives you some idea of why Snow is so 'special.' We're talking about a man who can kill you with a sheet of paper, for chrissakes. If there's a way to murder someone, he knows it. The man is a walking, talking killing machine. So maybe you can appreciate something of my desire to see him brought down as soon as possible."

McCall could not quite get the image of the carotid paper cut out of his mind. He found himself unconsciously rubbing his throat. Beneath his fingers he felt the first sharp whiskers of a missed shave.

"Do you think he'll try to leave the country?"

Lincoln shook his head. "He's too smart for that. He'll know we'll have the airports alerted. Buses are another matter. But we've done our best to make them aware of the situation. On the other hand, Snow likes nothing better than the chance to show off his brilliance. And there's no telling how long or how well he's planned this breakout. For all we know, he might have provided for a false passport while in prison, had it hidden by someone on the outside, and altered his appearance. He may be on a plane to South America right now.''

''So what do we do?''

''The only thing we can do under the circumstances.''

''Which is?''

''The hardest thing of all: wait.''

14

Kate dumped the sodden mass left by yesterday's coffee in the trash and lay a crisp, fresh white filter into the coffeemaker. She measured out three scoops of decaffeinated grounds, dropped them into the filter, and, thinking of Jeff, added enough water for six cups. She snapped the switch to the "on" position and listened to the comforting gurgle of the coffeemaker. All the while she tried to ignore her shaking hands.

Snow's message had really unnerved her, as it was no doubt intended to do. There was no denying it. She felt her breath coming in short, ragged gasps, the room around her contracting with every inhalation, and expanding with every exhalation.

In her crate by the heater, Penelope watched, her head on her paws, her large, sad eyes rolled upward, filled with compassion.

Recognizing what she was suffering were the symptoms of a classic panic attack, Kate knew the best thing to do was to distract herself. She reached up into the cupboard for her favorite coffee mug, only to have it slip from between her fumbling hands, hit the tile floor, and break into a hundred pieces.

"Shit," Kate muttered, grabbing the broom and dustpan that

stood by the refrigerator. She carefully cleaned up the scattered pieces of ceramic, knowing that a single stray shard could lodge inside one of Penelope's pads and lead to an infection. She mourned the loss of the mug as she slid the broken pieces into the trash.

By the time she'd thoroughly cleaned up the mess, the coffee was ready. Kate pulled down another mug and filled it, taking a first tentative sip of the steamy black brew, forgoing milk and sugar this morning. She turned her concentration to the small window over the kitchen sink. From a certain angle, on a clear day, she could see a small strip of the ocean. It wasn't much, but it was enough to allow the real estate agent to say the house had an ocean view and to tack a few thousand more onto the purchase price. And, in fact, Kate cherished her "view" of the ocean, no matter how small, though today that view was obscured by a lowering gray sky and a dirty-looking mist lit up from within by the first premonitory rays of the sun, which wouldn't rise for another hour yet.

Carrying her cup back to the table, Kate reviewed the events of the past five hours. Perhaps she was overreacting. As Jeff said, Snow would most likely try to leave the country, escape to Canada or Mexico. In any event, he would be too preoccupied with staying free to bother her. Most likely he'd be caught before too long. It seemed to her that Jeff was right, most escapees were apprehended within twenty-four hours of breaking out of prison. But even more important, and what consoled Kate most of all, was the possibility, no matter how slim, that Snow had no idea that it was she who'd betrayed him.

She finished her first cup of coffee and poured a second, feeling a lot better, but still a little wired. Though she had thought twice about it, and it was a little earlier than normal, she decided to take her usual morning jog along the beach anyway. The run would work off some of her residual nervous energy. Besides, there was no need to let Snow's escape disturb her normal routine. If nothing else, she was determined not to let Snow have that victory over her.

As if sensing the change in her mistress's mood, Penelope

raised her head from her paws, yawned, and thumped her tail inside the crate.

5:15 A.M.

Lincoln couldn't count how many times he'd been holed up in some hotel room with another agent while waiting for a case to break. Now that time was at a premium, he didn't want to remember how many hours of his life he had wasted in this fashion, hours he could have spent reading, fishing, or making love.

He looked over to the bed where McCall was still lying, hands locked under his head, eyelids fluttering on the verge of sleep, and envied the younger man his ease, his whole life in front of him. Lincoln would have liked to lie down, too, but he knew from experience it was better to sit up. Whenever he lay down, the pain inside his skull was ten times worse.

He felt a sudden desperate sense of loneliness, odd because he usually preferred to be alone. It was probably just the tumor talking; he'd grown used to sudden irrational swings of mood and emotion. Now, watching McCall about to nod off, Lincoln felt as if he couldn't bear to lose the younger man to sleep.

"You married?" he said.

"Me? Nah," the young agent replied sleepily. "You?"

"Married fifteen years. Divorced ten."

"That's tough."

"Thinking about it?"

"About what?"

"Getting hitched."

"Someday, I guess. Not in the near future. I'd like to raise a couple of kids."

"You picked a hell of a line of work."

"Is that what did your marriage in? The work?"

"No one thing kills a marriage, but it was definitely an accessory to the fact."

"Any kids?"

"One. Stephanie. She's a senior at UCLA, majoring in political science."

"You must be proud of her."

"I am. She's a good kid, not that I had a lot to do with bringing her up. My wife used to complain that I was married to the Agency. She said she might have even been able to accept it if I'd had a mistress instead, but she couldn't stand being the other woman. She didn't know how to compete. In the end she stopped trying."

"I'm sorry."

Lincoln shrugged. "She was right, I suppose. I was married to this damn Agency. But let me tell you something, McCall. The Agency won't grow old with you, it won't comfort you when you're down, it won't hold your hand when you get sick, it won't be there when you die. The damn Agency is just a job like any other, it's not a substitute for life or the love of a good woman. And when it seems like it is, that is the first sign that you'd better get the hell out while the getting is good. Of course, by then, it's usually too damn late."

Lincoln felt the tears stinging the back of his eyes and forced himself to shut up. He had no intention of saying half of what he'd said and couldn't help feeling embarrassed, rambling on like some senile old fool, giving advice where none was asked for. He was about to apologize when from across the room he heard the sound of McCall lightly snoring and looking closer, saw his eyes had closed. Lincoln had to laugh in spite of himself. How long had the kid been asleep? With any luck, long enough to miss entirely the last half of his eulogy to love lost, and long enough to forget the rest.

Lincoln shut off the laptop and closed the lid. He reached into his pocket, unscrewed the safety cap on the brown bottle and swallowed another grey pill. There was nothing new coming across the wire, probably wouldn't be for hours. He stared across the room at the television, which was tuned to an early-morning news show, the sound turned down. The story of Snow's escape had not yet made the networks. That was good. But it wouldn't last indefinitely. Snow's trial hadn't been big news five years ago, but his gruesome, bloody escape from a prison for the criminally insane would be impossible to squelch. Was that how the son-of-a-bitch had planned it?

Lincoln shut his eyes, rubbing them lightly with his fingertips.

He was tired, unbelievably tired, but sleep was impossible for him.

Behind his closed eyes, on the dark theater of his lids, he saw a vision of his tumor, red and tentacled, like a blood-fattened octopus, slowly and contentedly sucking his life away.

15

Dressed in a blue nylon jogging suit, with triple white piping, Kate stood with her heel propped on the steps of the front porch, stretching out her left hamstring. Beside her, Penelope sat panting expectantly. Kate obliged the dog, cheating a little, not taking as much time as she knew she should warming up. She wanted to get moving as quickly as possible.

She started out at a slow jog down the wet sidewalk, turning left at a short side street to the main avenue through town. She watched her feet. Last night's storm had blown the last of the dead leaves off the trees, leaving them scattered in slick patches on the pavement. One misstep and she could easily go sprawling.

Behind her Penelope kept pace, the short-legged little dog running with a barrel-chested wobble.

Most of the stores on Main Street were still closed. Only the newsstand at the corner and the luncheonette had opened their doors. The other shops—which sold handicrafts, souvenirs, shells, and the like—wouldn't open for hours yet, some closed entirely until next summer. Kate caught her first whiff of the sea, damp and salty, and felt spurred on, picking up her pace, breathing deeply of the invigorating scent. She passed the legendary Sampler restaurant, a favorite with the senior citizen crowd. The Sampler sold solid fifties fare cafeteria-style at reasonable prices. It, too, was closed for the winter. She looked up and caught a glimpse of the ocean, heaving up against the horizon, which was shot through with a few penetrating spears of pink light.

She crossed Ocean Avenue and climbed the stairs to the boardwalk, which stretched out gray and slick through the early-morning fog. From the boardwalk she got her first good look at the sea. The swells were swollen and brown, covered with elaborate foam lacework, white spray blowing off the top. The water ran nearly to the boardwalk pilings, though Kate could tell from the seaweed and other debris washed up on the gray boards that the waves must have reached all the way to the boardwalk sometime the night before. Penelope stopped to sniff some of the more pungent leavings and then hustled to catch up, following closely at her heels.

The beach itself was littered with huge beams of salt-rotten timber, like the ribs of some dead leviathan churned up from the depths of the sea. A few kids in wetsuits stood by the jetty, clutching their surfboards and gazing uncertainly at the ominous fat-bellied waves.

The salt tang in the air was more palpable close to the ocean and Kate swallowed it like fuel. On her right, weaving in and out of the fog, she saw the seagulls, searching the churning waters for food, ever the opportunists. She could never hear their piercing cries without thinking that they somehow seemed to give voice to all the rage and hurt in the world.

There were a handful of people out on the boardwalk, some just there to see the restless sea, dressed in slickers, shielding the lenses of expensive cameras from the corrosive salt spume; others, joggers like herself, not to be turned back by a little bad weather, were out trying to cheat age, melt the fat around midsections collected at sedentary jobs. For Kate, however, running wasn't a way to keep fit, but a means to burn off the toxic stress that built up in her system; it was a means of relaxation, a meditation in motion, and she pursued it with a religious fervor.

She hardly missed a day's running, rain or shine, in the past five years. As a result, she was probably in the best shape of her life. There were always plenty of excuses not to run: it was too cold, or her knee hurt, or she could use the extra hour's sleep, but there was only one answer to all the petty protests of her body: run, pure and simple. And Kate had done just that. She'd run every morning for so long now that her body protested on those rare days when overwhelming circumstances forced her not to run. She'd run until running had become a habit more easily indulged than denied. She'd run until her very life depended on it.

As she reached the end of the boardwalk, swung around, and headed back the way she'd come, the ocean on her left side now, the irony of her obsession with running wasn't lost on her.

5:45 A.M.

A knock on the door announced that the breakfast they'd ordered a half hour ago had arrived.

Lincoln opened the door to see the young cop assigned to babysit them while they were in town standing in the rain, holding two soggy white paper bags. No wonder local cops hated the Agency, Lincoln thought. He took the bags from the cop, who stood there awkwardly for a moment as if waiting to be tipped and then retreated back into the rain. Lincoln watched him a moment before closing the door.

"Breakfast," he announced.

McCall had swung his legs over the bed and rubbed his brush-cut.

"Good. I'm starved."

They ate at the small round table in front of the window. McCall unwrapped a breakfast sandwich from inside tinfoil, a sloppily made affair consisting of a fried egg topped with a slice of pork roll covered with melted American cheese, all sliding sideways out of its poppy-seed roll. With every bite a patter of grease hit the makeshift plate McCall had made out of the tinfoil wrapping. Lincoln could barely stand the sight of the food, let alone the smell. He nibbled on his dry toast, washing it down with a styrofoam cup of herb tea.

He had lost over thirty pounds since the diagnosis, as well as his pot belly, going from a husky 180 to barely 150 pounds, a weight he hadn't recorded since his high school track days. They had quit the chemo a year ago; it wasn't doing anything to shrink the tumor and only made him feel sicker. His hair had grown back, if slightly thinner and drier, his bald spot in back bigger and the hair itself shot through with more white than he remembered; but at least he wasn't cue-ball bald as he'd been for months on the treatment. He didn't get as many colds, either, but his appetite had never come back. The chronic nausea remained, no doubt a side-effect from the medication he was taking. He would have liked to do away with the medication as well, but a few brief experiments in that direction were enough to convince him otherwise.

The doctors had initially given him six months to a year. He knew that six months was tantamount to a death sentence. They just didn't cut it any closer than that. When they gave you six months, that meant you could die at any time. His doctor suggested that he consult with a hospice worker, and at first Lincoln was too shocked to refuse. He listened while the well-meaning woman explained the various stages a person went through when they learned they were terminally ill: denial, bargaining, grief, rage, acceptance. He didn't remember exactly what order they came in because it seemed to him he'd had only one emotion from the moment he'd been given his diagnosis, and he'd been stuck with it ever since: rage.

He remembered calling his ex-wife with the news because he needed to tell someone and she was the closest thing to family he had. Sarah was sympathetic but distant. He still remembered the words she had used: ''Jeez Tom, that's too bad,'' as if he had just told her he'd blown the radiator on his

Jeep. What did he expect? By that time they'd been divorced for six years and Sarah had remarried, started a new life with an attorney in Connecticut. Lincoln asked her if she would break the news to Stephanie, but she flat-out refused, telling him he couldn't shirk this responsibility, that he owed it to Stephanie to tell her himself. He was a little taken aback by her hostility, her lack of sympathy. After all, he *was* dying, but later he realized that she was right. He had been emotionally absent for most of Stephanie's life. The least he could do was to be there to explain in person.

He flew out to California and she knew there was something wrong the minute she saw him. It wasn't only the weight loss and the slight shuffle he'd developed. Lincoln knew it was because he was there at all that Stephanie suspected trouble, and that hurt him worse than anything. He took her to eat at a Pizza Hut just off campus and there, over a pan pizza with everything on it that sat between them uneaten, he told her the grim facts. Her eyes watered, but she didn't cry, for which he was grateful, though he couldn't help but wonder if her self-control was an indication of how emotionally detached from him she really felt. She asked some sensible questions about his condition, his treatment, his options. He awkwardly told her that he had made arrangements for his savings and pension benefits to be transferred to her when the time came. He could tell from the look in her eyes how much she despised him for bringing up the matter at all. It was a look much like her mother's.

They said goodbye in the parking lot, Stephanie holding out her hand and Lincoln taking it, all so very formal, then Lincoln saying to hell with it and grabbing her and pulling her close, burying his head in her hair, which smelled of wildflowers, letting his own tears loose, feeling the rigid self-control of the body in his arms, knowing that he had bequeathed this quality to her, and feeling both a profound sorrow and a tragic pride. He stood back and looked at his daughter for what he was sure would be the last time and didn't bother to wipe the tears from his face.

That was three years ago, and he was still alive. Three years of doing nothing in particular. Cashing his disability checks, watching television when his eyes weren't bothering him, doing the crossword puzzle in the daily paper to keep his mind sharp. But all in all he was just marking time, just waiting for the fall that took away his independence, the dizziness he couldn't shake, the blindness that made him an invalid, the coma he wouldn't wake from. He was just marking time, playing solitaire with a deck stacked against him, until last night, when the call came that Snow had escaped. Now, sitting in this hotel room, he had to admit, he was almost glad the bastard was loose.

It would give him something to live for.

Something to die for.

If he'd only known how sick he was the first time around, he would have killed Snow when he'd had the chance.

If he got the chance again, he wouldn't blow it.

"Penny for your thoughts," McCall said, wiping his mouth with a napkin.

"Life . . ."

"What about it?" McCall said, taking another bite of his breakfast sandwich, catching the flapping egg white between his teeth.

"It's like Mick Jagger says."

"You a Stones fan?" McCall asked incredulously.

"Hell, the Stones are as old as I am."

McCall grunted, nodded, conceding the point. "Well, what's old Mick say about life besides you can't get no satisfaction?"

"You can't always get what you want."

"That's for sure."

"But sometimes you get what you need."

16

5:55 A.M.

When Kate returned to the house, Jeff was already up, rummaging around in the kitchen. She found him standing at the stove, dressed in only his worn blue jeans from the night before, making one of his famous swiss cheese and sausage omelets.

Penelope went sliding across the floor to greet him and to beg shamelessly for a handout, which Jeff obligingly gave the little dog, who trotted back to her crate with her prize, a corner of buttered toast. She held it between her forepaws and gnawed contentedly.

"Thought you might be hungry after your run," Jeff said and grinned, looking undeniably sexy. It was a snapshot from a cozy domestic life that might have been, a life Kate didn't dare dream of as a possibility for herself.

It wouldn't work.

Not in a million years.

But she would enjoy the taste of it while she could. She crossed the floor and gave Jeff a kiss on the cheek.

"Smells delicious," she said.

She poured herself another cup of coffee from the pot.

"I made fresh," Jeff said, flipping over the omelette, sizzling in the hot frying pan. "That stuff you made tasted like mud."

"Hmm, good," Kate said, sipping the coffee. She had never gotten the knack of making a decent pot of coffee. It was one of the jokes she'd endured at the office, where the first person in was required to make the morning brew. Her coffee was so bad it was generally agreed that she was exempt from the task. She had never gotten the hang of working in the kitchen, one more reason she'd make a lousy wife.

Jeff got two plates out of the dishwasher and, using the spatula, cut the omelet evenly in two. He put the plates on the table along with the toast and fetched his coffee mug from where he'd left it on the stove. In the meantime Kate grabbed a couple of forks from the drawer under the sink. They sat down at opposite sides of the table and started eating. She had no idea how hungry she was, didn't think she could eat at all, until she dug into the omelette, cheesy and hot, the diced sausage adding a smoky tang.

"How is it?" Jeff asked.

"Delicious."

She watched him picking toast crumbs out of the thatch of red hair on his chest and wondered why it didn't disgust her. If anything, she felt an overwhelming surge of tenderness toward him. If that wasn't love, she didn't know what was.

"I really didn't think you'd run this morning."

"I was awake. I didn't get much sleep last night."

"Snow?" Jeff frowned.

Kate nodded. "I just couldn't get him out of my mind. Still, I was determined not to let him disturb my routine. I run every morning. Why should this morning be any different?"

"That's the spirit."

"Did you listen to the radio?"

Jeff nodded. "There was no news."

Kate tried to hide her disappointment.

"Of course, that doesn't mean anything." Jeff said. "The story might not have even made it to the press. For all we know, he's already been captured."

"Don't you think they'd have called? After all, they *did* call me when he escaped."

"Bad news travels fast. Good news . . ." Jeff shrugged. "They just might not have gotten the chance. I'm sure it's a pretty chaotic situation."

"Yeah," Kate said, unconvinced.

"Hey," Jeff said, changing the subject. "I missed you in bed this morning."

"I bet you did."

Jeff had a penchant for morning sex that Kate didn't share, not that she'd ever told him, but she didn't mind obliging him, especially since he'd been so kind to her over the last twenty-four hours.

"I've got to take a double shift at the ER starting in about an hour. Gives us just enough time to take a shower together."

"Sounds good to me. I could use a shower myself."

Jeff pushed his chair away from the table. "Well, what are we waiting for?"

Kate stood naked facing the shower head as Jeff gently shampooed her shoulder-length auburn hair. She stood with her hands against the tiles for balance, her eyes shut, her head thrown back as the warm water gently needled her bare breasts. Every once in a while she swayed backwards, feeling Jeff's hot erect cock between the cheeks of her wet ass. She could feel him rubbing it there, teasing himself, though he had never entered here there, knew he wouldn't try. She could hear his breath coming harder and faster as he squeezed her soapy hair, leaning forward to press his hard body against hers, kissing her on the side of the neck, his cock pressed up against her burning even hotter than the water.

He turned her around to face him, kissing her on the mouth this time, his tongue pressing her lips, gaining entry with its urgency. She let him pull her toward him, returning his kiss, throwing her arms around his shoulders, lightly raking her nails down his long, lean, muscular back. He whispered something and was aware of his hand sliding down to his penis as he inched closer, their wet bodies seeming to melt into one.

"No," she whispered, pushing him lightly on the chest, forcing him back an inch.

He looked puzzled for a moment and then his expression changed to one of pleased surprise.

Kate snaked her way down his body, leaving a trail of warm kisses as she went, traveling the route of his muscular contours, pausing at his nipples, licking his navel. She reached behind him and grabbed the firm, hard globes of his ass. His penis was bobbling only inches from her face, full and engorged; it looked like a thick pink cactus topped with an impossibly brilliant purple fruit. She gently nibbled the flesh along the underside and then slowly licked along the length of him, giving extra attention to the sensitive triangle of flesh just beneath the glans. She left him hanging while she turned her attention to his balls, tight and hard as walnuts, tucked up against his pelvis, ready to explode. She could sense his urgency as she returned to his cock, circling the head with her lips and then swallowing the length of it in one gulp, hearing the breath catch in his throat. She felt his hands twisting in her wet hair, the heat and electricity in his cock, and knew that he was close. She pumped her head up and down, proud of the pleasure she was able to give him, even as it made her feel envious. He came in a rush, the semen rising like a ball of fire through his cock, splashing like fireworks in her mouth. She winced at the bitterness of it but kept on working, her head, her lips, her tongue, while above her she heard him moaning her name, his gratitude, his love for her.

It seemed like it lasted forever, but it was over in a matter of seconds.

She let his penis, still at half-mast but slowly descending, slide from her lips. It no longer looked as imposing as it had a few moments before. If anything, it resembled a delicate flower, the kind that blooms for a day and dies overnight.

With the water beating down on them, it was easy for her to cup her hand, collect enough to wash out her mouth.

Still, the bitter taste remained.

The taste of pleasure.

He hadn't seen, his eyes still shut, still lost in reverie. He finally looked down to where she knelt, lifting her up by the elbows, his blue eyes sparkling with a foreign joy.

"Let me . . ."

He reached between her legs, but she stopped him.

"No." She smiled, murmuring, her words barely audible over the water. "That was enough for me, just making you feel good."

Wasn't that every man's dream, what every man wanted to hear?

Then why had the sparkle gone out of Jeff's eyes?

"Okay," he said quietly, pulling her close to him, embracing her under the falling water. He let the sound enclose them for a while, as if they were in their own private world.

6:05 A.M.

Snow parked the stolen BMW in an underground garage in the theatre district. He took the ticket for the car from a small, monkey-faced man. Then he walked halfway up the block before tossing the ticket into a wastebasket on the corner.

He bought a cheap umbrella from a black man standing against the wall of a porn theater and followed along with the workaholic early morning crowd. The rain gave a gray, dingy cast to the city, washing garbage into the gutters and raising a sickeningly sweet stench. New York City, Snow observed, was the only place he had ever visited that seemed dirtier after it rained than before.

On the stoop of an abandoned building a man sat hunched over in the rain under a cardboard tent. In spite of the cardboard, the man was soaking wet, his long gray hair and thorny beard matted and filthy. Still, in spite of the filth, his skin shone with a shiny alcoholic radiance. He sat with his head down, one dirty hand lifted, palm up.

Snow smiled.

Most people passing would assume the man was too lazy even to beg.

But in the simple gesture Snow saw an almost Zen-like beauty.

He stopped in front of the man.

"Hey there," he said.

The man looked up, his rheumy, red-rimmed eyes floating toward Snow.

"What's the face you had before you were born?" Snow asked.

"You gonna give me money or not, mister?"

"Excellent," Snow said. "When you're hungry, eat; when you're tired, sleep."

He handed the man a five-dollar bill.

Two blocks away, Snow descended to the subway, bought a token, and climbed aboard a train going uptown. At this hour finding a seat wasn't a problem. An hour or so later and the cars would be packed with straphangers. Snow looked around at his fellow passengers. Most of them were men and women in business suits and trenchcoats, hiding behind newspapers or cut off from the world around them by Walkmans. Snow was left free to examine their faces closely, faces tired and old before their time, dull eyes ringed with dark circles, jawlines puffy, flesh sagging with lack of sleep. Snow saw the shadow on each of those weakened faces, thinking of the poet William Blake, how two hundred years ago he'd seen the same look on the citizens of London, the indelible marks of weakness, marks of woe.

For many years Snow had been dedicated to erasing those marks.

But that was long ago.

He realized that people didn't want to come awak They had to be forced into it.

Most people, he had come to realize sadly, pre erred to remain asleep.

They preferred to be robots.

6:15 A.M.

Jeff dressed in the clothes he'd worn the night before. He didn't keep a change of clothes at Kate's house; he didn't even have so much as a toothbrush in the bathroom. It seemed to be an unspoken agreement between them, that there would be no symbol of commitment to their relationship, even if it were no more than a mere matter of convenience. It was the way they both wanted it.

Dressed in a bathrobe, Kate kissed Jeff goodbye at the door. "Thanks for coming over last night," she said.

He pulled her close, engulfing her in his muscular embrace, his body still radiating the afterglow of sex and the smell of soap. "You insult me," he said playfully. "You know I'm always there. Anytime."

"Thank you."

"There you go again."

"Sorry," Kate smiled. "What I mean to say is that it means a lot to me to know you're there."

"Now it's my turn to say thanks. I know how tough it is for you to admit you need anyone."

"Now you're insulting me."

"Sorry," Jeff said and kissed her again, taking his time. "Maybe we should just stay away from words."

"Hey, I've got a reputation to uphold. The neighbors are going to talk."

"Let them talk."

"Really," Kate said, pushing him away gently. "I've got to get dressed for work. And you're going to be late."

"You're right," Jeff said, looking at his watch. "After last night's storm, I'm sure someone's going to cut off a hand chainsawing a fallen tree. I'll call you later. Or you call me if you hear anything."

Kate nodded, holding her robe closed against the damp air, now that Jeff had stepped away.

"Promise?"

"Promise."

Kate felt a sense of relief when Jeff finally left. She couldn't quite explain it, but she suddenly wanted to be alone. She padded barefoot back to the kitchen where Penelope was waiting for her breakfast. Kate opened a fresh bag of Prime Cuts, emptied the contents in one of the dog's pink bowls, and filled the other with water from the kitchen tap. The dog watched her intently but sat patiently, not moving a muscle until Kate left the kitchen before clicking over the linoleum floor to begin eating.

Kate stood in front of her open closet looking for something to wear. She finally chose a black blouse and an ankle-length skirt whose brown and gold motif gave a nod to autumn. She added a gold blazer and a pair of brown boots. She checked herself in the mirror on the back of her bedroom door.

Not bad.

She pulled her still damp hair back, not feeling like setting it this morning, and gathered it at the back of her neck. Looking closer in the mirror, she could see some faint signs of the sleepless night before. She walked into the bathroom, where she applied some light makeup. No need to advertise the fact she'd been up all night. People might get the wrong idea.

Kate had been somewhat disingenuous with Jeff. She didn't have a class until later that morning, but she wanted to get to the office early. It would give her a sense that she was doing something. That today would be a day just like any other.

She grabbed her pocketbook and her leather satchel of books and lecture notes and headed for the front door. She checked the weather outside the window before deciding on her tan trenchcoat. Penelope lifted her head from where she lay on the living-room sofa. Kate walked back across the room to scratch the dog under the chin, bending over to kiss her on her wet black nose.

"Have a good day," she said.

Penelope licked her face.

17

McCall had dozed off again when the call came through. Lincoln grabbed the phone on the second ring.

"Lincoln here."

"I'd heard you been called in on this one. How the hell are you, Tom?" He recognized the voice on the other end as that of Henry Frank, an old-time friend and agent who worked out of Albany.

"Hanging in there. What have you got for me, Hank?"

"Missing persons report relayed from Hoboken P.D. They wouldn't have bothered to put it through because it hasn't been twenty-four hours, but they got the alert over the wire that anything coming out of this sector was to be given top priority. Good work. Anyway, a Mrs. Scheffield called it in. Seems her son Todd was spending the weekend upstate with his girlfriend. He was supposed to be driving home last night and promised to call to tell her he'd made it back all right, what with the storm and all. He never did."

"Scheffield," Lincoln said, cradling the phone on his shoulder, as he grabbed the pen and pad from his shirt pocket. How do you spell that?''

''S-c-h-e-f-f-i-e-l-d. He was driving a 1995 red BMW, New Jersey license plate number FYE68H.''

''The girl. What was her name?''

''Brenda Pilot.''

Lincoln scribbled the name on his pad, adding one more to the growing list of names, all of them Snow's victims.

''Have the next of kin been notified?''

''In Scheffield's case I instructed the Hoboken police to do it. No sense keeping the poor woman dangling on the hook. The girl lives in Summit. I informed their police department of the situation. They're going to take care of it. We're going to need someone from the families to ID the bodies. The Agency will send a car down to Jersey.''

Lincoln thought of the poor officers whose job it would be to tell the parents that their kids had been murdered. He'd had to deliver bad news like that on more than one occasion himself. It never got any easier. The Agency even held classes and seminars on how to handle such situations, but it was all a lot of bullshit. When you stood on someone's stoop at two in the morning to tell them that a loved one was lying on a steel slab in the morgue, there was no good way to break the news. It all came down to the same thing: a paralyzed terror in the face of the evil of the world. Lincoln had seen it more times than he cared to count. He had seen it in his own face while shaving on a number of occasions since he'd gotten his diagnosis, that completely dumbfounded look of ''Why me?'' Why anyone, stupid?

Whenever he could, Lincoln avoided mirrors.

''Anything else?'' Lincoln asked.

''Not on this end. It looks like you've got your getaway car, though.''

''It's probably history by now,'' Lincoln said, thinking out loud. ''But it gives us somewhere to start.''

''Oh, there is one more thing.''

''What's that?''

"The waitress you sent in."

"What about her?"

"We rubberized the rules a little interrogating her. We're sure she saw something, but she just wouldn't give it up. It was getting a little frustrating. You know how these things are. Then the call from Hoboken came in. Anyway, she's kind of broken up right now, not thinking too clearly. What I'm afraid of is that when this is all over and her head clears, she might get to thinking she has legal recourse, if you know what I mean."

"Send her to the psychiatric wing of the local hospital for observation. Tell them she broke down during routine questioning. Tell them you're concerned. You want to make sure she doesn't do anything to hurt herself. The Agency cares and all that bullshit. Cover your ass."

"Good idea. I always said you were the best, Lincoln. By the way, how are you feeling?"

"Like the Knicks and Bulls are playing game seven inside my skull."

"Sorry I asked."

"Sorry you had to."

McCall was standing expectantly by the table when Lincoln rung off.

"Well," he said. "Any news?"

"Yeah," Lincoln said. "It looks like we just got our first break."

6:45 A.M.

It was usually twenty minutes from Kate's house to the university, but this morning she ran into a roadblock where a fallen tree had downed some power lines. Kate saw two men in yellow hard hats sawing the entangled branches off the tree and thought about what Jeff had said about someone inevitably cutting off his hand today. No doubt it would be tough in the emergency room. She felt bad about giving him the bum's rush after their session in the shower. He was only trying to give her aid and comfort. Why was it so hard for her to accept that from Jeff?

She was brought out of her reverie by the frantic waving of a policeman, his face only a foot away from her windshield, his mouth moving.

Kate mouthed an apology and quickly turned toward the detour the policeman indicated.

She arrived at the university ten minutes later. Locking her green Toyota Camry, she crossed the parking lot and headed for the psychology building. There was a light rain falling, a mist, really, no need for the umbrella she hadn't bothered to bring with her. She passed the commons, where a few students and faculty were already heading for an early-morning breakfast. She walked down the wet, leaf-clogged asphalt paths between the rolling lawns, the gray sky overhead shattered by the slick black branches of the sleeping trees.

Monmouth University was a small private school that had just been officially upgraded to college status. It had had an enrollment of just under 4,000 full-time students when Kate had first started, but even in the short amount of time she had been teaching there recruitment efforts had raised that figure by nearly thirty percent. The school garnered most of its student body from New Jersey, though its current ranking as a university and its proximity to the Atlantic Ocean made it attractive to a growing number of out-of-state students. In trying to compete with other colleges, Monmouth had also recently developed a modest football program. The campus itself was attractively situated in a verdant corner of West Long Branch. Its most celebrated structure and the hub of the university was Wilson Hall, built earlier in the century, a stately pillar-and-marble building that had once served as the summer home of President Woodrow Wilson. Now it housed the university's administrative offices, though the English department also taught classes there.

The psych department was located in a newer albeit more prosaic building. Kate took the stairs to the second floor and headed for her small cluttered office at the end of the hall. She was greeted by Mary, who'd been there longer than anyone in the department and worked as the secretary for all four full-time and both part-time professors. She must have been at least seventy, but she somehow managed to escape the inevitable scythe of mandatory retirement. It was a good thing for the department, because she was the most efficient secretary in the university.

"You're here early this morning Dr. Bennett."

She lifted her leather satchel. "Thought I'd get an early start. Didn't get much sleep last night with the storm and all."

"Yes. It was awful, wasn't it? The people next door lost two trees. One went right through their living room window. I was up half the night myself. I figured since I was up I'd come in a little early."

Her punctuality was something of a departmental joke. Mary was always at the office by six A.M. No one could ever claim to have beaten her into the office.

The secretary held up an empty coffeepot and a fresh filter. "I was just going to put a pot on. Would you like a cup?"

"Yes," Kate said, feeling the chill of the wet morning. "I'd love a cup."

"You go on and get that wet coat off and I'll bring you one when it's ready."

"Thanks," Kate said. She unlocked her office and hung up her coat. She put her pocketbook in the bottom drawer of her desk and pulled out a folder full of notes for the lecture she was supposed to give that afternoon. Her subject was the schizophrenic personality.

Perfect.

Her mind went immediately to Snow. Where was he now?

She didn't realize how much time had gone by until Mary knocked lightly on the open door, startling her.

"I'm sorry," she said, holding out a steaming mug. "Coffee's on."

"Oh, it's okay. I was just daydreaming, I guess. I'm glad you snapped me out of it. I really have to get ready for this morning's class.'' She took the mug. ''This should help. Thank you.''

Mary smiled and left, and Kate took a sip of the hot coffee.

She opened the folder and stared at her notes, but no matter how hard she tried, she couldn't force herself to concentrate. Her own handwriting might as well have been some unknown cipher.

18

Julie Golden drove swiftly through the streets on her way to her law office in a well-kept Upper East Side brownstone. She was singing along to the latest Melissa Etheridge love song. She had an early-morning case scheduled at the city courthouse and wanted to go over her notes before the morning's preliminary hearings.

She ran into a traffic snarl about a block from her office, cursed silently under her breath, and turned up Melissa, drowning out the noise of car horns and jackhammers. Her new Lexus was her pride and joy, a masterful piece of engineering, so responsive to her every whim, sometimes it seemed as if the car were reading her mind. She had bought it as a reward for working so hard, for sweeping her sense of ethics under the carpet, though in spite of herself, she often felt more than a little guilty over the way she made her considerable salary.

As a case in point there was her latest client. A young mother had tried to kill herself and two young children by blowing out the pilot lights of her gas stove after learning that her husband had left her for his secretary. Julie learned that the woman was taking hormonal therapy as a result of undergoing radical surgery for ovarian cancer. She truly believed the woman was a victim, but she couldn't help feeling she was doing a disservice to the woman's children. The husband wanted the children, but so did the mother, and it was up to Golden to prove to the court that therapy and new medication had completely restored the woman to sanity. After spending almost thirty-six hours of interview time with the woman, Julie felt pity for her plight but little confidence that her children wouldn't be better off with her two-timing husband. Still, the politics of her practice dictated she defend the woman in spite of her personal convictions.

Julie sighed.

Sometimes being a confirmed feminist liberal had its downside. She'd learned long ago that conscience isn't often a lawyer's best friend.

She tried to think of more pleasant things, like the past weekend. The setting had been exquisite: the small A-frame she'd bought three years ago in the Poconos, making the perfect romantic getaway, including fireplace, jacuzzi, and a bountiful supply of whipped cream, strawberries, and Jacques Rémy champagne. The storm had passed to the northeast, delivering only rain, forcing them to stay inside almost the entire three days, making things even cozier. The sex was everything she could have hoped for, and then some. If she had any doubts that she had at last found her perfect soulmate, this weekend had chased them away. Even thinking about what they had done together in bed—and out of bed—was enough to get her hot and bothered all over again, not to mention successfully help her forget her earlier feelings of guilt over the case she was to prosecute later that morning. Indeed, it had been difficult to leave her love nest early that morning and drive back into the dirty city, but business called.

The traffic started moving up ahead and Julie tapped the gas, passing a group of men in Con Ed hard hats. They didn't seem to be working. Instead, they were just standing around, staring inside the opened street, as if they'd never seen a hole before.

Julie couldn't resist pressing her horn in protest.

One of the men looked up and flipped her the finger.

Julie flashed her blinkers and turned into the garage a half-block down the street from her office. She buzzed down her window.

"Hiya, Sal," she said to the good-looking attendant whose weightlifter's body wasn't concealed by his uniform of starched white shirt and black bow tie.

"You're looking well this morning," Sal said, grinning knowingly. "Positively radiant. Good weekend?"

"Great weekend." Julie grinned back. "What about yourself?"

"Same old, same old."

"Problems with Rosa?"

"You know how women can be."

"Yeah, I guess I do. Hey, take care of my baby, will you?"

"Don't I always?"

"No muddy four-wheelers . . ."

He placed his right hand over his heart. "I'll treat her like my own daughter." He handed her a ticket. "She'll be safe from harm in 2-D."

Julie took the ticket, waved to Sal, and pulled away from the booth, her tires squealing on the wet concrete, echoing into the labyrinth of passages ahead. She followed the numbers on the concrete pylons, descending to the lower level, where only a few cars were already parked, nothing of lesser eminence than an Acura. As Sal had promised, 2-D was off in a corner all by itself, the elevator bank on one side and a service closet on the other. There were no parking places on either side of her, no pipes overhead to drip onto her hood.

Julie turned off the engine, set her Cobra car alarm, and clubbed her steering wheel.

No sense taking any chances.

She climbed out of the car and locked the door just as she felt the arm circling her throat, the hand covering her mouth.

Instinctively she fumbled with her car keys, a key between each finger, forming a makeshift set of brass knuckles, and grabbed for the Mace dangling from the key ring. She was about to drive her left heel into her attacker's groin as she'd learned in her Tae Kwon Do class when she felt her right arm go numb from the shoulder, the keys dropping with an echoing *clang* on the concrete floor. But it wasn't so much the expertly applied pressure hold just under her collarbone that paralyzed her but the voice of the man tickling her ear.

It was the unmistakable voice of her old client.

Dr. Alexander Snow.

7:15 A.M.

Lincoln waited as the motel manager lit a fresh cigarette and then jabbed at the 8 × 10 with his nicotine-stained fingers.

"Yeah, that's him," he said.

The call had come through only moments after the identification of the car and the bodies at the toll booth. A Warwick police officer had answered a call of criminal vandalism at the Wander Inn motel, just off Route 80. He was writing it up as a typical report when he ran the license plate number and turned up the red flag. Lincoln was notified through the FBI's Albany office in a matter of minutes. Wilson, the young agent who'd driven Lincoln up from the airport, drove him and McCall to the location. All of a sudden things were happening fast. It was always like that. For an agonizing period of time nothing happened, and then all of a sudden there was more information flowing in than you could process. On the way down in the car, Lincoln had checked his Rand McNally road atlas to see just where in the hell Warwick was. Luckily, they weren't far from the small, mostly rural town; it took them less than half an hour to get there.

"He seemed like an upright guy," the motel manager said. "Drove a BMW. Had a platinum Amex card that checked out. Said he was a teacher, or something."

"When did you notice the damage?"

"About an hour or so ago, I guess." The manager took a deep drag on his cigarette and stared up at the clock on the wall behind him. "I was making my morning rounds, checking license plate numbers before my morning guy comes in."

"Checking plate numbers?" Lincoln turned his head to avoid the sickening stench of the cigarette smoke.

"Yeah. You never know when someone is trying to pull a fast one."

"His plates didn't check out?"

"No. But that wasn't the only thing. I noticed a lot of flickering light behind the window. I thought the room was on fire. I knocked on the door, but there was no answer."

"So you entered?"

The manager's eyes shifted away nervously. "It was unlocked."

"Look," Lincoln said. "I'm not interested in how or why you entered that room. The man is an escaped prisoner. All I'm interested in is catching him."

"I've been in this business a lot of years. I knew something fucked up was going on in there. I wasn't doing anything illegal. I have the right to protect my property."

"I already told you, I'm not interested in how you gained admission to the room."

The manager looked unconvinced. "I went in and found it just the way you saw it."

Lincoln nodded. "What name did he use?"

"It's right here," the manager said, lifting up the thin Amex receipt. "Todd Scheffield. I suppose that isn't his real name?"

"No, I'm afraid not."

"Shit. Then I'm screwed for the cost of the room, right?"

"Well, you might be in luck," Lincoln said drily.

"How so?" the manager said, crumpling the receipt in his hand.

"Todd Scheffield is dead. Chances are his family is going to have a lot more on their minds than clearing up a few unauthorized charges."

"I didn't mean it to sound like that," the manager muttered, but Lincoln noticed that he didn't throw the crumpled receipt into the trash.

"No," Lincoln said. "Of course not. If you don't mind, Agent McCall and I are going to have another look at that room."

"Sure."

Lincoln started out, McCall holding the manager's gaze for a moment as if he were staring at a roach and then following, but turned back at the door, unable to resist.

"How did he seem?"

"What do you mean?" the manager asked.

"What was your impression of him?"

The manager took another drag on his cigarette, now just a burning ember between his two fingers, and shrugged.

"He seemed like an honest guy."

Lincoln and McCall walked in the rain to the end of the row of small motel units. They stepped inside the open door to number 27.

All the movable furniture was stacked against the east wall. There were candles covering almost every available surface, about half of them still burning, others sputtering in puddles of melted wax. Indeed, the flickering light of the candles did give the impression that the room was on fire. On the walls of this particular hell were spray-painted various Chinese ideograms, and, given the medium used to create them, several surprisingly beautifully executed mandalas. Lincoln also recognized the four basic trigrams from the ancient Chinese oracle the *I Ching*, as well as the classic yin-yang symbol, rendered in white and blood-red.

Lincoln took in the bizarre scene and tried to imagine what Snow could have been thinking, what he was thinking now. If only he knew how to read the arcane language left on the walls, the shorthand of a madman.

Beside him, McCall took in the scene for a second time as well. His commentary hadn't changed.

"What the fuck is going on here?"

19

Julie lay with her cheek pressed against the carpet in the trunk of her Lexus.

The trunk was spacious enough and the automobile's suspension excellent, yet she was still knocked against the steel only inches above her whenever the car hit an occasional pothole. It was disorienting, being locked inside the trunk and jostled around. She was glad she wasn't claustrophobic.

She had driven out of the parking garage herself, handing the ticket back to Sal, explaining to him that she had forgotten some pages from the brief she was presenting that morning. She could only hope that her trained legal poker face hadn't fooled him, that he could see the terror she felt behind her calm, cool exterior. She was certain that he'd seen Snow sitting beside her, but what conclusions he had drawn she couldn't determine from the look on his face. To her dismay, Sal seemed to be paying more attention to some tasteless schtick coming from the shock jock on the radio behind him than to her.

That had been only an hour or so ago. Or was it more? She'd

lost all sense of time and couldn't move her arm to read the illuminated dial of her wristwatch.

She had driven out of the city and through the tunnel back into New Jersey, and after about half an hour, pulled off the turnpike at Snow's direction into a deserted area of swamp and dead cattails.

There Snow had politely asked her to get out of the car.

"Please leave the keys in the ignition," he said.

"Take the car," Julie said, hating the tone of pleading that had crept into her voice, certain that Snow was picking up on it. "Just leave me here. It'll take me at least an hour to get back to the nearest tollbooth. I promise I won't say anything for two hours after that. I give you my word."

Snow laughed. "What's a lawyer's word worth, anyway? Please get out of the car," he said again.

Julie did as he'd asked. To her dismay, Snow did not slide over into the driver's seat but climbed out of the car.

"Walk around to the back," he said.

Julie felt the heels of her pumps sinking into the soft mud beneath her feet. Her stomach churned; she felt like she was going to double over and vomit right there. But she forced herself to maintain control. She wouldn't humiliate herself in front of him, no matter what. She looked wildly around her. There was a part of her that urged her to make a run for it, to try to make it to the cattails and lose him, wondering how far the turnpike could be from where they'd parked and whether she could avoid the murky swamps spread all around them. At the same time, she knew that she couldn't make it ten yards before he caught her. Suddenly she was certain that he was going to kill her. At that moment her senses seemed to come alive: every sight, smell, touch, taste, and sound intensified. The glistening of water droplets on the heads of the cattails, the stench of rotten vegetation, the feel of the rain on her face, the all-too-distant sound of traffic. She was going to die out here in the swamp, her fine sensual body dumped in the mud and water, to be found and photographed by impersonal strangers.

She jumped when Snow whispered in her ear.

"Take your coat and shoes off," he said.

"My shoes?" she said, uncomprehendingly.

"You'll be more comfortable that way."

As if sleepwalking, Julie shucked off her trenchcoat, reaching down to remove her pumps. She felt the wet cold seeping through her stockinged feet and allowed a small glimmer of hope to spark deep inside her.

He's not going to kill me. Not yet, anyway . . .

For the first time she realized that he'd used the interior button to pop the trunk.

She was staring into the immaculately kept compartment, wondering how she was going to fit inside, when she felt a small stinging sensation where her left shoulder met her neck. Her body went numb on the left side. A similar stinging sensation on the right was swiftly followed by paralysis on the right side.

He caught her before she fell to the mud, lifting her into the trunk, arranging her limbs so that she fit snugly with the small of her back against the spare tire. A drop of rain fell into her staring left eye before he slammed the trunk shut.

Now she lay curled on her right side in a fetal position, paralyzed, finding it impossible to wriggle so much as her wet toes.

What the hell was he doing out?

What did he want with her?

The questions were coming fast and furious.

She felt the tire iron pressed into her side, giving her a little pain, and tried to shift her body without success.

She wasn't bound, and yet she couldn't move.

What had he done to her?

Injected her with some kind of paralyzing drug?

Her mind drifted back to the beautiful weekend she'd just enjoyed, of lying in bed until two in the afternoon, of long, sweet, delicious lovemaking. What she wouldn't give to be back in her lover's arms right now. Was it the last time she would ever have such an experience? No, Julie thought. She wouldn't let herself think like that. She had to think of some way out of this predicament. There *must* be some way out.

The first thing she had to do was remember not to panic.

7:25 A.M.

Lincoln stood outside the motel room, seemingly oblivious to the rain.

McCall stood beside him. They stood in complete silence for several moments before McCall spoke. "Maybe you'd better tell me what kind of nut we're dealing with here," the young agent asked. "What's all this occult crap? I thought he was a psychiatrist."

"He *is* a psychiatrist."

"What kind of a psychiatrist?"

"The kind that needs a psychiatrist."

McCall grunted. "Do you mind telling me what I just saw in there?"

"Snow is an adept of the Oriental arts, from Tai Chi to Nei Kung to others you and I have never even heard of before. He's made a life study of the most arcane spiritual and martial practices. He considers himself a bodhisattva warrior."

"A bodhi-what?"

"A bodhisattva. In Buddhist belief, a bodhisattva is a higher being who has delayed his own passing into nirvana until he has helped enlighten all other sentient beings."

"And he does this by torture and murder?"

Lincoln shrugged. "He is a mental and physical warrior. From his point of view, any means to enlightenment are justified. He is performing the greatest service he can for his fellow human beings."

"I thought Buddhism was a religion of peace."

"It is. But there is a lot of moral ambiguity to some of the more esoteric branches, especially sects such as Zen. Ever see the yin-yang symbol?"

McCall jerked his thumb over his shoulder in the direction

of room 27. "Yeah. He had it painted on the wall in there. It was the only thing I recognized."

"Light turning into dark, dark into light. There is no right or wrong. At the extremes, one blends imperceptibly into the other. The seed of darkness lies inside the light, and vice versa."

"What about the law of karma? Isn't he worried he'll come back in the next life as a fucking toad or something?"

"As a warrior, Snow considers himself superior to karma. He is willing to take on bad karma if necessary to carry on his work of liberating consciousness. To the bodhisattva, existence itself is hell. His very decision to come back is demonstrative of his willingness to suffer for the good of all."

"So he suffers."

"Every psychotic suffers."

"And does he really believe all this bullshit?"

"When we catch him, you can ask him."

McCall reached into his pocket and pulled out a stick of chewing gum.

"Want a piece?"

"No, thanks," Lincoln said.

He watched as McCall unwrapped a stick of gum, bent it in half, and popped it into his mouth. He carefully folded the empty foil and tucked it into his shirt pocket. He slowly, methodically, began to chew.

"This whole damn case," he stopped chewing long enough to declare, "is beginning to leave a bad taste in my mouth."

"I've had that taste in my mouth for five years," Lincoln said. "And I can tell you one thing for sure."

"What's that?"

"Spearmint won't take it away."

20

Kate sat staring at her lecture notes until Diane Patterson arrived.

Diane was the department's behaviorist—the rat-in-the-box gal, as their department head Dr. Policastro liked to call her. Policastro was an old-style Freudian who'd studiously ignored the recent revisionist trend in psychology that had rendered his intellectual idol all but obsolete.

Diane, on the other hand, wasn't your usual behaviorist. For one thing, she was totally unconventional, from her eclectic dress to the number and variety of erotic liaisons she'd had with what seemed like almost every single professor—and a few married ones—at the College. This morning she was improbably dressed in a gauzy peasant skirt and clogs, topped with a denim jacket emblazoned with the logo for the Hard Rock Cafe. Kate had her pegged as in her late forties, but her dress and infectious vivacity made her seem at least twenty years younger. Her office was directly across from Kate's, and more than once Kate found herself wondering what Diane was doing during a conference behind closed doors with one particularly good-looking upperclassman or other.

Kate often castigated herself for her suspicions. For all her unconventionality, Diane was a scrupulous person and a damn good teacher. Kate really didn't think she'd risk her position getting involved with a student. But it wasn't unheard of. More than one male professor had gotten caught with his hand in the cookie jar, and what was good for the goose was good for the gander. After all, this *was* the nineties. Kate had been tempted herself on one or two occasions. In spite of her strictly professional, if somewhat standoffish, relationship with her students, especially the male ones, she had easily seen what could have happened in one or two situations if she'd been a little less circumspect. Kate just wasn't interested in that kind of thing: no matter how you looked at it, it would bring more harm than good.

"Hiya, Kate," Diane said, dropping her load of nylon knapsacks and straw handbags inside her office, which she always kept open and unlocked, taking off her denim jacket and rubber rain hat, and ruffling her short, spiky red hair. "I'm surprised to see you here so early. I thought you didn't have a class until ten."

Kate felt a stab of annoyance. *Does everyone around here know my goddam schedule?*

"Just thought I'd get in a little early and go over my class notes for the day."

"Anyone ever tell you you're a classic anal retentive?"

"Yeah, as a matter of fact. My ex-boyfriend."

"Bet he never got in the back door, eh?"

Diane enjoyed a crude joke more than anyone. If she'd been a man, she'd have been bounced out of the university on sexual harrassment charges years ago. Her ability, even her willingness, to take it and give it back was one of the things that made her so popular with the male professors. Her lack of political correctness made her equally unpopular with the powerful feminist faction at the college. Kate found herself somewhere in the middle of the seemingly unending PC wars. On the one hand she wanted to be respected for her talent and intellect as a professor. On the other, she thought the countless sensitivity seminars and speech codes a ridiculous, unnecessary, and even psychologically unhealthy encumbrance on free expression.

"And I suppose you've got a revolving door back there that has let through more customers than Macy's?"

Diane laughed. "Not in this day and age, honey. The back door is locked up, barricaded, and manned by armed guards. Anyone even attempts entrance and they've got orders to shoot to kill."

"That's good to hear."

"Seriously, though. How are things between you and Jeff?"

"Good," Kate said, feeling a little defensive. *How were things between her and Jeff?* Did he have any idea of how blocked she was sexually, that to her, relations were just a duty, in spite of her willingness and inventiveness? If he did, he didn't let on. Christ, was she that good? She should win an Academy Award. She felt another stab of emotion, this time anger.

Diane seemed to pick up on it at once. That was the problem working with shrinks. You couldn't hide anything from them.

"You don't seem so sure."

"I'm sure. In fact we had a two-fer last night. Well, actually once in the night and once this morning." It wasn't the kind of personal detail Kate would ordinarily volunteer, but she knew it would lead Diane off the trail.

"A two-fer, huh? Well, I envy you. I didn't have much luck last night."

"You were with that assistant dean of economics?"

"Marty Lehrer. What a case. We get into it kind of hot and heavy in the bedroom, and I get up to go to the bathroom to put my diaphragm in. I don't care what the magazines say, there's no way to make stuffing that thing inside you sexy. Anyway, I'm in there a couple of minutes freshening up and when I come out, what do you think I find? Marty is sitting on the bed in my panties and slip and putting on my lipstick."

"Marty Lehrer?"

"Imagine my surprise."

"What did you do?"

"Well, I tried to be as diplomatic as possible. I told him to get dressed and get the hell out."

"What did he say?"

"He mumbled something about thinking that since I was a psychologist, I'd be more understanding.

"I told him understanding had nothing to do with it. If I wanted a woman, I'd have a relationship with a woman."

"He must have crawled out of there."

"You never saw a man get dressed so fast. Of course, he begged me not to tell anyone."

"And of course you told the first person you saw this morning."

"Of course. I guess he figured there was some kind of doctor-patient privilege working. *Wrong.*"

In light of Snow's escape, that last remark stung. But Kate forced the unpleasant thoughts it brought up out of her mind. Instead, all the unwelcome sex talk got Kate to thinking of her relationship with Jeff. How the hell could he be so oblivious to her dissatisfaction? He wasn't the type not to care. Was he so wrapped up in himself that he just didn't notice that the pleasure wasn't mutual? Of course, it was all so damn irrational. She didn't want him to know. Hadn't she done her best to keep him from knowing? Besides, wasn't it true that one time in the beginning of their relationship, in the dark, warm, damp intimacy of after-sex, holding her in his arms, he had in fact asked her if there wasn't something he was doing wrong, exposing himself, naked, vulnerable?

And what had she done? She remembered it well. Cut him off with some cold, clinical remark about everything being fine until he decided to analyze it, turning the tables, making it seem as if it was him with the problem, that he must feel some hidden inadequacy. He had never broached the subject again, which had suited Kate just fine.

Still, she couldn't help but blame him.

Like she said. Irrational.

"One good thing did come out of it, though," Diane said.

"What's that?"

"I finally finished that paper I've been planning to submit to *Psychology Today*."

"The one relating MTV to Skinnerian training?"

"Yeah."

"That's great."

"I've got a favor to ask you, though. I'd really appreciate it if you'd give it a quick read. I know you're not a behaviorist, but you're not a completely hostile audience. You've got an open mind."

"I'd be glad to."

"Thanks a lot. By the way, you really ought to get working on something. It would really help when they decide on tenure. You actually worked as a psychiatrist in the real world. Those who can, do; those who can't, teach, and all that; but in academia, it really is 'publish or perish'. Even Policastro keeps on publishing. Granted, it's the same damn thesis applied to everything he lays his eyes on, that old Freudian crank sees the world through Oedipal glasses, and most of the editors he submits to are personal friends, but he gets his name out there, and you can't underestimate that in this business."

"I know you're right," Kate said. "I just can't seem to get a handle on anything I care to write about."

"Oh, Christ," Diane said. "You've actually been out in the real world of psychiatry. You've seen more than all of us put together. I'll bet there are *dozens* of interesting cases you could write about."

This time the image of Snow came into her mind and refused to be dispelled. Kate had never told anyone about Dr. Snow or her real reason for leaving private practice, in spite of the fact that she knew her reticence would spawn salacious rumors, which it had. Academia was a swamp of gossip. But to her mind, the truth was worse than any rumors anyone could dream up She wondered if the story of Snow's escape had made the network news, if Diane had heard it and, like thousands of others, just filed it away because it had no direct consequence on her life.

She was dying to ask.

"Really," Diane was still talking. "There must be at least one case you'd like to write up."

There was, Kate thought. It had been a failure, but it could be an instructive failure. There was only one problem.

The case wasn't over.

7:45 A.M.

Once a monk walked a journey of a thousand miles to seek guidance from the great sage Bodhidharma.

He sat outside the sage's cave, waiting for the master to appear, but he waited in vain. Nonetheless he kept on sitting, day and night, through snow and rain, through heat and cold, and all to no avail. Finally, in his desperation to gain an interview, he cut off his own right arm and laid it in front of the cave to indicate his sincerity for the great man's teaching.

At this, Bodhidharma appeared and asked the monk what he sought.

"I want you to pacify my mind," the monk said beseechingly.

Bodhidharma stared at him from beneath his impressive brow and was silent for a long time. At last he said, "Bring your mind before me and I will pacify it."

The monk nodded his head. "That's just it!" he said excitedly. "Everytime I try to grasp my mind, I come up empty."

"There," Bodhidharma said. "I have pacified your mind."

And with that the great master turned and disappeared into the cave and the monk was enlightened.

Snow remembered the woman tied to the chair. She was naked, frightened, beyond pleading. He had stretched her right arm out and tied it down on a wooden plank, tying off the major arteries just above her elbow so she wouldn't bleed to death. As he'd lifted the ax, the fear on her face had been truly terrible to behold, and he'd felt a moment of pity, but he knew what he was doing was for the best. She had come to him sick, as they all did, pleading with him, as did Bodhidharma's monk, to make her well, and in his infinite compassion he was determined to cure her, to grant her what she'd come to him for: enlightenment.

It was over in a matter of seconds. The arm was severed neatly with one blow, the fingers grabbing on nothing, like the monk in the story trying to grasp his mind. The stump bled profusely for a minute or two before the makeshift tourniquet did its job, the blood pulsing slower and slower, until it finally stopped.

The woman stared disbelievingly at her severed limb, her lips moving but no sound coming out, the stench of urine rising off her as she lost control of herself, and then a glitter, just a glitter of what Snow knew to be illumination dawning in her pretty blue eyes, just before they glazed over with shock.

It would be good to be going back to the old house again. It was there that he had conducted his most interesting experiments. It was there that he had kept his voluminous notes— koans, really, sacred texts thorny with paradox and illogic as all great koans were, but all leading to enlightenment if read in the proper spirit.

That was the key.

To be shocked into the proper spirit.

Snow slowed for a tollbooth and handed the old man in the window a twenty-dollar bill.

"Sorry," Snow said. "It's all I have."

The old man muttered something and took his time giving Snow his change.

"Have a nice day," Snow said.

The old man cursed under his breath and Snow laughed. He would die of a massive coronary in less than eight months.

Snow pulled away from the tollbooth and enjoyed the feel of the luxury car beneath him. The Lexus rode a lot better than the tinny BMW. Even at a length of almost 197 inches and nearly 3,700 pounds, it was far more maneuverable than its smaller, lighter competitor. Its four-liter four-cam thirty-two-

valve V-8 engine was whisper-quiet and cruised from zero to
sixty in less than seven seconds. He stepped on the accelerator
and gave full rein to all 260 horsepower. Even with the transmis-
sion in the more aggressive sports mode, he could barely feel
the shift points. He could feel the all-weather tires beneath him
biting the slick road. Above his head, the rain was pattering
against the power moonroof. He flicked on the in-dash six-
compact-disc changer on the off-chance there was something
like Philip Glass or Ravi Shankar cued up, but he was out of
luck. He turned the CD player off and contented himself with
the meditative sound of the rain hitting the glass.

He didn't pay attention to the speedometer until the radar
detector went off on the sunvisor above his head, its shrill tone
accompanied by a rapidly blinking red light. He touched the
brake immediately and felt the car decelerate nicely down to
sixty-five, slower than the traffic moving around him, and then
down to sixty, just to be on the safe side.

Snow chuckled.

It wouldn't do to be pulled over now, not while driving a
stolen car with a woman in the trunk. The police were bound
to get the wrong idea.

A half-mile down the road he saw the state trooper parked
in a small culvert behind a green hill.

Snow checked the parkway signs.

He had to be careful.

He was still a good forty-five minutes from home.

21

Lincoln and McCall were in the car heading back to their headquarters at the Holiday Inn when the call came in on Lincoln's cellular phone.

They had finished investigating the break-in at a hardware store just up the road from the Wander Inn. The owner had come in to open up and found the deadbolt disengaged. For some reason the alarm hadn't gone off. He suspected one of his own employees of having seen him set the alarm and therefore getting the code to disarm it. He called the robbery into the Warwick Police Department, where Lincoln overheard the call on one of the squad cars parked outside the Wander Inn.

On a hunch, Lincoln had Wilson drive him and McCall to the hardware store. The owner seemed perplexed. Why would one of his employees go through the trouble of breaking into the store without even troubling the safe in back? As far as he could tell, none of the stock was disturbed, nothing major, anyway. Maybe a few cans of spray paint . . .

Was it just a case of vandalism?

Why not just throw a rock through the window? It didn't make sense.

Lincoln left the disturbed owner to his perplexity and climbed back into the car. They were on the road only ten minutes before the cell phone rang.

"Lincoln."

"It's Hank."

"You've got something?"

"Maybe. Maybe it's just nothing."

"Let's hear it."

"You remember Julie Golden?"

"Of course. Snow's defense attorney."

"She hasn't shown up for work yet. Her secretary placed a call to the NYPD. It seems she had a case scheduled early this morning and she's always very punctual about such things. The secretary was worried Golden might have gotten into a traffic accident. Then she got the call from the prison asking for Golden. When she told them Golden wasn't in yet, they gave the message of Snow's escape to the secretary. That's how we learned that she was missing."

"You mean no one got around to telling her of Snow's escape until this morning?"

There was an uncomfortable silence on the other end.

"I'm asking you a question, Hank."

"It seems they couldn't get in touch with her. Her beeper was turned off. There's no need to panic just yet. When pressed, the secretary agreed it was possible that she might still be on her way in to the office. Golden was supposedly spending the weekend with her lover in the Poconos and didn't want to be disturbed. That's why the beeper was turned off. To be honest with you, Tom, I think it's probably a non-issue. Just a case of a girl with hot pants."

"Who else on that list hasn't been called?" Lincoln asked sharply.

"No one. Everyone else was notified."

"No exceptions?"

"No."

"Good," Lincoln said, thinking of Kate. He made a mental note to place a personal call to her the first chance he got. "Keep me posted."

"All right, Tom."

Lincoln pressed the end button and folded the cell phone, thrusting it into his pocket.

"We've picked up the scent?" McCall said.

"Something definitely stinks."

"Let the chase begin."

"Wilson," Lincoln said.

The driver's eyes flicked to the rearview.

"Yes, sir?"

"Turn this car around and get us to Manhattan, pronto."

8:33 A.M.

Julie Golden blinked against the light as the trunk swooshed open above her.

Dammit. She had actually fallen asleep.

How long had they been driving?

She lifted her head a little from the carpet beneath her cheek and felt the cold rain spattering her face. The doctor was standing above her, looking down into the trunk. He reached toward her. She flinched away from Snow's touch, but it was useless; her body wouldn't respond to her mind's command. She saw the doctor smile. He really did have a nice smile. Open. Honest. No wonder she had once placed such trust in him. He reached gently behind her and she felt again the small sharp stinging on each side of her neck.

"You can move now," Snow said softly.

Slowly, Julie stretched her cramped legs. He was right, the feeling was rushing back into her limbs. She reluctantly stretched out her hand to allow Snow to help her from the trunk.

"Watch your head," he said.

Snow half-lifted her out of the deep well of the trunk and set her down on the ground. She felt the thick bed of wet pine needles beneath her stockinged feet and blinked the rain from her eyes. She seemed to be in the middle of some kind of dying forest. All around her were stunted black pine trees looking like malignant, gnarled gnomes out of a B-movie horror story. They seemed to be looking back at her with malicious glee. She shivered at the sight. A damp cold penetrated her clothes.

"Come on," Snow said, propelling her forward. "Let's get inside."

He was referring to a modest cabin of weathered gray wood behind a sparse stand of pines. Julie hadn't noticed the structure until he'd started her toward it. She looked wildly around her, trying to get her bearings, the thick stench of rotting vegetation assaulting her nostrils.

Where the hell was she?

"Let's go," he said, yanking her around.

Julie stumbled, her legs still wobbly, and Snow lifted her up.

"I'm sorry, dear," he said. "Just trying to keep you focused."

Julie let him lead her up a short hill toward the shack, waiting until she got her legs under her. They were within ten yards of the door before she went spinning out of his grip, delivering a front snap kick to Snow's groin. She had executed the move a hundred times, a thousand times, with Master Park and against the heavy bag hanging in his upstairs martial arts studio on Forty-seventh Street. Master Park had insisted that learning one or two moves to perfection was a lot better preparation for actual combat than learning a dozen moves imperfectly. As a result, Julie had always felt confident that the move would work in real life if she ever needed it. She had never needed it before, but as Master Park said, a true martial artist never has to fight. Julie was certain that the confidence she radiated had kept trouble away from her in many dicey situations. Now she needed the move to save her life and she was determined to deliver it to perfection, cocking her knee at the chest and whipping the instep of her right foot toward the vulnerable place between his legs.

There was only one problem.

Snow parried the blow expertly with a down-block, knocking Julie off balance.

My God, my God, Julie thought, panicking, fear draining her, *it hasn't worked.*

Stunned, she could do nothing but stand there as she saw him reach forward with a sword hand. But instead of the devastating blow to the carotid she expected, he merely touched her softly, almost gently, on the solar plexus.

Julie felt a shock go through her entire body as if her nerves were short-circuiting and then her consciousness was slipped into a black envelope and mailed away into nothingness.

22

Less than a half hour later, Lincoln was standing in the parking garage beneath Julie Golden's fashionable East Side office.

He was talking to a Sal Marino, who'd checked in Ms. Golden's silver Lexus SL400 at 7:08 A.M. and checked her out again exactly three minutes later, at 7:11. The garage attendant said she claimed to have forgotten some important papers. It was McCall who asked if there'd been anyone in the car with her when she'd left.

The attendant looked confused for a moment, then irritated.

Lincoln watched the play of emotions on the man's broad, no-nonsense face with interest. He'd seen the expression before. It was as if there were a place in his brain's hard drive that was inexplicably scrambled.

"I don't know," he said. "I didn't see anyone. At least, I don't think I did."

"What the hell is that supposed to mean?" McCall said. "Either you saw someone in the car or you didn't."

"Maybe there was. I mean, I just didn't notice." The attendant was growing agitated as his confusion mounted. The blood was rushing into his face. How many times had Lincoln seen this before? "It all happened so fast. She was in a hurry. There was another car coming in at the same time. My attention was distracted. It isn't my fault."

"It's okay, Mr. Marino," Lincoln interrupted. "We understand. You weren't expecting anything out of the ordinary. If you were, you would have been more alert. It was just another transaction. Do you remember the other car? The other car that was coming in as Ms. Golden was leaving?"

"Yeah. Red Mercedes 560SL ragtop."

"Who's it belong to?"

"Dr. Havermeyer. The dentist on the third floor."

"Thank you very much. Sorry to inconvenience you."

The attendant still seemed hostile, confused. "Is Ms. Golden in some kind of trouble?" he asked.

"We don't know yet," Lincoln replied honestly. "We're taking all the necessary precautions. Now, can you point us toward the elevator to her office?"

Inside the elevator on the way up to the office, McCall asked Lincoln why they hadn't pressed the attendant as they had the waitress earlier.

"Because he was really trying to remember and couldn't," Lincoln said. "You could see it in his face. He knew there was something wrong in his head. If we'd pressed him any harder, he could have had some kind of mental breakdown."

McCall looked at him disbelievingly.

"I've seen it happen," Lincoln said.

McCall shook his head. "To take her ticket, he would have had to come out of the booth, *right around* the passenger side. How do you figure he didn't notice if anyone was in the car with her?"

"He could have been crouched down in the back."

"But you don't think so."

"No. I think he was sitting in the front, right beside her."

"Then how do you explain why he didn't see him? What's

the next thing you're going to tell me, that Snow has the power to make himself invisible?''

"You wouldn't believe me if I told you.''

McCall was about to say something when the doors to the elevator slid open and they stepped out into a thickly carpeted vestibule in front of a pair of glass doors emblazoned with Julie Golden's name in no-nonsense gold leaf. Behind a wrap-around desk was a receptionist with a blonde bowl cut no taller when she stood up than when she'd been sitting down. Her name plate identified her as Samantha Lewis, but Lincoln already knew her name from the FBI report he'd received in the car on the way over.

"Ms. Lewis, my name is Tom Lincoln, and this here is Agent McCall of the FBI. We're here regarding your missing persons call.''

"Thank God you're here," the receptionist said. "Is Ms. Golden all right?''

"We're trying to determine her whereabouts right now. Anything you can tell us would be extremely helpful.''

"Well, she was due in early to go over the preliminary depositions of the case she's working on this morning. She's due at the courthouse in less than two hours.''

"Is she usually on time?" McCall asked.

"She's always on time. Punctuality is one of her pet compulsions. I make sure I leave the house a half-hour ahead of time so I can still get here ahead of her even if the train breaks down.''

"Sounds like a real ballbuster," McCall said, trying to calm the receptionist down a little. It didn't work.

"Is she all right? God, I hope nothing's happened to her.''

"You knew, of course, about the Alexander Snow case,'' Lincoln said.

"Yes. I didn't think she should take it, but I kept my opinion to myself. It wasn't my place to say. But as far as I was concerned, she didn't make a name for herself in this business taking on cases like his. That man was a monster. My God, do you think he kidnapped her?''

"Ms. Lewis, we aren't making any assumptions just yet. We're going to try to establish Ms. Golden's whereabouts as quickly as we can. The first thing I need to know is where was she driving in from this morning."

"From Pennsylvania. She has a place in the Poconos."

"All right. I need her home phone number here in the city and her number in the Poconos."

"I'm not supposed to give out her Pocono number," the secretary said without the least trace of irony, "unless it's an emergency."

Lincoln laid his hand on her shoulder, his voice calm, paternal. "I'd say this was an emergency. Wouldn't you?"

The home phone number turned up nothing but Julie Golden's answering machine. Lincoln dialed the Pocono number, waited three rings, and heard a woman's voice, deep and sexy, answer.

"My name is Tom Lincoln, and I'm working with the FBI. May I ask who I'm speaking to?"

The woman's name was Peema, or something like that. In spite of the smoky, sensual tone of her voice, she had a clipped, no-nonsense manner about her and she immediately wanted to know what was the matter, if anything had happened to Julie. Lincoln didn't need to hear anything more than the tone of her voice to know that the woman on the other end of the phone was Julie Golden's lover. He explained the situation and endured a stream of obscenities that poured through the phone from the other end.

"Why wasn't she informed of that bastard's escape?" Peema demanded to know. "Someone could have sent a car up here to tell her."

Lincoln lamely tried to explain the breakdown in communication the best he could. He didn't see the point in blaming Julie for turning off her beeper. He understood the woman's pain. She needed to lash out at somebody. Lincoln just happened to be there. There was enough blame to go around. If he took a little more than his share, that was okay by him. His back was strong enough to carry it.

For the time being, anyway.

"It's your fault, Lincoln," the woman fairly screamed over the phone. "You encouraged her to take the case. You were the one who talked her into betraying him. You were the one who guaranteed he would never get out. Now you let him escape and the bastard walks right back into her life."

"We're not sure yet that anything of the sort has happened. We're just trying to cover all the bases."

"You're just trying to cover your asses. But let me tell you, they're going to be mighty sore before this is over. I'll never let this rest. You and the entire bureau are to blame for this fuck-up, and I'll personally make sure that you get yours."

Lincoln could do nothing but stand there and listen to the woman's abuse. There was no sense in arguing his side of the story.

She was absolutely right.

"Tough call," McCall said sympathetically, when Lincoln finally extricated himself from the phone.

"Yeah. The toughest."

"Had a couple of those myself. I give you credit for taking it. You could have laid it all on the Agency. Or on the damn prison."

"It belongs to me."

"So that's what he meant."

"What who meant?"

"Kirkland."

"What did the tightass have to say?"

"That you were the last of a dying breed."

McCall seemed to realize what he'd said only after the words had come from his mouth."

"Thanks for reminding me."

"Sorry," he said, and blushed.

"Don't worry about it. What now?"

"There's always Havermeyer, the dentist," McCall said, seeming genuinely relieved to get off the subject. Maybe he saw something."

"Yeah," Lincoln said, pressing the button to the elevator, after checking the office directory. "And maybe pigs will fly."

8:47 A.M.

For the time being, Lincoln decided to set up shop in Julie Golden's office.

They really had nowhere else to go and nothing to go on. They'd sent officers over to Golden's Central Park residence, but Lincoln didn't expect they'd find her there. He had also ordered a tap on the office phones, just in case Snow made a call with a ransom demand—equally unlikely, but they had to cover all the bases. Finally, Lincoln issued the usual APB on Golden's Lexus, but that was a shot in the dark. If Snow was still driving the car, the chances were he'd switched plates. It was a common enough thing to do. He could get a new set from any parking lot or driveway in the tristate area and no one would be the wiser. After all, how many times did the average person check their license plates?

The way Lincoln thought of it, they were between rolls of the dice. The only thing they could do was wait until Snow made his next move.

Lincoln saw a fireworks display of colored lights explode in his right eye. He waited until it died away before carefully making his way across the room to the watercooler, standing between a potted ficus and an armchair, trying not to betray his sudden unsteadiness. He took a small paper cup, filled it with cold water, and sat it on top of the water jug while he reached into his pocket for his bottle of pills. He threw two more of the little blue pills into his mouth and swallowed them with the water, taking a second cupful to erase the bitter trace they left in his throat.

He stood for a moment, pretending to be studying a piece of modern art hanging above the watercooler. It looked like one of his tumor-induced visual disturbances.

For the first time since he'd disembarked from the plane, Lincoln wondered if perhaps this case was too much for him.

He took a deep breath, steadied himself, and turned, already feeling better, only to find McCall staring at him.

"Pretty damn ugly, isn't it?" the young agent said, indicating the painting.

"Yeah," Lincoln said. He could see by the way McCall was staring at him that he was evaluating him, wondering if Lincoln could go the distance, if he would be there when the chips were down. Lincoln didn't blame the kid. He'd do the same thing if he were in McCall's shoes. Before a fight, you kind of like to know who the guys are standing beside you. McCall had to know if Lincoln would be there if he needed him, so he returned McCall's level, steely-eyed gaze with one of his own. "Uglier than an elephant's hemorrhoids."

He must have passed the test. McCall's eyes softened and he grinned at the joke.

Lincoln made his way back to the receptionist's desk looking more confident than he felt and asked her if he might use her phone.

He wanted to place a call before the wiretap experts got there. He tried her at home first, and when he got no answer, he checked his watch. He figured she must be at work by now.

He squinted at the number inked into his weathered black address book, and holding the phone between his shoulder and chin, punched in the numbers. He gave the name and department to the woman on the other end and the switchboard shepherded his call through. He heard the voice on the other end before the first ring expired, almost as if she were sitting there, waiting for the call.

"Kate?"

"Yes?"

"This is Tom Lincoln."

There was a pause.

"Yes?"

A note of anticipation, an expectation of hope, perhaps? It made what Lincoln had to say next all the more painful.

"You've been informed that Snow has escaped."

"They called me around midnight last night. Have they caught him yet?"

"No," Lincoln said, and felt the disappointment, palpable even over the miles of wire separating them, like the dead weight of seaweed on a fishing line. "Not yet. But we'll catch him."

"I hope it's soon."

Lincoln let that slide. "I just wanted you to hear from someone, from me, actually, to assure you that something was being done. I don't want you to feel that you've been left hanging."

"I appreciate that, Tom. I really do."

Lincoln felt some measure of redemption. She seemed to mean it. If he were honest, there was more confidence in her voice than he felt at the moment.

"We're going to get him," he repeated, as if convincing himself. "We've already got a lead on him. I'm going to keep in touch with you, let you know how things stand. In the meantime, I'll give you my number, in case you need anything. You can reach me anytime. Don't hesitate to call, understand?"

"Yes, Tom."

Lincoln could tell by the tone of her voice that Kate knew the implications behind his giving her his number.

"Kate?"

"Yes?"

"I don't want you to worry."

"Just catch him as quickly as you can, please?"

"I promise, Kate."

He rung off, staring morosely at the office phone, feeling guilty. He purposely hadn't told her about Julie Golden's disappearance. Of course, there was still a chance that she would turn up.

Yeah.

And he still believed in Santa Claus and spontaneous remission.

23

Julie Golden opened her eyes.

To her it seemed she'd only been out for the space of a heartbeat. She felt refreshed and incredibly alert. In fact, she'd been unconscious for several minutes, enough time for Snow to carry her into the cabin, strip her naked, and secure her to a straight-backed chair. He sat across a plain wooden table from her now, dressed casually in a pale blue polo shirt and a pair of black chinos. His gray eyes regarded her curiously, as if staring at a specimen under a microscope.

Julie felt the goosebumps pimpling her naked flesh.

She sank back into the chair as much as her bondage would allow, which wasn't much, as if trying to make herself invisible.

"I hope you're not too uncomfortable," Snow said. "But given your recalcitrance, the binding was necessary."

Julie didn't answer. Instead, she noticed for the first time the blood pressure cuff on her left bicep, the band across her diaphragm, the foam sleeves into which the first two fingers of her left hand were thrust. She might not have recognized the device if she hadn't seen them enough times in her line of work.

It was a modified version of a lie detector.

Julie wondered how she could ever have seen Snow on a doctor-patient basis. She had chosen him as her psychologist because he'd come highly recommended from a close personal colleague and she had heard of his reputation in professional circles. She had gone to discuss her lifelong physical and emotional attraction to other women, half-hoping, half-expecting Snow to guide her past her aversion to men, which was part of the reason she had specifically chosen a male therapist. She figured he could find some deep-seated unconscious reason for her aversion to male sexuality buried in her past. But to her surprise, Snow did not try to dissuade her from her natural desires. Instead, he encouraged her to be true to herself. By the end of her therapy, aside from developing a certain unexpected erotic transference to Snow himself, Julie was content and happy to proclaim herself a lesbian for the first time in her life.

She owed a great deal of her personal growth to Dr. Alexander Snow, so it was especially difficult to accept the fact that he was a serial killer. She was prepared to defend him honestly, but when Lincoln had approached her with circumstantial, albeit clearly inadmissable, evidence of his crimes, neither her gratitude to the doctor nor her sense of ethics to her profession could stop her from performing what she felt was her true personal mission. She'd devoted her entire life to bringing down the male oppressors and abusers of women, and in spite of what he'd done for her personally, Julie Golden had no reasonable doubt in her mind that Snow was guilty—if not of murder, at least of highly suspect criminal activities, accomplished while hiding behind his patriarchal authority as a physician.

If she had any lingering doubts, they were dispelled now, as she sat tied to a chair in a shack in the middle of nowhere.

It was damp and cold in the cabin, with a musty smell in the air. She flicked her eyes behind his head, her own head immobilized, to the wall behind him. It was lined with built-in shelves crammed with green file folders, no doubt filled with case histories. Was hers among them? She couldn't help but wonder. There were several books whose titles Julie couldn't read from this distance, as well as folders of tightly typed loose papers, no doubt notes for future publications. On the wall just to the left of the bookshelves was a poster outlining the human body, its interior traced with various blue and red lines, like a state with a particularly complicated highway system. It didn't look like any anatomical chart Julie Golden had ever seen before.

She had to remain calm. Her life depended on it.

She could feel her heart thudding in her chest, skipping beats. If she panicked, he'd kill her for sure. Psychos always wanted you to be scared; they fed off fear. The longer she could maintain her composure, the longer she'd remain alive. It was as simple as that. The longer she remained alive, the more chance she had. For what? Who was going to find her, out here? How could she get away? She fought down the terror. She'd find a way, as long as she was alive. The important thing was to stay calm.

"What's your name?" Dr. Snow asked gently.

"You know that already. Why are you trying to play games?"

Julie knew he wasn't playing games. He was attempting to get a baseline reading on the lie detector.

"Don't make this difficult," Snow said, without the least trace of threat in his voice. "What is your name?"

She frowned. "Julie Golden."

Julie saw the needle scratching the graph paper in a regular sweeping stroke.

"What do you do for a living?"

"I'm an attorney."

"Do you defend the innocent?"

Julie glared at him with defiance. "Yes."

"What are you thinking right now?"

"I'm wondering what the hell you want from me."

The needle didn't waver, keeping up its steady sweep across

the paper, the tiny pencil sounding like a mouse chewing through a plaster wall.

Snow glanced at the graph paper. "Good," he said. "Very good."

He reached down under the table and retrieved something lying on the ground by his feet. It was a black nylon foldover case sealed by velcro. He tore off the tab and unfolded the case, revealing an array of glittering silver pins of varying lengths and thicknesses.

Julie felt her heart stutter once again and the bottom fall out of the pit of her stomach.

Keep calm, she told herself, *keep calm. Whatever you do, don't let him know you're afraid, or you're dead.*

"These pins," Snow said neutrally, "can elicit the greatest pleasure or the most intense pain. I spent three years in China under a master acupuncturist, learning the precise meridian points and chi channels. The choice is yours."

"I asked you before," Julie said, keeping her voice tight. "What do you want from me?"

"The truth, Ms. Golden," Snow said. "Nothing but the truth."

She was intensely aware of the shining pins, her naked flesh, the machine scratching away beside her. And then he asked his next question, the one she feared the most, the one she knew would defeat her right from the start.

Snow folded his hands on the table in front of the case of glittering pins, leaned forward, and almost whispered the words.

"Are you afraid?"

8:51 A.M.

Kate laid the phone back in the cradle with exaggerated care.

She stared at it for several moments as if it were an ominous black bird staring back at her. For the second time in less than twelve hours the phone had turned against her. She thought of Poe's raven, slowly but surely taking away every option for hope. A little bit of that hope had died when she'd heard

Lincoln's voice on the other end and then the news that Snow was still at large.

As she sat there staring at the phone, half-expecting it to squawk again with more bad news, she was startled out of her reverie by Diane, who once again stood in her doorway.

"Are you okay?"

Kate jerked her head up. For the time being, words failed her.

"You look like you've just seen a ghost."

Kate nodded toward the phone, thinking of Lincoln. *"Heard* from a ghost, sort of."

"Bad news?"

"Not good."

"How bad?"

"Just a voice from the past."

"Old boyfriend?" Diane said, almost hopefully, always ready to edge the conversation into some juicy gossip.

"You might say that."

"Feel like talking about it?"

"No."

Diane made a disappointed face.

"Spoken like a true psychoanalyst. Bottle it up until you explode. Would you like me to take your 10:30? Abnormal psychology is one of my favorite topics. I can tell 'em how we behaviorists fuck up perfectly healthy rats and turn 'em psycho. No rodent lovers in your class, I hope."

"No. I can handle it."

"Sure? I'm free during that section."

"No. Thanks anyway. I'm all right. Just need a minute or two to collect my thoughts."

"Okay. But if you need anything . . . "

Kate raised her hand. "I know. And Diane, thank you."

"Don't think anything of it. If you change your mind, just let me know. I really wouldn't mind talking about abnormal psych, especially not after my date last night."

Kate couldn't help but laugh. "You wouldn't dare."

"Mention Marty? Well, not by name. Let's just say I'd have an unusual case study to present."

"You're terrible."

"Hey, I work with rats all day. It's gotta wear off."

Diane swept out of the doorway with a swish of her colorful skirt.

Kate thought how easy it would have been to let Diane take over her class for the day, but that would be giving in, and she refused to do that. She refused to let Snow alter her life any more than he already had. She was taking her stand. Jeff and Lincoln were right. They would catch him. It was only a matter of time. In the meantime, she would go on with her life as usual.

Her decision gave her no little amount of satisfaction. She knew it was the last thing Snow would have wanted her to do.

24

"'I was born for this,'" Snow recited from memory. "'I came into the world for this, to bear witness to the truth; and all who are on the side of truth listen to my voice.' Do you know who said that?"

"No," Julie said.

"That's Christ speaking to Pontius Pilate, John 19:37. But when Pilate asked, 'What is truth?' Christ was silent. Why do you suppose that was?"

Julie didn't answer. She was still trying to think of a way out, but her courage and resourcefulness were fast diminishing. It was as if someone had pulled a plug inside her and hope was draining away. Snow was standing beside her now, his Velcro package of pins open on the table just beneath her naked breasts, his breath on her neck, feathery and intimate. Julie shivered, but not from the raw dampness inside the cabin.

"Pilate was a worldly man, a Roman governor, a man it might safely be presumed who was educated in the major philosophical schools of his day, of which there were no small number, all of which concerned themselves with the apprehension of truth to one degree or another. Certainly Christ could have found no better audience to discuss the matter of truth than with a man as philosophically minded as Pilate. If he had been successful, even entertaining, Christ might have saved his own life. It's clear throughout all four gospels that Pilate did not want to crucify Christ. Yet Jesus chose to remain silent even though his very life hung in the balance. Why?''

"I don't know."

"Think," Snow said.

"I really don't know," Julie said, trying to hold onto her thoughts, which were all focused in one direction: escape. "I don't see the point of your question. What has this to do with me?"

"Ah," Snow said. "A pragmatist. Just give you the facts, is that it? Well, don't you see, it has everything to do with you. Don't you see how similar your position is to Christ's when he was brought before Pilate?"

Julie felt a numb coldness fill her. She knew this was Snow's way of telling her he was going to kill her. Of course, she had known it all along, but it was different, now that the idea was actually in the air.

"Do you see the relevance now?"

"No," Julie said stubbornly, and saw the pencil swing wildly on the page of graph paper feeding through the lie-detector.

Snow shook his head. He reached down and elegantly picked out a long silver pin from the Velcro sleeve on the table. He held it in front of her eyes for a moment, the light traveling down its length, gleaming in a tiny white star at the point.

Holding it delicately between thumb and forefinger, he inserted the pin just above her left collarbone. Only the tip of the pin pierced her flesh, the shaft itself lying against her skin, and so there was a moment between the tiny pinprick and the sickening pain that filled the left side of her body like molten lead. She felt burning bile rise in the back of her throat and forced it back down to answer his question.

"Do you see the relevance now?"

"Yes," Julie gasped.

"Very good."

With the same delicacy, Snow removed the pin. The pain and sickness instantly vanished.

"You said you defended the innocent."

"Yes."

"When you defended me in court, did you think I was innocent?"

"Yes."

She was conscious of the scratching of the lie detector. She had heard there were ways of beating it. She wished she had looked into them a little more closely now.

"Julie . . . " Snow's voice was soft, insinuating.

"At first I believed you innocent."

"That's better. What happened to change your mind?"

"Nothing," Julie said. "I just changed my mind."

Once again the pencil swung wildly on the chart, but Snow wasn't even looking at it. Instead he was looking into her eyes—defiant, determined, the eyes of a liar, but a liar for a good cause. Snow's eyes were horribly patient, the eyes of a man with all the time in the world. The worst thing about them was that they were almost sympathetic.

Without a word he replaced the pin and added another one about an inch lower.

Julie stiffened with pain as if electrically shocked, her fingers and toes clenched, white lightning behind her eyes. She felt herself lose control of her bladder, the embarrassment lost in the confusion of agony that was scrambling her thoughts.

This time Snow removed the pins only halfway, leaving them dangling from her skin. She felt a dull sickness all through her body. For the first time she noticed the towel under her thighs, now wet, and realized the bastard had known this was going to happen all along. She could smell the sharp tang of urine in the air. She blushed with shame.

"There's nothing to be embarrassed about," Snow said gently. "It's merely a physiological reaction."

"You bastard," Julie whispered hoarsely.

"I don't enjoy doing this," Snow said. "I'm not a sadist. I

only want the truth. Now I'll ask you again. What changed your mind about my innocence?''

Her voice shook when she spoke. Julie was shocked to hear how weak and tentative it sounded. It was nothing like the voice she was used to hearing when she cross-examined some abusing husband on the witness stand.

''I was given information. It was inadmissable, but it clearly pointed to your guilt.''

''Is that why you didn't challenge the procedure that led to the seizure of my research papers?''

''Yes.''

''And who gave you that information?''

Julie thought of the pin between Snow's fingers, the sickness, the pain, the humiliation. She realized she couldn't fight it any longer. He would have to take care of himself. Besides, the last she'd heard, he had terminal brain cancer. He might be dead, or near-death, already. There was no sense in protecting a dead man. Julie pleaded her case, using her best arguments even though she knew they were merely rationalizations. She was trying to save herself. She had devoted her career to saving many others. Why not use the truth to save herself, even if it meant betraying an innocent man, a man who'd gotten her into this situation in the first place?

''It was Tom Lincoln.''

Snow smiled benevolently. He pulled a shorter pin from the sleeve and Julie stiffened, whimpering in anticipation of the sickness to come.

''I'm telling the truth.''

''I know you are, dear,'' Snow said. He reached down and deftly inserted the shorter pin about an inch below her navel.

Almost immediately Julie felt a not unpleasant warmth spreading from her wet buttocks over her thighs and stomach. She felt her nipples stiffening, her lips parting, panting for breath. Her heart gave a little jump-start and the warmth that started below intensified to a sweat-inducing heat centering on her genitals. Her fingers and toes curled, this time not in pain, but in unexpected pleasure as the first convulsion seized her.

It was not an orgasm, exactly, but something close to it. She hardly had time to process the sensation when it seized her again, wracking her body, as if years of chronic tension were being spontaneously released from her muscles. A third wave of pleasure shook her before Snow pulled the pin halfway out, leaving her on the brink of another release, but mixed with the sensation of the pins in her shoulders, blending into a curious mix of pleasure-pain.

Somehow what she had just experienced was even more humiliating than the agony he had put her through earlier, for this was something just as involuntary, but intimate—personal, even loving.

"Why . . . " Julie managed to say.

"I told you," Snow said. "I can give you pain or pleasure. The choice is yours."

Julie almost wanted to believe him, but the very calmness of his manner hinted at his depthless insanity.

"Where is Kate Bennett?"

It was the question she was afraid he'd ask next. The one question she had no defense for. The pencil swung wildly on the graph paper before she even had a chance to answer. But neither one of them were paying attention to the lie detector anymore. They were connected by more than mere wire and bioelectrical impulses.

"She's the one who really betrayed me, isn't she Julie?"

"Yes," Julie said dully.

"Where is she?"

Julie felt the tears leaking from the corners of her eyes, rolling hotly down her cheeks. There was no rationalizing her betrayal of Dr. Kate Bennett. It was she who had made possible—at the cost of her career, and now maybe her life—the conviction of Dr. Alexander Snow. She could only hope she was aware of Snow's escape and well protected.

"Come on, Julie," Snow said patiently. "Give it up. You know you want to."

That was the problem: she did want to. She didn't want to feel the pain anymore. She wanted this to end. She told Snow what he wanted to know, and when she was finished, she slumped forward in her chair, knowing that she was defeated. She had nothing left to hide.

She could not guess that there was one more question Snow wanted her to answer, the most painful one of all.

He lifted her sweat-damp hair in one fist, staring into her dulled eyes.

"What is the truth, Julie?"

Julie's lips were numb, the tears dry on her cheeks. She felt her body trembling uncontrollably. This was going to be the end, and it wasn't going to be quick or easy.

"I don't know," she said in a faint voice, barely a whisper, so soft she hardly heard it herself.

Snow shook his head sadly.

He removed another pin from his folder.

"Wrong answer."

9:15 A.M.

Just as he'd expected, Julie Golden wasn't in her penthouse apartment.

The doorman had explained that he hadn't seen her since the previous Friday. The officers had judiciously requested permission to investigate the apartment anyway, which was immediately granted, under the circumstances. They confirmed the doorman's statement, reporting that there was no sign that Ms. Golden had returned to the apartment after leaving her office.

The wiretap was in place on all the phones in Ms. Golden's office, as well as on her private line, but so far, no calls other than business ones had come in, including one from an irate client waiting for Ms. Golden at the courthouse. It was still too early to expect anything from the APB.

Lincoln had ordered a check of the traffic patterns on all the likely routes leading from the Poconos into the city. There were no reported accidents nor any major traffic tie-ups leading into or out of the city. Julie Golden, if she'd left her weekend getaway as her lover had reported, should have been in the city hours ago.

Still, Lincoln wasn't jumping to any conclusions. Even though the possibility of abduction was growing more and more likely with every passing minute, Lincoln clung to the narrow hope that Julie might still arrive. Perhaps her car had broken down somewhere on the way to the courthouse or she'd forgotten something back at the Pocono retreat? McCall wasn't buying any of it, of course. In his mind, Julie Golden had been abducted and they should be doing something about it.

"What?" Lincoln had asked.

McCall merely stared at him.

Lincoln had to smile. Once he'd been just like McCall, brimming with youthful energy and idealism, believing that because you were FBI you did something, dammit.

Looking at McCall now, Lincoln found himself thinking, *Was I ever really that young?*

25

Kate waited for the last of the stragglers to take their seats. She looked out at the sea of placid faces assembled this morning for Psych 262, Abnormal Psychology. She noted, not for the first time, how they seemed to take the same desks, even though she'd never assigned them seats. They just naturally gravitated to the same places. She mused on what Diane and her behavioral science background could make of that, making a mental note to mention it to her. Diane might be able to get a monograph out of it.

Kate also noted that the class was two-thirds female, though the psychiatrists she knew were at least two-thirds male. It was an interesting phenomenon. What made young women take advanced psych courses if they had no intention of going on to become psychiatrists? Was it just the well-documented general humanism of the female of the species, interested to know what made people tick? Or was there some hidden sexism at the heart of it that discouraged women from pursuing the technical medical training necessary to practice psychiatry? She thought bitterly of Dr. Policastro, the Freudian department head, and his condescending attitude toward female students. It was men like him who kept many promising therapists from pursuing careers in psychiatry just because they were women. For her part, Kate tried to encourage her most promising pupils, male or female, but especially female. She sought out the bright, eager face of Bonnie Kaplan, her best student, sitting, as usual, in the third row, third seat from the left. Kate had vowed to do her best not to allow Bonnie to become discouraged and slip away like so many others.

The rest of the faces in the class were a blur. Some looked simply tired, others obviously hung-over from a night of partying, still others looked vaguely bored, as if they would rather be anywhere but sitting in a classroom, listening to her lecture on abnormal psychology.

Kate stared up at the clock at the back of the class and saw the second hand sweeping around the face. It seemed to be moving at half-speed.

This session was going to be murder to get through.

She remembered how nervous she'd been when she'd first started teaching. She hadn't expected to be so jittery. But standing up in front of a group of students waiting to be taught was nothing like talking one-on-one with a patient, or even running a group therapy session. In her practice, she was merely a guide, a prompter; most of the talking was done by the patients. In fact, there were many patients and groups she'd have to fight to get a word in edgewise. Even after nearly four years in front of a classroom, she still felt butterflies. An English department colleague she'd dated briefly had told her it was good to feel butterflies. He still felt them after twenty years of teaching. When the butterflies were gone, that meant the life had gone out of your teaching; it had become nothing more than a stale routine. Like everything else, you needed to be on the edge to teach well.

Normally she felt the butterflies, but not today. Today they were all lying dead in the pit of her stomach, killed by the noxious thoughts of Dr. Alexander Snow.

She heard someone in the class clear a throat and was aware

of an uneasy rustling of bodies in the chairs ranged in front of her. Everyone's eyes were on her. They were waiting for her to say something.

Kate stared down at her notes, but they made as little sense to her as they had earlier that morning in her office. She shoved them back into her folder and came around the front of her desk, sitting at the edge. She decided to wing it today, to talk about what was on her mind. Suddenly her stomach was fluttering with the feathery wings of butterflies.

Kate was barely conscious of talking. Instead she seemed to hear herself as if she were sitting in one of the seats of the classroom.

"The schizoid personality is perhaps the most common mental aberration in modern man. In fact, radical psychologists such as R. D. Laing believed it was impossible for modern man *not* to be schizoid to one extent or another, given the materialistic nature of our culture, which has all but inculcated into man the idea that he is nothing but a machine. The schizophrenic takes the idea one step further, internalizing it, and literally believes he is a robot. Laing says this is a rational solution to an irrational society."

A boy dressed in baggy jeans, a plaid shirt, and a wispy goatee shot his arm in the air. Unlike other professors, Kate always encouraged questions during her lectures. It made for a livelier class, not to mention mimicking in comforting fashion her old psychotherapy sessions.

"Dr. Bennett, are you saying we should all be schizophrenic?"

"No, of course not. Only that for certain people it is an understandable reaction to an unreasonable society. You have to remember that Laing was arguing from the side of the schizophrenic, which was a revolutionary thing to do in his day. He located the problem outside the individual and saw his illness as a viable coping mechanism. It's a rather controversial theory, to say the least, but the undeniable fact is that most of us have elements of the schizoid personality."

"Then what keeps me from being a schizophrenic?"

"What separates a schizophrenic from the schizoid is that the schizophrenic has suffered a major psychic earthquake that has separated his psyche from the mainland. He is no longer able to maintain the tension between his inside desires and the public mask he wears as a contributing member of society. Wife, mother, businessman, doctor, professor, even student, these are all roles we play, they don't represent us in our totality. And so a tension builds up between what we are and what we represent ourselves to be. If we cannot assimilate enough of our true selves into our social roles, we break and become schizophrenic. But for most of us, this never happens. We are able to function normally in society, though we still bear traces of the schizoid personality. For instance, one schizoid tendency is to depersonalize the other, especially when he or she poses a threat to your ego. What you attempt to do is to turn the other person into a thing. To give a specific example, when I give a difficult assignment or request a paper, I'm no longer a human being, I'm a teacher, with all the stereotypical aspects that dehumanize me. I'm an object that stands in the way of your pleasure.''

There was laughter from the class and another hand rose, this time Bonnie Kaplan's.

"Yes, Bonnie."

"Didn't Laing also say that the schizoid personality fears being turned into an object himself?''

"Yes. He fears three things, basically. As you say, he fears being turned into an object by the scrutiny of another. In the schizophrenic, this is exaggerated into a fear of being turned into stone. He also fears that others will be able to read his thoughts. Again, in the schizophrenic, this is exaggerated into the fear of being transparent, like one of those plastic visible-man models. The last fear is of implosion. The schizoid personality fears that there is nothing of substance inside and that he or she is merely a shell that the least bit of pressure can smash into oblivion. I think that this is the most common fear in the functioning schizoid personality, but perhaps the most dangerous.''

"Why is that?" Bonnie asked.

"Because it signals a fear that there is no ego at the center of the self, no identity, no truth." Kate realized that she was no longer speaking to the class, but to herself, and that she was talking about Alexander Snow. "You see, the schizophrenic's need to understand himself completely is basically a defense mechanism. It is a defense against being turned into an object in the world of another. To allow himself to be consumed by his own self-love is the only way to prevent himself from being consumed by someone else. But such a search inevitably leads to madness, for just as the Chinese sages taught, no matter how hard or desperate his search, no matter where he looks, he will never find himself because," and Kate knew that her next words were a time-bomb planted in her subconscious by Snow, "there is no such thing as the ego. Madness is the result. Or," she was forced to concede, "enlightenment."

Kate looked up at the clock and realized that she had kept the class over five minutes.

"I'm sorry," she said. "I must have been rambling. Class dismissed. Oh, and please follow the reading assignment on the syllabus."

Kate walked back around the desk and started putting her discarded notes away, still feeling a little shaken by the unexpected turn of her impromptu lecture, when she heard a voice beside her.

"Dr. Bennett?"

Kate looked up. It was Bonnie Kaplan.

"Yes, Bonnie?"

"That was a great class today. I really feel like I'm learning a lot."

"Thank you."

"I was wondering if I could have a conference with you today."

"Let me check my book," Kate said, looking down the column of her black appointment book that outlined her day's activities. Except for a 3:30 Introduction to Psychology class, it was empty. "Sure," she said. "How is one-thirty for you?"

"That would be great. Thanks, Dr. Bennett."

Kate watched Bonnie gather up her knapsack and denim jacket from her desk and leave the room just as the students for Dr. Policastro's special honors class in Freudian Depth Psychology were straggling in. She hurriedly packed up her own stuff and left, being in no mood for Policastro's dry double-entendre attempts at wit.

They reminded her too much of a poor man's version of Alexander Snow.

10:35 A.M.

Snow used a long, flat iron bar to jimmy open the lock on the passenger door of a dark-blue Lincoln Town Car parked in the lot of a Foodtown in a small town called Wanamassa in New Jersey.

The parking lot was half-full and the car was parked between a van and Julie Golden's silver Lexus, so he was screened from the store. No one was making his way from the lot to the store or from the store to the lot, so he had enough time to work the lock. It took him less than a minute to open the door. He smiled at the club locking the steering wheel. Had he wanted, he could have removed it in seconds.

Snow straightened up, checked the lot once again, and walked around to the passenger side of the Lexus. He reached inside the cool interior of the car and half lifted, half slid the woman from the bucket seat into the gray drizzle.

She was wearing a long trenchcoat, but her legs and feet were naked. Understandably, she seemed to be shivering, walking in a jerky, spastic, unnatural way as Snow escorted her to the Lincoln, holding her up with one hand around her chest, reaching around under her shoulders. From a distance, if anyone was around to see him, it merely looked as if he was helping her move from one car to another.

She was still shivering when he sat her in the plush leather seat of the Lincoln, carefully swinging her spasming legs inside, her teeth chattering on something jammed between her swollen lips.

Snow kissed her on the forehead just before he closed the door with a quiet *click.*

Through the darkened, rain-splattered window the woman was jumping around in the seat. Her raincoat had fallen open, exposing the front of her body. She looked like a nervous wreck, like a mental patient.

She was far worse.

26

Kate saw the message on her desk blotter when she got back to her office.

She read it twice, even though there was nothing ambiguous about it.

Lincoln called, 10:21, the message read, *555–0635.* There was a small checkmark in the box labeled "Please return call."

Her finger trembling over the buttons, she misdialed twice before she got the number right. The phone rang three times before he picked up. Kate found herself wishing he wouldn't answer.

"Lincoln."

"Tom? It's Kate."

"Kate. I'm glad you called back." There seemed to be genuine relief in his voice. "Where were you?"

"I had a class to teach."

"I understand."

"Did you catch him?"

There was a heartbeat's pause that gave away the answer.

"No. Not yet. But there's been a development that I thought you should know about."

"Yes?"

"It's not good news, Kate. But I promised you that I would tell you everything, and so I am. I owe it to you."

"What's happened?"

"I'd been holding out hope to the contrary, but I think it's unavoidable at this point but to admit that Snow has Julie Golden."

"Oh God, no."

"She's been missing since early this morning. No one knows her whereabouts. We've been trying to trace her, but without success."

"How could this happen?"

"There was a glitch in communications. She wasn't informed of his escape. I'm sorry."

Kate knew he wasn't apologizing for the fact that Julie hadn't been informed. That wasn't his fault. He was apologizing for giving his personal guarantee that she would never have to worry about Snow again.

"Listen," Lincoln continued. "We still don't know for sure yet. I just thought I'd tell you because I owe you that much. For all we know, she might turn up at any time perfectly safe and well. The most important thing is that I don't want you to panic. Do you understand me, Kate? I need your assurance on this if I'm going to keep you a part of it."

"I understand," Kate said, forcing her voice into some kind of tone of command. "I understand perfectly."

"Good. I knew I could depend on you. I'm certain that Snow has no idea that it was you who leaked the initial information that led to his conviction. If he has Golden, and I stress we're still not certain he does, it's purely a matter of revenge against the attorney who betrayed him in court. You know how his mind works."

"Yes," Kate said tonelessly. She was thinking that was precisely what made her so scared. She knew exactly how Snow's mind worked.

"If anything new breaks, I'll be sure to let you know."

"Thank you."

"And Kate?"

"Yes?"

"Remember, don't be scared. We *will* get him. I give you my word."

"I know you will, Tom," she said, wishing she could say what she was really thinking. What good was his word when it had been broken already? But this was no time for accusations or recriminations. The unthinkable had happened, and the man was doing his best to make it right.

"All right, then, I'll let you go for now. If anything happens on your end or you just need to talk, don't hesitate to give me a call."

What would happen on her end? She let the phrase hang *in* the air. She didn't want to know the answer. Instead, she said, "I will" and placed the receiver back in its cradle, not noticing until that moment how badly her hand was shaking.

11:15 A.M.

Ed Brody walked gimpily across the parking lot to his car parked right next to the handicapped spots near the front of the store.

He could probably have qualified for a handicapped spot himself but even at seventy-one he refused to give in to the aches and pains and infirmities of old age. So he satisfied himself with parking as close to the prime spots as he could. Retired for the last fifteen years, he always did his shopping and other chores on weekdays, when most of the rest of society was hard at work helping to pay his social security benefits.

Weekends, he and his wife stayed holed up in their comfortable split-level house on a quiet tree-lined street and read the papers or went out for a quiet wade in the pool.

Ed felt the drizzle beating down on the top of his Greek fisherman's cap, the water pouring off in a little rivulet from the peak. He sniffled. Might be getting a cold. In each hand he carried a plastic bag full of groceries. They served to steady him somewhat. The damp weather was playing the dickens with his bad leg.

He frowned when he saw the beat-up old van that had pulled in beside him. It was parked at an angle, dangerously close to the right rear of his Town Car. He was in a sour mood already. At the deli, some old hausfrau in a red kerchief had tried to cut in front of him without taking a ticket, and at the checkout line another old biddy had kept pushing her cart into the small of his back until he'd finally had to turn around and tell her what for. On top of that, the cashier at the register, a young woman with orange hair and a nose ring, had rung up his package of Ballpark franks twice and he'd had to wait fifteen minutes for the manager to come over and void the sale. Where did they get these people, anyway? If the store wasn't five minutes from his house, he'd never shop there again.

He walked around to the back to make sure that the van hadn't scratched the dark blue paint, ready to march right back into the store and find the owner, when he noticed someone sitting in the passenger seat of his car. For one crazy second he thought it was his wife and was confused, because he thought he'd left her ensconced on the sofa in the family room in front of one of her morning talkshows.

He wiped the rain-spattered window and peered closer.

His fists unclenched and he dropped his plastic bags of groceries onto the pavement, cans and bottles rolling every which way. He tried to scream, but no words came from his twisting lips. Instead he turned and ran as fast as his gimpy leg would carry him back to the supermarket, his right hand clutching his wildly thumping heart.

27

Lincoln knew the call was trouble before he even picked up the phone

They were still in Julie Golden's office, awaiting word of her whereabouts, hoping beyond reason that she would suddenly show up wondering what all the commotion was. Instead, Lincoln listened as Henry Frank read the police report of a body found in a small New Jersey town called Wanamassa.

Listening to the gruesome details, Lincoln had no doubt the body belonged to Julie Golden. He instructed Frank to relay the message that no one was to so much as breathe on the crime scene until he got there. He knew how small-town police departments liked to get themselves all fired up over a murder. All of a sudden, cops who had nothing more exciting to do than break up domestic disputes or issue summonses for speeding became junior versions of Sherlock Holmes. The crime scene probably already looked like the Calgary stampede. He hated to think how much of the delicate evidence had already been disturbed or lost. He consulted the map of the tristate area he was carrying in his jacket pocket, spreading it out on the receptionist's desk, and located the tiny speck that was Wana-massa. It was about fifty miles south of Newark. He estimated that they could be there in just under an hour.

"I'll do what I can," Frank said.

"You do what I say," Lincoln corrected him.

He hung up the phone.

McCall was standing across the room, drinking a small cup of water from the water-cooler. His blue-gray eyes showed no emotion whatsoever.

"Where is she?"

"In the parking lot of a supermarket in some jerkwater Jersey town called Wanamassa."

They had completely forgotten about the receptionist, who was standing there shell-shocked, tears running down her face.

"Ms. Golden," she stammered. "Is she—"

"Positive identification hasn't been made yet," Lincoln said. "It's a matter we have to look into."

"But you think it's her."

"There's reason to believe it might be," Lincoln conceded.

"How will I know?"

"We'll check in to let you know one way or another. In the meantime, we're leaving a team of our agents here to handle the phones in case our suspect or Ms. Golden calls in."

"Should I call Peema? She's called in three times already."

"I'd hold off on that right now. As I said, there's no reason to jump to conclusions. If she calls again, let one of our agents handle the call. He'll know what to say. Right now, the important thing is to stay calm. For all we know, Ms. Golden is still safe and sound."

Lincoln hated lying; it was one of the worst parts of the job. But a lot of times it was necessary. In this case, he didn't need the receptionist, or Julie Golden's lover, falling apart on him emotionally. The news that they were checking on a deceased person would subconsciously help prepare them for the inevitable truth they would have to face later. He reflected for a moment how much his work with the Agency had made something of a psychologist out of him. It was a bond he shared with Snow. After years of giving bad news to parents, spouses, friends, and lovers, Lincoln had learned that truth often was best administered in small doses.

Too much at one time could kill you.

He thought again of Snow. And he wondered how many of Snow's victims had learned that lesson the hard way.

12:05 P.M.

Kate met Jeff at a dark, cozy restaurant close to the hospital.

It was one of those theme restaurants filled with memorabilia from the days when trains were the primary mode of long-distance travel in the United States. The restaurant was something of a throwback: an eatery that prided itself on large portions, reasonable prices, and quick, fast service. The latter was essential; the clientele might be called to surgery at any moment. Antique railroad signs, posters, and advertisements covered the walls, and one of the bars had been converted from an old railroad car attached to the restaurant. Across the street from both the hospital and restaurant was a stop on the New Jersey transit line, mainly servicing commuters in and out of New York City. At this hour the restaurant was filled with doctors and nurses on break, as well as people taking time out for lunch after spending the morning visiting sick relations.

They had taken their usual circular booth in the back and picked up their menus, even though they both knew them almost by heart. They ate here often, Jeff not getting much of a break and needing to be close to the hospital just in case they needed his surgical expertise.

He was still wearing pale green scrubs but had thankfully changed into a fresh pair. There were times when she met him at the hospital for a quick lunch only to find him unaware that he looked like a butcher who'd just carved up twenty pounds of sirloin.

They had each ordered the cheeseburger platter, prompting Kate to think how much they'd become like those old married couples she used to like to joke about who invariably ordered the same items. She wondered if they would soon start dressing alike on the weekends, wearing color-coordinated outfits, blue polo shirts, jeans, and Reeboks. Kate realized that Diane must have really gotten her thinking, because she found herself wondering if there wasn't also a paper in the strange symbiosis that couples developed over time.

They were a lot like a married couple already, her and Jeff, except their sex hadn't gone south, at least, not for him. He undoubtedly still found her attractive. Playing a little hard to get always had its advantages, Kate thought. She knew enough behaviorism to know it worked pretty well in the animal world. She wondered how he'd be if they got married.

Married?

What was she thinking?

If they got married, he was sure to notice the passion that was lacking in her, the block she couldn't get around or talk about.

Jeff sipped at his coffee, which the waitress had brought right after they'd ordered. "Well," he said. "Any news?"

Kate hated to say it; it forced her to accept the reality of the situation.

"Julie Golden is missing."

"Who—"

"I'm sorry. She's the attorney who handled Snow's case. Lincoln called me this morning with the news."

She tried to sound casual about the development, but her nervous fingering of a pair of sugar packets gave her away.

"What do you mean, she's missing?" Jeff prompted.

"Just that. She didn't show up for work this morning, and no one knows where she is."

"Do they think Snow has her?"

"It's a possibility, but Lincoln downplayed it."

The waitress interrupted them, bringing two heavy white plates with large burgers surrounded by mounds of hot french fries.

"Will there be anything else?" The waitress smiled.

"Just a refill on this coffee, when you get a chance," Jeff said.

"Sure. For you, miss?"

Kate stared at her cup, the coffee still filled to the brim.

"Nothing, thanks."

Jeff took a bite of his burger, chewed thoughtfully for a few moments, and swallowed.

"Are you having your pickle?" he asked.

"No. Take it."

"Thanks."

It was a little bit part they must have played a hundred times. He loved pickles; she hated them. So he always asked before hijacking the pickle off her plate. It was a routine, as comfortable and predictable as if they had memorized a script.

Just like they were married.

"So they're not sure of any foul play?"

"No, but it doesn't sound good. Julie Golden is apparently never late for a court date and she's already missed this morning's. As for motivation, she betrayed Snow in court. He may be seeking revenge."

The waitress returned and refilled his cup. He thanked her and jabbed his burger in the air for emphasis. "I still think he's got too much on his mind right now to be looking for revenge. He's got every police force on the East Coast looking for him, not to mention the FBI. It's only been, what, twelve hours? They'll get him before the day is over. Mark my words."

"I hope you're right."

"Hey, you're really worried about this missing lawyer, aren't you?" he said.

"Yeah, I guess I am."

"You think he might try coming after you?"

"The thought has crossed my mind. I don't mind admitting it's got me spooked."

"You do mind admitting it. That's part of the problem. You have so much trouble asking for help. That's why I was so surprised—and so honored—that you turned to me last night."

"Oh, come off it, Jeff."

"No, I'm serious. Sometimes a man needs to feel like he's needed. I know it sounds corny and chauvinistic, but it's true. Thanks for letting me pass your usual defenses. As for Snow coming after you, I'm no expert in the criminal mind, but I don't think you have anything to worry about."

"I hope you're right."

"You can quote me on it."

"Thanks."

She saw a troubled expression flicker over his face.

"What's the matter?"

"What do you mean?" he said guiltily.

"I mean, I can tell something's bothering you."

He shook his head, a slow smile spreading across his face. "You know me too damn well, Dr. Kate Bennett. If I wanted to have a private life, I should have known not to get mixed up with a psychiatrist. Something *has* been bugging me."

"Are you going to tell me what it is, Dr. Jeff Hudson? Or am I going to have to pry it out of you? I'd better warn you, we psychiatrists have ways of making our victims talk."

"It's the sex," he said, so softly Kate had to lean over to her.

"The sex?" Kate was feeling a dead sensation in the pit of her stomach. "What's the matter with the sex?"

"Last night and this morning."

"What about it?"

"You couldn't have been in the mood. I should have been more sensitive. Here you finally turn to me for support, and what do I do but turn it into an opportunity for a Roman orgy. I've been beating myself up about it all morning."

Kate breathed an inward sigh of relief.

"It's okay," she said. "Really."

Jeff looked at her incredulously.

"Really. I didn't mind."

"Not exactly a ringing endorsement."

"You know what I mean."

He smiled. "Yeah. I guess I do."

Of course, he didn't. He couldn't know that she used sex

like a vampire uses blood, to bind him to her, to steal his energy, but unlike your traditional vampire, she derived very little pleasure from the process. To her it was merely a means to an end. She didn't like facing the bald truth of the facts, but every once in a while they forced themselves upon her. The simple fact of the matter was, she used her sexuality as a means to power. She had gotten that far *in her own therapy,* but her shrink could penetrate no further. The walls surrounding her secret were too thick. Kate wouldn't let anyone inside.

"Enough about me and my problems," she said, feeling uncomfortably warm all of a sudden. "How was your morning in the ER?"

"Oh, about as bad as I'd expected. I have to admit I was somewhat surprised. No one cut off a hand." He knocked his fist on the wood of the table. "Not yet, anyway. We did have a chainsaw accident, though. A guy cut through a branch that had fallen across his walkway and kept right on cutting through the muscles of his right thigh. He didn't feel a thing until the chainsaw started spitting out bone dust. Let's see, we had an electric shock victim who tangled with a downed power line and needed cardiopulmonary resuscitation, a young woman who cracked three ribs and the crown of her skull in a traffic accident, and a surfer pulled from the ocean up in Allenhurst. Other than that, it's been a breeze."

As if on cue, Jeff's beeper began going off.

"Shit," he said, putting down his half-eaten burger to shut the thing off. "I've got to take this."

He went to the pay phones near the exit and returned about a minute later, his face bearing a mixture of annoyance and concern.

"I'm sorry," he said. "I've got to take this one. A guy working with Jersey Central Power and Light just fell off a telephone pole. They're bringing him in now. They think he might have broken his back. They need me there when he gets in." He pulled a twenty from the pocket in his scrubs and threw it on the table. "Someday I'm going to get out of the ER business."

"It's okay, Doctor. You get to work. Save that poor guy's life."

Jeff smiled, leaned forward, and kissed Kate on the cheek.

"I'll call you first chance I get."

"Okay."

She knew the chances of his calling her were as good as his chances of his leaving the ER. For all his complaining, he loved the excitement, the pure rush, the life-and-death crises. He could have made four times as much as a specialist and lived a relatively normal doctor's life. Office hours four times a week and a day off for golf. But the fact was that such a life would never appeal to a man like Jeff Hudson. He was an adrenaline junkie. Nothing would change him.

Not even marriage.

Perhaps that was why their relationship worked as well as it did.

It was impossible.

Enough self-analyzing, Kate thought. Playing doctor with yourself could be dangerous.

"Will that be all then?" the waitress said, arriving from out of nowhere.

"Yes," Kate said.

"Would you like me to have that wrapped?"

"No. It's fine. Thank you."

The waitress totaled the bill on her pad, ripped it off, and took it along with the twenty to the cash register.

12:25 P.M.

From behind his newspaper, the man with the white hair imperceptibly shifted position.

He reached for his dry martini, took a sip, and then put it down on the bar. Through one gray eye he watched Kate sitting at the table, collecting her things, getting ready to leave.

He had been watching her and her boyfriend all through lunch.

He had been especially pleased to note that she hadn't

touched a bite of her food. But it wasn't her lack of appetite that gave him the most pleasure.

It was the way she was sitting.

Her body language gave her away.

28

Kate heard a light, tentative tap and looked up to see Bonnie Kaplan standing in the open doorway.

"Come in, Bonnie."

"I hope I didn't disturb you, Dr. Bennett. We had a one-thirty appointment. If you're busy, I can come back."

"Of course not. I was just looking over some papers." She drew a thick red line through some absurd interpretation proposed by the boy with the goatee and wrote in the margin, "pseudo-Freudian crap." She motioned with the uncapped felt pen. "Please have a seat."

There were three chairs in the office. Bonnie chose the middle one. a conciliatory personality type, didn't feel comfortable with extremes, probably the peacemaker in her family—if you believed in that kind of analysis.

Kate looked up from the paper she was marking.

Bonnie was not just pretty, she was gorgeous: long blond hair parted perfectly down the middle, high cheekbones, large blue eyes with inviting black pupils. Perhaps the only thing that kept her from being a perfect beauty was her mouth. Her lips were a little too thin and a little too straight, but nothing a trip to the plastic surgeon couldn't correct. She didn't wear any makeup, which highlighted her girl-next-door freshness.

Kate didn't envy the girl her beauty. She knew from experience how difficult it could be for a woman to be taken seriously in the medical profession as it was, but add beauty to the equation and it only made it that much more difficult. Not that Kate was any covergirl, but she had fought her share of unwelcome advances and irrelevant comments on her way to becoming a psychiatrist. She knew for a fact that Bonnie had experienced some trouble with Dr. Policastro, who'd directed some sexual innuendos her way both in class and out. In fact, Kate had counseled Bonnie on more than one occasion regarding him, advising her to just go with the flow, offering suggestions on what to do and what to say to put him off, rather than lodging a formal complaint of sexual harassment. Kate had grown to womanhood before the days of speech codes and sexual harassment guidelines and so had developed her own sophisticated form of self-defense. As a result, she thought it far more important for women to develop their own modes of self-defense than to rely on legislation which reduced women to dependents on the patriarchal state for protection. The school-run programs all reminded Kate of a more complex form of running to daddy every time someone calls you a bad name.

"What can I do for you?" Kate asked.

Bonnie fidgeted uncomfortably in her chair, clearly not knowing where to start, or if she should start at all.

"I don't really know how to say this," the girl said, confirming Kate's suspicions.

"Why don't you just come out and say it?"

Bonnie set her thin lips in an expression of determination.

"Okay," she said. "It's psychotherapy. I'm not sure if it's what I really want to do."

Kate leaned back in her leather chair, which gave a satisfying little squeak. She capped the pen and held it across her own lips, regarding Bonnie over her reading glasses.

Bonnie continued.

"I mean, you're a wonderful teacher, Dr. Bennett. You've been a real inspiration to me. I probably would have given up long ago if it weren't for you. But I'm just not sure if this is the right field for me."

"Why do you say that?" Kate asked.

"I feel like I've lost confidence in it. I think of the founders of psychoanalysis, and sometimes it seems they just imagined all of it. I mean, does anyone undergoing psychotherapy ever really get better?"

Kate couldn't suppress a laugh.

"I knew this would sound stupid," Bonnie said.

"No," Kate said, shaking her head. "Just the opposite. There's not a therapist worth his salt who hasn't ask himself the same question. Lord knows, when I was in private practice, I asked it of myself with every patient I counseled."

"What was your answer?"

"There are no simple answers in psychotherapy, Bonnie. That's the most valuable—and toughest—insight any therapist has to realize. And each therapist has to realize it in his own way. No one can answer that question for you."

"The thing is, I go to my psychoneurology class and the teacher says the brain is nothing but an electrochemical machine. He reduces every psychological problem to a surplus or deficiency of brain chemicals. If it's all just a matter of pills, what's the point of psychoanalysis? What's the point of trying to analyze people's fears or understand their dreams?"

"What you're asking is the classic question: what came first, the chicken or the egg?" Kate said, thinking inevitably of Snow, who was obsessed with the same question. "Do our emotions control the chemicals released in our brains, or do the chemicals control the emotions? Perhaps the problem can be approached from both sides."

"I never thought of it like that."

"Let me ask you a question, Bonnie. Why did you decide to go into psychotherapy?"

"Because I've always wanted to understand the human mind. I find it fascinating."

"There are other fields that allow you to study the mind. Art, for instance."

"Art is just a hobby."

"You're very talented, I understand."

Bonnie shrugged. "I can't make a career of it."

"Who says?"

"I—don't know. I just—"

"Who says you can't make a career of art?"

Bonnie looked away. "My father, I guess. You see, he's an attorney, and he's always put a high value on professionalism. My brother's in pre-med and my older sister is in her final year of law school. I tried to find a profession that would allow me to use as much of my artistic intuition as possible. When I discovered Jung, I thought I'd found it."

"Why do you think you have to compromise?"

Bonnie stared down into her lap, where her hands were folded primly.

"To please my dad."

"Why do you feel you have to please your dad?"

"I don't know, Dr. Bennett. But it's always been like that. Doing things to gain his attention. Being the best in school, making first-team tennis. He wants us to excel."

Kate leaned forward in her chair which squeaked again, the noise bracketing their conversation.

"I'm afraid this is as far as I can take this, Bonnie. Our conversation is taking on the tone of a psychiatric session, and I'm your professor, not your psychiatrist. It wouldn't be ethical for me to go further. But I think we've identified the source of your problem. You might want to find a therapist you can discuss this with, but ultimately the answer can come only from within yourself."

"You're right," Bonnie said. "And thank you, Dr. Bennett. I think you answered my question. People can get better through psychotherapy. The only catch is that they have to cure themselves."

Kate smiled. "That's a lesson many of the best psychotherapists never learn."

She watched as Bonnie gathered up her knapsack and umbrella and followed her out the door. Her eyes drifted to the left where a framed Rohrshach blot hung. She stared at it for a full minute, not a single image rising to her overwrought mind.

She thought of Bonnie and her dilemma and found herself wondering what she herself believed in anymore.

1:45 P.M.

The dead woman was still jumping around on the car seat.

It wasn't as bad as it had been about an hour ago, when Lincoln had first arrived at the scene, but the effect was disturbing enough. Her arms and legs were rising and falling, the muscles in her face twitching, her eyelids fluttering in a grim but unconvincing parody of life. Upon closer inspection, the cause of her dance-of-death was evident: a series of well-placed silver pins buried halfway into the flesh behind her ears and at her shoulders, her elbows, her stomach, and the rest of the way down her otherwise unmarred body.

Lincoln ran a practiced eye over the woman's body, unable to help admiring it, lifelike as it still seemed. Forty-two years old and she was still as fit and trim as a twenty-five-year-old. No doubt long hours at the gym and no little money spent at the plastic surgeon had kept the telltale signs of age at bay. Ordinarily there was nothing remotely sensual about a dead body, in spite of what bad crime novelists often wrote. If only once such authors could witness firsthand the agony of death stamped on the face of the victim, the stiffened limbs, the blood and the stench of incipient decay, they would put that particular fiction to rest once and for all. But here there was no obvious cause of death and no way to estimate the time of death, for there were no outward signs of rigor mortis. The constant twitching of the nerves in her limbs had prevented the usual telltale signs, such as blood pooling in purple welts under the parts of the body resting in this case on the car seat. She would have to be taken to the coroner's office and examined thoroughly at the lab. Even then Lincoln suspected that Snow's treatment of her corpse would frustrate all attempts to pin down the exact time of death.

From between her clenched teeth Lincoln had extracted with no little difficulty a miniature tape cassette. He had borrowed tweezers from one of the coroner's assistants and pulled the cassette free, wiping off the bloody saliva from its plastic case, not worried about fingerprints. It was more important that he hear what was on that tape than hope Snow had left any fingerprints on it, which he doubted. He had asked one of the local cops if there was a Radio Shack in the area, and getting a positive response, Lincoln gave him his credit card and ordered him to buy him a microcassette recorder. The cop seemed glad to comply, glad to be doing something useful—anything to get away from the unnatural corpse in the car.

The locals had done a fair enough job isolating the crime scene, moving the cars in a twenty-square-foot quadrant away from the corpse, stretching yellow police tape around the area, and posting an officer or two at each cardinal point directing away the eyes of curious passersby. Lincoln was informed by the chief of police that the old man who'd found the body was rushed by ambulance to Monmouth Medical Center for observation but that he was in stable condition and was expected to come out just fine. He'd already been questioned and hadn't seen anything except for the woman in the car, which damn near gave him a heart attack. Lincoln trusted the local cops competence on this score. He didn't expect it would be necessary to question the old man further.

Still, the scene was the usual circus that Lincoln had expected it to be. The scent of more than one weak stomach was wafting in the air. The whole thing was overkill. A half-dozen police cars, three ambulances, and even a firetruck were on the scene, lights flashing, uniformed personnel milling about aimlessly. Not to mention the local cable television vans Lincoln had spotted. The police chief, a stout, bald, bullet-headed man was doing a good job keeping reporters at bay, but Lincoln had spotted a couple of cops off to the side talking to the reporters. No one, it seemed, could resist their fifteen minutes of fame.

McCall was standing beside him now, shaking his head.

"I've never seen anything like it. What the hell did he do to the corpse?"

"Acupuncture. You saw the needles."

"But how?"

"It's one of his specialties. You ever read about those experiments where they apply a charge to a dead frog's muscle and it contracts? I suppose it's the same principle."

"But why would he go through the trouble of doing something like this?"

Lincoln shrugged. "Perhaps he's mocking the difference between life and death. To him, we're all nothing but puppets jerking around on invisible strings."

"Fuck him."

"Yeah. Fuck him."

Lincoln gazed one last time at the dead woman, but this time it was a look emptied of all misplaced lasciviousness and clinical detachment. Instead, it was a look of genuine pity. He'd known and worked with this woman. She had helped him to put Alexander Snow in prison, and now she was dead and Lincoln had to admit to himself that in a large way he was partly responsible for her death. He had let McCall identify her to the local police chief, though it was the first time the young agent had ever seen her. Lincoln himself had tried to depersonalize the corpse sitting in the front seat of the car, tried to protect himself from the full impact of the pain, but now he forced himself to swallow it, along with another pill for his aching head, both as bitter as a poison that was slowly but inevitably killing him.

"Goodbye, Julie Golden," he whispered. "I'm sorry it went down this way. You did the right thing. I'll get the bastard. I promise."

He finally granted permission for the coroner's people to move the body, the black bag already spread out on the ground, unzipped down the front like an enormous pod.

He turned away from the car and almost ran into the cop he'd sent to Radio Shack. He handed Lincoln his credit card and a Panasonic microcassette recorder. Lincoln tore away the packaging on the recorder and motioned to McCall.

"Let's listen to this in the car. I don't want anyone overhearing."

They sat together in the car, Wilson, the driver, standing outside, leaning against the door with instructions to keep any would-be interruptions at bay. With slightly trembling fingers, Lincoln slipped the tape inside the cassette recorder and pressed the play button.

What they heard first was a woman panting, and underneath it, the sound of scratching, as of a pencil on a sheet of paper. And then, a voice as calm and soothing as those one might hear on self-help tapes of affirmation, beckoning one to greater self-esteem or peace of mind.

"Tell me the truth, Julie."

"I—I'm trying, Dr. Snow."

"You don't have to try to tell the truth. The truth just *is*. Just let it happen."

"I want to understand . . ."

"No, no, no," the doctor said softly.

"I don't understand . . ."

"There's nothing to understand."

"Then what am I doing wrong?"

"You're lying.

There was a bloodcurdling cry of pain, and then sobbing. Lincoln felt McCall stiffen beside him.

"I'm—not—lying," Julie sobbed.

"You're lying right now. You're lying about not lying."

"But—"

"Julie," Snow said, his voice taking on the tone of a father with his daughter. "You're only making it worse on yourself."

"I want to tell the truth. I do. I really do."

"You're lying to me again, Julie."

"No, Dr. Snow. No!"

There was a manic nature to this exclamation that made it

clear that the same pain that had wrenched the earlier scream from Julie Golden's throat was being proffered again.

"Then tell me."

"Yes." Julie's voice was dull, defeated.

"What is the truth?"

"What is—"

"It's a very simple question, Julie. What is the truth?"

"I don't—I don't know."

"Of course, you do," Snow said evenly.

What followed was a scream that raised the hairs on the back of Lincoln's neck, a scream of such pain and outrage that McCall felt sick to his stomach, a scream that didn't end, that wouldn't end, until Lincoln pressed the stop button.

McCall was the first to speak.

"What the fuck kind of monster is he?"

"Monster is the right word. Don't forget it. It might save your life," Lincoln said. "You know the funny thing about all this? I could have stopped it. I had a chance to plug him the first time around. I had the chance, and instead, I did the right thing. Let me tell you. If I get a second chance I'm not going to let it pass."

Lincoln stared down at the now silent tape recorder in his lap. He thought of Kate Bennett. He knew he was going to have to make the most difficult call of his life.

29

"Excuse me. Can you tell me where I might find Dr. Bennett's office?"

The question came from Bonnie's left, and she turned to follow the voice, spotting a handsome middle-aged man in a three-piece gray suit standing under an umbrella, leaning on a bamboo cane. His gray hair was combed straight back off his high forehead and just brushed the back of his white shirt collar. He was dressed too well to be a professor, his suit impeccably cut, reminding her of one of her father's specially tailored suits. He was standing close enough for her to notice that the color of his hair nicely complimented his sharp stainless-steel eyes.

"Yes," Bonnie said. "It's in the applied sciences building. The one behind this one." She pointed to a glass-and-steel structure two hundred yards from where they were standing.

"You don't know by any chance if she's in?"

"Yes," Bonnie said, somehow eager to be of help to this man 'I just came from her office."

' Thank you,'' the man said, and seemed about to turn when he stopped. "I was wondering. I have two boxes of books and seminar papers in the trunk of my car that I'm returning to Dr. Bennett. Would you mind helping me take them to her?''

Snow had moved imperceptibly closer to the girl, gazing down toward the tip of his nose, his breath relaxed on the exhalation, in what was known in Tantric lore as the ''petrifying gaze.'' Card sharps, mesmerists, mind readers, and even used car dealers were familiar with it in one form or another. He used it now to bring the girl toward him, reeling her in slowly, like a fish who'd swallowed his bait.

For her part, Bonnie didn't know why she had agreed to help the stranger. She had just enough time to grab a cup of coffee in the school cafeteria before heading to her fourth-period Shakespeare class, and she was already running late. She hadn't carried an umbrella, and though the drizzle was minimal, it had a cumulative effect and her jacket was getting damp. Besides all that, she knew enough not to go off with strange men. But there was something about this man. If she'd stopped to analyze her reaction to him she might have thought it had something to do with the fact that he knew Dr. Bennett, or that he seemed too cultivated to be dangerous or demented. Maybe it was that he seemed somehow vulnerable, leaning on the cane, or even that it was broad daylight and bad things didn't happen in broad daylight. But it had nothing to do with any of those things. It was the strange way he was looking at her that drew her to him, a glance so subtle and powerful she was completely unaware of it.

They headed toward the parking lot, Bonnie slowing up a little to allow for the man's slight limp as he shifted his grip on the umbrella to offer them both partial coverage from the rain, which was suddenly falling more heavily. She was close enough now to smell his aftershave, something unpretentious, clean, and crisp, reminding her again of her father. She felt an embarrassed attraction for this middle-aged man. Still, she couldn't help but smile to herself. Dr. Policastro would be delighted. It would seem that Freud's much maligned theory of the Electra complex wasn't completely dead, after all.

"Allow me to introduce myself," the man beside her said. "My name is Dr. Alexander Snow."

2:35 P.M.

Kate could tell the news was bad from the sound of the ring.

She picked up the phone, held it at her ear, and barely croaked out the words.

"Dr. Bennett."

"Kate. It's Lincoln."

The tone of his voice was funereal. It told her everything she needed to know. The rest of the conversation would be a mere formality. Yet somehow she knew she had to go through with it.

"Yes."

She said it flatly, no question, no hope left in her voice.

"It's bad news. We found Julie Golden."

Kate knew he didn't mean alive.

"Where?"

"In the parking lot of a supermarket in Wanamassa."

There was a silence between them but each knew what the other was thinking. *Why so close?*

"She's dead, Kate."

There was no need to say it, but perhaps as an ex-cop he was following some kind of protocol.

"I see," Kate said. It was the best she could come up with, under the circumstances. She hoped it sounded neutral, but she knew it didn't. Her tone gave her away.

"There's no need to get overly concerned at this point, Kate. The location may be just a coincidence. Fact is, we suspect he may just be traveling down the coast, or he may have a place somwhere within a fifty-mile radius of the town. Somewhere secluded. Evidence at the scene left no doubt that he is in possession of his . . ." Lincoln paused for a moment, as if trying to choose his words carefully, ". . . of his medical supplies."

Kate was doing her best not to imagine what he meant by that.

"I'm trying not to worry about this, Tom, but it's getting harder by the minute."

"I know it's difficult, Kate. Losing Julie Golden was a fluke. He got lucky; he got the jump on us by sheer chance. It won't happen again. I've already made arrangements with the Neptune and Long Branch police departments to provide an escort for you over the next twenty-four hours. "You're not to leave the university until they've arrived."

"Is that really necessary?" Kate said. "On the one hand, you tell me not to worry; on the other, you tell me not to go anywhere until a squadron of cops arrive to lead me home. Isn't that a little inconsistent?"

"I'm just trying to cover all the bases. Like I said, we're not going to have any more accidents. Listen, I've got a couple of things to work out up here. I'd like to join you early this evening at your house, if that's okay."

"Why not? The more the merrier."

"Right," Lincoln said, ignoring the sarcasm. "You'll be home by six?"

"Before."

"Good. See you then."

Kate sat with her hand on the receiver for less than a minute before she dialed the hospital. It took five minutes to persuade the receptionist to put through the page and another five for Jeff to make it to the phone, though when he did, he sounded out of breath.

"Kate. What's up?"

He knew it must be important, because she never called him in the middle of a shift.

"They found Julie Golden. In Wanamassa. She's dead."

"Oh, Christ."

"The nightmare is coming back."

"I wish I could get out of here right now, but a call just came in. There was a seven-car pile-up in front of the Sheraton out on Route 35. About a half-dozen people look to be seriously injured. They're bringing them in right now. I can try to get Dr. Baldini to cover me, but—"

For once she wanted to tell him the hell with his patients, to rush home and tend to her, she needed him more, but once again her rational side won out.

"No. It's okay. You stay there and take care of business. They need you. I'm probably just being hysterical again. Lincoln himself said there was probably nothing to worry about. Besides, he's ordered a police contingent to escort me home. I'll be okay. I just needed someone to talk to."

"I get off around five. I'll come over then."

"That sounds great."

"I'll bring a pizza."

"Okay," she said, though she couldn't imagine eating. "And Jeff?"

"Yeah, baby?"

"You've been wonderful through all this."

"Listen, I hear the sirens already. It sounds pretty bad. I've got to get down to the ER *stat*. I'll see you later."

Jeff hung up before she got a chance to say goodbye.

She leaned forward at her desk and put her head in her hands, pretending to be reading the essay in front of her, just in case anyone stopped by. She didn't even have the energy to get up and close her door. She wondered what she was going to say to her colleagues when the police arrived. She couldn't even think about that now. All she could think of was what she and Lincoln had left unsaid. Only two people connected with the case against Snow knew of Kate's current whereabouts. Now one of them was dead. And the odds weren't good that Julie Golden had gone to her death with the secret intact.

If there was one thing Kate had learned about Alexander Snow in the time she'd been his therapist, it was the doctor's almost preternatural ability to uncover the truth.

3:15 P.M.

The funny thing was that somewhere deep inside, Bonnie Kaplan knew she was doing the wrong thing even as she followed the man back to his car.

She had bent over to take a box out of the back seat of the silver Lexus when she'd felt him press his fingers ever so lightly at the base of her backbone. There was pain, excruciating pain, as if a rope had been wrapped around her lower spine and two muscular dwarves were pulling it in opposite directions. She felt nauseated, her legs gave out, and then everything went black. She didn't remember any of what happened next, coming back to consciousness to the sound of rain spattering against a tin roof, her body wrapped in a blanket. She opened her eyes and found herself lying on the wooden floor of a cabin, the smell of must and mold assailing her nostrils.

She didn't seem to be bound, yet when she tried to move, she found herself paralyzed. She felt a great rush of warmth rise through her and two tears trickled down her cheek, between her lips, bitter on her tongue. Whatever was going to happen here would be terrible, would scar her for the rest of her life, if she was lucky enough to survive. Suddenly she felt nauseated again and was barely able to swallow the bitter bile that burned its way up her throat. What would her family think? Her friends? Especially her father? How could she have been so stupid?

She heard the ticking of a clock. It seemed like hours passed. The waiting was unbearable. But what would happen when the waiting was over?

And then the man came.

He was dressed casually now, in a black T-shirt and tweed sportcoat, a pair of loafers at eye level. He stooped down and slowly unrolled her from the blanket like a mummy, leaving her face-up on the floor, staring at the rafters of the high-pitched ceiling. Now it was happening. With long, perfectly manicured fingers he was slowly unbuttoning her sweater, then her blouse. He unzipped her Scotch-plaid skirt and slid it down over her legs. He undid the laces of the funky nylon hiking boots she'd worn to protect herself from puddles and carefully rolled off her socks. She had imagined a thousand times what she would do if something like this happened, but nothing could have prepared her for the reality of the situation. She knew what was coming next and tried to speak, but it seemed her vocal chords were paralyzed along with the rest of her body. What had he done to her? He removed her bra and panties and she lay there naked before him, helpless and vulnerable, without even words to protect her.

He looked down at her and smiled benignly before stooping over to lift her effortlessly from the floor. She felt dizzy, but only for a moment, until her senses reoriented themselves. She smelled again the tang of his aftershave and thought of her father. There was something about the man that reminded her of him. Was it a dream she'd once had of him?

He carried her to a chair in front of a plain wooden table and secured her lifeless limbs to its arms and legs with thick leather straps. Her jaw fell open and to her embarrassment a string of drool dropped from her lips to her bare breasts. He took out a monogrammed handkerchief from inside his jacket and delicately wiped away the spittle. He replaced the handkerchief and then reached out toward her face. She would have flinched if she could have. He stroked her cheek gently and smiled. He placed what looked like a blood pressure cuff around her upper arm and a tight nylon band around her waist. He slipped her left index and middle fingers into two foam sleeves. Her eyes followed the wires connecting her to what she could only assume was a lie detector machines in front of the empty chair at the other end of the table.

Her mind was a flurry of mixed thoughts and emotions. If this wasn't rape, what was it? Had she been mistaken for someone else? Was this man a cop? No. No cop would be authorized to do this. Was he a spy? Was this whole bizarre scenario something out of a spy novel come to life? If so, how could she convince him that she was not who he was looking for, that she knew nothing, that the whole thing had been a terrible mistake? And how would he take it, once he knew? Her eyes flicked involuntarily to the table in front of her and the dark, unmistakable stain worked into the grain of rough wood.

Death, she thought, and the thought numbed her inside as his touch numbed her outside.

One way or another, he was going to kill her.

Unless she could somehow talk her way out of it.

With a movement of his hand so quick she didn't catch it, he pressed his fingers at a point just beneath her second vertebra and she felt the feeling flow back into her chilled limbs and with it the power of speech.

Her last and only hope.

"What," she stammered, her voice still not completely under her control. "What do you want from me?"

The man folded his hands in front of his waist and looked down at her. His eyes were clear and sharp, without a hint of the madness she expected to find there. His answer surprised and confused her.

"The truth, darling," he said softly. "Nothing but the truth."

30

They took up headquarters at a Holiday Inn on Route 36 in Long Branch.

Lincoln couldn't count the number of times he'd been in a Holiday Inn on some case or other. They were strangely comforting, in a way. There was that perfect sameness to the rooms that made him feel at home no matter where he was. In fact, when he thought about it, he felt more at home in a room in a Holiday Inn than he ever did in his own home. It was an observation that at this point in his life he rather didn't think about.

He was sitting at the usual round table by the window, plugging in his laptop. He flipped on the switch, waited for the little computer to make its internal checks, then logged onto the mainframe in Albany, hoping to get back the preliminary lab reports on the victims from the night before. To his annoyance, he merely got a screen with the message that the reports weren't ready yet. He wondered what the hell was taking so long. He hated to admit it to himself, but the waiting was starting to get to him. After seeing Julie Golden's body, it was hard to muster the usual patience.

But no matter how impatient he was getting, it was worse for McCall. He was pacing from one end of the room to the other. If he smoked, Lincoln was sure McCall would be doing so right now. Lincoln was thankful the younger agent didn't; he didn't think his stomach or his head could stand the stench of burnt tobacco right now. As it was, McCall did have a stress-reducing oral fixation of sorts. He pulled out a stick of chewing gum and worked it furiously between his broad jaws. Lincoln could smell the refreshing tang of spearmint in the air.

"We've got to catch this bastard," McCall said.

"That goes without saying."

"No. I mean, we really have to catch him. And fast."

Lincoln nodded. He'd been in enough of these situations to know that the younger agent had to talk. Hell, once, a thousand years ago, he'd been a rookie agent himself.

"What he did to that woman. Did you know?"

Lincoln shook his head. "Until the last twenty-four hours we've never had a body before. No forensic evidence. Nothing but his papers and the inadmissable testimony of his psychiatrist, Kate Bennett."

"What's his deal, anyway?"

"He's obsessed. Obsessed with the truth."

"The truth? What is the truth?"

"The truth of human nature."

"And what is that?"

"That is what he's trying to find out."

"I don't understand."

"Neither do I. But Snow is not like other men. There's something special about him. He's gone beyond what other men are. I've told only one other person about this because it sounds so fucking crazy. But he diagnosed the tumor growing inside my head six months before a CAT scan picked it up."

"A man is a man," McCall said stonily. "I worked on the Kalinsky case. You might remember it. The bastard thought he was some kind of latter-day John the Baptist spreading the news of a new messiah named Manson II. He left gutted bodies along roadsides all across the Southwest until we caught him. He claimed to have supernatural powers, but in the end he was just a dimwitted pervert with a sub-moron IQ.''

''Snow is no moron. I'd bet dollars to donuts he tests out as a genius. And he's no simple thrill killer,'' Lincoln said.

''I don't believe in the supernatural,'' McCall said flatly.

''Neither do I. But I believe a man can go beyond what we generally consider natural.''

''What you're talking about sounds like tabloid crap. You sound like Captain Ahab going on about the white whale, making him some grand embodiment of all human evil, instead of just a pitiful warped psycho who needs to be brought down. You build up a mystique about him in your mind, and that makes him even harder to catch. We've got to hunt him down for what he is. You saw the body of that woman. He's an animal.''

''No,'' Lincoln said, this time more forcefully. ''He's not an animal. But if I sound like Ahab, so be it. I've stared into his eyes. Alexander Snow *is* the embodiment of human evil.''

''Well, he sure as hell ain't no Superman. I told you, I don't believe in the supernatural.''

''And I told you, neither do I. But if you're not careful, what you don't believe can get you killed.''

4:15 P.M.

''Once a very wise man went to a certain master to learn the secret of Zen. When the wise man was seated, the master brought out a pot of tea. He proceeded to pour the tea into his guest's cup. The wise man watched as the master filled the cup and continued to pour. The tea overflowed the edge of the cup and still the master continued to pour. Finally, unable to tolerate the situation any longer, the wise man pushed himself from the table and shouted, 'Stop! Can't you see there's no more room in the cup?' The master nodded. 'Your mind is like that cup,' he said. 'How do you expect me to teach you Zen when your mind is already full?' ''

''I—don't—understand,'' Bonnie rasped. Her naked body was shiny with sweat and bristling with slender steel pins. Her head had fallen forward, her eyes were fixed on the table in front of her, as if trying to find the answer in the meaningless swirls of wood. ''What—do—you—want—from—me?''

''I told you already,'' Snow said, his tone unerringly patient, even though he'd answered the same question at least ten times. ''I want you to tell me the truth.''

Bonnie was openly sobbing now, at the end of her rope. She had lost all sense of time, but in that indeterminate period she had experienced the pinnacle of ecstasy and the pit of agony. It had been a physical and emotional roller coaster that had left her as limp as a rag doll. And in between, there was always that same maddening, infuriating question.

''What is the truth?''

''About what?'' Bonnie whined, a small, wounded, animal sound that, coming from her, shocked her.

''About yourself.''

''I don't know what you mean. I've already told you everything about myself.''

''Everything but the truth.''

In spite of her earlier appraisal, she now knew for certain that her captor was insane. She tried to remember everything she'd ever learned about psychology, especially in Dr. Bennett's Abnormal Psychology class, to break the spell of the man's fixation. If only she could penetrate his obsession and reach the tortured soul within. Confronting madness in the flesh for the first time, she realized how little she really knew about the workings of the mind, yet what knowledge she had managed to gain represented her only hope for survival. It took all her strength, but she lifted her head and stared into those empty gray eyes. ''Maybe you can explain to me what the truth is.''

''Only you know your own truth,'' Snow replied.

''Do you know yours? If you told me yours, it might help me understand.''

"No one can help you to your own truth; you must bring it out of yourself."

Bonnie thought of Dr. Bennett's class that morning. Was it only that morning? It seemed like a lifetime ago. She remembered what Dr. Bennett had said about the schizoid personality and the schizophrenic. Bonnie wasn't certain, but this man seemed to fit the criteria of a full-fledged schizophrenic. She had to be careful that he didn't feel threatened, that she didn't challenge his sense of inner security. She'd made a dangerous mistake asking him to tell her his truth; the last thing he'd want to do would be to reveal himself. She had to be more careful. She wouldn't make the same mistake again. If she did, it could cost her life.

"I know how you feel," Bonnie began slowly and evenly. "I feel that way myself. As if the whole world can see right through me. I feel that way now, as if you can see right through me. I feel as if you're turning me to crystal, paralyzing me, and the truth is," she stopped for effect, knowing everything depended on how much he believed her performance, "the truth is, I'm empty inside."

There was a short silence in which the only sounds were the ticking of the clock and the scratch of the pencil over the graph paper feeding through the lie detector. Her captor didn't bother looking down at the readout. He merely stared at her for a moment or two, and then laughed. It was a genuine laugh, not a laugh of madness, and for a moment Bonnie felt a sense of relief, but it was short-lived.

"R. D. Laing. *The Divided Self.* I met Ronnie in England shortly before he died. An interesting man. An interesting mind. But basically deluded. He had quite a drinking problem, you know. I suspect his works were a reflection of his own inner conflicts. It's the same with all the great psychologists. Freud, Jung, Rank, Adler, you name 'em. They can't get out of their own way. Their theories merely present their own psychopathologies. You have digested their writings like the good student you are and have come to the conclusion that I'm schizophrenic. But the fact is, you are just like that wise man in the parable of the Zen master's tea. Your mind is too full of theories. How do you expect to see the truth when your mind is so full of lies?''

Bonnie felt her heart sink, and with it, the last of her hope and strength.

Her head sagged back down with her breath. She was too exhausted to meet his eyes any longer.

She felt him cup her chin and gently lift her face. On the table in front of her was a crude-looking icepick with a worn wooden handle. She felt her blood run cold.

''With all the knowledge in psychology you've acquired, did they ever tell you how, in the dark ages of psychiatry, which were not so long ago as they'd have you believe, they used to perform lobotomies?''

''I—don't—''

Snow waved her off. ''No matter. No one likes to talk about it now. But I'll explain the procedure. It's alarmingly simple. They would take an icepick like the one I have here,'' he said, picking it up from the table, ''stick it through each eye of the patient, and jiggle it around, destroying the brain tissue in the front of the skull. You'd think they'd have come up with something more sophisticated, of course, and eventually they did. But for a long time and for many patients that was the prescribed treatment. Crude, but effective. Now I'm going to ask you one last time. What is the truth?''

And suddenly Bonnie knew what the answer was, the answer he wanted, but it gave her no comfort; for the answer was no escape from what lay in store for her.

The answer he was looking for was death.

31

4:25 P.M.

Kate unlocked her front door and stepped inside after the two policemen had dutifully checked all the windows and doors for any signs of forced entry and given her the all-clear.

She had been undeniably shaken after the call from Lincoln confirming Julie Golden's death, but police protection now seemed more than a little melodramatic. She had been met at the university by two uniformed members of the Long Branch Police Department. They'd caused something of a stir among her colleagues who'd at first wondered if something was wrong and had then relapsed into those stale, awkward jokes about the law finally catching up with her. Behind both reactions was an insatiable curiosity that she couldn't ignore or wholly condemn, just because she was its focus. She decided to tell the truth—or half of it, anyway—and told them that a former patient of hers had escaped from a mental asylum and that the police were there as a precaution. She assumed the story of Snow's escape had made the news by now, but that none of them had heard the story yet. Maybe they would figure it out later, but for now the excuse sufficed. Policastro, for one, seemed impressed, and told her to take the next day off, if necessary, he'd cover her classes. Kate told him she didn't think it would be necessary. Diane offered to stay the night with her. Kate thanked her but told her that wouldn't be necessary, either, she'd be perfectly okay, and besides, she'd have the cops to protect her. Diane winked, made a lewd comment, and swished away.

Kate was happy to get out of the office, feeling the curious eyes sticking to her back as she left. The police followed her home in their squad car, forcing her to pull over twice as she inadvertently lost them behind the early afternoon traffic. They didn't drive off until they'd deposited her safely in front of her house, where she found a Neptune Township police cruiser parked and waiting for her with two officers inside. As she walked up the path to her house, she could sense the eyes of the neighborhood on her, eyes furtively glancing from behind parted curtains, looking up from their chores, slowing down as they passed by in their cars. Maybe she was just being paranoid. In any event, she had never developed more than a passing acquaintance with any of her neighbors, valuing her privacy, and therefore was virtually guaranteed that none would come by now, bothering her with questions she didn't want to answer. Not that she wasn't something of a curiosity to them already or that she wouldn't become the fresh focus of speculation among them, but at least they would leave her to herself.

The four cops climbed out of their patrol cars and talked for a few minutes on the sidewalk, looking awkward, like rival gang members on neutral turf, which it was in a way, as Ocean Grove didn't have its own police force and were served by the police from neighboring Neptune. Finally the Long Branch cops got back in their car and drove away. That's when the two Neptune patrolmen spotted her about to open the front door and stopped her.

One of the cops was medium height, heavy-set, with a five-o'clock shadow. He introduced himself as Officer Bob D'Angelo. He had an easy smile and a gentle, friendly way about him. Kate didn't think he seemed at all like a cop. His

partner was a tall, ramrod-thin, taciturn black man with eyes
that shifted nervously in their sockets, as if he expected a hidden
gunman at any moment to start firing. He was introduced by
D'Angelo as Officer Otis Miller. If opposites made a good
team in police work, these two were well matched.

Miller walked back to the squad car, where he would stay
posted while D'Angelo followed Kate into the house.

Penelope scrabbled over the hardwood floors to greet her,
rolling up her big eyes suspiciously to look at the policeman
still standing in the doorway.

"It's okay, Penelope," Kate said, feeing a little bit stupid,
as she always did when talking to the dog in front of anyone
besides Jeff.

"Does she bite?" D'Angelo asked.

"No," Kate said. "But she's a little shy with strangers."

The warning didn't stop the policeman from settling on his
haunches, letting Penelope sniff his hand, and then scratching
her behind the ears.

"We've got to learn to be buddies," the policeman said to
the dog. "After all, we both want to keep Dr. Bennett safe and
sound."

The dog looked directly at him, her tail low, and for a split
second Kate was concerned she might snap. But the policeman
rose to his feet with his face and fingers intact.

"Nice dog," he said. "Do you mind if I take a walk around
the house to familiarize myself with the layout, Dr. Bennett?"

"Kate," Kate said. "Please call me Kate. And no, I don't
mind." She thought of the unmade bed upstairs and minded
very much. "Just try to ignore the mess."

The policeman looked around as if appraising the house.
"They all say that."

"You mean you're called to do this often?"

"Not offer personal protection, no. But it happens even when
we go into a house during a drug raid or a weapons search.
The place could be the worst stinking hole this side of hell. It
may sound sexist, but if there's a woman on the premises, she
invariably apologizes for the mess. Don't worry, this place

looks immaculate compared to some of the places I've been. Even compared to my place." He smiled that same easy smile of his.

"Thank you," Kate said, a little sarcastically. The tone was lost on the policeman.

"And by the way."

"Yes?"

"You can call me Bob."

"Okay, Bob." This time more sincerely, realizing she was just being oversensitive.

The policeman proceeded to look through her house, Penelope watching closely at his heels, while Kate went back out to the mailbox to get her mail. She saw the other officer behind the wheel of the cruiser turn to her, and she gave him a wave. He returned her greeting with a curt nod and returned to his vigil. Kate wondered if he was pissed at pulling this duty, or if this was his ordinary behavior. She thought of asking Bob, but she could hear him already moving around upstairs. She shrugged off the question. After all, what difference did it make to her? She felt like going down to the car and telling him she didn't want him there any more than he felt like being there. Instead, she flipped through her mail. A couple of bills, two sale announcements from major department stores, and a thick envelope informing her that she might be holding the winning number entitling her to become a ten-million-dollar winner. She threw everything away but the bills, putting them in a basket she kept on a desk in the foyer.

She felt silly having the police in her house. Snow wasn't going to come back. She should have told Lincoln to forget the police protection, not that he would have listened. Within a matter of hours her whole life had been transformed. The situation was taken out of her hands and not the least of her anger was caused by the inevitable invasion of her privacy.

Damn Snow. Damn him to hell.

Kate was brought out of her misanthropic musings by the cheerful voice of the policeman descending the stairs, Penelope coming down a cautious distance behind him.

"I checked out the house and everything seems to be in order," he said.

Great, Kate thought wryly.

"Everything," the policeman went on, "except the third floor. The door seems to be locked."

"It's just the attic. I use it for storage. There's nothing up there but some old furniture and a leaking roof. A little storm damage after last night."

The policeman nodded, looking as if he were about to ask for the key to the room, but he let the subject drop.

"Okay. I'm just going to have a seat in the living room, if you don't mind, maybe put on the television. Just go about your usual business."

"Can I get you something to eat or drink?"

"No thanks," the policeman said and smiled again. "Like I said, just go about your usual business. Pretend I'm not even here."

Yeah, Kate thought. *Fat chance.*

4:45 P.M.

There it was.

Lincoln finally had what he'd been waiting for, but what he saw on the screen of his laptop didn't make him happy. According to the preliminary report, there was absolutely no trace of Snow at either the tollbooth or in the elevator in which the two guards had been killed. No hair, no blood, no skin, nothing. As far as forensic evidence was concerned, Snow should still be sitting where he belonged: in his cell in the bowels of the Hudson Valley Correctional Institute for the Criminally Insane.

"It's not possible," McCall protested, staring over Lincoln's shoulder at the screen. "He had to leave *something* behind. He's not a ghost, goddammit."

"He can control his body," Lincoln said. "He's like a yogi. Nothing happens involuntarily. He leaves no traces."

"I don't believe that."

"Well, it's only a preliminary report. Maybe they'll find something later."

"But you don't think so?"

Lincoln shook his head. "Shortly after I became sick, I made a study of Eastern thought in the hopes of trying to understand Snow's mind. What I learned stunned me. Snow has tapped into an esoteric tradition thousands of years old originating in India and spreading to China and eventually Japan. My sources were secondary and merely descriptive of the extraordinary powers believed to be possible to one trained in these secret arts. The real teaching is passed on orally from master to pupil. I'm certain that Snow received such personal instruction as well as using his powerful mind to extract the rest from certain rare and sacred texts."

"What kind of powers are you talking about?" McCall asked skeptically.

"For instance, in yoga and the martial arts as practiced by such groups as the ninja, there has always been a mystical, even supernatural component. The ninja, for instance, has long held a reputation for scaling walls or walking on water, becoming invisible, wielding the power to read minds or anticipate events in the future. The master ninja was believed able to control the consciousness of others and even hold power over death itself."

"You're talking nonsense now. Hocus-pocus."

"Of course I don't believe Snow can literally do these things. But I'm convinced that there is more to our reality than meets the eye. How do accomplished yogis stay buried underground for hours without air or walk on hot coals without injury? How do martial artists break a stack of cinderblocks with their bare hands? How do you explain that Snow feigned his own hanging, was pronounced dead by an experienced doctor, and then killed six people without leaving so much as a hair of himself behind?"

"I don't know, but I assume there must be a logical explanation."

"We're not dealing with a logical man," Lincoln said.

''That's just the point. He's tapped into the power of the irrational, the illogical.''

Lincoln turned off the laptop and its useless display of information disappeared in a wink of light and static.

McCall went to the sink to get a glass of water. As he drank
he stared at Lincoln's slumped form in the chair by the round
table. He suddenly looked ten years older than when McCall
first met him. The last couple of hours had really taken their
toll on the man. No matter how good he was in the past, the
fact was that Lincoln was tired and sick now, maybe even a
touch senile. He was positively addled on the subject of Snow,
making the man out to be some kind of god. The tumor must
be affecting his reasoning. McCall began to wonder why the
dying man was put on the case in the first place. McCall decided
he would have to watch out for himself. One way or another,
the young agent figured he'd have to take over in the end.

32

Jeff stood on the stoop, fumbling with the door with one hand and precariously balancing the pizza box with the other.

Kate had to smile.

She opened the screen door and grabbed the box as Jeff stepped inside. Penelope came dashing out of the kitchen and around the armchair and danced around Jeff's legs on her hind paws. Jeff bent to pet the dog and glanced up to see the policeman getting up from the chair in front of the television set.

"This is Officer Bob D'Angelo," Kate said, "of the Neptune Police Department. He's been assigned as my bodyguard." She said it as if it were all a joke, but Jeff caught the note of concern in her tone. "His buddy is outside in the car."

"I know," Jeff said. "I met him on the way in. He checked my driver's license and just about gave me the third degree before he'd let me pass. I presume it was you he was talking to on the radio to confirm my identity."

"Otis can be a little overzealous," Officer D'Angelo smiled. "I hope he didn't give you too hard a time."

"It's okay," Jeff said. "I'm glad someone is taking this seriously."

D'Angelo's smile faded. "You can be sure we're taking this seriously, Mr. Hudson. We wouldn't be here if we weren't."

Jeff nodded, but he let his blue eyes linger on the cop a half-beat longer than necessary to let him know he still wasn't satisfied.

Meanwhile Kate had set the dining room table with paper plates, napkins, two glasses, and a bottle of diet Coke. Jeff took a seat at the head of the table. He was still wearing the clothes he'd worn the night before, obviously not wanting to take the time to return to his place for a change. Kate felt a touch of tenderness for his concern. His usually unruly red hair was wet and slickly combed back from his forehead. He'd no doubt taken a shower in the doctor's lounge at the hospital. Kate placed a slice of pizza on his plate and a smaller one on her own before calling in to the living room, where D'Angelo had returned to his chair in front of the television.

"Would you like a slice of pizza?"

D'Angelo turned round, his head emerging from behind one of the wingbacks. "No, thank you." He checked his watch. "We should be off-shift in about another hour or so. My wife has a pork roast in the oven."

"Something to drink?"

"I'm still working on the soda," he said, holding up his glass as if to provide evidence. "Thanks anyway."

"What about your friend in the car?"

"He'll be okay."

"You sure?"

"I'm sure."

It was awkward having the policeman around. Even as nice as he was, it leant a tension to the atmosphere in the house. His mere presence was an admission that something was dreadfully wrong. On the lighter side, she felt as if she and Jeff were being chaperoned. Kate found herself talking to Jeff in hushed tones, as if the policeman in the next room might be there to overhear their every word.

Jeff had already finished his first piece of pizza and handed down his crust to Penelope, who was sitting expectantly beside his chair, occasionally shifting impatiently on her haunches. She grabbed the crust from Jeff's hand and trotted off to the corner, where she lay down with it between her front paws, thoughtfully chewing.

"What happened with the accident?"

"It was a real mess," Jeff said, reaching for another slice. Kate was always amazed at how he could eat even while delivering the most graphic descriptions of carnage, but she supposed it came with the territory. After a while you must just get used to it. If you didn't, Kate mused, you'd wind up starving. "Two of the cars were so folded up they had to use torches to cut away the twisted metal. Unfortunately, three people bled to death before they could get them out. Two people lost legs, another an arm. I lost a patient on the table, a girl no more than eighteen. Massive head injuries and severed femoral artery. I'm still not sure which she died of. It was a damn shame."

Kate nibbled at the end of her slice and put it back down on her plate. She, too, had gotten used to Jeff's battle stories. It wasn't that that had ruined her appetite. Not totally, anyway. It was the gray light coming through the windows as the sun made its early retreat in the west. It was the long shadows starting to creep across the room like a leak from some deep dark pool. It was the fact that *he* was out there somewhere, and the feeling, probably totally irrational, that he was closing in on her.

5:15 P.M.

Snow leaned back against the motel bed's cheesy headboard.

He was eating Moo-Shu shrimp out of a small white box with a pair of chopsticks and watching the five o'clock news.

He made the news right after stories about the storm and a jewelry heist in Manhattan. The newscasters who regularly giggled through the newscast like a couple of preteens who'd heard someone fart in church maintained their serious masks long enough to deliver a "late-breaking" story. Snow saw a quickly edited montage of the prison, the tollbooth, and the parking lot of the New Jersey Foodtown where he'd left Julie Golden's body. Then he saw a brief interview with Tom Lincoln. Snow had figured they might call the agent out of retirement for this one. In a way, he had counted on it. Nonetheless, the ex-agent looked the worse for wear: sallow, sagging skin, a slight droop of the left eye, an all but imperceptible tremor. He mumbled a few words about how dangerous Snow was and cautioned listeners to report any possible sightings to local authorities. Snow didn't hear the words; he read Lincoln's muffled lips. He had the television turned down to mute. He always watched it that way; it made the images more interesting and allowed him to pick up more easily the subtle visual cues often masked by the words people used.

Words lied. Faces didn't.

And Lincoln's face told the plain truth about the progress the tumor had made in his brain. Snow had no doubt it was bringing the former agent ever closer to the truth. In a way, he envied the man.

There followed a screen showing Snow's original FBI mug shots, neither the frontal nor the profile shots looking anything like him.

Snow smiled as he expertly scooped another mouthful of Moo-Shu shrimp out of the container. On the television there was a car advertisement. The spokesperson, a famous basketball coach noted for his flashy wardrobe and rugged Irish good looks, was lying. The newscasters, the reporters, the advertisers, they were all lying. Was it any wonder that no one had any idea of the truth?

Only Lincoln had some glimpse of it.

And he would soon be dead.

6:05 P.M.

Kate tried to hide her shock when she saw Lincoln at her front door.

She was familiar with the usual advance of inoperable brain cancer, but she was unprepared for the ravage the disease had worked on the man who stood before her now. He must have lost close to fifty pounds, his face sallow and sagging slightly on one side, and he stood with a slight stoop to his shoulders. He was not the same, strapping, healthy middle-aged man she had spoken to less than five years ago. She could see the recognition in his eyes and knew she had not done a very good job of concealing her surprise at his condition. Still he merely nodded, and from his slightly skeletal face came the words, almost apologetic, as if by way of explanation.

"It's been a long time."

"Yes," Kate said. "It has."

"How are you, Kate?"

"All right until about eighteen hours ago. How are you?"

"As well as can be expected from a man who is supposed to have been dead for the last four years."

So there it was, out in the open. As a psychiatrist she was trained to handle such situations, but they were still uncomfortable. They still hurt, especially when it was someone you knew and trusted as intimately as she'd known and trusted Lincoln.

"This here is Agent Ryan McCall. He's in charge of this case. I'm just along as an adviser."

Kate shook hands with the tall, broad-shouldered agent who with his chiseled good looks and brush-cut looked like he'd just stepped out of Central Casting.

"Pleased to meet you, Dr. Bennett."

"Kate, please. I'm afraid I can't say I'm so glad to meet you, though, under the circumstances."

Just then Jeff emerged from the basement holding a package of ten-penny nails in one hand and Kate's battered all purpose wood-handled hammer in the other. He'd just finished nailing all the basement windows shut. He glanced from Kate to Lincoln to McCall and back again. He didn't need any introductions. Kate could see the blood coloring the fair skin under his red beard an instant before he started shouting.

"How in the hell could you have let something like this

happen?'' Jeff yelled, the note of command in his voice honed by years of emergency room experience. "You were supposed to take care that nothing like this would ever happen."

Of course Jeff had oversimplified the situation. Or had he? Kate was running much of the same script through her mind herself; she just could never get her mouth to say it, especially after getting a good look at Lincoln and realizing how the man was already paying the highest possible price for his decision to come here.

Psychologically, Lincoln did the best thing he could in the face of Jeff's attack. He admitted being wrong. Kate wondered whether it was just a strategy he'd learned at the agency to gain Jeff's compliance or an actual expression of his contrition. "You're right, sir," he said. "I screwed up big time on this one. I would like to say that it couldn't be helped, but it should have been helped. I made a promise that nothing like this would ever happen, and I broke my promise. I take full responsibility. That's why I'm here."

Jeff wasn't completely won over. "What you want to do," he said angrily, "is to use Kate as bait to undo something you should never have done in the first place. You're just here to save your own ass."

"No, sir." Lincoln's voice was soft but emphatic. "I no longer have a professional stake in this case. I'm on medical retirement." He touched a finger to his forehead like the barrel of a gun. "A brain tumor that should have killed me four years ago ended my career. I'm here to do my best in keeping my word to Kate and protecting her as best I can. The only way to do that is to catch this bastard before I die." He said the last without the least trace of bravado or self-pity.

A certain bitterness still lurked around the edges of Jeff's face, but the color had drained away, and with it his justified rage. Lincoln had somehow defused the situation.

"Now you can help me," Lincoln went on, the note of contrition gone, replaced by a cold professionalism Jeff couldn't help but appreciate, "or you can go on hating my guts. Actually, you can do both. But either way, I won't allow you to get in the way. I intend to make certain that until Snow is apprehended Kate is kept safe. That's my number-one priority. I think we can both agree on that. What do you say, Mr.—"

"Hudson," Kate interrupted. "Jeff Hudson."

"What do you say, Mr. Hudson?"

"All right," Jeff mumbled, and moved the hammer and nails over to his left hand to take Lincoln's frail, almost delicate hand.

"Are either of you hungry?" Kate asked Lincoln and McCall, as a way both to break the ice and get the image of that handclasp and all it meant out of her mind.

"I'm not," Lincoln said, "but Agent McCall here might be."

"I've got some leftover pizza from dinner," she offered.

"That sounds great," McCall said.

Kate turned to Jeff. "Would you bring Agent McCall a couple of slices of pizza? Please?"

Jeff clearly didn't like being sent from the room, but after half a beat, he nodded grimly and retreated. McCall stalked off to oversee the men putting a tracing device on the living room telephone. For a moment she and Lincoln were alone.

"Your husband?" Lincoln asked.

"Boyfriend."

"I just assumed after all this time someone would have grabbed you. You're quite a catch."

Kate smiled. "Thanks. I'll take that as a compliment. Actually it may come to that, who knows? I'm sorry about Jeff's reaction. He gets a little emotional at times."

"That's okay. I don't blame him. If it were my wife or daughter, I'd put the son-of-a-bitch responsible to the wall myself."

"You're not responsible."

"I take responsibility."

"You take too much on yourself."

Lincoln shrugged. "What's it gonna do, give me a tumor?"

Kate smiled with Lincoln. "It's good to see you again. Just you being here makes me feel safer."

"Thank you. Believe it or not, hearing that makes a big difference to me."

For the first time Kate could see a touch of sadness in the old agent's face. "It's true. I haven't been quite myself since I heard the news. This whole thing has got me unnerved."

"We'll catch him, Kate. I promise."

She nodded in the direction of the living room. "You really think he'll try to contact me?"

"Maybe, maybe not. It's just a precaution. We're covering all the bases."

"Did we do the right thing, Tom? I mean, entrapping him the way we did?"

The answer came so swift and unequivocally it startled Kate. For a split second Lincoln looked like the man she remembered.

"Don't ever doubt it. Doubt anything else, but never that. You helped save innocent lives. There's no telling how many."

"Not Julie Goldens."

"Julie Golden wasn't innocent. She didn't deserve to die for doing the right thing, but at least she had a choice. She knew what she was getting into."

"So did I, Tom," Kate said. "And that means I'm not innocent, either."

"No," Lincoln said. "No, you're not."

6:35 P.M.

Snow sat cross-legged in the damp motel room.

It had started raining again, the drops spattering against the windows, the sky darkened so that the only source of light in the room came from the television. It was still on, muted, but Snow was no longer looking at it. Instead, his attention was focused on the fifty yarrow sticks laid out on the worn carpeted floor in front of him. He set one aside as the "observer" and then grabbed the other forty-nine sticks in his left hand. At random he separated about half the sticks with his right hand and placed these on the floor in front of him.

With the sticks remaining in his left hand he phrased the situation in his mind again and then began removing the sticks four at a time until four or fewer sticks remained. These remaining sticks he placed between the ring and little fingers of his left hand. He then gathered up all the discarded sticks, separated them again, and began the process a second, and finally, a third time. He picked up the fifty sticks again and repeated the process 17 more times until he had formed a complete hexagram from the *I Ching*.

The hexagram made up of two broken and four unbroken lines was that of Chun, indicating difficulty and danger at the beginning of the enterprise he was about to undertake. He knew what the hexagram would be before he'd even cast the oracle sticks, but he enjoyed the process; it put him in a mood of deep contemplation. There were two moving lines in the hexagram, changing it to number forty-nine, Ko, whose meaning was, not surprisingly, ''time for a change.''

Snow had committed to memory all the important major translations of the *I Ching,* such as those by James Legge and Richard Wilhelm. He also knew by heart the commentaries, including those attributed to no less an authority than Confucius himself. He therefore knew what the all-important fourth line was telling him. Before he could move forward, before he could successfully make the needed change, he would have to secure the aid of a talented adviser.

Snow knew who that meant.

He thought of Kate Bennett.

He smiled tightly against the steady wave of pleasure-pain washing through his body.

In the dim blue light cast by the television, one could just make out the dozens of silver pins puncturing his face, arms, chest, and loins.

Snow was ready.

He was ready for the final steps of the journey of a thousand miles he had begun so long ago.

The journey each conscious man and woman must take to reach enlightenment.

The journey to self-revelation.

It seemed to him he had taken the first painful step of that journey a thousand years ago.

33

Jeff returned from the kitchen with two paper plates of pizza, a can of diet Coke under each arm, two straws. He passed by Lincoln and Kate with a disapproving sidelong glance and joined McCall in the living room where the young FBI agent had settled on the couch in front of the TV beside D'Angelo. Jeff plopped down in the easy chair, balancing his pizza on his knees and popping the top of the Coke can with his thumb. Kate could hear the opening theme of *Jeopardy* playing from the other room.

Kate turned her attention to Lincoln. The last hour had not softened the ravages of disease on his face. If nothing else, the lines around his mouth and eyes had grown deeper. Earlier he'd asked for a glass of water only to wait until he'd thought Kate wasn't looking to slip a pill into his mouth from a small brown bottle he kept in his breast pocket. She wondered why he was ashamed to take the pill in front of her, why men in general had so much trouble admitting their vulnerabilities. She thought of Jeff, working double shifts in the ER with walking pneumonia.

In Lincoln's case, it was somewhat different. The man was clearly dying, and dying could be an intensely lonely and private affair, especially for someone as proud and used to being in total control as Lincoln was. Kate wanted to reach out and tell him it was okay, that he could talk to her, but her instincts told her that her efforts would not be appreciated, that he'd only resent the intrusion. Instead, in a hushed, gravelly voice, he asked her about her last sessions with Alexander Snow, hoping there was something he might have missed in their earlier conversations, something that might give him a clue to the doctor's next move.

"What do you think he was looking for?" Lincoln asked. "Why had he come to see you?"

"I don't know, really," Kate replied. "He seemed haunted by something."

"Do you think it was guilt? That he felt the need to confess his crimes?"

"No," Kate said emphatically. "It wasn't guilt. In all my years as a therapist I never met a man so thoroughly devoid of a sense of guilt. The normal person always feels some guilt over something. The way they treated an aged parent, something said years ago to an ex-girlfriend, a lie told to a business associate or friend, those kinds of things. Snow felt absolutely no guilt."

"A sociopath," Lincoln said.

"A perfect sociopath. The gold standard of the type. Right out of the textbook. As you know, he never killed a regular patient, anyone who could be traced directly back to him. He was too smart for that. But then he all but told me about the ones he'd taken all the way and I put two and two together with that rash of missing persons. In all that time, there wasn't the slightest sense of guilt or regret about him."

"You think he knew you knew?"

"He all but spelled out his theory. Whether he actually believed I thought he'd put it into practice I couldn't say. But I think he did. The fact is, I feel he was proud of his work, and maybe he wanted to share it with someone, even if he couldn't come right out about it. Maybe he wanted recognition for his theories. Like every scientist, perhaps he thought he was doing something good for humanity and wanted to be acknowledged and understood, if only by one person.''

"So he *is* psychotic. He doesn't know good from evil."

"He doesn't believe in good or evil."

"But why you? Of all the eminent psychiatrists he could have chosen?'' Lincoln blushed beneath his pallor. "I'm sorry. I didn't mean it to sound like that. It's just—''

"No offense taken. Believe me, I've been wracking my brain over the same question ever since he first came to see me. I remember him telling me that he'd read some paper I'd published about memory that had impressed him. Maybe he saw me as some kind of potential protégée.''

"Still, Snow doesn't seem like the kind of man who'd need anyone's approval. He seems totally self-sufficient. I know it fits the profile of the ordinary sociopath to flaunt his superior knowledge right under the unsuspecting noses of authority, but you yourself said he's no ordinary sociopath.''

Kate nodded. "Which puts us back at square one.''

From the living room Kate heard the three men playing along with the contestants on *Jeopardy.* She heard Jeff's voice quicker and more often than McCall, D'Angelo lagging far behind. Jeff had a wide range of knowledge that had always impressed Kate, and it often amazed her how many questions about arcane subjects he could answer. She often teased him that he should try out for the show.

Lincoln seemed to be thinking out loud. "If not guilt, if not recognition, what *did* he want from you? You said he'd read a paper you'd written on memory.''

"Yes. It was about how we often invent large chunks of our past to compensate for details we really can't remember.''

Lincoln's gaunt face suddenly seemed to light from the inside. For the second time since he'd arrived, he didn't look like a terminally ill man. "Maybe that's the answer!'' he said excitedly.

"What?'' Kate said, not following his line of thinking.

"Maybe he wanted you to help him remember."

"Remember what?"

"Something in his past so horrible he'd suppressed it all his life. Something that was keeping him from complete liberation."

"But what in the world could it be—"

"I don't know. But if we found out, it would answer a lot of questions."

Kate felt herself shudder. "I'd hate to think your theory was correct."

"Why?" Lincoln asked.

"Because considering what Snow has done, I wouldn't want to be the one to find out what made him what he is."

7:20 P.M.

Snow knelt naked, cross-legged on the floor in front of the television watching *Jeopardy*.

He had removed all of the pins except those along his hairline and at his temples, those running in a line from below his left eye to his chin, and those along his jaw to his left nipple.

He answered the questions flickering on the screen in quick succession far ahead of the three contestants:

> *Charles Fairbanks*
> *The Dutch East India Company*
> *The Truth in Lending Act*
> *Carlos Montoya*
> *Titian*

Meanwhile, Snow watched the expression on Alex Trebek's face, easily able to determine when the gameshow host really knew the answers to the questions and when he was only pretending erudition. By the end of the game Snow had answered every question correctly, amassing a total of $136,000. He bet it all on the final *Jeopardy* category, which was "Playwrights." The question was ridiculously simple: "In

1936 he wrote his last play, *The Boy David*. An actress played the title role.''

Snow chuckled.

He felt refreshed, alive.

On top of that, he had won a *Jeopardy* record of $272,000.

The answer to the final *Jeopardy* question was, of course, James Barrie, the author of *Peter Pan*.

7:30 P.M.

The closing music of *Jeopardy* was playing when the phone started ringing.

Kate could feel everyone's eyes turn toward her. Lincoln covered one of her hands with his own.

''Answer it,'' he said quietly. ''It may be him.''

Kate nodded. She walked slowly across the room, as if she were sleepwalking. The phone rang a second time. The technicians were sitting beside the phone, ready to monitor the call. Lincoln had followed her into the living room. Behind her he whispered, ''Keep him on the line as long as you can.'' Kate nodded. She picked up the phone in the middle of the fourth ring.

''Hello?''

''Hello, Katherine. How are you?''

Kate felt her stomach flip-flop.

''What do you want, Dr. Snow?''

Lincoln motioned from the corner of his eye, pulling his fingers apart slowly, as if stretching taffy. *Stretch it,* he mouthed.

Kate nodded.

''So abrupt, Katherine,'' Snow tsked. ''Surely they want you to keep me talking. You'll have to do better than that.''

''I'm sorry. Your call comes as kind of a surprise.''

''Now you're lying to *me*, Katherine. Surely you knew I'd be getting in touch with you.''

''I guess I was hoping—''

Kate stopped herself. She knew it was too late. She'd already said too much. There was no way Snow was going to let her get away with such a gaffe.

"Hoping for what?"

There was no choice but honesty.

"That you'd forgotten about me."

"You mean forgiven."

That's exactly what she'd meant, but she didn't dare say it.

"But I *have* forgiven you, Katherine."

"The way you forgave Julie Golden?"

Kate couldn't help herself.

"We have unfinished business, Katherine."

"With all due respect, Dr. Snow, I think our business is finished."

"I beg to differ, Katherine. Our relationship was prematurely interrupted. By the way, it might interest you to know that I've been tutoring a pupil of yours."

Kate felt her blood run cold.

"What are you talking about, Dr. Snow?"

"A very bright girl. Her name is Bonnie Kaplan."

"Jesus, she's got nothing to do with this, Dr. Snow. Please, I'm begging you. Let her go. I'll do whatever you want."

"*Whatever* I want?" Snow sounded amused.

"Anything. Just let her go. She's only a kid; she's innocent."

"No one is innocent. Certainly I've convinced you of that by now."

"I'll do whatever you want," Kate repeated, desperate now.

"I want to finish my therapy with you."

Kate was stunned into silence.

"Are you still there, Katherine?"

"Yes, I'm still here."

"Good. Please put Lincoln on. I'm sure he's been listening in on the other line."

"I'm here," Lincoln said.

"How's the tumor, Tom?" Snow said. "I saw you on TV tonight. You didn't look so hot."

"I'm still getting around."

"Any visual disturbance yet? Any paralysis?"

"I'm sure you didn't call to give me an examination, Snow."

"Still the unrepentant curmudgeon. That's the spirit. Studies have shown that it's the patients with attitude who survive the longest. I understand it's inoperable. That's too bad. On the other hand, at least you've got all your faculties. There's no guarantee with brain surgery. By the way, do they still let you carry a gun?"

"I've got my own licensed firearm. I intend to use it if you give me a good excuse."

Snow laughed. "I'll keep that in mind. I have to tell you, though, from what I saw, I'd say you have only another three good months left."

Lincoln gritted his teeth. "That'll be long enough to bring you down."

"You sound awfully sure of yourself, Tom."

"I am, Snow. We're going to get you this time."

"Well, the gauntlet's down. I wish you the best of luck. I really do, Tom. You want it so badly."

"Save it, Snow."

Snow laughed again. "I guess you've got what you want by now, unless your people screwed up. Good evening, Tom. I'll see you in your dreams."

Snow hung up.

Lincoln looked over at the FBI techs working the phone tap. One of them gave Lincoln the thumbs up. They did it. They had a make on the number.

34

7:45 P.M.

Lincoln had to do some wrangling about available manpower with the local police chief but he finally got the okay to have a second officer assigned to watch over Kate inside the house, in addition to the two agents manning the wiretap and the officer watching the house from the car outside.

Still, Jeff wasn't satisfied. He wanted Kate moved to a neutral location. He suggested bringing Kate to his own condo, or even taking her out of town, putting her up in a hotel in some randomly chosen locale. Lincoln nixed the idea out of hand. He maintained that Kate should be around just in case Snow called back. Jeff was incensed. Once again he accused Lincoln of using Kate as bait, dangling her in front of Snow, waiting to see if he'd bite—and guaranteeing nothing in the way of safety.

"We're doing everything we can to protect her," Lincoln said, sounding weary.

"The way you protected Julie Golden?" Jeff snapped back.

McCall took over. "We weren't prepared for Julie Golden. She wasn't under our protection. Look, we've got three uniformed officers and two agents on the premises. Not even Snow can get past that. Besides, we're not even sure he wants to. He may just be taunting us. I can guarantee Dr. Bennett will be safe here.''

"Oh, well, if you *guarantee* it," Jeff said sarcastically. "You're the ones who guaranteed Snow would stay in prison in the first place."

It was Kate who broke up the dispute. She would stay in her house. She wasn't going to be chased away because of a phone call. She was tired of running from the past. Besides, she felt herself responsible to those who had died to bring Snow to justice. The fact he had kidnapped Bonnie Kaplan, or so he'd claimed, made it even more impossible for her to abdicate her responsibility. Snow would have guessed as much, which meant he wanted her in the house, which meant she was putting herself in greater danger by playing into his hands. She didn't care; she had no choice. She'd stay and wait for his next call. If it came, she'd be there to answer it. She'd see this thing through. One way or another, she would help Lincoln get the bastard.

Jeff tried to talk Kate out of staying in the house, but in the end he had no choice but to abide by Kate's decision. He knew from experience how stubborn she could be. Besides, deep down he knew she was morally right. There was no way she could turn her back on this thing now and be able to live with herself. She was staying as much for herself as for Bonnie Kaplan and the others.

In the back seat of the car that was to take them to the motel where they'd traced the call, Lincoln sat looking out at the old Victorian house, every light in the lower two floors lit up like there was a party going on. He was satisfied that Kate's safety was secure, at least as far as conventionally possible, which in spite of McCall's claim, Lincoln knew was no guarantee. Snow was not a conventional man.

Jeff was right.

Lincoln was using Kate as bait.

7:55 *P.M.*

Bonnie Kaplan was dead, just as Lincoln knew she would be.

Her nude body was sitting upright in a chair placed right in front of the television. There was a sitcom playing on TV, the sound turned up so loud Lincoln wondered why neighboring occupants hadn't complained. The inane laughter on the soundtrack jarred with the sickeningly gruesome scene. Bonnie Kaplan's once pretty face had been skillfully removed from her head like a mask, leaving only the white, grinning skull beneath the long, straight blond hair. Judging from the lack of blood and residual tissue, Lincoln deduced that Snow must have performed the operation somewhere else and carefully scrubbed the glaring white bone.

"Jesus," McCall said, holstering his gun. "Jesus."

The local cops who'd accompanied them to the motel and broken-down the door still had their weapons out, throwing open the doors to the closet and bathroom. Lincoln could have told him that Snow was long gone, but he let them go through the motions, realizing it was their way of avoiding the horror in the chair. Meanwhile, two other cops stood outside the door to keep any curiosity seekers away, though their very presence had already attracted a couple of drunken motel residents.

It was Lincoln who'd spotted the tape between the girl's gritted teeth.

He removed a handkerchief from his pocket and used it to pull the cassette free. He inserted the tape into the microcassette player and pressed the play button.

The girl's voice was reedy and tremulous, interrupted by gasps as she struggled to catch her breath. Lincoln had heard such "confessions" before. To his ear, this one didn't seem forced. He could only wonder what unspeakable tortures the girl had been forced to endure before she'd been broken to the point of making this statement.

"My name is Bonnie Kaplan and I'm a liar. I've never told the truth in my entire life. I want to do so now. I've never dared face myself as I really am. I've always been afraid; I'm afraid even now. But I know the time has come. I'm ready for enlightenment. I'm ready to understand. I'm ready to learn the truth—''

Lincoln had heard enough. He clicked off the recorder before the inevitable bloodcurdling scream.

''I've had enough of this shit,'' McCall said. ''I want this guy. *I want him now.*''

Lincoln didn't say anything.

Inside his skull he felt the tumor pulsating like a surging and fading radio signal.

What was it trying to tell him?

35

Kate did not take the news of Bonnie Kaplan's death well.

In spite of herself, she clung to the wishful fantasy that Snow had just been bluffing, that he had not really kidnapped Kaplan but was just using the threat to keep Kate in place. Now there was no choice but to face the bitter truth. She was responsible for yet another death, and this time it was that of an innocent young woman.

Lincoln had spared her the ugly details of the Kaplan girl's death as well as the taped message. He could tell Kate was close to snapping. The last twenty hours had taken a tremendous toll on her. She didn't need to know the circumstances in which they'd found her former pupil.

"Why?" she asked. "Why her?"

A simple question with no simple answer. How many times had Lincoln heard it during his many years in the Agency? How many times had Kate heard it herself in her practice? They both knew the answer.

There *was* no answer.

Still, Lincoln felt the need to say something.

"It isn't your fault, Kate."

They both knew that was a lie. Bonnie Kaplan had died because she was connected to Kate.

Kate nodded, accepting the consolation for what it was worth, which wasn't much. Jeff was pacing back and forth in the living room. He resumed his argument for moving Kate out of the house for the night. Lincoln didn't object. It was Kate who cut Jeff short.

"I'm not going anywhere, goddammit. I'm staying right here. I don't want to hear any more about it."

There was a harsh strength to Kate's words, but Lincoln could hear the exhausted desperation under them. She left the room without looking at anyone, passing both Jeff and Lincoln as she headed upstairs.

In the bathroom off the bedroom Kate turned on the faucets and let the water run cold. She placed her wrists under the flow and looked at her face in the mirror. She was almost as white as the stucco wall behind her. There were dark purple pouches under her eyes and the lines extending from her nose to the corners of her mouth were pronounced.

She looked absolutely awful.

She cupped her hands and collected the cold water, took a deep breath to brace herself for the shock, and splashed the water over her face. She did this twice before looking at herself in the mirror again. She looked worse than before. She felt nauseated.

She opened the medicine cabinet and took out a small brown bottle of tranquilizers. It was always a dangerous proposition to prescribe yourself drugs but knowing the dangers, Kate had been especially judicious in their use, taking them only to help her over the rough spots when she'd first moved down to the shore. She hadn't taken a tranquilizer in two and a half years. Now she stared down at the egg-shaped light blue pills and shook two into the palm of her hand. She noticed her hand was shaking. Her whole body was shaking, and two hot tears were running down her cold, cracked white face.

Bonnie Kaplan was dead and it was all her fault.

She popped the two Xanax tablets into her mouth and filled a cup with cold water, swallowing both pills with one practiced gulp.

If she was going to get through this thing, she was going to have to remain calm.

Dead calm.

8:30 P.M.

The phone rang just as Kate was coming down the stairs.

She crossed the living room with grim determination. She ignored the looks trailing after her. She grabbed the receiver and pressed it against her ear.

"Dr. Snow," she said matter-of-factly.

"I'm glad to hear you've got a grip on yourself, Katherine. I had begun to worry that this would all be too much for you."

"Why did you kill the girl, Dr. Snow?"

"I didn't kill her. I enlightened her. You should know the difference by now."

"She was innocent."

"No one is innocent, Katherine. You know that." Snow breathed a long, bored sigh. "We've been through this already. Why do you insist on making it so difficult? We're all guilty of something."

"Even me?"

"Oh, you know the answer to that better than anyone, Katherine."

"You left me with no choice, Dr. Snow."

"We all have choices. Therein lies the rub."

"Then why all these games? Why don't you just kill me?"

"Because we have unfinished business, Katherine. I want you to finish my therapy."

"I can't help you, Dr. Snow."

"Oh, yes you can, Katherine. You're the only one who *can* help me. You're the only one who can give me what I need."

"What is it you think I can give you?"

"Why, the truth, Katherine. That's all. The plain and simple truth."

Kate listened for a long time to the dead line before carefully replacing the receiver. On her empty stomach she could already feel the effect of the two tranquilizers she'd taken, but they didn't prevent the chill plummeting down her spine.

8:35 P.M.

They couldn't trace the call.

"Was he on long enough?" Lincoln asked the two technicians, listening in on earphones by the extension.

"I'm sorry," Kate said. "I couldn't think of anything to say. I froze."

"Don't worry about it," Lincoln said. "You did just fine." He turned back to the technicians, who looked confused.

"He was *on* long enough," one of the technicians said, a tall sandy-haired man with thick, wire-rimmed glasses, "barely. But we can't get a make on the call."

"Why the hell not?"

The tech shrugged. "Not sure. He might be calling from a cellular phone. Maybe from a car."

"A car!" Lincoln shouted. He might as well have shouted *Eureka!* "That's it!"

Lincoln knew tracking down a killer was like playing a game of chess. No matter how good the player, he always made a mistake somewhere in his game. You just had to be ready for it. The question was, why hadn't Lincoln thought of it sooner? It must be the damn tumor. But then, neither Mccall nor anyone else had thought of it, either. The car was Snow's mistake. As far as Lincoln knew, he was still driving Julie Golden's Lexus. The APB had turned up nothing; Lincoln figured Snow had switched plates, but he'd bet Golden had had the car equipped with Lo-Jack. The radar-oriented tracking device was a favorite with theft-conscious luxury-car owners. It was a long shot, to be sure, but something told him he had locked onto the target this time.

"Get on the phone," Lincoln said, turning to McCall. "Double-check and make sure Golden had a Lo-Jack system installed in her car and have it activated. Then coordinate the activation of every police station equipped with a Lo-Jack tracking system in Monmouth and Ocean Counties. If my hunch is right, we can pinpoint exactly where this son-of-a-bitch is in a matter of minutes."

36

It did not take long for them to locate two cars reported stolen on the Lo-Jack system. One was traveling about fifty miles south through Brigantine, the other was heading east somewhere between the small towns of Clarksburg and Siloam.

Lincoln unfolded his map and spread it out on the table in Kate's living room. He placed his little finger on Ocean Grove, this thumb on Brigantine, and his middle finger on the blank space between Clarksburg and Siloam. He couldn't trust himself to a hunch now: he had to reason this out. Unfortunately, with cancer eating his brain cells by the minute, he wasn't in top form. As he looked at the map he felt his temples ache, each throb answered by a nauseating echo in his gut. The points on the map blurred into one amorphous blob and he had to make a conscious effort to concentrate, forcing his eyes to focus. In the chess game between him and Snow, his opponent had just made a blunder, and it was up to Lincoln to press the advantage, to back Snow into a corner.

Lincoln looked at the map and in a moment of crystal clarity decided that Brigantine was out. It was too close to well-populated areas as well as being the location of a famous bird sanctuary that drew thousands of tourists every year, any of whom might have stumbled on Snow's hideaway. On top of that, it seemed too far away, considering the speed which Snow seemed to be commuting back and forth between Ocean Grove and there. The area between Clarksburg and Siloam was fed by I-95 running east and west like a belt around the middle of New Jersey.

The area was right at the heart of the pine barrens, a huge, blighted stretch of sand and stunted pine trees legendary for its insulated, inbred, rural population, its cranberry bogs, and the Jersey Devil, a cloven-hoofed, horse-headed, winged monstrosity that had been sporadically sighted haunting the barrens ever since it had been born to a certain Mrs. Leeds back in the late 1870s. The area officially designated as the pine barrens stretched throughout about the entire state and was bigger than any natural park in the United States. Much of it was protected from development by state and local environmental law. Lincoln had a passing familiarity with it, as it was occasionally used as a dumping ground for victims of mob hits on the Atlantic City–Philadelphia organized crime axis. Isolated, off-limits, and with a hint of menace, it was a perfect place for a man like Snow to carry on his gruesome research.

Lincoln thumped his middle finger on the green space between Clarksburg and Siloam.

"This is it," he said. "This is where he is."

He instructed McCall to phone the surrounding towns as well as the nearby state police barracks and the Agency headquarters in Trenton to send all available back-up to close in on the signal.

"Use your authorization," he said to McCall. "You've got the pull."

If the young agent resented being ordered around like an underling, he didn't show it. Instead, he made his way to the phone and began dialing the appropriate numbers. In a matter of minutes they were both in the car heading for that blank green space on the map, the next move on the chessboard in

Lincoln's game plan. The decision had been easy; now came the hard part—waiting. Because Lincoln knew that if he'd guessed wrong, there'd be hell to pay.

9:05 P.M.

Heading east on the interstate, Alexander Snow was driving a black Ford pickup.

He was doing an exercise from the Gurdjieff tradition—the Armenian mystic—called "self-remembering." It consisted of taking a mental inventory of what one was perceiving through each of the senses in the present moment: the sound of the Ford's engine, the feel of the phosphorescent lighting running up his face from chin to forehead, the big green sign with white reflector letters reading "Shore Points." The goal was to be fully in the moment, to achieve true objective consciousness. The idea was to snap out of the trance of everyday consciousness, to stop running on automatic pilot, to wake up.

With great deliberation, Snow reached beside him, picked up the microcassette recorder lying on the seat next to the black briefcase containing the lie detector.

He brought the voice-activated microcassette recorder, brought it to his lips, and watching the white lines slip beneath his left front fender one by one, spoke, his voice barely above a whisper.

"Hello, Katherine . . ."

37

They found the car half-buried in a cranberry bog about fifteen miles outside Siloam, emitting a weak, barely discernible signal.

Lincoln stood beside McCall on a soft bed of pine needles and looked at the moonlight glancing off the roof and the bit of chrome that hadn't yet been sucked under the greenish-black muck.

"I've radioed for a tow truck to get in here and pull it out," McCall said. "We'll dust it for prints. My bet is that our boy got careless. Never thought we'd find his wheels."

Lincoln didn't say anything. He was running various possible scenarios through his mind. He turned and watched the bright eyes of the maglites searching the forest behind them. He was not surprised when he saw one light growing larger, looking almost as big as a headlight. Lincoln shielded his eyes, the pain stabbing like a knitting needle deep in the soft tissue of his brain.

"For Christ's sake," he barked, "turn that thing off."

"Sorry, sir," the agent replied. He was dressed in a large

windbreaker stenciled with the letters FBI across the breast just in case anyone got confused in the middle of a crossfire. He clicked off the light. He was looking at McCall. "Parker told me you were down here, but I wasn't sure it was you."

"What do you want?" McCall said.

"We've found something. A cabin about two hundred yards up the slope. Can't tell if it's inhabited or not. It's completely dark. Might just belong to some toothless old cranberry farmer, but we thought we ought to check it out."

"What do you think?" McCall said, turning to Lincoln. "Feeling lucky?"

"We're due for a little luck."

"Let's go."

They hiked their way to the spot, following the agent with the light, watching their feet with every step over the treacherous ground below, veined with shallow roots and pitted with chuckholes. By the time they got there, everyone had already converged on the spot. From the moment he saw the cabin, Lincoln had no doubt it was Snow's. He was back to thinking in hunches, and something about the place repelled him. State troopers, local police, and FBI agents were milling among the trees just beyond the clearing. Most of them had the good sense to turn off their maglites, but a few stray beams played up and down the weathered clapboard structure. The shadows of the law enforcement personnel looked like dark ghosts in the bluish half-light of the moon shining through the trees.

From out of the shadows a tall, broad-shouldered trooper emerged, the edges of his aging but still chiseled face limned silver in the moonlight. He was a full head taller than either Lincoln or McCall and wore a large Stetson.

"Captain Hansen," he said, by way of introduction. "We've got a cabin here. Occupant unknown."

Lincoln nodded, all too familiar with the peculiar penchant the state police had for stating the obvious.

"We've got to get in there," Lincoln said simply.

"I'm afraid we're still waiting for authorization. No warrant. No reasonable cause."

"I've got reasonable cause," Lincoln said. "That cabin belongs to an escaped convict. A serial killer who has already killed at least eight people. We *have* to get in there. He might be cornered inside right now. This might be our best chance to nail him."

The state trooper shook his head. "Sorry. No can do. I can't deploy my people unless we have proper authorization."

"I've got the authorization," McCall interrupted. He took his leather billfold from inside his coat pocket and flipped it open, flashing his credentials, including the warrant to enter any premises if he felt there was reasonable cause. The captain borrowed a flashlight from a trooper standing behind him and looked them over. He drew a deep breath, held it, and exhaled.

"I don't know. We're not even sure it's his cabin."

"Listen," McCall snapped. "We've got a dangerous fugitive on the loose, and he may be holed up in that cabin. We found the stolen car he was driving only a couple of hundred yards away. There *is* no other habitation in the area. Now, I'd say that's reasonable cause to suspect he might be hiding inside. So let me make one thing perfectly clear. We're going inside, with or without your men. This operation is under my jurisdiction. The decision to enter is mine, and I'll take full responsibility. Your men can either join us or pull back. But while you're waiting for authorization, we're goint to be catching a killer. You got that, Captain?"

"I hear you, McCall," the captain said, reining in the anger edging his voice. State troopers were bred to be aggressive, never-give-an-inch sons-of-bitches. More than anything else, they didn't like other law enforcement agencies muscling in on what they considered their turf. As a result, Lincoln could only stand back and admire McCall's tenacity. If he had to admit it himself, Lincoln couldn't have handled the captain any better.

"So what's it going to be, Hansen?"

Hansen's jaw jutted even further, his temples throbbed, and he shifted his weight. Finally he turned his head and spat on the ground as if ridding his mouth of something particularly distasteful. He lifted his head and leveled a steely gaze at McCall.

"All right," he said. "Give me a couple of minutes. At least let's coordinate this thing right. As long as its agreed you're taking the fallout if anything goes wrong. And it better not."

"I already said I would."

"Fine," Hansen said, and squared his considerable breadth of shoulder. "I'll order my people up just outside the doors and windows. Meanwhile, I'll pull up the cruisers in a line in front of the cabin and turn the floodlamps on the front of the place. We've already got officers stationed out back, in case he tries to make a rear exit into the woods. We'll move in on your orders."

McCall nodded and Hansen was off, giving instructions to his second-in-command.

It didn't take long to deploy everyone, state troopers and FBI side-by-side with a handful of local cops looking on from the fringes. Hansen ordered the floodlights on the cruisers turned on, and the whole area around the cabin was illuminated in a harsh, cold glare. The place jumped out of the dark in sharp relief, and Lincoln thought he could see every nail hole in every plank of weathered board.

"Let me talk to him first," Lincoln said. "It's a long shot, but I might be able to talk him out."

McCall stood behind the line of cruisers with a bullhorn in his hand, which he handed over to Lincoln. There were a pair of snipers, crouched, poised on either side of them. Lincoln raised the bullhorn to his lips.

"Snow, this is Lincoln. If you're in there, I suggest you come out now. The cabin is surrounded. There's no escape. There are only two ways out of there: through the front door, with your hands behind your head, or in a body bag, and I know you're not ready for that. When the time comes, you'll want to pick your own way. We both know this isn't it. Now, what say we end this thing right here and now? This part of the game is over. You lost. Take it like a man."

They waited for what seemed like hours, though only a

handful of minutes passed. There was no sound or movement from inside the cabin.

Only deadly quiet.

And the impregnable glare of the spotlights rebounding off the windows like blind eyes.

"I've had enough," McCall said, and took the bullhorn from Lincoln. "We're going in after this bastard. If it's a shootout he wants, then that's just what he's going to get." He lifted the bullhorn to his mouth and shouted through it. "We've given you your chance, you son-of-a-bitch. Now you've got exactly ten seconds to come out, or we're coming in. Ten," McCall rasped. "Nine. Eight. Seven . . ."

It wasn't until McCall had gotten to three that Lincoln got the bad feeling in the pit of his stomach. Something wasn't right. He looked across at the cabin, the agents and troopers ready to burst through the doors and windows, he looked at McCall, shouting out his inevitable countdown, but it was already too late to warn him; he had already reached zero. The men and women rose into action and the forced entry into the cabin had begun.

Lincoln didn't know exactly what his bad feelings intimated until he saw the flash of orange-white light from inside the cabin and saw the three agents who'd broken down the front door thrown backwards outside the cabin with a deafening roar. He had been suckered. Snow had led him here; he'd *wanted* Lincoln to find the cabin. It was a chess game, all right, and Lincoln had jumped at a valuable but expendable piece that Snow had decided to sacrifice in defense of an even more valuable piece. Lincoln had jumped to take the proffered piece like a fool, not seeing the powerful piece it concealed, which now swooped as if from out of nowhere to put Lincoln in check.

There was another flash of light from inside the cabin and then another, and all of a sudden agents and troopers were stumbling out of the cabin holding various parts of their bodies or shielding their eyes, some falling to the ground, those who were still on their feet helping up their fallen comrades. The place was booby-trapped, goddammit. That's what Lincoln's sixth sense had been trying to tell him: Snow had turned the cabin into a death trap.

There were what sounded like a series of explosions, and then a fire started that quickly climbed the walls and made its way to the roof. A couple more people staggered from the quickly burning building, running pell-mell, blinded by smoke and blood. The weathered wood burned like dry hay. The flames leapt in a nightmarish dance against the surrounding darkness of the woods, illuminating the grotesquely stunted trees as well as the shell-shocked looks on the faces of those who'd somehow escaped the cabin.

"Look what the hell you've done!" Hansen came up screaming at the top of his lungs, his face red in the firelight. "Look what the hell you've done! I've got at least six men down! This was your call! *Your call!*"

McCall looked shaken. He hadn't expected anything like this, even as he'd watched the cabin burn to the ground and heard the groans of wounded and dying police.

Lincoln stepped between Hansen and McCall.

"We know it was our call. We stand behind it. You go inform whatever authorities you have to inform and get enough ambulances here to care for the wounded. Right now, on this site, at this time, we are the authority."

"This isn't the last you've heard from me," the captain growled. "You can stick that where the sun don't shine and collect interest on it."

"I'll take that under advisement," Lincoln said drily. "Now I suggest you go and do your duty, Captain."

Hansen gave him a look that might kill a man not already dying, turned sharply on his heel, and stalked away. He started shouting orders to his subordinates, who gathered around him in a confused hive of pointless activity. Meanwhile, Lincoln took McCall by the arm and led him a few feet from the line of cars where he seemed to be standing paralyzed. Lincoln grabbed the younger man's shoulders and shook him.

"It's not your fault, son," he said. "Get that through your head right now. If anyone's to blame, it's me."

"I gave the order," McCall said dully.

"But I know Snow. That's why I'm here. I should have seen what he was up to. I did, but not until it was too late."

"I gave the order," McCall said again.

"Listen to me, McCall," Lincoln said. "There's a long way to go yet. We've made a mistake. But we can make an even bigger one. And that's to let this cripple us. It's just what he wants. So pull yourself together and let's get on with it. I need you."

The flames were dying in McCall's eyes.

"I'm finished."

"Maybe, maybe not."

McCall waved to the stretchers bearing off the wounded.

"The Agency will never forgive this. *I'll* never forgive it."

"Then there's only one question left: how do you want to go out?"

McCall wiped the sooty tears away from the clean planes of his young face.

"What do we do now?"

"We order backhoes to get in here and dig up the land around his damn place, sift through the ashes of the cabin, see what we can find."

"You don't think he's in there?"

"No," Lincoln said. "I don't think he'd choose to go out this way. But we'll look anyway."

"In the meantime?"

"What else? We wait."

9:30 P.M.

Kate heard the muffled sound of a phone ringing, not in the living room or kitchen, but the cell phone buried in the briefcase she'd earlier put down in the dining room along with her car keys.

She'd been standing nearby in the kitchen, emptying the

dishwasher, trying to keep busy, when she'd heard the short, staccato ringing. She walked quietly into the next room, grabbed the bag, and glanced into the living room to make sure no one else had heard the phone. Jeff and the four men sent to protect her were watching a football game on TV, cheering a touchdown. Penelope was barking.

She brought the bag back into the kitchen, laid it on the table, and rummaged around inside until she found the compact gray phone. She unfolded it and silenced the ringing with the push of a finger.

She kept her voice low so as not to be overheard.

"Yes?"

"Hello, Katherine. I thought I'd try a phone that wasn't bugged this time. Now we can be alone."

Somehow, Kate had known it would be him, but another part of her mind was rapidly thinking how—

"Wondering how I got your cell-phone number?" Snow completed the thought. "Don't waste your time worrying over details like that. Your life is not so private as you'd like to think. No one's is, for that matter. All it takes is a little observation and the secrets are revealed to those with eyes to see. But enough about that. Our time is short." There was a crackling of static on the phone and Snow's voice came back faded. "You really should make sure your battery is charged. You never know when you're going to be getting an important call." It was something Jeff was always reminding her about, especially in case she needed the phone in an emergency, but hearing the warning from Snow made her feel sick to her stomach.

"You betrayed me, Katherine."

Kate swallowed hard. So there it was, out in the open. He knew it was she who'd turned over the confidential files to Lincoln.

"Is that what this is all about, Dr. Snow?"

"Only peripherally. I told you, I wanted to finish our therapy. I want to get at the truth."

"The truth about what?"

"You know better than to ask that question, Katherine."

"What if I refuse to see you?"

"Then the killings continue. And I'm sure you don't want that on your conscience—do you?"

"No," Kate said.

"So predictable," Snow sighed. "Conscience does us all in at the end. Oh, well. Lucky for me. Then we have a date. There's a phone booth on the boardwalk where you run every morning. Why do you insist on concerning yourself with how I know these things? It's unimportant now. But if you must satisfy your curiosity, it's simply a process of symbolic synchronistic logic, a form of intuition, in layman's terms. You have a lot to run away from, Katherine. The Chinese believed that the past, present, and future are encoded in any particular moment. They expressed these snapshots of reality in the hexagrams of the *I Ching*. To the expert eye, every object, every situation, every personality becomes a hexagram of the *I Ching*. All you have to do is look at the hexagram and its meaning becomes clear . . ." The rest of what Snow said was broken up by a long stretch of static. Kate thought the battery had gone dead and she'd lost him. Sure enough, the indicator light was on.

Unexpectedly his voice came back on the phone, so soft and intimate, she felt as if he weren't using the phone at all, but whispering in her ear, speaking directly to her through telepathic means.

"This is your last chance, Katherine."

"But they won't let me out of the house."

"You'll find a way," Snow replied. "I have confidence in you. You're a very good liar, Katherine."

38

Under the harsh glare of portable phosphorescent lights, yellow backhoes dug up the ground surrounding the scorched patch of earth that had been Snow's cabin hideaway. The portable lights were suspended on long rickety silver poles buried precariously in the sandy earth, which was now a snakepit of black wires. The wires were running to a JCP&L generator making enough noise that it was necessary to shout in order to be heard.

"They want me to suspend all operations pending further notice," McCall said glumly, returning from the cell phone in the black LTD, picking his way carefully over the wires. He waited until he was close enough to Lincoln so as not to be overheard.

Lincoln nodded, expecting the directive. The damage had been bad. Of six troopers down, two had been killed outright, another had lost his leg in the series of explosions, and the other three looked to survive their wounds. Five agents had also gone down. One was dead, another was three-quarters of the way there, and a third had probably lost his eyes. The last two Lincoln had spoken to himself. They were dazed, bleeding, and in terrible pain, but they would recover. A half dozen others had gone off in the ambulances called in from surrounding towns, all suffering from minor burns, abrasions, and smoke inhalation. All in all, by Agency standards, the raid had been a major disaster.

"They told me not to do anything until authorized personnel gets here. Do you understand what that means? I'm being relieved of my command."

"I understand."

"All this," McCall waved his hand at the backhoes overturning the sand, "is supposed to stop."

"We can't stop now," Lincoln said calmly. "We're in the middle of the chase. If we let up he can get away."

"What the hell can I do? I've been given direct orders. If I disobey them . . ." McCall shrugged. "I'm fucked."

"Don't you get it, kid? You're already fucked. What happened here will have you riding a desk for the next thirty years. You've seen all the field action you're ever going to see. That is, if you quit right now."

"Well, what the hell would you do if you were me?"

"If I were you, I'd probably follow orders and hope for the best. But knowing what I know now, I'd go ahead and finish what I started, knowing it'll be my last chance, one way or another. I'd get the bastard who did this to me and my men."

"You don't give a damn about me or anyone else, do you, Lincoln? You'd sacrifice anything to catch him. You don't care if you take us all down in the process."

"You're right, kid," Lincoln said. "Maybe that alone should tell you something."

"Yeah, it tells me—"

McCall was interrupted by an agent clambering toward them, holding a soot-blackened handkerchief over his face. He pulled it away as he approached and shouted over the grinding sound of the generator.

"You've got to come see this, sir," he said to McCall. "We found . . . you've got to come."

They picked their way over the sand and wires into the patch of harsh blue-white light. Lincoln felt as if he were being x-rayed, as if every bone in his body were visible, as if the tumor in his brain could be seen as clearly as if his skull were made of cellophane. He had to shield his eyes from the glare with one hand and fight the urge to place his other hand against the left side of his head.

They finally got to the place where the agent was leading them, a roughly dug trough in the sandy loam about four feet deep and about twenty feet long. Lincoln and McCall stood at the edge and looked down into what was a makeshift burial plot. They could see the yellowed bones in sharp relief against the light: rib cages, leg bones, arms with skeletal fingers still attached to fleshless hands, and, of course, the skulls, their staring black eyeholes looking up at Lincoln in mute accusation, their grinning jaws full of sand, dropped open in what looked like dumb surprise at having been found. It would take some time for a forensic team to piece together the bones, but Lincoln estimated that he was looking at the remains of at least twenty bodies.

"I've got him," he shouted over the roar of the generator, pointing into the mass grave. "I've finally got him now. There are the bodies."

"I'd say you still had one last thing to do," McCall shouted back.

"What's that?"

"Catch the bastard."

"Are you with me, son?"

"Wouldn't miss it for the world."

For the first time in close to five years, Lincoln grinned.

10:05 P.M.

Kate couldn't wait any longer.

She had walked back and forth into the living room, gone upstairs, and come back down, letting the men see her. She couldn't leave too soon or they would surely miss her presence in the house and come looking for her. But if she waited any longer, she'd miss the rendezvous at the phone booth. She knew from her past sessions with Snow what a stickler he was for punctuality, always arriving at exactly the right time, never a minute early, never a minute late. She felt the butterflies in her stomach at the prospect of meeting him after all these years. She could hardly believe she was actually going through with the clandestine meeting, but deep down she knew she had no choice. She could not be responsible for any more people dying. Besides, he had not threatened her, only expressed a desire to finish his therapy, whatever that meant.

Kate double-checked on the men in the living room, satisfying herself that they were still engaged in the football game, before going to the cellar door.

She winced at the grating sound the skeleton key made in the lock and paused a moment, before opening the door and making her way carefully down the creaking wooden stairs to the basement. She had read in some mystery novel that if you kept your feet to the edges of stairs they were less inclined to protest your weight, so that was what she did, half-expecting, half-hoping that with each step she would hear Jeff's voice from the head of the stairs, demanding to know what she was doing. Still, having decided to meet Snow, she felt good to actually be getting on with it. The last half-hour of waiting had been murder.

She made it to the foot of the stairs and across the concrete floor to the window over the workbench. It was a typical rectangular wood-framed basement window, small, just barely big enough for an average adult-sized body to squeeze through, as if specifically made for burglars. She examined Jeff's handiwork. He had driven the large nails three-quarters of the way into the frame so that the window, which opened inward, could not be forced from the outside. Kate searched around the workbench for the hammer, cursing herself when memory supplied her with the picture of Jeff emerging from the basement with the hammer and nails in hand. She futilely tried to pry the nails up with her bare fingers before accepting the fact that she'd have to go back upstairs to get the hammer.

She picked her way up the stairs as carefully as she had come down, cringing at the occasional squeak from the warped wood, and cracked the door to the kitchen. Certain no one had gone out there for a soda or anything, she spotted the hammer on the counter by the microwave, grabbed it, and started back down the stairs. This time she moved quickly and more confidently and seemed to make less noise. She climbed onto the workbench, and crouching on her heels, used the hammer to pull the ten-penny nails from the window frame. It took less than a minute. She undid the hook-and-eye latch at the bottom and pulled the window open. She then shimmied through the frame and climbed to her feet on the small patio in her tiny fifteen-by-fifteen foot backyard, standard issue in Ocean Grove, where space was at a premium, and the houses built close enough together to reach out your window and hand a cup of sugar to your next-door neighbor.

She thought of the policeman sitting in front of the house and realized she'd have to cut through the backyard bordering her property to get to the street behind hers. A shiver ran down her spine when she realized how pointless it was for the cop to be sitting outside the front of her house when Snow could just as easily approach from the back, as she was doing. Kate had thought to wear her thick rubber gardening gloves to avoid the thorns of Mrs. Adams's bramble roses, which sprawled in rich profusion over the picket fence bordering their properties. Still, as she climbed over, she felt the thorns catch her jeans and her thick sweatshirt. With more than a little caution, she cleared the fence, hoping Mrs. Adams or any of the other neighbors didn't happen to be looking out the window, and moved quickly down the path to the front of the elderly widow's house. She opened the gate to the white picket fence surrounding the front yard, glanced quickly behind her, turned left, and started jogging down the street toward the damp, salty smell of the beach.

10:10 P.M.

Penelope was barking.

She had trotted off into the kitchen only a few seconds earlier on a mission of canine urgency that Jeff and the others had ignored until the barking had started. One of the cops turned to Jeff, a question on his face, a vague look of indecision.

Jeff shook his head. "She's probably trying to get at the pizza box I threw in the garbage. I'll check on her."

The policeman nodded.

Jeff went into the kitchen and found the dog standing not on hind paws, her muzzle buried in the trashcan, but in front of the cellar door, which was slightly ajar. Penelope was staring intently at the crack, barking, her curled, bushy tail waving excitedly back and forth.

"You silly mutt," Jeff said, stepping forward and opening the door for the dog, who went bolting down the stairs. A moment later the barking stopped.

Jeff saw the light coming from the side of the basement where the washer and dryer stood. He figured Kate had gone down to do some laundry. He grinned. And they said there was no difference between the sexes. Here they were in the most dangerous situation of their lives, and how did they respond? The men were all gathered around the television, watching football, while the woman of the house was downstairs, washing clothes. He made a calculated decision not to point this out to Kate; she'd deck him with a left hook.

He was halfway down the stairs, ducking under a low beam and calling "Kate," but he got no answer. He laid his hand on the railing and walked the rest of the way down the stairs and passed the boiler and the oil burner, looking around the corner to where the large white washer and dryer stood. There was no one there. Jeff looked around for Penelope, whistling softly for her, but the dog was nowhere to be found.

"What the hell," Jeff muttered, his heart rate tripling.

It was probably nothing.

Still—

He was about to bolt back up the stairs, alert the cops sitting in the living room, and begin a search of the house for Kate. But before he could turn, he felt the numbness in his limbs and the darkness rising up from the pit of his stomach like black water, turning his cry for help into a gurgling moan as he sank unconscious to the cold concrete floor.

39

Kate jogged down the wet street, trying to avoid the puddles.

She could hear the crash of the waves, the long sussurating ebb tide as the water was dragged back into the sea. She ran through curtains of mist, her face and sweatshirt damp, the taste of salt in her mouth. She lifted her left wrist and pressed a button on her watch. In the soft aqua glow she could read the digital display: 10:15. She should have started earlier. She was already late.

She doubled her pace and then doubled it again until she was sprinting toward the boardwalk, careless of the puddles, her feet splashing cold water onto her socks and jeans.

She ran down the slick gray boards, heedless of her footing, staring at her goal, a pay phone illuminated by an overhead streetlamp. Even at this distance, even over the roar of the angry sea, she could hear it ringing.

"Damn!"

It stopped ringing by the time she had closed the distance by half. By the time she got to the phone, she was doubled over, her hand on her knees, gulping for breath. The phone above her was dead silent. When she finally caught her breath she lifted the receiver, heard the dial tone, and slammed it back down in disgust. No sooner had she done so than the phone rang. Kate snatched it up in the middle of the first ring.

"You disappoint me, Katherine. You know my insistence on punctuality."

"I'm sorry, Dr. Snow. I had trouble leaving the house. The windows were nailed shut and the hammer was upstairs. I forgot. It took me longer than I'd expected. You've got to believe me. Certainly you're not going to punish me over a couple of minutes."

There was a long silence on the other end. Kate held her breath.

Snow said only two words.

"You're late."

And hung up the phone.

Kate stared at the receiver in disbelief, hearing the dial tone. She finally hung up.

She looked at her watch.

It was 10:18 P.M.

She jogged her way slowly back to the house.

10:18 P.M.

Lincoln watched the lightning fall.

It was falling inside his head alone, a private storm, the phosphorescent light zigzagging through his skull, scorching brain tissue, leaving vivid after-images behind his closed eyes: old memories, old dreams, new nightmares. They were in the back of the black car speeding toward Ocean Grove. Lincoln opened his eyes and stared out the darkened window only to see his own face reflected back, white, haggard, lifeless. He wondered how much longer he could go on: he looked like a walking dead man.

The lightning fell again, a bolt that went down his backbone, grounding itself in his feet, making them tingle. His left arm flopped involuntarily, the movement catching McCall's eye.

"You okay?"

"Yeah," Lincoln snapped.

McCall nodded and turned back to his own window, staring at his own face, no doubt contemplating the premature end of his career. Lincoln took the opportunity to reach into his jacket pocket and pull out the brown pill bottle. He shook two pills free and dry-swallowed them. Funny how, even now, he was embarrassed to let someone see him taking his medication. He saw it as a sign of weakness and realized with some surprise that although he had fully accepted it himself, he wasn't yet willing to let other people know how close he was to dying.

He picked up the cell phone on the seat next to him and dialed Kate's number.

The line was busy.

Lincoln wondered if it was Snow calling Kate back to inform her of what had happened in the cranberry bog. Certainly Snow had good cause to gloat over that: Lincoln had fallen for it hook, line, and sinker. No doubt Snow was having a good laugh at Lincoln's expense.

Well, Lincoln thought, we'll have to correct that situation.

He didn't know a lot of Oriental philosophy, certainly not as much as Snow, but he did know the old Confucian axiom, more true in Lincoln's line of work than most others: he who laughs last laughs best.

10:20 P.M.

Snow lay the receiver on its side and turned to Jeff, lying flat on his back on the floor. He stood over him, staring into his face.

"Do you know why I left you alive?"

Jeff tried to make a fist with his right hand, but his fingers wouldn't respond. Instead, he attempted to lift his arm to grab hold of the man's throat. But like his hand, his arm wouldn't work: it felt as if it weighed a thousand pounds; he couldn't lift it an inch from the floor.

In the end, he found himself staring into the strangely vacant eyes of the man standing over him, like two rooms whose occupants only just left. Hypnotic, the eyes seemed to draw him in, forcing him to fill the void, until he was locked inside those empty gray rooms.

"I let you live because I want you to testify to what is going to happen. You shouldn't consider yourself lucky. What you will see will curse you for a lifetime. You've got the most painful job of all. I want you to witness the truth."

Jeff tried to move again, but the effort was only half-hearted. He already felt separated from his body.

"Don't bother trying to move," Snow said, reading his thoughts. "It's quite useless. The impulses from your brain to your nerves are blocked by the pins I inserted into your chi meridians. You are effectively paralyzed."

Jeff felt the rage and helplessness build inside him as he paced the empty gray rooms that were Snow's eyes. In the distance he heard the recorded voice of an operator informing him that if he would like to make a call to please try again.

40

10:30 P.M.

Kate jogged home, slowing to a walk as she turned down the street behind her house.

She darted down the path through Mrs. Adams's backyard and climbed over the fence covered with bramble roses, dropping unscratched into her own yard and heading toward the basement window illuminated from within by the light she'd left on over the washer and dryer.

She knelt by the side of the house, pushed open the window, and climbed through backwards, careful not to catch her head on the jamb, letting her legs dangle until she felt the workbench under her feet. She crouched there for perhaps half a minute to collect herself and listen to the noises coming from the house.

Everything was quiet.

She slid down from the workbench and crossed the concrete floor toward the wooden stairs. This time she didn't need to be careful not to make any noise and ironically seemed to make less than when she'd been creeping down the stairs, afraid each footfall was going to give her away. She pushed open the kitchen door at the head of the stairs and peeked into the living room. Somehow, she'd expected to find the house in a whirlwind of police activity centering around her disappearance. She figured someone would have discovered her absence and all hell would have broken loose. Instead, the four agents were still sitting in front of the TV in exactly the same positions as before she'd left.

Some bodyguards they made, she thought.

Still, she had to admit she hadn't been gone long, and she'd done all she could to disguise her absence.

But how much more could Snow do?

She couldn't stop the thought, which made the small hairs at the back of her neck stand up and tingle.

She noticed that Jeff wasn't among the men, seated around the living room and she saw no sign of Penelope. She figured Jeff must have take the dog out for her last pee of the evening.

Kate walked out of the kitchen, behind the seated men, none of whom turned around to acknowledge her passing, and up the stairs, stopping only briefly in her bedroom to get the key, before making her way up to the third floor.

From the moment she'd heard Snow say he wanted to finish his therapy with her, Kate was more convinced than ever that the secret to his twisted psyche lay buried in the tapes of their sessions. Now she crept quietly up to the third floor, not wanting to be disturbed, and placed the skeleton key into the lock. She turned the knob and opened the door. She ran her hand along the wall for the light and switched it on, holding her eyes closed for a couple of seconds to give the mice a chance to scamper away into their hiding places. After a few seconds she opened her eyes, but what she saw was worse than a mouse. What she saw were—

Pins.

Hundreds of them. Stuck in the walls, the floorboards, the old furniture, the boxes, the desk. Kate felt her heart thump in her chest and felt a brief moment of dizziness shadow her brain before the adrenaline took over and her head cleared. He'd been here. The bastard had actually been in her house. She walked slowly, as if hypnotized, toward the tape recorder situ-

ated so perfectly on the pin-studded desk she had no doubt that
that was where she was supposed to go next. She pressed the
play button and heard his voice come through the speaker.

*"Hello, Katherine. I hope you're not too surprised to hear
from me. Certainly you didn't think I would refuse you a second
chance, after all we've meant to each other. I'm forced to admit
that I have a certain weakness for you. It must be karma. I'm
inclined to believe that we must have been linked somehow in
a past life. Perhaps I've killed you before. I know that's not
terribly scientific, but sometimes emotions are more important
than science, wouldn't you agree? There are some things science will never be able to fully explain. Like love and hate,
synchronicity, and destiny. Our relationship has the form of
destiny. But alas, our drama is playing to a close. You have
one last chance, Katherine. One last chance, and I hope you
won't disappoint me. I want you to meet me at the old Palace
Amusements on the boardwalk, I'm sure you know the one. I
want you to meet me inside the fun house. We are going to
have some fun there, Katherine, you and I. Certainly I don't
have to tell you to come alone and to come punctually this
time. Life on this earth is shorter than you think. As the sages
said, we should live each moment as mindfully as if it were
our last. And by the way, please take this tape with you when
you come. We don't want anyone interrupting our last session,
do we, Katherine? You've got thirty minutes. The clock is
already ticking. See you soon. Alex."*

The voice ended and the tape spooled through the sensor,
emitting the sound of empty static. Kate pressed the stop button,
rewound the tape, but did not listen again. She didn't need to.
She remembered all too well what Snow had said.

She crept back down the stairs, passed the men in the living
room, and went back down the basement stairs. As she climbed
through the window she heard the upstairs phone ringing. She
was sure it wasn't Snow. She had her instructions; he wouldn't
be calling the house again. This was between her and him alone
now. Nonetheless, she thought it more than a little odd that no
one was picking up.

10:35 P.M.

Kate never saw the dog.

Penelope was lying on her back between the washer and dryer, her black lips pulled back in a silent snarl, her paws twitching, her soft pink belly lined with a double row of silver pins.

10:36 P.M.

Something was wrong.

Lincoln didn't need his intuition to tell him that. He punched the number on the cell phone again, waited eight rings, and terminated the call.

"What's wrong?" McCall asked.

"No one's answering at the Bennett house."

"Shit. We left four men there. You don't think—"

"I don't know what to think," Lincoln snapped. He dialed the Neptune Police Department, identified himself, and ordered them to get every available car to Kate's house as soon as possible.

He pressed the button on the cell phone and let it rest in his hand beside him on the car seat. He felt a hollow feeling in the pit of his stomach. If this was a chess match, Snow was clearing the board of pieces, setting Lincoln up for the inevitable end game.

For the first time since the hunt had begun, Lincoln allowed himself to admit that he was no match for Snow. The doctor had been in charge of the game from the start, leading Lincoln around by the nose, forcing him into blunder after blunder. Lincoln realized that his last and only hope was to get lucky. No sooner did he have the thought than he felt the distant throb of the tumor inside his skull, just enough to remind him that his luck was quickly running out.

41

Jeff sat on the dusty wooden floor, staring at a reflection of himself in the mirror.

His face was grim, determined, red with pointless effort. He had once seen a demonstration of acupuncture at the hospital. A Chinese surgeon had come to America to show how operations could be performed painlessly without anesthesia, using only the correct application of needles. The surgeon removed a man's diseased appendix to the amazement of all, cutting through the fat and muscle of his abdominal wall while the patient remained talking and fully conscious. Aside from a few of the Asian doctors, the staff had remained skeptical. The performance was a medical curiosity, little more, and had no true application in a modern Western hospital, even if it did prove itself not only safer but just as effective as conventional methods, significantly reducing a patient's recovery time.

Jeff had watched with more interest than most but knew that he'd have no use for the procedure. There was precious little time for the subtleties of acupuncture in an emergency room.

Now he was experiencing first-hand just how effective acupuncture could be.

As he sat on the floor virtually paralyzed, he wished he hadn't been so quick to dismiss the relevance of acupuncture to his practice. He wished he had read up on the subject and payed closer attention to the little visiting Chinese doctor.

If he had, perhaps he wouldn't be in this position right now . . .

10:50 P.M.

The black car eased up to the front of the house, double-parking behind two police crusiers, their lights flashing wildly.

People were standing on their front porches trying to get a look at what was going on. A few others gathered on the sidewalk and were held back by a uniformed cop.

"Oh, no," McCall muttered. "Not again."

Lincoln didn't say anything. He yanked open the car door and went straight past the harried officer to the front steps. He grabbed the bannister, took a deep breath of the cool night air, and prepared himself for what he would find inside.

There was another cop standing guard at the front door. McCall flashed his ID and both he and Lincoln went into the house. Inside, a plainclothes detective was questioning the policeman who had been sitting guard outside in the car.

"I didn't see anything," he repeated over and over again. He was a tall, gangly, greasy-haired man with a premature paunch and tears running down his pockmarked face. "I didn't see anything."

Lincoln stared stonily at the carnage in the living room. All four men were dead, their erect posture on the chairs surrounding the television belying their glassy-eyed gazes. A casual onlooker would have mistaken them for alive, four men watching a Monday night football game. From what Lincoln could see, there wasn't a mark on any of them, but that was a job for the medical examiner. They had obviously been taken completely unawares, dispatched with all the skill of a master assassin, a look of faint surprise on each frozen, slightly discolored face, as if to say, "Why didn't you warn me what we were up against?"

"How?" McCall asked. "That's what I want to know. How did he get in here and kill four men without any of them so much as moving a muscle?"

There was no answer to that question. If McCall didn't realize that by now, he never would. Lincoln's gaze shifted to the TV set just to have somewhere else to look. It was late in the third quarter. The Bears were losing 31–0.

Lincoln thought he knew just how the Bears felt.

Just then two uniformed officers emerged from the basement, their guns unholstered, pointing at the floor.

Lincoln snapped out of his trance. He crossed the floor in three large strides, grabbing one of the uniformed cops by the shoulder.

"The woman and the man," he said. "Kate Bennett and Jeff Hudson. Did anyone find them?"

"No," a young black officer replied. He pointed over Lincoln's shoulder to the living room. "Just the bodies that are in there."

Lincoln exhaled a sigh of relief. At least there was still a chance that they weren't dead yet.

"It looks like the perpetrator came in through the basement window over the workbench," the black officer's partner said. "All the other basement windows are nailed shut. Why that one wasn't—"

He shrugged.

Just then a rumpled-looking plainclothes detective with a short gray crew cut came down the stairs from the second floor.

"You guys Lincoln and McCall?"

"Yeah," McCall said.

"Then you're going to want to see what we found up here." Lincoln's heart skipped a beat.

"More bodies?" he asked, the words forced between pursed lips, trying not to let the emotion escape.

"No," the detective said gruffly. "Even weirder."

42

Kate wondered how he'd known to pick the fun house.

As she ran along the rain-slicked streets, passing under the streetlamps shuttering between light and dark like blank movie film, she forced the memories back into the black sack of subconsciousness where she'd confined them nearly three decades ago. She crossed the bridge between Ocean Grove and Asbury Park and saw the pale green Palace Amusements building rising beside the boardwalk. The place had been closed for years. Economic collapse, a failed renovation project, and a growing crime rate had turned the once-thriving boardwalk into a wasteland.

Kate wasn't taking any chances at being late this time. She ran at top speed, feeling a stitch in her side, the chill sweat on her body.

How many times had she passed the boarded-up building in her car or seen it in the distance on her morning runs? Somehow it gave her a sense of comfort that it had been closed, as if it ended a chapter of her life, and she waited for the day when the place would be torn down to make room for an apartment complex or a parking lot. She never dreamt she would one day be forced to return there.

Kate stopped about ten yards in front of the building to catch her breath.

Across the way, in the shadows of a store that had once sold saltwater taffy, two young men seemed to be engaged in some kind of drug deal. They didn't pay her any attention. But a voice came from behind her, startling her.

"Hey, baby, whatcha lookin' for?"

She turned and saw a tall, skinny, bleary-eyed black man with wooly white hair and a gray stubble along his chin. He was dressed in an army surplus jacket and holding a dark brown bottle. She could smell the stench of alcohol and stale sweat coming from inside the folds of his coat. He grinned and in the dim light she could see a sparse row of yellow teeth set in his shriveled gums.

"Hey, where ya goin' so fass?" he slurred, grabbing for her awkwardly, as Kate twisted from his grasp and ran the final thirty feet to the fun house.

"Ya goin' in the spook house?" The man laughed, attracting the scowling attention of the two young men by the saltwater taffy store, who shortly turned back to their business. "Ya doan' want to be goin' in there. The boogie man'll git ya for sure."

Kate was afraid the man would try to follow her, but he was more drunk than sexually interested. He laughed again, turned, and shuffled slowly away into the wind, toward a bench fronting on the dark ocean.

Kate found herself standing in front of the fun house, its main entrance blocked by a sheet of corrugated steel, its surface covered with the stylized signature of graffiti artists. Kate looked to her left and saw a light shining over a side door. She walked around the front of the building, put one hand on the knob and the other against the door, and gave a firm push. She half-expected, half-hoped it would resist her efforts, but instead it easily slid inward as if welcoming her inside.

She carefully closed the door behind her and let her eyes

adjust to the gloom. Above her head the ceiling soared into a dizzying blackness. She felt her heart beat double-time and gritted her teeth, remembering the first and only time she'd been here. Somehow, it all seemed appropriate that it would end here. Everything she was afraid of was in this building. The fears she thought she could run away from were waiting for her, as fears always did, and this time she wouldn't turn away. This time she would face them head-on.

She had no choice.

A light came on and Kate turned to see the line of cars illuminated against a painted background of drooling, hulking monsters. Over the pounding of her heart in her ears she could hear the febrile tension of the electricity running through the rails under the cars wheels and knew what she was expected to do next.

Sure enough, no sooner had she settled herself into the third car from the front than the train of cars began to move along the rail with a loud grating sound, as if they hadn't moved since she'd last sat in them. She looked up and saw a devil's face painted on the wall above her, the archway designed to represent Satan's open mouth, complete with jagged white teeth, the cars rattling their way down his black gullet, presumably into the bowels of hell. She had just enough time to read the inscription between his blood-tipped horns: *Abandon hope all ye who enter here . . .*

The car moved forward through the open mouth and Kate felt the black straps flapping over her head and shoulders. She threw her hands up to fend them off, ducking her face, as they continued to beat over her back. From somewhere far off she heard the recorded sound of insane laughter. Suddenly her stomach lurched as the car plunged on the rails down a short, steep embankment toward a series of red lightbulbs disguised to look like glowing coals. The effects were cheap, but Kate still screamed when a dummy dropped from the ceiling suspended at the end of a hangman's noose. It was all coming back to her now. She felt her heart pounding, pounding just as it had that day nearly thirty years ago, but for an altogether different reason. She couldn't have known then what real-life horror awaited her in this place; nor did she know now why Snow had chosen the fun house for their final rendezvous, but this time she was no longer innocent.

A light came on to her right and a moldy-looking vampire rose from his plywood coffin. In another lit alcove a stocky man in a blue workshirt stood holding his head at his hip, the head warning her not to go further, except at her own peril.

The car rounded a pitch-black corner and Kate brushed away the cobwebs clinging to her face and neck, probably the only real effect in the place, and all the more unsettling for that.

When she came out of the dark she was confronted with the spectacle of a witch being burned at the stake, her recorded screams still creepily realistic enough to raise goosebumps on Kate's arms. There was a depiction of a charnel house where rats crawled among human remains, and another sharp, dark turn where lights suddenly flashed to reveal a group of skeletons reaching toward the car to pluck out its still-living occupant. Something screeched overhead and Kate looked up in time to see a shriveled human head on a pair of batlike wings diving toward her only to follow the trajectory of its invisible wire back up into the recesses of the ceiling.

The car came to a grinding halt in front of a labyrinth of black-painted walls.

It figured.

Kate knew that this was where the ride ended for her, where it would always end for her. She had made her mistake here last time, and she was making it again. Beyond that labyrinth was where Snow would meet her.

She climbed out of the car and the train moved on without her, leaving her alone to face the labyrinth.

She took a step forward and then another, hesitating before the labyrinth, before slowly walking inside. The light behind her grew smaller and fainter and then was extinguished entirely as she felt around with her hands to find her way. The place was full of odd angles, blind corners, dead ends; it was impossible to stay oriented. She felt the panic rising up inside her as the dark pressed in around her from all sides. She wanted to run, but knew that was pointless; there was no place to run to. She would have turned back, but the way out was already as incomprehensible as the way forward. She heard the laughter—not the canned laughter of the fun house, but the mocking laughter of her memories, the laughter that greeted her screams as hands reached out for her from the darkness, the laughter of those who misunderstood her cries for help as part of the game, instead of a genuine plea for help. She remembered how she ran, crashing into walls, the hot breath of her pursuers right behind her, the pain, the anger, the frustration, and most of all, the fear. Even now, trying to control her emotions, she felt breathless, claustrophobic in the utter darkness, the black walls drinking up every atom of light, forcing her to follow the thin lifeline her memory threw out. She grasped it with all the concentration she could muster and followed it, a kind of intuition, a trail of crumbs that led her out of the blackness, the nightmare, the howling hell of memory.

At first it was just a tiny flicker, but a few steps forward and it grew to the size of an orange, and then it enlongated into a blinding white pillar—a pillar of pure white light.

Kate stumbled out of the dark labyrinth as if she were being expelled from the winding interior of a snake and found herself where she knew she'd find him at last.

In the hall of mirrors.

She took a step forward and saw Snow at last, multiplied a hundred times in the mirrors surrounding her.

A voice came from somewhere in the room.

His voice.

"Welcome, Katherine," he said.

10:59 P.M.

Jeff watched helpless, trying to cry out, his tongue dead in his mouth.

Until he saw Kate, he had all but given up hope of escape. Now that she was here, he knew he had to do something, anything, to save her. He might not be an expert in acupuncture, but as a doctor, he knew what nerve Snow had paralyzed with his needle. If only he could muster enough willpower to move the knotted muscle in his arm a little bit, he might be able to dislodge the needle just enough . . .

It was a big if—

Kate was already standing at the entrance to the hall of mirrors, ready to meet Snow for the last time.

43

He was performing the ritualized forms of Tai Chi, his movements slow, smooth, graceful, almost balletlike.

It was truly a beautiful thing to behold, and Kate found herself watching in spite of herself, entranced by his beautiful dance, knowing that the soft, flowing movements of the Tai Chi form could be used as one of the most deadly of martial arts. She waited until he finished his set, watching not one Snow, but hundreds of them, approach her until the real one emerged from the maze of mirrors.

"I'm so glad you could make it, Katherine," he said, smiling. He was dressed casually in a gray pullover, blue jeans, and a black sportcoat. "Please follow me."

He turned back toward the mirrors and Kate quickly followed behind him. It was all she could do not to lose him in the angled reflections. She saw the table just over his right shoulder, a small square of wood, complemented by two straight-backed chairs. Behind the table, angled sharply down, was the source of illumination: a high-intensity stagelight.

But what caught her attention was the single object resting on the table: it was a lie detector.

"Please," Snow said, gesturing to the chair facing the lamp. "Have a seat."

Kate slid the chair out, hearing its legs scrape against the dusty wooden floor, the sound echoing in the empty building. She saw the repeated image of herself sitting down in the chair reflected from the mirrors all around her as if she were on stage in front of an audience of unblinking eyes. She tore her gaze away from the mirrors and focused on a single set of eyes, those of Alexander Snow.

They were even more unsettling than the mirrors because they belonged to a human being. Gray, empty, reflective. Kate had the feeling that if she looked closely enough, she would see herself reflected there a hundred times, just as she did in this hall of mirrors.

"Comfortable?" Snow asked, taking the seat opposite her.

"I'd like to get this over with, Dr. Snow," Kate said, trying to sound more in control than she felt. She tried to remember that she was the doctor in this relationship, that by his own admission, it was Snow who was the patient, and that he had specifically summoned her here for a final session.

"You cannot rush enlightenment, Katherine," Snow said, "although it can fall like lightning when the time is right. I think the time may be right."

"Where do you want to begin?"

"First I want you to put on that blood pressure cuff."

Kate saw the cuff lying on the table in front of her and slowly picked it up. She stared at it for a moment and then back at Snow.

"I thought this was about you."

"It's about *us*, Katherine. Every therapeutic relationship, by its very definition, is about at least two people. No one is cured in a vacuum."

"I don't understand, Dr. Snow. It's not me who's come to you for help. It's *you* who's come to *me*."

"Perhaps that is precisely the problem. Before you can help me, you must help yourself, Katherine. Put the cuff on."

Kate rolled up the sleeve of her sweatshirt and wrapped the cuff tightly around her biceps, securing it with a Velcro strip.

"Good," Snow said. "I think you know what to do next."

Kate secured the strap that measured her breathing and slid her hand forward, inserting the first two fingers of her left hand into the foam-covered sensors lying on the table.

"What is it that you want from me, Dr. Snow?"

"The truth, Katherine. Only the truth."

"I think you know the truth," Kate said, "or we wouldn't be here now."

"If you're talking about the fact that you betrayed me, yes, I know all about that. You might even say I foresaw it. No, I'm asking for a confession of your sins, Katherine. What I want is your secret. The truth that will set you free."

"I'm afraid I don't understand, Dr. Snow. I don't have any secrets."

"Oh, but you do, Katherine. Aren't you in the least curious about how I happened to pick this particular location for our last session?"

Kate felt her heart skip a beat, a band of sweat suddenly standing out just below her hairline. She was conscious of the needle scratching the paper on the lie detector. When she finally answered, the voice didn't sound like hers at all.

"Yes."

"Little cues, inadvertent comments, unconscious references. We give ourselves away in spite of ourselves. Isn't it curious that you moved back only minutes from the place that gave you the most pain? Did you feel that you needed to punish yourself after you betrayed me?"

"No," Kate said softly, honestly.

"Then why here?"

"It's the place I knew best. I'd always dreamed of living here. I wasn't going to let what happened spoil it."

To her surprise, the needle spiked on the page, calling her a liar.

"You're not being honest, Katherine."

"I am. If there were other motives, they were subconscious."

Again the needle spiked.

"It happened in the labyrinth, didn't it?"

"Yes," Kate said dully.

"How many of them were there?"

"Two."

While the memory had returned in staccato bursts during her frantic journey through the labyrinth, it was flowing back now, along with the tears running down her face. Her whole body was shaking; her eyes, unable to meet Snow's, fell to the table in front of her.

"Tell me what happened."

Kate's voice trembled. "I don't want to."

"You have to, Katherine," Snow said consolingly. "It's the only way out. We all have to face the truth sooner or later. You must know that by now."

Kate lifted her face, her eyes locked on Snow's, a fire burning inside her.

"All right, you bastard. You want to know what happened? I'll tell you. The car stopped outside the labyrinth, just as it did tonight. I got out to walk through, and once I got inside they began to touch me. I tried to run, but I couldn't find my way out. I screamed, but everyone just laughed, assuming it was all part of the fun. I was lost, confused, terrified. They dragged me down and took me right there. I tried to fight them off, but I was too scared and shocked to do much but lie there and take it. It was all over before I even knew it had begun. I'd never felt so powerless in all my life. Are you satisfied?"

"But it wasn't all over, was it?"

The fire inside Kate died. She stared into Snow's empty eyes as if wandering around lost in a snowstorm.

"No. I told my mother."

"And what was her reaction?"

Kate tasted some of the old bitterness on her tongue. "She acted as if it was my fault."

"How did that make you feel?"

"How do you think it made me feel?"

"I'm asking you, Katherine."

"It made me feel like dirt."

"Why do you think your mother blamed you? Why didn't she suggest going to the police?"

"How the hell should I know?"

The pencil spiked on the paper again.

"I think you *do* know, Katherine."

Kate gritted her teeth. "Because I knew them."

"You knew them?"

"They were my cousins, my goddamn cousins, all right. Is that what you wanted to get out of me, you son-of-a-bitch?"

"It's a start, Katherine."

"What's left?"

Kate was weeping openly now, her whole body deeply wracked by spasms, the tension of a lifetime convulsively being released.

"Just a little bit more, Katherine."

"I can't."

"You've come this far."

"What else?" she sobbed, her voice half-choked. "What else do you want to know?"

"Why your mother blamed you."

"Because she saw—"

"She saw what, Katherine?"

"She saw. She caught us—"

"Tell me, Katherine."

"She caught us making out one day in my bedroom. It didn't mean anything. It was innocent."

"No one is innocent, Katherine."

"*I* was innocent."

"No, Katherine, you weren't. Not then, not now. You've never put it behind you. Do you know why?"

"Isn't it obvious, dammit?"

"Only the truth is obvious."

"And what is the truth?"

"Why don't you tell me?"

Kate felt the spotlight over Snow's head beaming down on her like God's eye, burning, white, omniscient. She squinted against its silent accusation.

"I still think about them, about it—"

"And?"

"And I blame myself for what happened."

"But that's not all, is it, Katherine?"

"No, I—"

"Come on, Katherine. We're so close. So close."

The words came convulsively, as if she were spitting them out one by one.

"I fantasize when I make love—"

"And you can't do it—"

"Because I think, I think—"

"Yes?"

"I think I enjoyed it."

"But you didn't Katherine, did you? You really didn't enjoy it. It was a horrible, frightening experience. You didn't enjoy it at all. You hated it. You wanted to kill them. You still want them dead for what they took from you."

Kate felt something hard and cold inside her melt, an impenetrable mass of ice, and from behind it came a rush of warmth and passion, a life she had forgotten even existed.

"Yes, dammit. Yes. I hate them. I hate what they did. I didn't enjoy it. I don't hate myself."

Kate screamed the final words, slumping in the straight-backed chair, soaked in sweat, the tide of pent-up emotion washing through her.

"Who are you, Katherine? The woman who is telling me this story now, the frightened girl, or the unsatisfied lover who relives her own humiliation over and over again in sexual fantasy? Which Katherine Bennett are you? And are you really telling me the truth, or some flawed remembrance biased by emotion? Which one of you is speaking? Whose truth are you telling me?"

"I don't know," Kate said in a small, defeated voice. "I don't know."

The lie detector scratched quietly in the silence.

"It's okay, Katherine," Snow said. He reached out and touched her wrist and Kate felt the warmth of true compassion in his touch. "You did very well. There's only one more question I have to ask you."

Kate didn't have the strength to lift her head. She merely shrugged her shoulders. What else was there? She had told him everything. There was nothing left to hide.

"Did you bring the tape?"

Kate held her breath in mid-sob, her head snapped up, and she caught herself in Snow's uncompromising gaze. She already knew there was no lying to the man.

"No," she said.

Snow didn't seem perturbed.

"Then we had better hurry," he said.

"Hurry?" Kate repeated.

"Yes," Snow said. "It's my turn now."

11:15 P.M.

Lincoln stared around the attic room in quiet amazement.

In spite of himself, Snow's theatrics had an undeniable effect on Lincoln's consciousness. No doubt it was intended to. Lincoln hadn't chased the man this far without realizing that Snow was a master of mind-play. Still, the surrealistic spectacle of the pin-studded room had not prevented Lincoln from seeing the tape recorder centered on the desk beneath the window. He walked over to it, shielding it from the grizzled detective. He noted, beside the desk, the box of audio cassettes and had no doubt what they contained. Why had Kate kept them secret? They might have provided the clues Lincoln had needed to nail Snow the first time around. Perhaps she felt a need to protect some aspect of her code of confidentiality.

Kate's crisis of conduct—or code of honor—however you wanted to view it—could cost her her life.

Lincoln turned from the desk to the grizzled detective. "Do

you mind leaving Agent McCall and me alone for a few minutes?''

''No,'' the detective said, his tone clearly insulted, not caring to be dismissed so summarily, but at the same time glad to be given an excuse to leave the bizarre room. ''You can have the place to yourselves. Frankly, it gives me the willies.''

The detective left and McCall came forward.

''What's up? What did you find?''

Lincoln waited until the detective's footsteps were halfway down the stairs before stepping aside to reveal the tape recorder.

''You think he left a message?''

''Only one way to find out.''

Lincoln listened to Snow's voice through the machine. The sound of it—so smooth, so confident, so earnest—set his teeth on edge. They listened to the entire message, including the part where Snow told Kate to bring the cassette along with her, that they didn't need any uninvited guests. He was glad she hadn't obeyed his request. It gave them a chance to save her. If they could get there in time.

''She left it behind on purpose,'' McCall concluded.

''At least she's not suicidal.''

''Do you know where this fun house is?''

''I saw it on the way in. It's right up the boardwalk.''

''So what do we do now? Call in the troops?''

''No,'' Lincoln said, shutting off the recorder. He pressed the eject button and pocketed the tape. ''We go in alone. The last thing we need is a convoy. He'll slip right past us in the confusion.''

''So I guess we're throwing out the book?''

''Where has the book gotten us so far, son?''

''Good point.''

44

11:17 P.M.

"It's time, Katherine."

Kate was still shaken. She had been aware of Snow's gentle ministrations, removing the blood pressure cuff, the diaphragm belt, sliding her hand from the sensors, but through it all she had remained as limp as a rag doll. If he had wanted to kill her, he could have done so. Clearly there was more to come. But what else could he have in store for her? Nothing could be worse than reliving the memories she had just been forced to relive. At least she had thought so, up to a few moments ago. Now that it was over, she realized she had her whole life in front of her. She realized that she wanted nothing more than to live.

It seemed to take almost all her effort to lift her head. She saw that Snow had donned the blood pressure cuff and diaphragm belt, his fingers slipped inside the sensors on the table. He was sitting cross-legged on his chair in the lotus position. His eyes were fixed on Kate with a strange expression, an expression she had never seen in his expressionless eyes before. It was a look of fear.

From below the table he lifted his left hand and she saw the revolver. He placed it against his left temple.

"I want you to analyze me, Katherine. I want you to analyze me the way you never have before. I want you to ask me the questions I am afraid to answer. I have such a short way to go to enlightenment, but the gap seems impossible to cross. I am caught between two iron mountains, as the Chinese say. I need you to shock me into awareness of the truth."

"Dr. Snow, I don't think I can do this. I'm not qualified. I'm not enlightened myself."

"Nonsense, Katherine. You found *your* truth. I can see it in your eyes: a look of sadness and triumph." He waved his hand in the air. "Look in the mirrors. You've passed through. From this moment forward your life will never be the same. Everything is new. Tell me I'm not correct."

Kate could say nothing. Sure enough, she did feel a change inside her, a lightness, as if a heavy storm had passed over her psyche.

"To realize what drives you is to acknowledge you're only a passenger. To realize you're only a passenger is to allow yourself to sit back and see the world. Unfortunately, it's been my gift and my curse to help others without being able to help myself. But now you must help me. I've waited a long time to prepare you for your ultimate role. You are going to assist in passing me over into nirvana. In spite of all my efforts, I am still suffering, Katherine. I need to know. I need to make the leap. I am prepared to die in the attempt." He cocked the hammer of the gun and nodded toward the lie detector. "It's simple at this point. You ask the questions. If I lie, I die."

11:25 P.M.

They pulled up at the curb in front of the fun house.

"You wait out here," Lincoln said to the driver. "We're going in alone. If the police arrive, tell them the FBI has jurisdiction over the situation and is in the process of apprehending the suspect. Make sure that they keep back, and under no circumstances allow them to enter the building. You got all that?''

''Yes, sir,'' Wilson said.

''You're not going to be satisfied until you've wrecked every-one's career are you, Lincoln?'' McCall quipped, when they were out of earshot.

''I'm not going to be satisfied until we catch this bastard,'' Lincoln said. ''That's all that counts. Careers can be resurrected. Murder victims can't.''

Lincoln looked up at the large face painted on the side of the building, a grinning idiot's face that looked something like that of Alfred E. Neumann.

''Cheery place, huh?'' McCall said.

''Looks like it's been out of operation for some time.''

''You think he's trying to psych us out?''

''Sure. What better place for a showdown? It goes with his warped sense of humor.''

They tried the old metal door at the side of the building and found it open.

''He's making it easy for us,'' Lincoln said.

''Are we walking into a trap?''

''Yes,'' Lincoln answered, without emotion.

''Thanks for telling me.''

''It's the least I can do.''

They stood inside the gloomy interior of the fun house, staring at a papier-mâché cave.

''What now?'' McCall asked.

Lincoln spotted the empty rail tracks to his left. ''I'll follow them. They're bound to lead through the fun house. Look for the emergency stairwell. All these places have one just in case something goes wrong.''

McCall nodded. He took his gun from the holster.

Lincoln put his hand on McCall's arm. ''Be careful.''

''You, too.''

Lincoln watched McCall disappear into the shadows and then turned towards the rails. He followed them through the open devil's mouth and passed the glowing coals. He saw the body hanging from the ceiling and pushed it out of his way. All the while he peered into the shadows, looking for some sign of Snow. He could be waiting for him anywhere. Lincoln grew itchy with paranoia. He felt his head begin to throb, the dim red light making it worse, forcing him to squint in order to see. The macabre surroundings, sordid and cheesily constructed as they were, seemed to be getting to him. Was it because they reminded him of his own impending mortality? He tried to ignore the dizziness, but it was affecting the way he walked, as if one leg was a good six inches shorter than the other. In a room full of skeletons he stopped and sat down on a black plywood coffin.

He reached for his pills. He pulled out the small plastic bottle, twisted off the lid, and shook free three pills. He cupped them in his hand and dry-swallowed them with one gulp. He took a deep breath and slowly stood up. The room did a quick half-spin and then settled into position. He took a step and then another. He still didn't feel right. It would take a while for the pills to kick in.

Perhaps he was a fool for coming here alone. Perhaps it would accomplish nothing but to get him killed. If that was the case, so be it. He was a walking dead man, anyway. But he didn't have the right to drag another man down with him, a young man with his whole life in front of him. If that happened, he'd never be able to forgive himself. The bitch of the matter was that he already had more on his conscience to forgive himself for than he had time left to live. He should have started the process a long time ago, when he was still well. If he had one piece of advice to offer the living, it would be that: start forgiving yourself now.

Funny, the things that went through your head at times like these. The imminence of death made you philosophical. It wasn't the tumor. It had been like this in every potentially lethal situation he'd ever faced.

He reached behind him and took out his Beretta automatic. The feel of the gun in the palm of his hand brought him back to the here-and-now, the life-and-the-death of the matter before him.

Lincoln listened to the creaks and groans of the old fun house. One thing the tumor hadn't impaired was his sense of hearing. If anything, it seemed more acute than ever. From somewhere above him he thought he could make out the faint sound of two people talking.

Lincoln stepped forward as quickly as he could on his uneven legs. He knew he had to find Snow before McCall did. The young agent still had no idea what kind of real-life monster he was up against.

11:30 P.M.

Kate was stunned when she realized what she had to do.

She had to make him lie and the whole thing would be over. She had no doubt he'd remain true to his word. If she could make him lie, he'd squeeze the trigger and blow his brains out and this whole nightmare would be over. She had never literally realized the destructive potential of her work as a therapist before, the power she had, the power to change lives, even destroy them, until Snow's dramatic and drastic gesture. She had always thought of herself as a healer. The thoughts that were going through her head now went against every instinct and belief she'd ever held. Was this Snow's final lesson? Could she live with the realization that she had been the instrument of this man's death as surely as if she had pulled the trigger herself?

She remembered Julie Golden. She remembered Bonnie Kaplan.

Damn right she could.

"Why are you here, Dr. Snow?"

"I told you, to seek myself."

"You can't find yourself on your own?"

"No one can. We need mirrors."

"You've come to seek my help, but you consider yourself superior to me."

"That's not so, Katherine."

"Certainly you consider yourself superior to most men and women."

"No, I don't."

Kate jerked her head to the lie detector read-out. He couldn't be telling the truth. But the pencil scratched evenly over the paper; there was no indication that he was lying.

"If that is so, Dr. Snow, how do you justify killing all the people you killed?"

"I didn't kill them, Katherine. Don't you understand? I merely liberated them from an intolerable situation."

"Which was?"

"Why life, of course."

The pencil continued to scratch evenly over the paper, leaving Kate with a queasy feeling in the pit of her stomach. There was no doubt that he believed what he was saying. His combination of murder and humility was totally unexpected, not to mention extraordinarily disturbing, but unimpeachably authentic. For the first time Kate had to consider that the man on the other side of the table was either a complete lunatic, or some kind of mad saint. She felt the sweat stand out on her brow, a different sweat than before, the icy cold sweat of someone confronting something totally alien to her comprehension. Snow sat as before, the barrel of the gun pressed against his temple, his face calm and composed, only his eyes betraying him. What secret did they hold, what had he seen and yet kept even from himself?

"You're a fraud, Dr. Snow," Kate said quietly. "That's your secret, isn't it?"

"You're going to have to do better than that, Katherine."

"I'm doing the best I can."

"No, you're not. Think, Katherine."

Kate listened to the rhythmic scratching of the lie detector, let her eyes drift beyond Snow to her own eyes confronting her from one of the angled mirrors behind Snow's head.

"You know, we've never really talked about your childhood."

"That old Freudian crap? There's nothing there. It's a dead end."

"Are you sure, Dr. Snow? You sound defensive to me."

"I'm not sure. Perhaps I am defensive."

"About what?"

"I don't know."

Both Snow and Kate looked at the lie detector. The pencil did not spike, indicating that Snow was telling the truth.

"So far, so good, Dr. Snow. Tell me, how was your relationship with your father?"

"My father was a scientist. He was an important man, aloof and reserved. But he was devoted to his family. He made as much time for us as his work allowed."

"And your mother?"

"I loved my mother. She was warm, intelligent, passionate. If she had been born thirty years later, she would have made an excellent psychiatrist. Instead, she was confined to a mental institution. After several attempts, she finally succeeded in committing suicide when I was twelve."

Kate sensed something the lie detector did not—or could not—pick up. It had nothing to do with the truth or falsehood of his answer, but with the answer itself. She was going strictly on instinct now, an instinct honed by years of clinical practice.

"What is your earliest memory of your mother?"

"So predictable, Katherine. I knew you'd ask me that."

"That doesn't surprise me, Dr. Snow. We are both trained in the same discipline. It also doesn't answer my question. What is your earliest memory?"

Her voice had an edge to it as she repeated the question, remembering how ruthlessly he had questioned her about her own past only minutes before. She had the sense that she was going for the jugular, that Snow was becoming increasingly uncomfortable, that she was finally breaking through that maddening facade of otherworldly serenity.

Let him lie, she thought, concentrating on the cocked revolver at his temple, as if by contemplation alone she could make it fire. *Let him lie.*

"All right, if you insist on this line of questioning."

"I do, Dr. Snow."

"Then let's have at it. I'm in the bathroom. My mother is helping me undress. I'm going to take a bath."

"How old are you?"

"I must be about two, maybe three."

"What happens next?"

"I step into the tub. The water is too hot."

"What does your mother do?"

"She makes me get in anyway. I start to cry."

"And then?"

"Then she undresses. I remember my mother's body quite clearly. She has large full breasts and hips, a tiny waist. She is quite beautiful. She climbs into the tub with me. I am leaning back against my mother's breasts. She is naked in the tub behind me. We are together in the water. It doesn't seem so hot anymore. It seems warm, fluid, natural."

"Go on."

"I can't."

"Why not?"

"I don't remember anymore."

The line laid down by the lie detector didn't so much as waver. He was telling the truth. At least, the truth as his conscious mind knew it. But for the first time she saw a tic starting at the corner of his mouth. Kate decided to press him further.

"The memory is there, Dr. Snow. You know that as well as I do. Everything that happens to us is recorded in our brains."

"I try to remember, but all I see is a black wall."

"Break through the wall, Dr. Snow. Tell me what's on the other side."

"An iron cow sits on top of a hundred-foot pole and gives birth to a calf."

"You're on the hundred-foot pole, aren't you Dr. Snow?"

"Yes. Dammit, yes."

"You can give birth to the calf. You can midwife the truth. Tell me, *tell me*, what do you see?"

The gun at his temple began to shake, and the words spilled

out in a jumble of images, coming so fast they left him breath-less. "Water, the ceiling, the bathroom tiles, splashing, the ceiling again, black, black hair, gasping for breath, my mother's cunt, breaking the surface, the pink porcelain, the peace, the calm, so much love, no suffering, no suffering anymore."

Kate stared at Snow, his body still erect in the lotus position, but trembling uncontrollably, his eyes burning straight ahead into the past, suddenly filled with the light of knowledge.

Kate had to force the next words from her mouth.

"How did it end, Dr. Snow?"

"Burning, a fire in the chest, fists pounding, choking, vom-iting up my heaven, my father's face, blood in the water, my mother's blood, so much blood. she tried to release us both from the pain of this world, from the lies, the heartbreak. She tried to take me with her, but she failed. My father spoiled it. I hated him. I will always love her. She was truly enlightened."

"Was she really?"

"Yes. I'm convinced."

"Go further."

"There's nothing else."

"You know that's not true."

"I can't remember any more."

"You don't want to remember."

"I want to—I can't."

"What is the face you had before you were born?"

Snow's appearance suddenly changed, twisted, his lips drawn and pale.

"I think I'm going to be sick. God, the pain. *The pain* . . ."

Snow doubled over in his chair and vomited on the floor. He writhed as if there were something loose and alive inside him. Suddenly he threw back his head and let loose a loud wail, the wail of an infant screaming out its terror and outrage.

Kate felt shaken. She thought of making a run for it, but it was more than fear that kept her at the table. It was professional curiosity. She had never seen anything like it before. As far as she could tell, she had taken Snow all the way back to his origins. The man was reexperiencing his own birth.

"Tell me," she said, fighting to keep her voice steady, "what do you hear?"

The wailing stopped, but not the expression of pain on his face. Snow spoke, but it wasn't in his own voice. His voice had changed. It sounded clipped, cold. He was straining to maintain composure.

"Why did you wait so long to decide, you stupid bitch. I can't kill it now."

His voice changed again, breathless and hysterical, filled with pain and anger, but it was clearly a woman's voice.

"Kill it, kill it, kill it."

The other voice came through again, the composure eroding, the coldness turned hot with anger and fear. "I can't. I can't kill it. The goddamn thing is *alive.*"

Snow stared glassily forward into emptiness. Kate felt spent. He had told her the truth; she didn't need the machine to confirm that. He had told her the truth hidden at the center of the twisted labyrinth of his psyche, and now she had no idea of where to go from there. She just sat there exhausted, amazed, stunned, and shocked. There was nowhere to run. She had come to meet him purposely to stop running. Their fates were strangely intertwined. But where they led, she couldn't guess. At last, Snow came out of his reverie and back into himself. He reached into his sportcoat, took out a handkerchief, and wiped the vomit from his mouth. He replaced the handkerchief and spoke, his voice returning to normal.

"So that's the secret," he said, more to himself than to her. "I should never have been born at all. It's all been a kind of lie, hasn't it? An ego trap, this constant search for the truth. I was programmed from the start to seek to destroy my ego, and yet as a defense, I had the biggest ego of all, so big I couldn't see it. I saw the mote in my brother's eye, but not the beam in my own. I was all ego, pure ego, pure evil. The rest I can't put into words. Only this."

Kate could see his finger tightening on the trigger and instinctively shouted "No!" just as the barrel turned and the hammer clicked down, but there was no gunshot.

Snow laughed.

"One empty chamber. The rest loaded. Truth is, I guess I'm just lucky." He looked up at Kate. "You did it, Katherine. I knew you could."

"What now, Dr. Snow?"

Snow slowly lowered the gun from his temple and pointed it at Kate.

"Well, to paraphrase Lin Chi, if you meet the Buddha on the path to enlightenment, kill her."

11:35 P.M.

Jeff might not have known much about acupuncture but he didn't have to be an expert in chi meridians to know that what paralyzed his right arm was a pin in the superior cervical ganglia controlling his ulnar nerve.

If he could only move that pin a fraction of an inch . . .

He bunched the muscles in his right shoulder, trying to dislodge the pin. His first efforts met with failure, but he kept trying. He could see Kate and Snow sitting at the table not twenty feet from where he sat, and the frustration of not being able to go to Kate's aid was unbearable. He tried again, shifting the muscles in his shoulder, and thought he felt the pin move ever so slightly. Feeling momentarily flooded back into his hand and he was actually able to make a fist. From there he bunched the muscles as he'd originally done. The pin moved again, this time allowing him to lift his arm an inch off the floor.

Jeff felt a surge of adrenaline pour through his body.

He could do this. He had to do this.

Meanwhile, he was listening to what was going on at the table. He had heard how ruthlessly Snow had broken Kate down, getting her to reveal what she had tried so hard to keep secret, and if for no other reason, he wanted to kill the man for it. He had also heard Kate give it right back to him, the two going at it like expert swordsmen, slashing away at each other, but using words instead of blades.

Now it was over and Snow was pointing a gun at Kate, saying she had to die.

Jeff clenched his right fist, squeezed his eyes and muscles, and lifted his arm off the floor as if he were lifting a fifty-pound weight. For a moment he thought he might pop an artery in his temple, but the violence of the motion was enough to dislodge the pin blocking the impulse through his ulnar nerve. His right arm was free, and soon he was plucking at the other pins paralyzing his body. He did not even try to remove them all. But he removed enough of them to enable him to stand up and lumber out of his corner, heading straight toward Snow, his hands up to grab the doctor's wrist when the first shot was fired and a burning hole opened up in his left palm and the smell of singed flesh assaulted his nostrils. He didn't hear the second shot, only felt the searing pain in his ribs.

The last thing he saw was the shattering mirror on which Kate's horrified face was silently screaming.

45

11:38 P.M.

11:38 P.M.

Lincoln heard the shots and followed their echo through the labyrinth like a line in the darkness.

The rush of adrenaline momentarily chased away his dizziness and disorientation and he silently prayed that he wasn't already too late to save Kate.

He stepped on a stretch of floor strewn with rubber squeaky rats—at least, he assumed they were rubber—turned a blind corner, and stopped short, squinting against the light reflecting at him from a thousand different angles. He raised his hands to his face to shield his eyes, pointing his gun at nothing in particular, hoping by chance he was locked in on a target. Instead, all he could see when his eyes grew accustomed to the light was his own image, gun drawn, looking haggard and disheveled, multiplied countless times in the hall of mirrors.

11:39 P.M.

McCall also heard the shots.

He had found the emergency stairwell leading up the side

of the building and was taking the steps two at a time. He emerged in a huge room that looked like a cross between a storage room and a theater. In the dark he could just make out the shadows of old trunks, props, rope, sandbags, and plastic skeletons. On one wall hung a row of sagging rubber monster masks. The sounds of shots reverberating from within the old building was hard to pinpoint, but it sounded like they were coming from somewhere above him, yet the stairwell had ended on this floor. Perhaps there was another stairwell on the other side of the doorway, across the dark room.

He hurried across the creaking boards beneath his wingtips, gun probing the darkness in front of him, toward the dull red exit sign floating near the ceiling above the door.

From the sounds of the shots, he could tell that only one gun had been fired.

Was it Lincoln's, or was it Snow's?

He had no idea; all he knew was that he had to get up to the floor above him as soon as possible. He didn't see the black rectangle of the trapdoor left open under his feet, nor did he understand he was falling to the floor below until he was half-way down. His eyes registered the image of a stuffed mannequin hanging from a rope moments before he hit the ground, his right leg doubled up under him at an impossible angle. He felt nothing for several seconds, and then the pain forced him to double over and momentarily black out.

Only sheer willpower drove him to his feet, his left shoulder leaning against the black-papered wall. He limped forward, testing his broken leg, a jolt of pain frying his brain, leaving him winded and dizzy. He stepped forward again, depending on the wall for support, the pain just as bad, blood filling his shoe. He was sure each step would be his last, but he kept on anyway, determined to go as far as he could before the matter was taken out of his hands and he collapsed once and for all into unconsciousness.

11:40 P.M.

"You surprised me, Lincoln. I honestly didn't think you had it in you."

Snow stepped forward, blotting out Lincoln's image in the mirrors with his own, multiplied a thousand times. He was holding a revolver in his left hand. To Lincoln, it looked as if he were facing an army of Alexander Snows.

But which was the real one?

He suddenly felt the dizziness come back and with it the familiar sensation of nausea. His damaged brain was working overtime, stressed to the maximum. For the second time he wondered if he was a fool for coming here. If he shouldn't have just turned the tape over to the police and let them handle it. He wasn't just putting his own life in jeopardy, worthless now as that may be, but the lives of Kate and McCall.

"Where's Kate?" he called to the audience of Snows.

Snow frowned. "You mean, is Kate still alive? Why can't we say what we mean, even in the most extreme circumstances?"

Lincoln wasn't sure, but he had to assume Snow had a clear shot at him. He was determined to rectify that situation and let the maze of mirrors work for him as well. He moved quickly to his right into a mirrored hallway. He advanced forward cautiously, his gun held in both hands, level with his chest. He ignored the persistent throbbing inside his skull.

"It's over, Snow—you know that, don't you?"

"Yes, Lincoln, I suppose it is. But I suspect the end will still surprise you."

Lincoln advanced down the corridor of mirrors and turned left, following the sound of Snow's voice. He crouched down and peered around a corner and saw himself crouched down and peering around a corner a dozen times over.

"Guilt drives you, doesn't it, Lincoln? Even though you're dying, you couldn't help trying to bring me down alone. Guilt is a powerful emotion, but its quite useless, quite pointless."

Keep talking, Lincoln thought, as he turned another corner. *Keep talking. That's what you goddamned shrinks do best.*

"We can't help but do what we do at the time. We are driven to it by forces greater than ourselves. We do the best we can under the given circumstances, given the irrational and unconscious drives that control us. I only recently learned that the hard way. I've spent my life searching for the truth in others when I myself have been living the biggest lie. But therein lies no blame. The problem is that the ego is powerless. The ego is just an illusion. So therefore it is a mistake to regret our past actions. We can't help ourselves. It is all out of our hands."

Lincoln followed the voice. He stopped when he saw the table, or rather tables, and sitting at the end of each of them, a hundred Kates. She looked pale and shaken but otherwise unharmed. Lincoln wasn't sure if she saw him or not, but he put a finger to his lips just in case.

"No, Lincoln, we can't help ourselves. That is the great tragedy of the human condition. You couldn't help yourself when you compromised your integrity to put me away. As a result I bear you no ill-will. You couldn't help yourself when you were offered the chance to track me down. In spite of your condition, you had to do it, isn't that so? In spite of the fact that it might—and did—cost innocent lives?"

That last stung Lincoln, for the thought of those killed in the last twenty-four hours hung heavily over him.

"Don't feel guilty, Lincoln. You couldn't help yourself, any more than I can help myself. No one can. The real pity is that you've never lived your own life. Few of us have. Until only a few minutes ago, I, too, was a prisoner of the ego. But don't worry. Before it's over, you'll be enlightened, I promise you."

Lincoln turned another corner and saw what he had been waiting to see: the back of Alexander Snow. He was talking to a bank of mirrors, each reflecting his own image, as if he were lecturing to a classroom of Alexander Snows.

Lincoln emerged from behind the mirrored wall, straightened up, and settled into a shooter's stance. He wasn't sure which was the real Snow, but he chose the most likely looking target.

He mustered all the authority left in his quavering voice. He had dreamed of this moment for five years. He just never thought he'd ever live to see it.

"Drop it," he said.

46

Snow did not answer, nor did he drop the gun.

Lincoln called out again, softer this time, his voice almost pleading.

"Drop it."

"I don't think so, Tom," Snow said finally. "You see, from where I'm standing, I've got a clear shot at Katherine. Take a look to your left."

Lincoln shifted his eyes quickly and saw Kate sitting at the table. He looked quickly back at Snow, or at least, at the one image out of a dozen he thought was the real Snow.

"Now, you may *think* you know where I am, but the fact is that appearances are deceiving. Which is the real me? You aren't really sure, are you, Tom?"

It was true. Lincoln couldn't be sure. He moved his gun to the figure on the right. But he couldn't be sure it wasn't a reflection, too. The voice was no help; it seemed to be as fragmented as the images on the mirrors. Was Snow purposely throwing his voice?

"Where do we go from here, Snow?" Lincoln shouted,

unable to hide his frustration any longer. His head was throbbing, the lights and mirror images making him light-headed. He fought the urge to rub away the spots dancing in front of his eyes. He didn't know how long he'd be able to hang on.

"Not feeling too well, are you, Tom?"

"You don't need to worry about me."

"Of course. A will of iron. At least, it's always been that way until now, hasn't it? It must be tough to see it all slipping away. You're the quintessential man of ego. Mortality is always toughest on such men. I truly pity you."

"I'm asking you again, Snow. How do you want this to play?"

"First you drop the gun."

"Will you let Kate go?"

"Yes."

"How can I be sure?"

"I'm a man of my word."

Lincoln had no choice. If he made a mistake and shot at the wrong Snow, Kate would be killed for certain. Reluctantly, he let the short barrel of his gun slowly drop a little. He had no sooner begun to do so, however, than he saw a dark shape scuttling along the floor and rising to its feet. He lifted the gun, tightening his finger on the trigger, and instinctively took aim at the moving figure, which turned to him and shouted two words.

"Shoot him!"

At the same time a mirror to Lincoln's right exploded outward, obliterating the image of Snow he'd gambled was the real one.

Lincoln watched as the lumbering form collided into Snow, knocking the gun skittering across the floor, exposing the doctor behind the mirrors. Lincoln recognized the dark figure as Jeff Hudson and saw the blood soaking the front of his shirt as he fell heavily to the floor, his last heroic act done. Lincoln couldn't worry about him now. He only had the strength to focus on one thing.

Lincoln stood facing Alexander Snow and aimed his gun at the center of Snow's chest, just a shade to the right, exactly over the heart.

11:45 P.M.

"Well, I guess it's just you and me again, old pal," Snow said.

The doctor was smiling. He looked completely unruffled, except for Jeff Hudson's blood staining his sportcoat.

In spite of the fact that he had the man dead-sight in front of him, Lincoln was still seeing double. The throbbing in his head increased to a blinding pitch. He wished he could reach into his pocket for the bottle of pills, but he couldn't take the risk of diverting his attention from Snow for an instant. Nor did he want Snow to see how close he felt to collapse.

"It's over now, Snow," Lincoln said.

"Do you really think so?" Snow answered, sounding slightly amused.

"We found the bodies at the cabin. We've finally got you right where we want you. There'll be no tricks this time. We'll go straight for murder one. You'll go down as the worst serial murderer in state history. What's better, they've got the death penalty in New Jersey. You didn't think ahead, or maybe you'd have set up shop in New York. This time you won't get away. You'll fry for what you've done, Snow."

"Too bad you won't be there to see it, Tom. You'll die long before me. With appeals and a possible insanity plea, I'll be around for a long time to come. Who knows, I may even have a chance to escape again. You never can tell about these things. And that's what really eats at you, doesn't it, Tom? There's no appeal from cancer. You'll never know for sure what happens unless you pull that trigger. But we both know you won't. You won't do it because you're going to die soon and you're not sure what comes after. It's a common emotion with the terminally ill. Not that you believe in heaven or hell in the conventional sense. You're much too sophisticated for that.

You're agnostic. But you do believe in a psychological manifestation of hell. You believe it possible that a man's guilt can make the dying of his consciousness an unbearable hell, a terrifying dissolution into an abyss of pain and suffering. And so you'll let me live because it's the right thing to do. It might give you some degree of comfort to know that in the Tibetan tradition, we look upon each other and see that we are all dying. Thus compassion is born.''

"Yeah," Lincoln said. "We're all dying. Some of us just not fast enough."

Snow laughed. It was not an unpleasant sound. He didn't even flinch when the bullet exploded in the center of his forehead, throwing his body back into a mirror, which shattered into ten thousand pieces. Snow lay face-up among the scattered silver shards.

Lincoln walked slowly up to his body. The doctor's face was perfectly composed. His gray eyes were wide open. He stared up at Lincoln, his unblinking gaze fixed around the bullet wound, opened like a third bleeding eye between his brows. With his dying breath he exhaled a single word.

"Nirvana."

47

Lincoln turned to McCall.

"You shouldn't have done that."

Blue smoke drifted over the mirrors. The metallic stench of the gun blast hung in the air between them. McCall was standing on one leg, his pants torn, a shard of white bone peeking shockingly from the blood-soaked material.

"Are you going to report me?"

Lincoln glanced up from McCall's wounded leg to his face, pasty white and twisted with pain. He wondered how in the world McCall had managed to make it up to the hall of mirrors. It must have taken a superhuman effort of will. There was something, alas, to be said for the human ego. He tried to read the expression in the younger agent's eyes, looking for anger, revenge, or righteousness, but all he saw there were shock and exhaustion. He knew the expression well. Lincoln reached into his pocket, removed the bottle of pills, and shook a couple into his palm. "I'm going to report what happened. You're going to report what happened. Maybe you saw a reason to shoot him I didn't. Who's to know the truth?"

McCall grinned, his lips white. He leaned against the mirror behind him and slid like melting ice to the floor. He looked up at Lincoln.

"It won't bother your conscience?"

Lincoln nodded toward the dead man lying among the shards of the broken mirror.

"He always overestimated the development of my conscience. Besides, as he liked to say, no one is innocent."

48

Midnight

Kate drew a deep breath of sea air.

She was standing by the fun house, shivering inside Lincoln's trenchcoat, watching the pandemonium around her. Police cars and ambulances had surrounded the building and patrol officers and first-aid volunteers were scrambling around in a frenetic swarm of activity. Kate saw the stretcher bearing Snow's covered corpse being wheeled from the building, a single red spot, like an angry eye, soaked through the sheet where he'd been shot. A moment later she saw the stretcher bearing Jeff. There were already tubes running from his arm and he held a great swath of bandage pressed tightly to his side. Kate stepped forward and he raised a free hand wearily for his bearers to stop a moment.

"Jeff—"

"It's okay," he said, and tried to smile. "I've lost quite a bit of blood, but I should be all right. See? I told you they usually catch them within twenty-four hours."

He began to shiver uncontrollably.

Kate could hear his teeth chattering.

She smiled, tears running down her face. She let them fall without trying to brush them away. It would have been a typical gesture before, but now it no longer seemed necessary. There was nothing left to hide.

"I wanted to thank you. I wanted to tell you—"

"How much you love me."

"Yes," Kate said. "How much I love you."

"I know."

She took his hand and was shocked at how cold and limp it felt. She grasped it all the more tightly, willing her strength into his body, like a transfusion. She was staring into his still-sharp blue eyes. She had never before felt so close to him.

One of the stretcher bearers interrupted their silent communion.

"Ma'am, we've really got to get him to the hospital."

Kate backed away. "Yes, sure, I'm sorry. Jeff, I'll be there as soon as I can."

"No rush," Jeff laughed and coughed. Kate hoped it sounded worse than it really was. "I won't be going anywhere for a while."

She watched as they loaded Jeff into the ambulance beside the one they'd put Snow inside. From the open back doors she could already see McCall sitting against the wall, his damaged leg stretched out in front of him, a medic cutting away his blood-soaked trouser leg.

God, what a mess.

"Kate—"

She turned and saw Lincoln.

"Tom."

"I can't tell you how sorry I am it came to this."

"It wasn't your fault."

Lincoln shook his head. "I gave you my word."

Kate pointed to the ambulance bearing Snow's body. "He had a way of making liars of us all."

"Yeah," Lincoln nodded. "I suppose he did."

"It's really over now, isn't it?"

"Yes," Lincoln said. "It's really over."

They stood there and watched them close the doors on the ambulance as if they were closing the covers of a book.

Lincoln turned back to Kate. "Do you want me to get them to assign you an agent to stay with you tonight? It's been a rough twenty-four hours."

"That's okay. I'm a psychiatrist, remember? I know how to deal with emotional shock."

She couldn't help paraphrase to herself the old expression about lawyers: *the doctor who treats herself has a fool for a patient.* She also couldn't help but think again of another old expression: *physician, heal thyself.* It was about time she began the process of healing. Ironic, that it should have been Snow who'd prompted that process to begin.

"Are you sure?" Lincoln prompted.

"I'm sure. Thanks anyway."

"Okay. Well, I guess this is goodbye." He held out his hand and Kate took it.

"Goodbye. And thank you."

Lincoln shook his head. "There's nothing to thank me for."

"You finally got him," Kate said. "It cost more than either of us thought it would, but you finally got him."

"Yeah," Lincoln said. "I guess there's that."

"Oh, your coat—"

"Keep it," Lincoln said, and turned away.

Kate knew it would be the last time she'd ever see him again. She wasn't sorry.

She watched the ambulance bearing Snow's body slowly pull away form the curb. The ambulance in which Jeff and McCall had been loaded had long since left for the hospital. In Snow's case, there was no hurry. As Lincoln said, the story was over.

Somehow, Kate didn't think so.

16 NOVEMBER

"Do you understand? If you open your mouth and say that you understand, I will hit you thirty times. If you say that you don't understand, I will still hit you thirty times."
Master Seung Sahn

"You've been asleep for millions and millions of years. Why not wake up this morning?"
Kabir

Epilogue

Kate spent most of the evening in the emergency room.

By the time she left early that morning Jeff was sleeping comfortably in his hospital room. It had taken much persuasion from the staff to convince her that there was nothing to be gained by staying beside his bed. She had returned home around 5 A.M. She didn't have a class until that afternoon and hoped to catch a few hours of sleep. She had just taken a Valium and undressed when she'd found the portable tape recorder under her pillow.

She crossed the sand up to the boardwalk and headed north into the wind. There was still a light mist in the air and the waves were still coming in, high and brown. She nodded at a jogger passing in the opposite direction. The boardwalk was relatively crowded with cyclists, runners, and those driven to meditate on the effects of the recently inclement weather.

Once she'd found the recorder, sleep was out of the question. She sat up until the light tinged the eastern sky and then slipped into her sweats and headed for the beach.

She ran until she reached the end of the boardwalk, turned,

and started back. Penelope followed eagerly behind her, nipping affectionately at Kate's heels. Apparently, she was no worse for wear after a veterinarian had removed the pins from her body. Kate headed down the short flight of steps to the sand and walked toward the tideline. She stopped and unzipped the fanny pack around her waist, taking out the tape recorder. She looked over to where Penelope was sniffing at a dead horseshoe crab, giving it her undivided attention.

She took out the microcassette labeled 7:02 A.M. She checked her watch. Sure enough, it was 7:02.

She was about to throw the tape into the ebb of a large brown wave, but something held her arm back.

She put the tape back into the recorder and pressed the play button.

"I knew you wouldn't throw it out without first listening, Katherine. You couldn't resist hearing from me one last time. Maybe you hope I'll put some kind of closure on things. I hate to disappoint you. But you see, the end of one man's life is never the end of the story. I congratulate you on surviving; it's what you wanted. Your life should have an enhanced quality to it now. You should be able to see the world through new eyes. Though it seems inconceivable to you now, I suspect you'll thank me someday.

"Remember that koan I gave you: How can the eye, without reflection, see the eye? No doubt you realize now it was a play on words. How can the "I," without reflection, see the "I"? The answer is, we never can. I think you realize that now. Can you live with that truth? Will it drive you mad? For your sake, I hope it will. Because if it does, it will be the madness of the blessed. You were my best student, Katherine. You can take some pride in that. I had so many. So many who never survived.

"I, on the other hand, have passed beyond the simple matter of life and death. By the time you are listening to this tape I will have achieved my goal. You helped me find the release I sought, whether you meant to or not, and for that I thank you. Of course, it's not quite so simple as you might think. I didn't die on the floor of that fun house, Katherine.

"Not really.

"Do you remember how I told you that I hadn't had a sexual release in ten years? I'm sure you do. Well, the fact of the matter is that before my voluntary abstention from sexual activity, I traveled the country donating sperm to hundreds of sperm banks all over America. I would guess that many prospective parents would be eager to procure my seed, after reviewing my genetic profile: award-winning psychiatrist, genius IQ, perfect physical health. How many women have already had my children? How many more will continue to have them, each bringing a different aspect of me into being, a different facet of my potential, a different reflection of my true self, so that all together they will embody every possibility of the man that was Dr. Alexander Snow? They are no doubt out there already, bright, fresh-faced ten-year-olds, each one seeking the truth. Perhaps we will even meet again, Katherine.

"By the way, I'd be disappointed if you thought I'd harm the dog. Animals and infants never had anything to fear from me. They are the only forms of consciousness that never lie. Alas, if we could only recapture such innocence, eh, Katherine?"

7:05 P.M.

In the end, there was only the sound of Snow's laughter and then the scratch of dead tape.

Kate stood a long time by the sea until the sound of the waves finally washed away the echo of that terrible laughter.

Then she cocked her arm, threw the recorder as far as she could from the shore, called to Penelope, and walked away up the beach.